SMOOTH HOPERATOR

A FAKE-RELATIONSHIP ROMANCE

LOVE ON TAP
BOOK 2

SYLVIE STEWART

Edited by My Brother's Editor

ISBN 978-1-947853-53-9

ALSO BY SYLVIE STEWART

Ale's Fair in Love and War (*Love on Tap*, Book 1 - *Free with Kindle Unlimited*)

Deja Brew All Over Again (*Love on Tap*, Book 3 - *Coming Winter 2023*)

Asheville Collection (Standalone Stories from the *Love on Tap* World)

* * *

Poppy & the Beast (*Free with Kindle Unlimited*)

* * *

Between a Rock and a Royal, Kings of Carolina, #1 (*Free with Kindle Unlimited*)

Blue Bloods and Backroads, Kings of Carolina, #2 (*Free with Kindle Unlimited*)

Stealing Kisses With a King, Kings of Carolina, #3 (*Free with Kindle Unlimited*)

Kings of Carolina Box Set

* * *

The Fix (Carolina Connections, Book 1)

The Spark (Carolina Connections, Book 2)

The Lucky One (Carolina Connections, Book 3)

The Game (Carolina Connections, Book 4)

The Way You Are (Carolina Connections, Book 5)

The Runaround (Carolina Connections, Book 6)

Carolina Connections Box Set 1

Carolina Connections Box Set 2

* * *

The Nerd Next Door (Carolina Kisses, Book 1)

New Jerk in Town (Carolina Kisses, Book 2)

The Last Good Liar (Carolina Kisses, Book 3)

* * *

Full-On Clinger (FREE for a limited time)

Then Again

Happy New You

About That

Nuts About You

Booby Trapped

ABOUT THIS BOOK

After tanking my career in politics, I'm looking for a new direction. But my GPS must be broken because it keeps leading me to a kooky librarian's front steps.

It's not easy, but I'm doing my best to let go of my old ambitions and embrace the simple life of slinging beer at my family's brewery. But some powerful players from my past are determined to cause problems for my family and me.

When a chatty local librarian with the wardrobe of a third grader and the optimism of a Disney cartoon begins sticking her nose into my business, I want to tell her to get lost. As fate would have it, though, Sunny and her equally odd grandfather are my only remaining option to get free of my past for good.

It will take some convincing to get this goofy, goat-loving librarian on board with my risky plan. But if she does things my way, I'll return the favor by playing her fake boyfriend to make her true love jealous and finally take notice.

But the deeper we get into this venture, the more I

realize there's nothing fake about Sunny at all. Including the way I'm beginning to feel about her.

Smooth Hoperator is book 2 in the Love on Tap *series which follows the Brooks family and their adventures in love and brewing beer in Asheville, North Carolina. Each book can be enjoyed as a stand-alone romantic comedy with an HEA and no cheating.*

To Katie, my sister. Not my sister-in-law. My sister.

CHAPTER
ONE

MUSHROOMS AND MUSES

SUNNY

"I WONDER IF HE'S FAMOUS," I consider as I bite down on the end of my pen.

Mia taps away at her keyboard beside me at the circulation desk. "Unless you tell me otherwise, I'll keep assuming you're talking to yourself."

"That would be wise," I respond, my eyes never leaving the tall, scruffy figure hunched over the desktop computer at station five. He never uses the same computer two visits in a row. Is that intentional or simply happenstance? Maybe he's superstitious. Yes, that must be it. It's very on-brand for a tortured artist.

Because that's what I've decided he is.

"Please tell me you're not still analyzing that poor drifter," Mia cuts into my musings. "The last thing you need is another man to take care of."

"He's an artist. But I suppose he could be both." I prop my chin on my hand and watch as the guy scratches his unkempt beard. The flannel isn't one I've seen before. I assume his usual green one is his lucky shirt because he wears it almost every time he visits the library.

The skepticism in Mia's stare is so strong I can feel it without even glancing over. When I do, her expression is the same one Duke gives me when I tell him Greek yogurt tastes like ice cream if you close your eyes.

"Well, he *could* be." I raise an eyebrow at my coworker. Mia doesn't share my passion for people-watching, despite its ability to turn a quiet day as a public librarian into a forum for delicious fantasies.

"That's like saying I could be the Queen of England because I occasionally drink tea and own a fancy-ass hat."

"Well, now you're just being ridiculous. You'd need a tiara, at the very least." I grin at her, and she shakes her head, hitting the logout button on her screen and sliding her chair back. Mia meets her boyfriend for lunch on Tuesdays, but from the glow on her cheeks on her return each time, I don't think much food is being consumed.

"Whatever you say. But if I walk in this afternoon and you're posing naked on a reading table and asking him to draw you like one of his French girls, I'm staging an intervention—and I'm inviting Duke."

I glance back at the computer station to see that the guy has taken off his flannel, exposing muscular arms and shoulders that might recommend a step up in size for his next T-shirt purchase. He could be handsome if he ever stopped frowning—and maybe combed his hair. Not that it makes any difference to me, but his dark wavy hair is the exact rich color of potting soil, and his cheekbones appear to have come directly from a sculptor's hands, even under all the scruff.

"Duke would be on my side," I respond. "He never takes anything at face value." My grandfather and I don't have a lot in common, but our well-developed imaginations find a way to connect us. Although his generally leads him down a conspiracy theory rabbit hole while mine only makes people scratch their heads before ultimately choosing the word "interesting" to describe me. I could do worse.

Mia retrieves her purse from the bottom desk drawer and flips her long braids over one shoulder. "I don't know how I always forget this is the same man who insists *Twilight* is based on true events."

This makes me grin to myself and feel sorry for boring people. The world is a much more interesting place if you allow for possibilities.

But that doesn't mean I'm a sucker. "If it makes you feel any better, I swear on my gnome collection not to pose nude for the bearded mystery man." Not that I can see myself posing nude for anyone, let alone an artist. There's a reason clothing was invented, and I choose to believe it wasn't just so we don't accidentally drop our boobs into a pot of boiling water.

Mia considers me for a second before nodding. "Thank you. It does." Her dark eyes flash to the computer stations before returning to me. "Just do me a favor and keep your distance, okay? I have a bad feeling."

Although I think she's being paranoid, I agree because she's my friend and it's always nice to have someone care enough to worry about you.

While Mia is gone, I help an older woman find a Swedish cookbook and I fill out order forms for new digital books we're acquiring. I'm thrilled to see a new embroidery pattern book on the list and make a note to myself to check it out as soon as we get access. In fact, I'm so engrossed examining the new titles that I don't notice the patron standing across the counter until he speaks.

"Excuse me, could you please grab my document for me?"

It's the artist. And his voice is the exact one I'd give him if I were anointed voice fairy of the world. It's deep and textured, like a well-loved vinyl record that has you leaning in to catch every rise and fall under the crackling overlay.

And now that I see him up close, it's clear that his frown is no match for his natural handsomeness. The man is ruggedly beautiful—and, indeed, tortured, if the circles under his eyes and the tension in his jaw are anything to go by.

"Your document?" I ask absently, noting that his eyes are the most beautiful mix of sienna and sun-drenched moss.

"Uh, yes." His dark eyebrows lift. "From the printer?"

"Oh!" Shoot. I shake my head and offer a weak smile. "I was staring, wasn't I? Sorry." He probably gets that a lot. The fact that he's never printed anything in all his visits over the past months is no excuse for my brain to forget my job entirely. I glide on my wheeled chair to the opposite corner of the circulation area, snatch the warm papers from the printer tray, and sail back to hand them over.

We're instructed to avoid reading the content printed by the library patrons, but that's like dropping hot bacon in front of a dog and expecting him not to scarf it down. I only catch a glimpse of the top sheet and the word "Addiction."

Ah. Poor man. Poor tortured visionary with anguish so haunting and all-consuming it's rendered him a slave to alcohol and porn to get through the day.

Relax, I'm just spitballing, okay?

"Thanks," he mutters, the rumble of breath over his vocal cords causing the hair on my arms to stand on end. I watch him wander back to station five, his attention never leaving the pages in his hands. It's another couple minutes before I shake myself out of it and get back to the digital books. And another thirty until Mia returns, a twig poking out from one of her braids and a satisfied smile resting on her lips.

I wonder if the artist would make love outside or if he prefers the comfort of a bed—or maybe he's into kinky stuff—satin-lined handcuffs and sex swings. Red rooms? My imagination starts wandering.

"Whatcha thinkin' about?" Mia's voice has a knowing sing-song quality I'm sure I deserve.

There's no helping the heat that paints my cheeks at being totally busted. "Nothing." I rush to occupy myself, stacking books from the return bin as Mia chuckles to herself. Darn it. "If you must know, I was thinking about something Sebastian said the other day."

The amusement dies on her lips, but I pretend not to notice. "Oh."

Sebastian is not everyone's cup of kombucha, but he's definitely mine. Although I don't really like kombucha—but Sebastian does. He says it's invaluable for gut health, which I'm sure is true. It doesn't change the fact that it tastes like poo, however.

"How is Sebastian these days?" Mia asks, clearly trying to make up for her initial reaction to his name. I'm afraid Mia doesn't find him as interesting as I do, but that's okay.

Everyone has their preferences. Mine happens to lean toward serious, intelligent men with integrity not even Keanu Reeves could question.

"Did you know it takes *ten years* of persistent herbicidal treatment to get rid of kudzu?"

"You don't say? No, I didn't." Mia's eyes drift to her screen.

"Well, Sebastian says most people don't. He's organizing a rally next weekend to petition the state to use goats instead of harmful chemical herbicides. They're marching at the Capitol building in Raleigh."

This has her swiveling her chair my way. "I'm sorry, did you say goats?"

I nod, scanning a book for reshelving. "Yeah. You can rent them to graze."

"Rent goats? I can't imagine that turning out well." Her chair returns to its original position and she resumes her scrolling.

"Sebastian said they'll even have a few at the rally. I can't wait." If there's a baby one, I can't be held responsible for the complete loss of self-control I'll experience.

"You're going?"

I glance over from my stack. "Of course I'm going. Sebastian needs me."

Mia's brow crinkles. "Did he, um, say that?" Maybe she has a headache or something.

"Say what?"

"That he needs you?"

My scanner hand stills as I consider her question. "Well, not in so many words, but you know Sebastian." I shrug.

"Not really," Mia mumbles before greeting a patron carrying an armful of books to check out.

I wait until the man leaves before responding, "I always forget you've only met Sebastian that one time. His activism takes up so much of his schedule." Sebastian is such a dedicated steward of the earth. He works tirelessly for environmental causes, is completely vegan, and he doesn't even own a car!

Mia scrunches her nose at me as she pushes a wheeled book trolley my way. "Does he have a nickname or something? Sebastian is so… unwieldy."

"No." I try to imagine calling him Seb or Bastian, but neither rolls off the tongue in the right way. "But it suits him." I shift the pile of scanned books to the side and wave to one of our regulars who just walked in the doors.

"Do you want to come to Raleigh with us?" I ask Mia.

Her chin dips as she eyes me. "Does anything about my person say I want to spend my Saturday lecturing people about weeds and farm animals?"

I reflexively scan her outfit, noting the shiny patent leather heels and the perfect state of her red nail polish. "I'll take that as a no."

My phone vibrates in my pocket, and I pull it out to see a text from Duke. We're not technically supposed to keep our phones with us during our shifts, but I worry if I don't have a tether to Duke.

DUKE:

The UPS man put a hidden camera in our eaves.

I narrow my eyes at the screen before moving my thumbs across it.

ME:

Why would the UPS man want to watch us?

DUKE:

He doesn't. It's the people he works for.

ME:

The shareholders?

He ignores me, as usual.

DUKE:

I'm knocking it down.

ME:

Don't you dare! It can wait until I get home tonight. No ladders! I mean it!

"Duke?" Mia asks as she slides a copy of *Now You're One of Us* across the counter to a sullen teenager with ink stains on her hands.

"How did you know?" I frown at my phone.

"Your face puckers like you're sucking on Sour Patch Kids when you text with him."

Well, that's not good. I chew my lip and continue watching the screen, willing my grandfather to text back that he's rethought his plan to break his one good hip.

"Go on," Mia says. "You've still got your lunch break, and I'll cover for you if it takes longer."

I don't even pretend to think about it. "Thanks, Mia. You're the best." I abandon the returned books, snatching up my bag and keys and practically sprinting for the door.

In my distracted state, I don't look where I'm going and plow directly into a solid object covered in cotton. I bounce off, barely catching myself with a foot behind me.

I blink to regain my bearings and bring a hand to my

throbbing forehead. "Oh my goodness. I'm so sorry." The scent of yeasty beer fills my nostrils as I look up to find I've nearly concussed myself on the scruffy artist's shoulder blade. The one covered by an army green T-shirt that highlights the moss in his eyes. This man would be any artist's perfect muse if you ask me.

But my heart squeezes at the thought that it's only midday and he's already drunk so much it's coming out of his pores. Perhaps alcohol is the only way he can access his own muse, and he's slowly lost control of it. Does he have anyone in his life to turn to?

That reminds me! I read an article last month about magic mushrooms' potential use in addiction treatment. Or was it LSD? No, that doesn't sound right. Now I can't remember, but I should definitely dig up the article again. Where might one procure magic mushrooms here in Asheville? Hmm.

"It was my fault," the guy responds in a curt tone, hiking a worn leather satchel up on his opposite shoulder as he steadies me with a hand. He radiates warmth—and beer, but that's neither here nor there. He's looking right through me, though, clearly anxious to get on his way. Which reminds me I need to move my butt as well.

"Not at all," I reassure him, and he releases his hold on my upper arm. "My head is hard as a rock." I give my skull a couple good knocks with my free hand. "Anybody home?" I grin.

The artist makes a sound somewhere between a groan and a hum and continues on his way, throwing a mumbled, "Sorry. Have a good day," over his shoulder.

I pause where I am so I don't accidentally assault him again. "You too." But he's already gone. Like I should be.

There will be plenty of time later to consider how I

might help this man on a mushroom hunt, but right now is not the time. There's a certain pig-headed octogenarian in Black Mountain who needs a lecture on the detrimental effects of his behavior on my mental health.

I swear that man will drive me to an early grave. And I refuse—absolutely *refuse*—to die a virgin.

CHAPTER
TWO

HOME IS WHERE THE BEER IS

CARTER

JEREMY:

The hot blonde from Pulaski's office asked about you again. When are you coming back to D.C.?

LEAVE it to my old coworker to abandon common sense in favor of pussy. I scroll to the next waiting message, though I know I owe Jeremy a call.

RUTHANNE:

Congresswoman Hopkins wants a meeting. Are you still in the District? Call me NOW!

It takes no struggle of conscience at all to swipe right past that one.

CAPITOL STORAGE:

> Payment on your storage unit is past due.
> This is your final notice. Contents of the
> unit will be forfeited if payment is not
> received by April 15th.

Shit.

JULIET:

> Screw you, asshole!

Now, that one… is entirely justified. And better left alone.

UNKNOWN NUMBER:

> Remember, we've got eyes on you. Don't
> be stupid.

Fuck me.

I jam the phone into my pocket, trying to remember why I pulled it out in the first place. Honestly, I should have chucked the damn thing in the Potomac on my way out of D.C. last year for all the good it does me. Except that my mama would blow a gasket if she didn't have a way to contact me every time a member of my family did something stupid. Which is often.

Despite these messages all accumulating in the last twenty-four hours or so, they're from my old life—the one I had to leave behind. The same one the unknown number keeps reminding me to let go of.

The article from the library starts burning a hole through my bag at the thought, but I've already promised myself to wait until I'm in the privacy of the attic to pull it out again. I roll my shoulder where I can still feel the impact of the librarian's head from earlier.

She smelled like vanilla and had the power of a linebacker, despite her short stature. My manners surely could have been better, but my mind was whirling too much to devote any effort to a conversation with the woman. Her vibe is the kind of eccentric that tells me conversing with her is more of a sport than a leisurely activity. I should know since I grew up with a mother who's exactly the same.

"What'll it be?"

A voice snaps me back to my surroundings, and I look up to see the line of customers between me and the coffee counter has disappeared.

I approach the waiting barista, my boots scuffing the tile floor as I scan the unfamiliar shop. "Yeah, sorry. Coffee. Black," I mutter.

I don't know what made me choose this coffee shop—I generally go to the one a few doors down from the brewery.

But walking around my hometown in a stranger's skin has had me seeking out unfamiliar habits and haunts that might fit this new me better. Maybe if I can relax in a fresh environment, I'll get some peace and stop feeling like a fish flopping around on a hot sidewalk sucking on air.

I'm not ready to accept this hand I've been dealt and leave the past where it is. Logically, I know the safest move is to let sleeping dogs lie and move on. Not every problem is mine to solve.

My phone vibrates in my pocket again as if reinforcing those very sentiments.

"Carter?" the barista asks. My eyes flick to him as adrenaline spikes from my lower back, singeing every nerve ending on its rush to my heart.

I'm not sure what I'm expecting to see, but each time one of those warning texts comes from the unknown number, my brain envisions every blind corner as a possible cliff's edge. The vigilance required is exhausting.

But the adrenaline dissipates when the face opposite me registers. I'll put it down to distraction that I didn't recognize him before.

"Pete?"

The guy swings a hand across the counter, his mouth spreading in an open smile that reminds me of sunny afternoons spent tossing the football and chasing girls.

"How the hell are you?" Pete grips my hand in a hearty shake, and I reflexively smile back at my old classmate. "I haven't seen you in… shit, probably ten years."

"At least that." I was never great about visiting, and when I did make it home to Asheville, my time was consumed by family. I never expected to move back, so maintaining relationships from the old days wasn't a priority. "What've you been up to?"

He releases my hand and spreads both of his to the sides as he surveys the coffee shop. "You're lookin' at it."

My brain connects the obvious dots. "Pete's Coffee. This is *your* shop." I take in the vintage tables and chairs bordered by nooks filled with overstuffed cushions and colorful artwork. It's got a comfortable-but-hip vibe my brewery couldn't touch. We're all kitsch and old-school wood.

"Going on eight years now." He grins and pumps dark coffee into a cardboard cup with movements so practiced, he doesn't need to take his eyes from me. "You home for a visit or you change careers to undercover ops?" He gestures to my shaggy beard and my hair that hasn't seen a barber shop in months.

"Right." I run an awkward hand through the mess on

my head. "I, uh, actually moved back. Cash and I opened a brewery." Why do I sound like I'm apologizing?

"Seriously? Very cool, man." He's nice enough not to ask more questions. My grand plans in politics were never a secret, and I know what people must be thinking—because I'm thinking it too. "I'll have to come check it out. What's it called?"

"Blue Bigfoot. Just down the road." I hook a thumb over my shoulder.

"No shit? I've been meaning to stop by there. Had no idea you guys owned it."

"Definitely stop in. I'll buy you a beer." It's the least I can do.

He slides the cup of steaming black liquid across the counter. "Then this one's on me, man."

A woman behind me clears her throat, and I realize we've been holding up the line. It's the first time since I've been home that I'm disappointed to cut a conversation short. Is that a good sign? I sure as hell hope so.

I'm getting sick of my own self, so I can only imagine how insufferable I've been to be around these last seven months. I owe my brother more than I can probably ever repay. Cash has single-handedly kept our business afloat while I've stumbled around only half conscious.

He and I co-own Blue Bigfoot Beer, a craft brewery and taproom in the River Arts District here in Asheville. When we started the business, I was essentially the money while Cash was on day-to-day operations. We both conceived of the vision for Blue Bigfoot and developed the initial beer recipes, taking inspiration from the summers spent helping our dad with his homebrewing operation way back. It's been a labor of love in a lot of ways—but, for me, it was only supposed to be a hobby. I had a career in politics that held 99 percent of my focus and energy.

Being the money made sense when I lived seven hours away and had more resources. But it's safe to say any of my cash reserves and connections dried up the minute I torpedoed my career and came crawling back home. Now I'm half-assing it as brewmaster for Blue Bigfoot while Cash still does the heavy lifting. And the fact that my brother hasn't given me one ounce of shit over not pulling my weight tells me I must look even worse off than I've been feeling. It's embarrassing if I let myself think about it too long.

Case in point, Cash spent the last few weeks single-handedly dealing with a disastrous inspection from the Health Department without telling me—something I'd have spotted if I'd been paying attention like I should. Luckily, we're now on track to hopefully pass our re-inspection in a couple days. Which reminds me I really should get my ass back to the brewery. I already wasted too much time at the library today.

Pete lifts his chin in farewell and takes the woman's order as I step aside and make my way out to the sidewalk. With the cup warming my hand and the spring sun filtering through the trees, my mood lightens a little.

That article needs to stay right where it is—or better yet, I should burn it. Only a fool would keep torturing himself with shit he can't possibly change. It's time to move on and focus on Blue Bigfoot and my family. Lord knows there's enough there to keep ten of me occupied.

But something inside me keeps clinging to the past, hoping it might rewrite itself.

"MILLER!" Cash's surly growl emanates from the taproom. The guy has had a rough week with this inspection business looming over us—not to mention an apparent breakup with his girlfriend, Hollis. Although the way those two fight, I'm guessing they'll be back to defiling the office desk any day now. I haven't so much as set one foot in that room since hearing them going at it like feral warthogs in there last week.

"What the hell does he want now?" Miller drops the mop he's been halfheartedly pushing around the brewhouse for the past ten minutes. The handle hits the concrete floor with a loud *crack*.

"Best to get it over with." I glance up from the fermenter leg joint I'm scrubbing as my youngest brother swipes at the curtain of hair that's trying to blind him. His only response is a grunt as he trudges to the door.

It's no secret Cash didn't want Miller working here, but family is family, no matter how many times they mess shit up. Miller's like a cat with nine lives, only by my count he's gotta be on at least his twentieth by now. His most recent was driving my car into a fence two weeks ago and escaping with only cuts and a broken arm. Just as well he's staying tucked in the fold where we can keep an eye on him and his dwindling lives.

Miller swaggers back into the brewhouse only seconds later, shit-eating grin in place. I don't ask.

Needing no prompting, he explains, "Turns out it wasn't my fault."

Again, I don't ask, and again, my brother expounds

anyway. "It's awfully rewarding seeing Cash eat his words, ain't it?"

Those two could argue about the color of a dog's asshole, so it's never a good idea to get involved. I pull myself to standing and admire my work before moving on to the next cleaning item on my list. We're making damn sure the inspector has nothing to say this time around. Miller natters on about whatever he and Cash were arguing over. Once he's done pretending to mop the brewhouse floor, I'll send him out to bug Cash while I clean it for real. It's quite the fall I've made going from future congressman to glorified janitor in less than a year.

But maybe I'll stick around and enjoy a beer with my brothers and the other staff when I'm done. It could keep my mind off that article I printed at the library. And Grace. And D.C. as a whole.

"So, if you think about it, I'm actually kind of the hero of the situation." Miller's words finally penetrate, and I blink over at him. He's fiddling with his earrings and paying me no mind at all while he props his casted arm on the mop handle.

"You think you can talk and mop at the same time?"

"Huh?" He glances at me and then the mop as if he's forgotten he's holding it. "Oh, right." He resumes his lackluster swiping of the floor.

"Quittin' time!" Cash shouts from the taproom. Miller's out the brewhouse door before the handle even hits the floor this time.

Cash's head appears in the doorway a second later. "What are you drinkin'?"

Decision made for me, I toss my rag onto a worktable and head for the door myself. "Whatever's cold," I respond. It's the same thing we always say when someone asks that question. It's what our dad always said too.

Cash grins and gestures for me to go ahead of him to the bar. Miller already has a beer in hand, listening to Oscar—one of the bartenders—tell some story that has him performing what looks like a belly dance. Kelsie snort-laughs and chokes on her drink while Cash slides behind the bar to pour me an IPA.

A reluctant smile crosses my face. Of all the places in the world to end up, I suppose I could do a lot worse than home.

CHAPTER
THREE

CATTYWAMPUS KIMCHI

SUNNY

Dear Mona,

My boyfriend has been going out with his friends almost every night and leaving me home alone. I thought it was just a phase, or him blowing off steam after a hard day's work, but he didn't even come home at all last night. When I confronted him, he told me it was no big deal. What should I do?

Sincerely,

Lonely in Leicester

Dear Lonely,

Key his car and tell him to get bent.

Sincerely,

Mona

I LIFT my eyes from the monitor to find Duke's grin staring back at me.

"You can't send this." I push the chair back from the desk.

"Sure I can." My grandfather raises a finger in lecture mode. "It's clear, it's concise, and that's a faultless piece of advice."

"Duke, it's rude."

"No, it's not. Now, the boyfriend? He's rude." The finger drops, and he turns to the office doorway. I scramble from the desk chair to follow him. "I hardly went anywhere without your grandma, God rest her soul."

"Yes, I agree. But people don't write in to advice columns for feedback like 'key his car.' This woman is hurting. It calls for a more thoughtful response—something constructive."

"Then you write it," he throws over his shoulder as he slowly hobbles his way to the kitchen. His mustard-yellow cardigan has a new stain on the back, adding to the variety of colors spotting the garment.

"This is so irresponsible. What was Randy thinking giving this column to you?" Randy is an old family friend who publishes a long-running local online newsletter. He has a surprising number of subscribers for a guy who doesn't believe in grammar.

"He was thinking his divorce means he can't ask Mona to keep writing it for him."

"Maybe so, but surely there's someone better suited." I pass in front of my grandfather to open the refrigerator.

"Like I said, you should take it. You're a writer, and you have more patience for morons at your age."

I glance up from my perusal of the fridge's contents. "I'm a librarian, not a writer."

"Same thing. It's settled then." He and his trusty cardigan inch toward the kitchen table by the window. Why isn't he using his cane?

I want to tell him I know absolutely nothing about

love, but he won't understand what that has to do with anything. Instead, I wait for him to settle at the table before moving on to the reason I sought him out in the first place.

"Mrs. Browning said she caught you looking in her window with your binoculars."

He barks out a laugh. "Why would I want to look at that bag of bones?"

"I don't know. You tell me." I finally decide on a pitcher of iced tea and close the door.

"I wasn't looking at *her*. I was looking at her roof." His amusement gives way to a scowl.

"Whatever for?"

"Drones."

Ah, I should have known. Ever since those things started coming out of the woodwork, he's been on high alert. Drones alone might explain his high blood pressure. "It was probably just some neighborhood kid." Why Duke is convinced us Underwoods are interesting enough to warrant surveillance is beyond me.

"In the middle of a school day? I don't think so." He shakes open today's newspaper and spreads it before him on the table.

I hand over a glass of tea, condensation already forming on the sides.

"Well, some retailers are experimenting with drone deliveries. Maybe we'll be able to get toilet paper dropped directly on our doorstep someday soon. Wouldn't that be nice?"

Duke is undeterred. "If I see it again, I'm shooting it with the BB gun." He takes a deep swallow of the tea, eyeing me over the glass with a raise of his furry white eyebrows.

Good gravy. "Well, whatever you do, don't shoot Mrs. Browning." I'm not confident he could hit anything past the front porch with that old BB gun in the first place, so it's not a battle worth fighting.

"I'm leaving for work. Promise me you won't send that response to Lonely in Leicester while I'm gone."

He sets the glass on the table with a satisfied "Ahh" before continuing in his usual raspy tone, "Fine. I won't send it. But that means you need to write something by Friday—*every* Friday. I promised Randy I'd take it off his hands."

"Okay, okay." It's only a letter or two for a friend. No biggie.

"Good. I'll forward the rest to you."

"The rest?" I'm afraid I'm not going to like his response.

"Yeah. There are only maybe fifteen this week. Randy will pick his favorite to publish."

Okay, no need to panic, I instruct myself. There's plenty of free time in the evenings. And, honestly, it can't be that big of a deal answering a few letters from people who probably already know what they should do in the first place. All they need is reassurance.

Easy squeezy.

Dear Mona,

My girlfriend refuses to try anal even though she knows it's important to me. I think it will bring us closer, but she's caught up in her head about it. How do I bring her around?

Sincerely,

Butt-Blocked and Blue

MIA CACKLES around her bite of chicken sandwich as she slides the phone back across the break room table to me.

"It's not funny! I have to respond to this guy!"

Her shrug is way too casual. "Just tell him to buy a dildo and let her do butt stuff to him first. What's good for the goose and all that. Maybe they'll both turn out to love it, and they can name the dildo after you."

"I'm not writing that." I knead my forehead and re-read the letter for the tenth time, my cheeks heating again. I've never even had sex, much less anal. I mean, sure, I've read about it in books, but that's like trying to coach some-body up Mount Everest when all you've done is read *A Walk in the Woods* from the safety of your couch.

"Why not?"

"The list of reasons would take longer than the remaining days I have left on this earth."

"You know this is the dictionary definition of irony, right? You getting stuck with this column when you never *ever* talk about S-E-X." She clutches at pearls that aren't there.

I glare at her and stab unenthusiastically at my salad with a plastic fork. Sebastian would be appalled, but I forgot to pack a metal one.

"You won't be laughing so much when I turn this column over to you." Mia is much better suited. If it were a column about manners or family relationships or crafts, I could power my way through with a combination of research and personal experience. But love and sex? I've never experienced either. Well, not really.

I mean, I've only ever had one boyfriend, and he

wanted to wait until marriage. Turned out he meant marriage to someone else. But it turned out for the best in the end because I don't think I was really in love with him. I wanted to be, but I never got that feeling people talk about—the one where you ache when you're not with that person. Where your entire body sighs when they look at you, and even the way they snore or chew their food is endearing.

Sebastian, on the other hand? I could fall hard for him. I'm halfway there already, and we've never even kissed. But I feel like I know his heart, and it's a perfect match for mine.

"No way," Mia cuts into my thoughts. "This will be good for you. Stretch you out of your comfort zone."

I jab the air between us with my fork. "I spend plenty of time outside my comfort zone, I'll have you know."

"Taking up crocheting in place of knitting is not what I would classify as a stretch." Mia pops her last bite of sandwich in her mouth and starts wiping stray crumbs from the table.

"I embroider too," I mutter.

"Well, then. I stand corrected."

"I can't believe you're going to make me do this." Am I whining? This won't do. I hate whining.

"Believe it, babe. Now, let's get back to work before Meredith gives us the boot."

"Fine." I snap the lid back on my salad and consider my fork before tossing it back in my lunch bag to reuse at home. I can picture Sebastian's nod of approval. "But if Duke takes on any more projects, I'm volunteering you as tribute."

She pauses to give me the full side-eye treatment. "It's cute you think you can boss me around."

The afternoon is uneventful, apart from an argument Mia breaks up between a couple of high school students. I'm unsure if I've ever heard the term "assbadger" before, but I file it away in my list of words that are fun to say. Cattywampus is my current favorite, but assbadger has a fighting chance to overtake it—not that I can imagine a scenario in my daily life that would call for it.

I spend a good part of the day reshelving books and researching a community program I've been working on. When I notice my attention drifting to the front doors of the library one time too many, I explain it away as eager anticipation of after-school Story Hour. The elementary school children are always so enthusiastic; it's lovely to share their energy—especially when they let me do all the voices.

In the back of my mind, of course, I know I'm waiting for the artist.

He tends to come several days in a row and then disappear for a week or so. I can only assume he's doing research for a project because he spends most of his time scrolling and taking notes on a spiral-bound pad.

The fact that he doesn't appear to have his own phone or computer is consistent with the entire artist vibe. I feel an instant kinship with anyone who uses physical notebooks as opposed to phone apps. It's my theory that the mechanical process of writing with pen and paper releases dopamine in the brain. At least, it does for me.

When the artist doesn't show by the end of my shift, I tell myself it's a good thing. But I might be lying to myself.

"DUKE? I'M HOME!"

"In the den."

I round the corner to find my grandfather in his recliner and Sebastian sitting on the sofa eating some concoction from a mason jar. Duke has his favorite true-crime podcast blaring from his phone from the arm of the recliner.

Sebastian grins my way, voice raised over the host. "Sunny. Just the girl I was looking for."

My cheeks warm at his greeting. "Hi, Sebastian." He's wearing one of his hemp shirts today paired with cotton pants and his usual slides from a sustainable shoe company. A portion of his sandy hair is gathered with a hair tie at his crown while the rest barely dusts his shoulders. How does he keep it so shiny? I should ask what conditioner he uses.

Duke mutters something too quiet for me to make out before he hits the pause button and allows my ears to stop ringing. Using the chair arms for leverage, he hoists himself up and I stem the urge to go and help. His doctor said he needs to keep working that hip, but it's a delicate balance between exercising it and overdoing it. He grabs his cane and shuffles to the hall. His scowl as he passes me is summarily ignored. Duke is not a fan of visitors in our house, even ones as familiar as Sebastian.

"You want some tea?" I ask my guest reflexively, pointing toward the kitchen.

He chews and swallows whatever it is that he's eating. "Is it sustainably grown, GMO-free, and organic?"

"I, uh." I pause, unsure how to answer. I go with, "It's Lipton."

Sebastian shakes his head and I decide to leave the tea right where it is. Instead, I plop down on the sofa next to him.

"It's great to see you. How are the rally plans going?"

"Good." He sets his jar and fork on the coffee table and turns to me. "That's actually why I stopped by."

Sebastian rents the room above our neighbor's garage, so despite his lack of car, we can easily see one another whenever we want. Which is, unfortunately, less often than I would like.

Eager to be of help, I lean closer. "Oh yeah? What can I do?" Maybe he wants to brainstorm slogans for protest signs, or he needs help with his speech. Or I could put my research skills to use for the cause.

"I need somebody to pick up the goats."

My smile falters at that.

He sends me a chagrined smile. "I know it's a lot to ask…" he trails off.

"I drive a MINI Cooper, Sebastian." How does he imagine I'll fit even one goat in Delilah the MINI?

He lays a hand on my knee, and that small gesture alone has my pulse kicking up. He is so going to be my boyfriend. "I'm so slammed with all the other preparations. Saving the earth isn't for the faint of heart."

Well, I'm not faint of heart, that's for sure. So, I summon my best smile. "I'll figure something out." A positive attitude is everything. I've got this. I *love* goats.

His responding smile is dazzling, and my body sings when he comes in for a fierce hug. "Thank you so much. I knew I could count on you, Sunny," he says into my hair.

Warmth spreads through my chest cavity at his words, and I inhale his scent of tea tree, eucalyptus, and… something sour. But who cares. He's such a wonderful person, and I'm so lucky to have someone like him in my life. The least I can do is haul some goats around.

"Absolutely," I respond as he releases me. I know my

cheeks are pink, but there's no helping it. "Do you want to watch a movie tonight or something?" I gesture to the TV. "Or maybe a documentary? There's a new one on Netflix about bees."

He turns forward again, reaching for his jar. "Oh, sorry, I can't. Too busy with the rally." He screws the lid back on and tucks the fork in the breast pocket of his shirt.

"Of course you are." I shake my head. "That was silly of me." Duh.

Sebastian stands and bends toward me. I lift my face, longing for the feel of his lips on mine.

As always, the kiss lands on my cheek instead. "Sorry about the kimchi breath," is all he says before straightening and heading for the back door with his jar. Just before it closes behind him, though, he turns and smiles again. "You really are the best, Sunny."

I sigh as the door settles in place. One of these days, I'll work up the courage to pounce on him.

But it's probably for the best that tonight wasn't the night. There's dinner to cook, goat herding to organize, and a letter about butt stuff that I can't even begin to imagine how to answer.

Whoever said being a librarian isn't challenging clearly hasn't walked a day in this librarian's platform sneakers.

CARTER

"YOU WANNA RIDE with Miller and me, or are you taking the pimpmobile?"

I rub the sleep from my eyes as I all but stumble into the kitchen. I'm too tired to trade insults with Cash.

"I can't wait to get rid of that thing." The loaner car from my insurance company looks more like a neon green circus on wheels than an automobile, and no one in my family appears even remotely ready to stop finding it amusing as fuck.

It's the morning of the re-inspection, so we're all heading into Blue Bigfoot early to triple check our list before we open for the day. There's no telling when the health inspector will show up, so we'll be on alert all day.

Since Miller has no vehicle and he crashed mine, I'm either bumming a ride with Cash in his piece of shit or getting strange looks at stoplights in my current ride.

"That reminds me. Which one of you assholes decorated my dashboard?" When I got in the car last night, there was a figure of a bulldog smoking a cigar dangling from my rearview mirror and plastic gold chains strewn across the dash.

My brothers both do a shit job of hiding their smiles. "I believe you have Denny to thank for that," Cash finally divulges, ratting out our other brother who's not around to defend himself.

"You should keep the pimpmobile. Maybe install a custom horn and some LED lights," Miller suggests, pushing the toaster lever down on his Pop-Tart. The guy still eats like he's twelve instead of twenty-one.

"Who's buying the Popemobile?" Mama wanders into the kitchen, wringing water from her masses of curly hair with a towel.

Yeah, we live with our mom. Big fuckin' deal. I suppose if I can convince myself I'm stuck here, it's about time to get my own place and move out of my mother's attic.

"Nobody." I don't bother to correct her, instead shuffling my way to the coffee maker to pour myself a cup. I slept like shit last night—no newsflash there. Adrenaline used to keep me up at night, and I thrived on it in a way. Now it's regret, anger, or frustration waking me up at all hours.

When I got home last night, the itch to go down the wrong rabbit hole wouldn't let me rest, so I decided to send Jeremy, my old coworker from D.C., a long-overdue text. As I suspected, the guy was awake at two a.m.

JEREMY:

He's alive! How the hell are you?

ME:

Good. Sorry for ghosting.

Jeremy doesn't know why I left my job; I assume Grace made up some bullshit reason. It doesn't matter, really. All that matters is that I'm here now and not there. We've exchanged a few texts since I've been gone, but not much. I blame myself for that.

JEREMY:

How would you like a visitor? I'm thinking of coming down and trying that beer you're always talking about.

ME:

Anytime, man.

It would be good to see him. We worked side by side for four years and shared way too many late-night shots and early morning coffees. Just because I don't live near him anymore is no reason to end our friendship.

JEREMY:

The April recess starts on Saturday, so we'll be headed to Raleigh. How about if I swing over your way on the front end?

Maybe this is exactly what I need.

ME:

You're on. Fly into Charlotte and I'll pick you up.

He'll have a field day with my loaner.

JEREMY:

No way. I'm driving my new Mercedes. Got the executive package and everything.

Of course he has a new Mercedes. The guy grew up

without two pennies to rub together and feels the constant need to play catch-up now that he's an adult with a decent-paying job. A thought occurred to me, and I went with it before I could think too hard about it.

ME:

> Does that new ride happen to have a hitch?

By the time I finally hit the hay, I'd tied up the last remaining loose end from my former life—or at least the last one that won't get me in trouble. In three days' time, my storage unit will be empty and my belongings on their way to North Carolina via the Jeremy Ricci pussywagon express.

In other words, I might want to move my ass on that apartment hunt.

"Cart's gonna keep his loaner and start a side business as a sex worker," Miller supplies as he tries shoving a fork between his cast and skin. That thing must itch like a son of a bitch. Good. He deserves it for totaling my car.

Mama doesn't blink an eye. "I'll give Regina a call. You can work for her if you need money that badly."

Cash chokes on his coffee in the corner and Miller guffaws, so I grab an orange from the fruit bowl and chuck it at him. It hits him in the back of the head, which makes me smile for the first time this morning.

Our mama knows everyone in town—or at least it feels that way—and she counts among her friends a woman named Regina Caldwell who runs a high-class male escort business out of a Victorian in Montford. They belong to the same book club, and I've learned the hard way never to ask about their current book selections.

I fill another coffee mug and hand it over to Mama. "I think I'm good."

She only shrugs and continues drying her hair with one hand while she cradles the coffee in the other. "Thanks, baby."

I glance over to see Mango, Mama's pet skunk, trot into the kitchen. He ignores the rest of us and heads straight for his mistress, as usual. She spoils that thing rotten. Case in point, when she doesn't immediately bend to pet him, he stomps his feet on the worn wood floor.

"Well, good morning, my little sweetheart," Mama coos, tossing her towel over a chair and picking Mango up with one hand. I swear he smirks at me. "Do you want some breakfast?"

We brothers come to a silent agreement that it's time to take off, so I quickly shrug on my flannel and go hunting for my boots. It's time to get this inspection off our backs and return to business as usual.

BY NOON, I'm watching the bald spot on the back of the inspector's head as he pushes through Blue Bigfoot's doors on his way out.

Cash stands in the center of the taproom, dressed in a checked flannel like me, his dark head bent to inspect the report. "Thank God." He sighs in relief.

Kelsie, Oscar, and Miller start whooping and hollering, but my eyes are on the inspector as he walks to his car. Something feels off, so I'm not ready to celebrate.

"Was that weird for anyone else?" Cash asks, glancing my way and reading my mind. "I mean, he didn't check half the stuff we were cited on, not that I'm complaining."

He's not wrong. The guy gave Cash a laundry list of violations last time he was in, threatening to shut us down if we didn't get up to whatever new code he outlined. I honestly didn't even know about it until a couple days ago when Cash finally sat me down and explained what had been going on right under my nose.

But the guy walked in this time, only glancing at a couple things before signing off and taking his leave. It makes no sense at all.

I wander closer to the door, and the hairs on the back of my neck stand on end when I see the inspector approach a car with the familiar red, white, and blue "Taxation Without Representation" license plates.

My pulse rockets, but I do my best to temper my tone as I stop next to Cash. "What did he say when he came in last time?"

Cash's response is flippant. "Hey, man, it's over."

I pin him with a stare until he answers.

"You know how they operate. He gave himself free run of the place and flashed his badge when I walked up."

My brother is not understanding me. "But why did he come when we'd just had our usual inspection the month before?" I'm keeping one eye on the inspector who has his phone to his ear and is fiddling with his car keys. Maybe I'm looking for trouble where there is none, but what the fuck is a health inspector with D.C. plates doing checking on bars in North Carolina? My pulse kicks up another notch as I see those warning texts run through my mind's eye.

"Oh, I see what you mean." Cash taps on the new inspection report. "When I went to the Department of Health, they checked the record and said he got an anonymous tip. Which is weird, now that I think about it, because he's a regional supervisor or something. He doesn't work in Buncombe County, so I can't imagine why somebody would call *him*."

My frown intensifies. Why would a regional office get a call about a nothing bar in Asheville? And how would that translate to bringing someone from D.C.?

It wouldn't. That's how.

"And you don't have any idea who might have called?" I glance around at the group of jackasses pouring beers behind the bar without a care in the world. "We didn't piss someone off earlier that week or something?" I'm grasping at straws now.

"Why are you looking at me?" Miller throws his hands up.

But Cash reels me back in. "No. Like I said, I assumed it was a joke at the time." He and Hollis had been in the middle of a prank war, and my brother assumed it was Hollis's doing. Which it turned out not to be.

I snatch the paper from his hand and skim the text, my gut gurgling with bile. "You remember what day that was?"

My brother frowns back at me. "Sure. It was the tenth. One week before St. Pat's. What the hell is going on, Cart?"

The tenth. I flip backward through the days in my head. Shit. The first text from the unknown number came in on the eighth. The timing is dead-on.

Was this threat to shut us down supposed to be a warning to *me*?

There's nothing helpful on this report or anywhere in this brewery. But there's no sense in worrying Cash about something that's my business alone. So I muster my best carefree shrug. "Nothing. Just my imagination getting away from me." I clap him on the shoulder, turning to the bar. "Great job, everybody. Thanks!"

I leave the crew to their celebrations and haul ass to the brewhouse, where I pull off my apron and toss it on the worktable. After committing the dates of all the warning texts to memory, I toss my phone on top of it, and I'm out the back door of the building seconds later. There's only one place I need to be right now, and it's not here at Blue Bigfoot.

I need to get to the library. Right fucking now.

CHAPTER
FIVE

WOULD JOHN WICK WEAR
FLANNEL?

CARTER

THE CAR GROANS and sputters before the engine shuts off in the parking lot of the library. The sun nearly blinds me as I climb out and hustle to the brick building's doors. I need to log into the chat rooms and message boards and verify my suspicions.

But, sure enough, I'm waylaid by the cheerful librarian almost the moment I cross the threshold.

"Hello again!" Her voice is chirpy and her smile indicates she's been mainlining caffeine all morning. She's cute, I'll give her that, but I don't have time for cute right now.

"Um, hi." I'm determined not to be rude after yesterday, but my anxiety has other ideas.

Possibly sensing my urgency, she gets to the point by bringing her hands around from behind her back and extending a magazine covered in plastic.

"What's this?" I ask, absolutely perplexed as to why she's giving me a back issue of *Car and Driver*.

She blinks up at me, her long eyelashes sweeping her cheeks and lending her an uncanny resemblance to a wide-eyed anime character. "I thought you might like it."

I consider this odd creature for a moment. Short and nicely curvy, she has reddish hair and an uninhibited smile that highlights the gap between her two front teeth as she smiles at me like we're old friends.

Whatever she's thinking, I need her to go think it about someone else. "Thanks, but I'm okay." I put a palm up.

She persists, even moving to intercept me as I try side-stepping her. "I don't know about you, but when I'm researching so intensely, I like to take a break and read something else for a bit." She shakes the magazine in another invitation to accept it.

I do, if only to end this interaction. "Uh, thanks." I nod and step aside again to bypass her.

Thankfully, she allows it this time, only saying, "There's a fantastic article on page seventy-six, in case you're looking for a place to start."

I lift my hand in acknowledgment and keep walking. Probably rude but I've got shit to do.

"It's really, *really* informative," she tells my retreating back, her eagerness palpable.

I'll have to take her word for it because the moment I sit down and plug in my thumb drive, my focus is fixed on the monitor.

Call me paranoid, but ever since those warning texts started, I've been careful as hell not to use my own phone or the Blue Bigfoot laptop to check in on my old bosses—or even read articles like the one I printed the other day. Whoever is texting those messages could be tracking me or hacking into my devices to check up on me. And I don't want to invite that kind of trouble.

But those D.C. plates are burned into my retinas—including the numbers—and they're telling me I may not have covered my tracks as well as I thought.

It only takes a few minutes to find what I'm looking for. I scroll back in the server search results to a post I made earlier this month. The date is March seventh. Three days before the out-of-state inspector showed up on our doorstep and one day before my first warning text.

Shit.

Kayak224: *"Anybody heard of a supplement called Nutri-Slender? It's being developed for weight loss."*

It took me three months to find the right chat rooms and message boards on the dark web. Honestly, the first challenge was figuring out how to access the dark web on a library computer in the first place. But the guy who runs the smoke shop a few doors down from us turned out to be surprisingly helpful on that count. I'm guessing his need for anonymous web surfing is a little less legal than mine.

The dark web is a maze of disorganization, so it took time to find what I was looking for: namely, other people interested in investigating and exposing corruption and disinformation. Not an area I thought I'd end up in, yet here I am.

My usual MO is that of a lurker more than a participant in the conversations. These range from discussions of suspected kickbacks enjoyed by members of the government to completely out-there conspiracy bullshit that makes me wonder if I'm in the middle of The Matrix. And while I don't believe the Denver airport hosts the international headquarters of the Illuminati, I do find it plausible that certain people of power cross a lot of lines that shouldn't be crossed.

The day I posted my question, I was feeling frustrated by my lot in life, and I took a chance.

The replies to my post from the seventh were vague at best, nothing attention-grabbing or particularly helpful. I remember feeling surprised that NutriSlender wasn't on anyone's radar since it had been consuming my thoughts for months. But I should have expected the parties involved would be taking great care.

The first warning text came the next day, but I didn't make the connection since the dark web is both anonymous and a bitch to navigate. I thought I was safe.

I keep scrolling and switching to different boards and rooms until I find the other post I made a week later. It was in a server for North Carolina based users.

Victor676: *"Looking for anyone with intel on Clarence Cody, congressman from Tennessee's tenth district."*

In retrospect, posting a name was foolish. I'd done it on a whim, but even then, I knew digging into this could spell trouble. It's why I'd abandoned the notion on my drive out of D.C. last year, the henchmen's warnings fresh in my ears. Casually gathering information and staying up to date was one thing; embarking on an investigation was another.

A few hours after posting that last one, my second warning text arrived, which finally had me connecting some dots. I worried the chat rooms and boards were no longer safe and decided to give them a rest for a couple weeks to test my theory.

But when the warning texts kept coming, I wasn't so sure.

Until today. Now I'm positive that whoever is behind that unknown number is the same person who tried to put Cash and me out of business with those bogus violations. When it looked like I was sticking my nose where it didn't belong, they sent a threat in the form of fucking with my livelihood. When I appeared to back off, no longer posting on the dark web, *poof*, the brewery was off the hook.

They can consider their message received. Loud and clear.

But their strategy has one giant flaw I'm guessing they never considered. I may be intimidated, but I'm also good and pissed.

Jaw clenched, I skim over the three responses to my post about Congressman Cody that I received but never had a chance to check. One is pure gibberish, the second suggests checking out another server, and the last responder says they may have something, and I should reach out via private chat.

The voice that told me to let sleeping dogs lie and only worry about making beer sounds a lot less convincing now that these assholes have come for not just me but my family.

You fuck with my family and I find it damn near impossible not to fuck with you right back. The last time I felt this motivated by revenge was when my dad died due to negligence from a surgeon and an OR nurse. If Mama hadn't insisted on taking the first settlement offer, the lawyers I hired would have kept after the doctor, the nurse, and the entire damn hospital until there was nothing left. The doctor and nurse lost their jobs, sure, but I would have taken it further if Mama hadn't insisted we move on.

It's not lost on me, though, that I don't have the kind of resources it would take to bring people this powerful down. I'm merely a reluctant brewmaster from a mountain town in the middle of pretty much nowhere. But that doesn't mean I can't at least do my best to protect my own.

I quickly type out a private message to the last responder, someone with the screenname MarsOrBust. This user generally posts about unsolved cold cases and some out-there conspiracy theories, but some of the context tells me that he or she is local to this area. It's got to be worth at least hearing what they have to say.

But even the dark web isn't safe anymore, so I log off as soon as I press send. I need a plan to get these bastards off my back for good and make sure my family isn't caught in the middle of my shitstorm again.

I may not be a hotshot anymore, but that doesn't mean I'm not still up for a good challenge.

CHAPTER
SIX

ARE SUPERMARKETS SEXY?

SUNNY

TO KEEP my behavior from bleeding into stalker territory, I vow to avoid the handsome artist for the rest of his visit. It was bad enough I forced the mushroom article on him earlier, but it really did have some fascinating information. There was nothing about porn, in case that is another issue he's grappling with, but I assume all addiction starts in the same place. And, really, I have zero evidence he has a porn problem. He could be addicted to shopping or exercise—or eating paint chips, for all I know. People are very complex.

I probably should have listened to Mia and kept out of this man's business, but there's no stopping me once I get an idea in my head.

For instance, the newest Mona response I'm determined to nail.

Dear Dayglo Princess,
   While I'm sure glow-in-the-dark vibrators can be fun, I

suggest you and your boyfriend stop using this one immedi-
ately and call your doctor. I hope the swelling goes down soon.
  Sincerely,
  Mona

This week is giving me a whole new appreciation for Randy's ex-wife.

I drop my pen to the table and yawn before closing the notebook and pulling out my yarn and crochet hook from my bag. While I have yet to figure out how to transport goats to Raleigh in my MINI Cooper next weekend, I did decide that the protesters could use some mascots to get their point across.

So, I'm crocheting little goats for them to wear as pins on their shirts and jackets. Kind of like a calling card for goat-rental enthusiasts. I stayed up late and finished five last night, so I figure if I work on them over my lunch hours and in the evenings, I can churn out at least thirty of them with no problem. Who needs sleep when there's a planet to save?

Sebastian is going to *love* them.

As if thinking of him had the power to summon the man, my phone vibrates on the lunch table with a text from Sebastian. Nothing can stop my grin.

SEBASTIAN:

Any chance you're free tomorrow night?

My belly flips, and I abandon the goat I was working on to text him back.

ME:

For you? Absolutely ☺

I can't believe it's finally happening. He's asking me out! This will be so terrific. We can go out to dinner, then maybe stay in and watch that bee documentary. Oh, or I could cook for him. I've been meaning to experiment with vegan recipes. Maybe I'll rent a movie for Duke to stream in his bedroom to give us privacy. Especially in case things get sexy.

SEBASTIAN:

Great! You want to run errands together?

Okay, not exactly the romantic date I had in mind, but spending time together is the most important thing. Heck, even the supermarket can be romantic if you have the right mindset. And I'll need those vegan ingredients anyway.

ME:

Sure. I should be home by 5:30.

SEBASTIAN:

Okay. I'll be over around 6:00.

ME:

Any signs of tiredness I might have been feeling evaporate at the prospect of an evening alone with Sebastian. Doing real couple things like running errands and doing favors for one another have all the earmarks of dating, right?

I decide they do and find myself wearing a silly grin the rest of my lunch break. By the time I return to Mia's side at circulation, I've finished another goat and my mood is even cheerier than usual.

"What got into you?"

"Oh, nothing. Just thinking about my *date* with Sebastian tomorrow night." My joy radiates from every pore.

"A date? Wow, that's great!" She knows how long I've been waiting for this. "Where is he taking you?"

"We're running errands together." Pretending not to notice how her smile drops, I hurry on, "I need to pick up Duke's prescriptions, then we'll probably hit the grocery store and maybe pick up some supplies for the goat rally. Then we'll watch some TV or something, I'm sure."

"Sounds cozy." Mia's tone carries the reassurance I need.

I grin at her. "That's exactly what I was thinking."

"Excuse me."

Our heads snap in the direction of the voice. The beautiful, tortured artist stands across from us.

"Hello again." I offer him an encouraging smile, hoping to appear more professional this time. I wonder if he read the article. Would it be weird to ask him if he knows where to get mushrooms?

"Is there a public phone I can use?"

"I'm afraid not," Mia replies before I can. While she's technically correct, exceptions can always be made.

"Is there any way we can help?" I ask, abandoning my vow to avoid him since he's the one who approached me this time.

"No." He runs a hand through his thick waves, and I notice he's back to his lucky flannel shirt today. It's green and ivory, with a tartan that has me thinking he's the kind of guy who'd look darn good in a kilt. "I just need a phone. My car battery is dead, so I was going to call for help."

"If that's all, I can help." I rise from my chair, ignoring the sharp tug on the back of my shirt from Mia. I was so preoccupied by my impending date with Sebastian I hadn't even noticed the artist leave—or try to, as it happens.

"No. No, you don't have to do that." He waves me off.

Mia tries to cut in, but I beat her to the punch. "Why not? I've got jumper cables, and it will be a lot faster—and cheaper—than calling someone else." I reinforce my statement with a wide smile. "No problem at all."

"Are you… sure?" His hesitation is entirely unnecessary.

"Absolutely." My smile tenses as Mia yanks so hard this time I hear a stitch pop in my T-shirt. "You go on and I'll be out in a minute."

The nanosecond he's out of ear's reach, Mia pulls me back down to my chair. "You are not going out to the parking lot alone with that man."

I roll my eyes. "Why not?"

"Because first, you have no idea who he is." She ticks off a finger before moving to the next. "Second, I'm pretty sure he lives off the grid in his car—which may or may not be a windowless white van." Another tick. "Third, he talks to himself—while scowling, no less. And fourth, he has a penis." She drops her hand only to point a finger from the other one in my face. "This is clearly not a man living his best life, and on the off chance he decides wearing a jacket made of your skin will turn things around for him, I'm putting my foot down."

"All the more reason to make his day easier." I pluck my keys from my bag and sidestep her chair.

"At least wait until Tanisha gets back from lunch so I can go with you."

I pause and turn back to my friend with a reassuring smile. "You worry too much."

"You worry too little."

I pat the butt of my favorite harem pants. "I have my phone, and I won't get into his car. I swear."

Mia's lips twist to the side. "You know my hair is going prematurely gray because of you, right?"

"Liar."

She sighs. "I hate you."

"I love you too."

Mia has nothing to worry about. I have no further intention of inserting myself into this man's life in any way apart from offering a simple jump to his car battery. Well, and advice on fungi.

But you know what they say about good intentions and handsome men... The road to hell is lousy with both of them.

CARTER

"YOU SURE I CAN'T..." My voice trails off as the librarian grunts again, her generous backside jiggling under the satiny fabric of her pants while she shoves aside another pile of books and yarn. I'm not trying to be impolite by looking, but the woman's upper half has been buried in the trunk of her tiny car for the last ten minutes, where she's trying to uncover the jumper cables she's sworn are inside. I never realized so much crap could fit in a MINI Cooper.

I wish I'd brought my phone, but it's best to remain careful.

"Aha!" the girl exclaims, straightening and drawing my attention back to her face. Locks of thick auburn hair obscure half of it and she blows them aside with a quick puff of breath before grinning widely. That gap between her two front teeth pairs with her exuberance to give off a childlike energy, yet I'm sure she's in her midtwenties.

"You found them." My response isn't a question because what else could "aha" possibly mean?

"Yes!" But as her eyes meet mine, her grin loses some of its enthusiasm. "Well, no, but I've been looking for this forever!" She lifts her hand up between us, and sitting on her upturned palm is what appears to be a tiny plush toadstool.

Christ. Exactly how big a risk would bringing a phone really have been?

As if reading my thoughts, she tosses the toy over the back seat of her MINI and dives back in. My field of vision is once again consumed by her ass encased in what I'm fairly certain are pajama bottoms. I avert my gaze again.

Not that her ass isn't perfectly nice, but my thoughts are occupied with topics more important than this woman's body. Besides, she's much too scatterbrained to be of any interest to me even if I did have the bandwidth to consider it.

No, my taste has always leaned toward ambitious, stylish women with just enough conceit to make it interesting. Not true assholes or sociopaths, but females who like to put on a little bit of a show—ones who know the game well and are good at playing it. After all, if you don't have to work for something, is it really worth it?

Something tells me that while this librarian may be skilled at Scrabble or possibly Dungeons & Dragons, she's no master of seduction.

But why am I even thinking about this? I need to get my ass back to the brewery to avoid raising suspicion after my interrogation of Cash earlier. I can come back tomorrow to check for a response from MarsOrBust.

My jaw tenses again at the nerve of these assholes. Ruining my chosen career wasn't enough? Now they try to ruin my backup plan—and my family's livelihood? Not fucking okay.

"Got 'em!" The librarian shoots upright again, this time with a pair of cables grasped in one hand. "Told you I had them."

"Great." I move to take the bundle of wires and clamps, but she pulls them out of reach. My jawbone may actually crack at this rate.

"I can do it." She tries taming her mess of reddish waves with her free hand while her spine snaps straight at her proclamation.

"I'm sure you can. But I figured since I'm already dirty…" I glance down at my clothes, aware of how disheveled I appear. But what's the point in grooming myself if all I'm doing is making beer? Hell, I don't even interact with customers. Her eyes drop down my frame before we both switch to examining her attire.

Either she borrows her clothes from someone's grandmother, or she hasn't updated her wardrobe since childhood. Her orange pajama bottoms pair tragically with a lime green T-shirt bearing the slogan "I wet my plants."

Not that I have room to talk, of course. My current wardrobe was pulled from a box in the attic—all relics of my youth in Asheville. There had been no need to schlep worn-out jeans, old T-shirts, and flannels to D.C. when I moved there after college. Just thinking about the price of a suit from my storage unit should make me want to vomit, but habit has a way of making things feel normal.

House staffers don't get paid all that much, but there's an image to maintain in that town and in the halls we occupy. Expensive but not too expensive. Sharp, clean, conservative, manicured—only to remain invisible beside more important individuals whose presentation is often nine-tenths of the job.

The girl surrenders the jumper cables and rounds her car to re-park it next to mine. "Which one's yours?" she asks out her open window.

I have no choice but to point to the massive bile-green Oldsmobile at the edge of the lot.

"Oooh, pretty," is her inexplicable response.

As soon as we're resituated by the Olds, she pops her hood. I do the same, then start prying off the terminal caps on my battery so I can attach the clamps. It takes some elbow grease to loosen them, and my hands are mostly black by the time I finish. I wipe them on my already dirty pants.

"Sorry about before," the librarian says from behind me, "with the cables, I mean. I know your day has already gone cattywampus, so you didn't need the attitude. But people assume women don't know basic things, and it makes us a little stabby."

My head jerks sideways, instinct taking over in case she is indeed standing there with a knife to stab my ignorant ass.

"Not at all." I place the last clamp and straighten. I must be a good foot taller than this girl. "You should meet my mother." That woman has tried her hand at a million things and succeeded at most of them. Gender has nothing to do with it. She's living proof that curiosity and determination trump any advantage gender might ever offer.

"Thanks, but I barely know you." The girl's brow creases as she winds her loose hair up into a knot on top of her head.

Wait, what? Shit. I throw my grease-streaked hands up between us. "Sorry, I didn't mean—"

"I'm messing with you." Her gap-toothed smile breaks through the feigned tension, and her gray eyes sparkle with amusement.

I cannot handle this today.

For reasons I can't explain, she continues, "I'm dating someone anyway. His name is Sebastian. He's an environmentalist." She punctuates her statement by shoving a pencil through the hair knot and dropping her hands to her hips.

I decide to go with, "Good to know," hoping it suffices as both a satisfactory response and a safeguard from getting stabbed by her hair pencil.

I step toward her, eager to finish connecting the cables and get this piece of junk running again. But if I thought she'd make things easy by stepping aside, I'm mistaken. She doesn't budge, meaning I can't access her car battery.

"Are you an artist?" she asks, her tone strangely breathy now.

"Am I what?"

"An artist."

"Um, no." I lift the clamps in a silent request for her to move aside, which she does this time.

"Are you sure?"

Her terminal caps release with much more ease than mine. "Am I... yeah, pretty sure." Praying that this conversation doesn't escalate into a dissection of my life choices, I secure the second set of clamps and straighten again. "You wanna start your car?" When she ignores me in favor of further silent examination of my person, I tack on a "please?"

She finally moves ass and heads for the driver's side again. The insurance company has *got* to give me a different loaner after this. I swear the guy who hooked me up with this giant eyesore enjoyed fucking with me.

The librarian's engine comes to life, and I go take a seat in my car. Maybe if I sit here while my battery charges up, there'll be no need to engage in conversation about toadstools, artists, or *Car and Driver* magazine. But luck is not in my corner today because she appears beside me only a moment later.

"So, if you're not an artist, what do you do?" Her hands are perched on her hips again, and she's squinting at me as sunlight bears down on her face.

It's not like I'm going anywhere anytime soon, so I may as well accept my fate. I sigh and say, "I make beer."

"Oh." She thinks on that for a second, and then her expression sags like something awful dawned on her. "*Oh no.*"

"Lemme guess. You're more of a wine girl?" I tap the steering wheel, wondering when the last time was this woman successfully kept a thought to herself.

"No, it's not that. It's just… Did you read that article on page seventy-six?"

"Sorry, no. I didn't get to it."

She chews her lip for a few moments before asking, "So, when you say you make beer, what exactly do you mean?"

"My brother and I own a craft brewery in the River Arts District. I'm the brewmaster." I manage not to make it sound like an apology this time. That's progress, I suppose.

"Oh." Her brow creases until her eyes widen almost comically and another smile overtakes her face. "Oh, my gosh. That's so wonderful to hear!"

I cough out a laugh at her enthusiasm, unable to help

myself. She must *really* like beer. "Don't be too impressed. We're minuscule in comparison to a lot of the local breweries."

She's undeterred. "What's your place called?"

Shit. I hope I won't regret this. "Blue Bigfoot Beer."

There go her eyes again, this time accompanied by a gasp and a hand to her ample breasts. "I've been there."

"Really?" This is unexpected.

"Yeah. My grandpa has a thing for folklore—so I took him there on his birthday last month. He even rubbed the sasquatch's head for good luck."

"Larry." I smile back at her, supplying the name of the Bigfoot statue that stands on our bar. It belonged to our dad, and we like to think it keeps his spirit alive in some way. Color me surprised that this peculiar librarian turns out to be a bar patron of all things.

We both fall silent while the hum of her engine fills the air. Not that she's appeared to need much participation from me, but the awkwardness of our interaction is ironic, really. I've always wielded words and conversation as both a weapon and a magic wand of sorts.

Convincing people to do what you want or to believe what you say is only a matter of figuring out the right words. All successful politicians know that, and it's something my bosses and colleagues have recognized in me—and exploited in the pursuit of our shared agendas. They used to send me in to grease the wheels with assistants and aides. I'd leave with a hard-to-win appointment or a handful of favors every time.

But clearly, I've lost my touch.

I take a breath and release it. "So, uh, how long have you worked here?" Wow. Step aside, Rachel Maddow. The master has arrived.

"About four years. I used to be a substitute high school teacher but then I went back to school for library science."

"What did you teach?"

She shrugs and rests her pajama-clad hip on my door-frame. "All sorts of subjects. But it was mostly a lot of glorified study halls."

That sounds like my idea of a fresh hell. "Sounds tedious."

"Only if you let it be, you know what I mean?"

"Not really," I admit. "I think I thrive on chaos." Isn't that the truth.

"Oh, high school can be chaos, alright." She brings a hand up to shield her eyes from the bright March sun. "One time, some students locked me in the boys' locker room while the baseball team was showering. I had to find a phone with one hand over my eyes." She demonstrates, smiling at her own antics.

I frown at her. "That's awful. Did the students get busted?" This sounds exactly like a stunt Miller would have pulled at that age.

"No. I never turned them in. It was just teenage girls testing limits and looking for attention. Best not to give it to them."

I think about my baby sister, Lynn, and imagine a bunch of mean girls doing that to her. It makes me want to break something. "Well, you're a bigger person than I am, that's for sure." I'm torn between admiring her and feeling sorry for her.

"We've all got our issues," she responds as she straightens and pushes off my car. "I think your battery might be all charged, don't you?"

"Yeah, maybe." I readjust my position and press the brake while turning the key in the ignition. The engine sputters a few times before finally catching and revving to life.

The librarian and I exchange smiles, and she raises her fists in an awkward cheer. "Yay!"

She's a little goofy, but she's clearly a nice person, and she certainly didn't need to interrupt her day to help a stranger. I extend my hand her way. "I'm Carter, by the way."

She takes it and offers me a firm shake. "I'm Sunny."

I fight the urge to laugh. Of course her name is Sunny.

After detaching the cables and handing them back, I climb into my car again. "Well, Sunny. I truly appreciate your help."

She flashes her wide smile at me again as the sun highlights a spray of freckles across her nose and cheeks. She really is cute. "No problem." She steps backward toward the library as she points a finger gun my way. "You know where to find me if you ever need to get jumped."

All I can do is shake my head as I pull out of the parking lot and head back to Blue Bigfoot. It takes me a minute to realize I'm still smiling, something I'd have found impossible to imagine thirty minutes ago—or thirty days.

CHAPTER
EIGHT

GERIATRICS MAKE TERRIBLE
SPIES

SUNNY

"WHAT DO you think about this one?" Sebastian holds up a mud-brown T-shirt for my consideration.

While I think it looks exactly like the last three he showed me, I nod anyway. "Definitely the one."

He turns the hanger to inspect it more thoroughly and then replaces it on the rack before moving on to the next batch of brown.

As it turns out, the supermarket was not on Sebastian's list of errands for the evening. Nor was the pharmacy, as he explained he couldn't in good conscience join me in the drive-thru to procure "chemicals to poison an old man." He suggested we pick up some Chinese cat's claw for Duke's blood pressure instead, but I told him I'd get it later.

The thrift store, on the other hand, was at the top of Sebastian's list. That and the organic community garden, where we dropped off a giant bag of Sebastian's compost in exchange for a trunkload of kale and a few radishes.

"I'm going to check out the books," I tell him, but I'm not sure he hears me.

As I wander over to the opposite side of the store, I check the time and press Duke's contact on my phone. He doesn't pick up, so I leave him a voice mail telling him to call me.

As Sebastian and I were leaving the house earlier, I noticed Duke slipping his shoes on and rummaging in the closet for his hat. When I asked where he was going, he was evasive, which is usually a sign he's up to something I won't like.

But Sebastian was waiting, so I let it go, assuming my imagination was getting the better of me. Duke was probably going to monitor for drones on our street and get some fresh air. After all, the doctor did recommend short daily walks.

Mia has suggested I get one of those apps where you can keep track of people's locations, but Duke is way too paranoid to allow that. His phone is a high-security device the CIA would probably envy. I've never asked where he got it because I don't think I want to know the answer.

And now he's not picking up, which means he's either feeling salty or he's wrapped up in something he shouldn't be. I'd give them both equal odds.

I trace my finger across the spines of the books as I skim the titles. It's a mix of everything from historical fiction to romance to autobiographies. When I spy a book on home brewing, I pluck it from the shelf and tuck it under my arm. As a librarian, it's my duty to educate myself on all manner of subjects. You never know when a patron will need information on brewing their own beer.

Thirty minutes later, we're headed back home, each of

us with our spoils from the thrift shop and the car smelling of earth and fresh greens.

When I pull up to the red light by the neighborhood park, I glance over to see a familiar mustard cardigan disappearing behind a tree. Without thinking, I jerk the steering wheel to the right and turn onto the cross street without even checking for traffic.

Horns honk behind me, and Sebastian grips the dashboard. "What are you doing?!"

I don't respond, pulling up along the curb with a squeal of Delilah's tires and jamming the car into park. I'm out the door with Sebastian trailing behind me only a second later.

"Duke! I know you're out here!"

I round a huge evergreen, but he's nowhere to be seen.

"Duke!"

"Quit your screaming, girl. You're making a scene!" he hisses as he emerges from behind a hedge, pine needles clinging to the cardigan and his favorite fedora askew.

"What are you—" I begin but fall silent as another figure emerges behind him.

It's the artist. I mean, the brewer.

"Sunny?" he asks at the exact same time as my, "Carter?"

Before I can even begin to puzzle this out, Duke spins on Carter with an accusatory finger. "I knew it! You're an impostor. You're in cahoots with my granddaughter!"

Carter throws his hands up in defense, backlit by a flickering streetlight and looking like a character from an old western. "I'm not in cahoots with anybody. I had no idea she was your granddaughter."

"How do you even know each other? And what are

you doing sneaking around the park?" I spear my fingers through my hair, glaring at Carter and Duke at once, unsure whom to accuse of what.

"None of your business," Duke replies while Carter opts for a more tactful, "It's business."

"What kind of business?" Sebastian chimes in from behind me.

I hook my thumb over my shoulder. "What he said."

"The private kind," Duke growls at my sort-of date as he swipes at the pine needles on his sweater, to no avail.

My hands hit my hips as I growl right back, "They have beer at the supermarket, you know? It doesn't take a secret rendezvous or a clandestine mission. Just put it on the shopping list."

Duke shoots me a perplexed lift of his bushy eyebrows as Carter steps closer, hands out again. "He's helping me with a little project. Nothing more."

"This, uh, sounds like a family thing," Sebastian interjects as he backs up a few paces toward the street. He's not a fan of yelling, being a pacifist and all. "I'll walk the rest of the way." He turns and retreats before I can so much as send another glare at Duke for scaring him away.

"I'm walking too." Duke straightens his hat and turns.

"No, you're not. My car is right there." I point in the direction of Delilah. He and I both know his hip won't let him walk the five blocks between the park and our house twice in one night. He changes direction and shuffles toward the car, relying more on his cane than he did earlier in the day.

Carter steps closer and sinks his hands into his pockets as I watch Duke's retreating back and catch my breath. "So, I take it that was the boyfriend?"

Adrenaline is still racing through my blood, so it takes a second for Carter's question to penetrate.

"Duke?" The notion makes me laugh, despite the perplexing circumstances.

He nearly chokes on his own spit. "No. At least I hope not. The other guy."

"Oh. Sebastian. Yes." Maybe I'm stretching the truth a little, but what's the harm in that?

I exhale to calm my pulse, and Carter falls silent, which I find a little odd—but it's not the oddest thing about this situation by a long shot.

"How do you know Duke?"

"I don't. Not really. I met him online." He shrugs before his eyes widen like SpongeBob's. "Shit. Not like that!" Despite the suspicion that should probably be consuming my thoughts, I can't help but find his reaction sort of adorable.

I bite my lip to keep from laughing. "I assumed as much." I exhale again, the situation finally clearing itself up. "Is that what you've been doing at the library? Working on unsolved mysteries with my grandfather?" Those podcasts will be the death of Duke if his blood pressure doesn't get to him first. Honestly, Carter doesn't strike me as the type, but what do I know?

"Not exactly."

"Well, to give you a heads-up, he's got a bad hip, no driver's license, and a record of offending people that has him banned from numerous local businesses. I'm unsure how far you'll get with him as your partner on *The Case of the Boone County Cat Strangler*." At least this whodunnit is closer to home. I caught Duke trying to board a bus last year because he was convinced he had the key piece of evidence in a serial killer case in California.

Carter's lips quirk, amusement sparkling like pixie dust in his eyes. I run a quick hand over my face to check for stray boogers or something. Why is he looking at me like that?

"I did get the impression he's a little obsessive about some of these things. But I promise you, he was only passing on information about something unrelated."

"Okay, well, I hope you got what you came for then, I guess." It's a little surreal seeing Carter outside the context of the library; I'm not sure what to do with my hands.

"Not exactly. You and the boyfriend showed up before we could discuss it." He smirks. Did he just put silent air quotes around the words "the boyfriend"?

I circle a finger in the air between us. "What does that face mean?"

The smirk disappears, only to be replaced by innocent doe eyes. Ah, I see. He's angling for a helping hand on whatever this thing with Duke is.

Glancing toward Delilah, I make up my mind. Carter may be a stranger, but he loves the library, drives a pretty car, and prefers pen and paper—all of which means he's a harmless human in my book. Yeah, he's meeting an old man in the park at night, but I'm chalking that up to a fabulously active imagination. Besides, I owe him one for trying to shove my addiction counseling down his throat without actually asking if he needed it.

"Look, I can't have Duke traipsing all around town or his doctor will have my head. But I can have him call you or something."

Carter is already shaking his head. "Can't. It has to be in person."

"Oh, right. You don't have a phone." I'm choosing to find that charmingly quaint.

He only shrugs again, this time raising an expectant eyebrow in a way that I'm confident works on a lot of people. Women, in particular. I wonder if he does this on purpose or if it's reflexive. He's always so intense and distracted when I see him at the library, this new encounter is giving me an entirely new picture to examine.

But first things first.

"You're not in… *real* trouble, are you?"

His hand goes to the back of his neck, and I'm sure of it now. He's trying to charm me. That gesture is laden with sheepish guilt that I'm supposed to find endearing in some way. Which, of course, I do. He may as well go all in and say, "Aw, shucks, ma'am."

Instead, he says, "I'm not trying to be." But he phrases it almost like a question. Oh, he's good.

I summon steel to my spine and back up a step. "Look, I can't let my grandfather get wrapped up in anything illegal or dangerous. Surely, you can understand that."

"Of course." His words are the right ones, but why do I feel like there's a silent "but"? "I know this is going to sound crazy, but I can't trust phones or devices on this." There it is.

It's no wonder I was drawn to this guy from the start; he's a younger, taller, and way more handsome version of Duke! Which tells me that trying to reason with him will do me no good.

Before I can respond, he continues, "If I could just have five minutes with him, I'm sure that's all I'll need."

I'm already shaking my head, but then he takes a direct shot at my Achilles heel. "I promise, it's for a noble cause."

The full tabernacle choir, in my conscience, starts belting out gospel hymns and fainting on the floor at that.

Well, shoot. His aim was impeccable, and from the expression on his face, he knows it too.

"Darn you, Thetis—you just had to skip the heel, didn't you," I mutter as I turn for the car with a resigned sigh. Mentally adding "tabernacle" to my list of fun words to say, I motion for Carter to follow me. "Come on. You can ride with us."

THE WONDERFUL WIZARD OF BLACK MOUNTAIN

CARTER

EXTRACTING myself from the back seat of Sunny's MINI Cooper is now on my top ten list of most humiliating moments as a grown man. That car was not made for anyone over five feet. But I'd do anything to get this chance to talk to MarsOrBust, or Duke Underwood, as I now know his name to be.

I'm not sure what I was expecting after our brief online chat where we arranged to meet up, but it definitely wasn't a stocky, sharp-tongued senior citizen and his cute librarian granddaughter. Her protective streak revealed a different side of her than the absentminded goofy one I saw earlier. I kind of enjoyed going toe-to-toe with her.

Duke wasn't happy when I tagged along on the ride back to their house, but Sunny has a way of disarming him that left him only grumbling a few words to himself while he allowed me to wedge myself into the back seat.

I'm thinking "the boyfriend" had the right idea about

walking, but since I don't know the address, that wasn't an option.

I'm generally not an air quotes guy, but this Sebastian dude did not give off boyfriend vibes at all. Not that it's any of my business, but what was with him leaving Sunny and her grandfather in a situation that could have been dangerous? He didn't know me from Adam, and let's just say Sunny got her height from her grandpa. But, hey, she could be a mixed martial arts master for all I know. She's been nothing but a surprise thus far.

Duke shuts the door to the tiny office and flips on a white-noise machine to full volume before settling in at the ancient desk at the center of the room. Equipment overflows from the desktop, wires snaking every which way, and a series of gadgets lines the wood floor beneath. I suddenly feel all kinds of stupid for using a library computer as my only attempt at protecting myself from discovery.

He nods to the white-noise machine and beckons me closer. "My security is tight, but it never hurts to be careful."

I'm unsure who *he* needs protecting from, as I'm fairly confident he's not on any terrorist groups' radar, but I suppose he does have a point. I, myself, was careful to leave my devices behind when I drove to the designated meeting spot, and I kept one eye out for any suspicious vehicles on my way to Black Mountain. It occurs to me, not for the first time, that maybe I'm dramatizing things beyond the reality of the situation in some attempt to add some excitement back into my life. But then I remember Cody, Grace, the henchmen, the texts, and those damn D.C. plates, and I become convinced I'm right all over again.

I was quick to press for a meet-up with MarsOrBust since his comments sounded promising. He wouldn't give too much detail on the private chat, but when he suggested a meeting spot only twenty minutes from my mama's house, I jumped on it.

All I know to this point is that Duke is ex-military and has a well-connected friend in the security business in Memphis—aka Clarence Cody's stomping grounds. Duke also has a contact to run license plates, like the one belonging to our inspector friend.

My plan is still in the formulation stage, espionage not really being my forte and all, but I figure if I can get some leverage, I won't be a sitting duck anymore, just hoping Cody or Grace—or whoever is behind this—stops messing with me. And my family.

My life wasn't always the mess it is now, believe it or not.

There was a time when I strode through my days with my head high, my mind sharpened to a fine edge, and my schedule packed with policy meetings, lunches, and conferences.

All in the name of Grace Hopkins—Congresswoman Grace Hopkins of the second district of the great state of North Carolina, that is.

She was everything I wanted to be. A self-starter with a dream to affect change who'd pulled herself up by the bootstraps out of a working-class neighborhood and catapulted herself onto the national stage through indomitable will and a whole hell of a lot of hard work.

Congresswoman Hopkins was the real deal. The fact that she made it clear there would be no free passes or riding her coattails to a future in office made me respect her even more.

I started volunteering for her first campaign when I was in college and interned for her the summer after I graduated, eventually beating out a hundred other candidates for an entry-level position on her staff. And I loved every minute of it.

By the time I turned thirty, I had risen to the position of Communications Director and, maybe more importantly, personal sounding board to the congresswoman. She never failed to impress me with how thoughtfully she considered each move, each decision, each detail leading up to what was sometimes an impossible choice. But she was determined to represent her constituents with integrity and a strong backbone.

Which was why it took me by such surprise when the shit hit the fan and *I* was the one left with an impossible choice: keep my mouth shut and support my mentor and her subcommittee colleague Clarence Cody on a legislative decision we all knew was unethical, or leave D.C.—and my career in politics—behind.

In the end, the choice was taken out of my hands, but I'm unsure I'll ever get over the resentment that I was put in that position in the first place.

So, sure, I kept abreast of the shady legislation's status and the associated developments as I licked my wounds and wandered around the brewhouse these last seven months. It was impossible not to. But every time I'd see my former mentor's face smiling for the news cameras, the itch to expose her and Cody grew a little more.

One little exploratory post didn't seem like a big deal. And one more couldn't hurt, right?

But I'd been so wrong. I knew powerful people played dirty, but I honestly never thought they'd come after me once they kicked me out of town.

As unfathomable as it would have seemed a year ago, Grace Hopkins has to be behind those messages and the little scheme to mess with my business when I stepped one toe out of line. She and Cody have someone monitoring chat rooms, that's clear. I can't possibly be the only person with a bead on this potential scandal. And they clearly mean business. Nothing makes a person as desperate and cruel as the prospect of riches.

There's no choice but to secure my family's protection, and Duke may be my ticket in.

"So," Duke begins, speaking barely loud enough to be heard over the whooshing sounds of the noisemaker. "You know who I am now."

He says it like I've just pulled back the curtain to expose the Great Wizard of Oz, so I summon my most sincere expression to lend some of the gravity he's clearly expecting. The guy has got to be pushing ninety, with a pot belly, a bad limp, and eyebrows furrier than Eugene Levy's.

"I assure you, we're on the same side." I swipe my wallet from my back pocket and withdraw my driver's license before handing it over. "And, if it helps, now you've got all my info."

He examines the piece of plastic, tilting it to catch the light from his table lamp and glancing from me to the card repeatedly. "If *Carter Brooks* is, in fact, your real name." He coats my name in enough skepticism, I'm half tempted to question it myself. "How do you know Sunny?"

"I've been doing research at the library."

"Convenient," is all he says, steepling his fingers like a true mafioso as he props his elbows on the arms of the desk chair.

He's making this way harder than it needs to be. Since I

have nothing to lose at this point, I take my license from the desk where he dropped it and get right back to the part where we were interrupted at the park. If he wants to kick me out after, so be it.

"There's a piece of legislation up for a vote soon that would clear the way for a class of supplements to sail through FDA red tape and reduce liability for manufacturers. Among this group is a product called NutriSlender. They're billing it as a game changer in the field of weight loss. I overheard a conversation I wasn't supposed to and learned that campaign donors are behind the new product and have promised to share the wealth with certain members of Congress if the legislation goes through."

"That happens every day," Duke responds with the bored confidence of someone who's been a fly on way too many government office walls. "It's not even illegal if it comes in the form of campaign donations."

"Yes, I know," I agree because it's true. Industry lobbyists make their entire living off the practice. "But I'm pretty sure this goes beyond donations. Setting that aside for the moment, this supplement is known to be dangerous. It has an undisclosed ingredient that leads to kidney failure, and the main study proving it has been buried. The plan is to get it to market fast, get people hooked, and then deal with any fallout through insurance and dodging liability—which the new legislation will facilitate."

His brow creases ever so slightly, telling me I've finally piqued his interest enough to consider taking me seriously.

"That's the part nobody wants getting out," I continue. "Plausible deniability can keep you in office. Conspiracy? Not so much. And I think at least one of them is personally invested in the manufacturer as well. But I have no proof."

"Clarence Cody?" He asks, fingers still steepled and expression as subdued as he can manage.

"Yes. And possibly others." I play back the shocked expression on Grace's face when I confronted her about the overheard conversation between her and Cody. The small trace of shame was quickly masked by a lift of her chin and a dismissive explanation that the situation was more complicated than I understood.

"And you what? Overheard this gossip at a truck stop bathroom?" Duke's gaze sweeps my casual attire and worn work boots. "You're grasping, kid." His voice sounds like he swallowed rocks.

"No, sir. I overheard it on Capitol Hill. In a congress member's office."

"Ha!" He tries pushing himself to standing but lands back in the chair, waving me off when I offer a hand. "Now I know you're full of shit. You can't just wander in and out of federal offices."

I fight an eye roll and reach for my wallet again, this time extracting a different card before extending it to the old man. "You can if you have one of these."

His eyes widen at my government ID—the one which I'm confident was deactivated the moment I was kicked out. But it does the trick.

"Well, I'll be darned." This time, when Duke steeples his fingers, I know I've been welcomed to the team—even if we're only a couple of underdogs on a doomed mission to fight for the little guy.

CHAPTER
TEN

PAJAMAS MAKE EVERYTHING
BETTER

SUNNY

AS SOON AS I heard the hum of the white-noise machine from the office, I knew it was no use trying to eavesdrop on Duke and Carter's conversation. So, I busied myself hauling all the kale to the kitchen and then settled in for some goat crocheting. Some date night, but at least it hasn't been boring.

I typed up all my *Dear Mona* responses and emailed them to Randy this morning, so I have the whole weekend to run some of my own errands and maybe plant some flowers to brighten up the yard. And I'll knock out these goat pins.

I never realized Mona responded to every letter received, and I'm a bit nervous to hear Randy's feedback. But I tried my best, even if I did end up copying some advice verbatim from the internet for Butt-Blocked and Blue.

I examine my handiwork, and it occurs to me that these goats would look even cuter if they were wearing pajamas, so I drag my yarn basket over and go digging for cheerful colors. By the time Carter and Duke emerge, I've finished adorning four of my goats with PJs and matching night-caps. They're adorable, if I do say so myself.

"What do you think?" I hold one up for the pair's inspection, if only to inject some lightheartedness into the tense energy surrounding those two.

Carter squints at my creation. "It's, uh…"

"That's the weirdest looking gnome I've ever seen," Duke finishes for him.

"That's because it's not a gnome. It's a goat."

"It's purple," Carter supplies, his tone neither questioning nor complimentary. The man is clearly under the misguided notion that when a woman asks what you think about something, simply confirming the color will suffice.

"It's wearing pajamas." I tuck the goat back into the bag with the other ones and shake my head. "Never mind. Did you get everything sorted?"

This has Duke's face lighting and his finger extending in a familiar gesture. "Tip of the iceberg, Sunshine, tip of the iceberg."

Hmm. This sounds a lot more involved than the simple five-minute chat Carter promised. I glance to the flannel-clad brewer for explanation, and there's that sheepish hand behind the neck again. *Jam in a jar!* I've been had.

Duke proceeds to play a one-man game of charades, telling me the two of them are either planning a road trip or he's becoming a sea captain. I'm not sure which I'd prefer.

I glare at Carter, but he's watching Duke hurry to the hutch under the TV. And by that, I mean he's watching Duke wobble like a lopsided bike with a broken chain. I pause to attempt formulating a charade for, "No effing way."

As soon as Duke opens the hutch door, about thirty gnome dolls and toadstools of varying sizes spill out onto the woven rug below. *Oh! There's Carl!*

What can I say? I like making gnomes.

But my attention is immediately diverted when I notice the bottle of booze in Duke's grip.

"Not so fast." I close the distance and swipe it from his hand. "How long have you been hiding this?" When I lift the bottle for examination, its half-empty contents give me a pretty good answer.

Duke says nothing, instead sinking into his recliner to catch his breath.

My mouth is a rigid line when I flash a look at Carter this time. His expression tells me I made my point.

"Duke," I begin, but there's a loud knock on the kitchen door that has all three of us snapping to attention.

My grandfather's eyes bug out of his head as he whispers, "Hide in the coat closet!" to our guest. Carter steps closer, clearly not having heard, which sends Duke gesticulating and playing charades again. While those two hash out whatever that is, I go answer the door.

It's Sebastian.

"Hey." I smile warmly in greeting and offer my cheek in case he wants to kiss it, but he must be distracted by Duke and Carter whisper-hissing at each other because he breezes past and into the kitchen without even a hello.

"There it is."

My momentary confusion is cleared up when I see the pile of kale overtaking the kitchen counter. I forgot to take it over to him when we got back.

"Sorry. I got distracted."

"So did I." He grins at me. He really is adorable. "Do you have a bin or something I could carry this home in? I'm making kale chips tonight for my rally co-organizer. She's coming over tomorrow."

A kernel of jealousy tries nosing its way in, but I force it aside. "Oh, that reminds me!" I scurry back to the living room to retrieve the bag of crocheted goat mascots before coming back to the kitchen. Duke and Carter have gone silent—perhaps they think Sebastian is in on the scheme with the UPS man—and Carter wanders over to lean a shoulder into the doorjamb at the kitchen entrance.

"I'm making these for the rally." I present Sebastian with the plastic grocery bag containing my pins. "I only have about ten right now, but I'm making more."

"Sunny." His tone carries a gentle scolding. Does he hate them or is he blown over that I went the extra mile for his cause? I get my answer a second later. "This is a single-use plastic bag." He shoots me a regretful half smile and gestures to the goat bag.

"Oh, right." I keep forgetting how easy it is to fill your life with all this plastic that's destroying our oceans. "Oops." Dumping the goats on the counter, I ball up the bag and stuff it in my pocket. Poof!

"I figured it would be fun for participants to wear them —you know, in solidarity." I grin up at him and he returns it, though his brow is still creased.

"Thanks. Uh, what are they?"

Doesn't anyone know what a goat looks like, for Pete's sake?

But before I can answer, Carter appears by my side. He selects a brown goat with pink and white striped pajamas and holds it up. "They're goats." His tone communicates that only a moron wouldn't know that—despite him being similarly confused not ten minutes ago! I don't know whether to hug him or point my finger in his face real hard.

"Oooh," Sebastian acknowledges, stretching out the long o like he knew all along and was messing with us. "But why are they—"

"They're wearing pajamas," Carter interjects in a new tone that invites no more questions.

Hug him, I've decided. Definitely hug him.

"Oookay," is Sebastian's only response.

The two men are now watching each other, and it's making me decidedly uncomfortable, so I choose to bail. "Let me find a bin for you." I retreat to the laundry room for an empty basket, but by the time I return to the kitchen, the room is empty. And the kale is nowhere to be seen.

Wait. Am I in the middle of a dream? The evening has been odd enough for that to be entirely plausible—even probable.

"They went next door!" Duke shouts from the living room. "Now, give me back my hooch!"

Nope. Not a dream. I'd like to think dream Sunny would have a grandfather who's a tiny bit less surly and maybe listens when his doctor tells him to rest and avoid alcohol.

CARTER

IT'S none of my business.

It's absolutely none of my business.

And yet…

"So, it must be nice living right next door." I pass through the door the Sebastian guy is holding open and precede him up a narrow staircase. My arms are too full of kale to open it myself.

"What? Oh, yeah. Duke is a little hard to take sometimes, but Sunny is always so good-natured."

Good-natured?

If "good-natured" was the first adjective I could think of to describe a woman I was dating, I'd tell her to dump me and find somebody better.

Sebastian opens another door at the top of the stairs, this one leading into a studio apartment with a minimalist vibe. Everything is tidy, what there is of it, including a neatly made double bed in the corner and a small kitchen at the far end. The only décor consists of a dozen plants, books lining a shelf under the single window, and a giant wooden bowl on the counter.

I follow him to the kitchen, where he pushes the bowl aside and dumps the leftover greens he was carrying. Sunny went to get a bin for it, but I didn't see any reason when we had four arms between the two of us. Besides, I wanted a minute alone with this guy.

Because I have the beginnings of a plan. But first things first.

If Cash were in my shoes, he'd be blunt and to the point by asking, "So, are you and Sunny fucking or what?" But that's why the guy doesn't have a lot of friends.

Instead, I drop my kale onto the countertop and go with, "There's something about librarians, isn't there?"

"How do you mean?" Sebastian bends to pick up a stray bunch of kale from the kitchen floor. His build is slim, draped in an oversized T-shirt and a pair of itchy-looking pants. He's also barefoot. Definitely gives off that earthy feel, which is apparently right up Sunny's alley.

"You know, the whole archetype of the buttoned-up, meek intellectual who—with a *nudge* in the right direction—has the potential to bring you to your knees. It's the whole fantasy."

His attention, unfortunately for Sunny, remains on the kale. "Uh, I guess."

It's as I suspected. This guy is oblivious. He's not Sunny's boyfriend; he's her unrequited crush. I clocked it from the second he walked into her kitchen and breezed past her upturned, hopeful face. The girl has got it bad, and the neighbor is clueless. For the moment, that is.

"It's just that I'd hate to step on your toes, but I was thinking of asking Sunny out," I lie. Maybe if my life weren't such a clusterfuck, she'd hold some interest for me

—I do love a nice round ass—but I'm anything but boyfriend material.

His eyes finally flash to me, and he blinks as he catches up. Who knew kale could be so riveting? Sebastian's gaze sweeps me from head to toe in an assessing manner, and I can perfectly read his thoughts. His "good-natured" neighbor has suddenly been repositioned in his mind as a potential sexual being of interest—and not simply a genderless person who lives next door and does favors for him. Instinct requires him to evaluate the competition.

It's human nature—it's man's nature. A woman is never more attractive than when another man shows interest. We're honestly a bunch of animals.

And that's what I'm banking on.

Sunny is not on board with Duke's involvement in my little project. And Duke is clearly not up for the trip to see his old friend and connection—a guy who goes by the name Knuckles (I have to assume he's given his fair share of knockdowns over the years, which could turn out to be good or bad for me, depending on how things go). Knuckles has zero reason to trust me, especially if he and Duke share the same level of paranoia and the same wicked temper.

Which leaves Sunny. The devil himself would trust that woman. She doesn't have a disingenuous bone in her body —and she knows Knuckles. Duke said she hasn't seen him since she was a kid, but I figure it's good enough.

"Sunny?" Sebastian's eyes return to my face.

"Hell yeah." Okay, that might be overdoing it, but I can tell he bites because his eyes narrow a touch.

Part of me wants him to tell me to fuck off, that he's staking his claim, but the other ninety percent needs him to give me the go sign.

"We're not… a thing, so go ahead, I guess." He shrugs.

That was way too easy.

"Cool." I give him a nod. "Well," I begin, letting my eyes slowly scan the sad room before dropping to the vegetables between us. I wait until he looks down as well and then finish with, "Enjoy your kale." The added "while I go fuck your neighbor" is unspoken, but we both hear it anyway.

It's the perfect punctuation to our talk, so I turn and head out the door, jogging down the stairs with a whistle that continues until I close Sunny and Duke's back door behind me.

Now I only need Sunny to bite.

You see, one thing I've learned over my years in the District is that you never go hunting for favors without learning exactly what makes the other person tick first. If you can offer something of the highest value to them, you can ask for just about anything in return and they'll hand it right over. And for Sunny, that high-value prize is Sebastian. The two of them are equally quirky, so it seems like a perfect match.

If I can bring Sebastian around, Sunny will happily give me what I need—her help with Knuckles in procuring some leverage. Duke can track the license plate and do a little digging from here, but his friend has the access I really need.

"There you are." Sunny's head pops around the corner, and I notice she's got not one, but two pencils stuck in her hair this time.

I throw a thumb to the closed door behind me. "I was helping haul lettuce to your neighbor's."

"What do you know about goats?" she asks, apropos of nothing.

What is it with this woman and goats? "Not a lot, I'm afraid. Hey, listen, can I talk to you in private for a minute?" I motion subtly toward Duke who's jamming his fingers into his phone screen with almost enough force to crack it.

"Sure." She gestures to the door I just entered, and I open it again to allow her through. "What's up?" She's wearing jeans and a short-sleeved sweater with a rainbow on it today, complete with two puffy clouds on either end like the kind favored by third graders.

"It's about Duke. And a guy named Knuckles."

Sunny's eyebrows spike. "Knuckles? What does he have to do with this?"

"I need to go see him with Duke." Her head is already shaking, but I forge ahead. "But I know that's not realistic."

"At least one of you is using your good sense." She frowns at me, her nose lifting in a way that's admittedly adorable.

"But I still need to go."

She reaches for her pocket, where I assume her phone resides. "Okay. Do you need his address or something? I'm sure I have it somewhere."

"Not exactly, although I suppose that would come in handy too." I try for a small smile of levity.

"Then what do you need?" She's so earnest, I hope I'm not crossing a line I shouldn't. This woman in no way strikes me as a game player. But…

"I need you."

She blinks, her long eyelashes brushing her cheeks and bringing back the anime resemblance. "Me?"

"Duke said this Knuckles guy knows you, and something tells me I might get shot if I stroll up his front steps by myself."

"I suppose that's likely." I don't exactly love how quickly she agreed with me. "But I can't go on some wild goose chase across the country."

"It's only Memphis. That's hardly across the country."

"I mean, I'd love to help, but I work five days a week, and I have Duke—and Sebastian's rally is next weekend, so I have no free days at all. Besides, I don't know you, and Mia will cut off parts of your body that you probably want to keep if I get in a vehicle alone with you."

I shake my head because half of that made no sense, but of course I'm not done yet.

"What if I told you I could do something to help you in return?"

Her brow furrows. "It's not about keeping score. Besides, I don't see how a lifetime supply of beer will help me much. I'm a total lightweight; I get drunk on one glass. And Duke is only allowed one a week. It would be a waste, really."

The part about her being a lightweight isn't at all surprising, given her short stature. Her curves prevent her from being mistaken as anything but a grown woman, but even those couldn't add much to her tolerance.

"Not beer. I can get you something better." I silently apologize to Cash for devaluing the nectar of the gods in such a way. But it's for a worthy cause.

"A plaid shirt?" She smirks, and her dig has me grinning despite myself. She quickly moves on. "A baby goat? Books? Oh! A puppy!"

"Sebastian." My tone is curter than I intended, but there was no indication her wish list of small animals had an endpoint.

Her head cocks in a way that makes her look like the puppy she guessed. "What do you mean?" Her voice is a whisper now as if Sebastian might hear us through his closed window. But a glance up to said window does, in fact, reveal a silhouetted profile, complete with tiny ponytail. This is going to be a piece of cake.

"He's not your boyfriend." I lay it out there.

Sunny sighs and drops her eyes to her shoes. The laces match the rainbow on her sweater. "I know."

Her guilelessness might actually kill me by the end of this plan. I've never met anyone so transparent and trusting.

"Yet," I finish, watching that brow furrow again as her gray eyes flick back to my face.

"What do you mean?"

I take a step closer, and her eyes narrow. I'm beginning to enjoy myself, which is curious. "If you come with me to see Knuckles and let me continue meeting with your grandfather, I will have Sebastian eating out of your hand by the time we wrap this thing up."

Her eyes are mere slits now, and I feel my lips twitch. Sunny is about as intimidating as a guinea pig.

"First of all, I can't have you bringing danger to Duke's front door. It's out of the question. You two will need to continue meeting online to collaborate on this mysterious mission. I'm sorry, but that's how it has to be."

Instead of arguing, I remain silent since it's clear she intends to say her piece.

"Second, while Memphis is not across the country, it is at least a two-day trip to get there and back. Like I said, I don't have the days. And third, I don't want Sebastian 'eating out of my hand,' and the idea that you think you have the power to control someone's feelings and behavior is outlandish. Last I checked, love potions don't yet exist. I prefer to continue my patient pursuit of his affections until it bears fruit on its own."

Sensing she's finished, I begin my rebuttal. "No eating out of your hand. Got it. How about desperate to ravage you?"

Her mouth drops open, heat immediately filling her cheeks. She's got it bad, that's for sure. But she shakes herself out of it in the next moment. "Still impossible. I just have to trust he'll come around one of these days."

"With my help, it could be as soon as tomorrow."

Her tone turns petulant, a perfect accessory to her sweater and shoelaces. "I'm not enjoying this conversation very much."

She's *this* close to giving in. "One tiny trip to Tennessee, and the absentminded tree-hugger will be yours." I'll work out the rest once she agrees.

Her arms are crossed over her chest now, propping her breasts up as she watches me. Sebastian would be a lucky guy if he got his head out of his ass. I maintain an expression of complete innocence as she replies, "If—I'm saying *if*—I agreed, exactly how would you make Sebastian… you know?"

I take another covert peek at the window to confirm that Sunny's beloved is still watching. No time like the present to kick this thing into action, so I snake an arm around her waist and pull her into my chest. Before she has time to do more than gasp, I lower my head and bring my lips to hers.

Let the games begin.

SUNNY

WHAT IS HAPPENING HERE?!

This is hands down the most bizarre evening of my life. Here I was, minding my own business one minute, and the next Carter's beard is brushing my chin and he's kissing me like a hero on a romance novel cover!

He doesn't smell like beer today, I notice, his scent kind of woodsy. It suits him better than the beer. But why am I smelling him? Why am I kissing him back? Wait! I'm kissing him! Oh no. This isn't good.

But it's impossible not to. The man's lips are supple and crafty, caressing mine with a warmth and softness that has my brain going all woozy. Oh, wow. This is… *oh, wow.*

His hands glide up my back and he presses me into his hard chest. He's probably got a foot on me in height, so he's angled down in a way that can't be comfortable at all.

But his comfort is taking a back seat to the zing of electricity popping up and down my spine and the hot ball of fire in my belly. I knew this guy had experience, but I'm beginning to think he could make a killing teaching lessons on making out.

Why is he kissing me again? I have no earthly clue. And I don't really feel like figuring it out right now because I'm more focused on the firmness of his muscles under my hands as I circle his shoulders and melt into him.

His kiss is soft and teasing rather than insistent, and *I* might have to start insisting he give me what I need. He must read my mind because he slants his head a little more and the tip of his tongue glides along my lips while his hands drop to my hips. My fingertips explore his back and—how is he so warm and solid? I need him closer. And I need a stool to stand on so I can kick this kiss up another notch.

When one of his hands drops to my butt, he makes a growling sound and squeezes. Oh my!

Something niggles at the edges of my brain, and as Carter moves to adjust the fit of his lips on mine, I remember.

Sebastian!

Bat in a belfry!

I push off the brewer with one hand to his chest and the other to my damp lips. "What are you doing?!" I whisper-hiss. He said he'd get Sebastian to ask me out, not ravish me himself!

Carter's composure is astonishing in comparison to my discombobulated state. I'm breathing like I just surfaced from a twenty-minute free dive, and my lips and face are a heated mess. But Carter? He could be watching an instructional video on pruning hedges for all the excitement he's showing. This is so wrong.

He doesn't offer any explanation, but I continue to

stare at him as my phone vibrates in my pocket. I automatically pull it out and glance at the notification, my mind still numb from the kiss.

It's Sebastian. My gaze flies to the window of his apartment, and there he stands, hand raised in an awkward wave.

No!

I return his wave with a halfhearted one of my own, knowing that I've completely screwed this up. He saw me kissing another guy! Why did I kiss Carter back like that?! My eyes drop back down to read Sebastian's text, and I'm hoping that by some miracle, he didn't notice the big scruffy guy attached to my face seconds ago.

SEBASTIAN:

Want to watch that bee documentary
tomorrow night?

I blink repeatedly at the device, wondering for the millionth time of the evening if I'm unconscious and dreaming. When I look up again, this time at Carter, he's wearing a smug grin, complete with matching dimples on either cheek that I didn't even know existed.

I suppose there's only one thing left to do. "When do we leave for Memphis?"

CHAPTER
THIRTEEN
ENIGMA, INDEED

SUNNY

"DUKE IS NO LONGER SPEAKING to me, thank you very much." I slide onto a bar stool and belly up to the long wood bar at Blue Bigfoot Beer the next afternoon. The place is peppered with themed décor lining the walls, giving off a homey log cabin feel with a side of camp. The high ceiling in the center lends an airiness that's a nice contrast to all the wood. The place is hopping.

Carter raises a brow at me from behind the bar where he's adjusting some hardware with a wrench. I've chosen to pretend the kiss between us never happened, because when I allow myself to replay it, my body temperature rises to an alarming level and my breathing turns to that of a twenty-year-old Labrador.

"And this is my fault somehow?" He asks over the din of customers' chatter and the music pumping from overhead speakers.

"I had to have his doctor tell him the road trip to Memphis was a non-starter, and now he says he'll never get to show the Presley family his proof that Elvis is still alive and living on Mars."

"Why is this unsurprising?" One corner of his mouth lifts in a way that reminds me how easily this guy can melt panties.

"Because this is the same man who thinks UPS drivers are installing spy cameras in our eaves."

"I've heard they're a crafty bunch." His attention returns to the repairs. "Not that I'm unhappy to see you, but what are you doing here? I figured we'd touch base at the library."

I glance around, impressed at the crowd these guys have. Two bartenders cross back and forth behind Carter to fill orders. One is a short, stocky guy with an open, friendly face and a buzz cut. The other is a woman with dark purple hair and a few tattoos poking out from the sleeves of her shirt.

"I wanted to talk to you. That, and before Duke commenced the silent treatment, he told me I had to hand deliver this note to you." I slide the folded paper across the shiny surface of the bar top. I already read it, but the name "Leonna Knotts" and the Washington, D.C., address mean nothing to me.

Which brings me to the first reason I came to find Carter.

He took off last night before we could hash things out —which I'm sure was intentional since he wouldn't want to give me the opportunity to back out, would he? He'd smooth-talked me into committing to a project I know absolutely nothing about.

Carter sets his wrench on the bar and picks up the paper to examine it. His expression tells me nothing.

"So," I begin, "exactly when are you going to tell me

what's going on?"

Before he can respond, a pretty blonde with long hair and square glasses sidles up next to me. "Who's your friend, Carter?"

Pig in a pen! Is this his girlfriend? Does she know we were swapping spit not twenty-four hours ago? I consider pretending I don't speak English to avoid any confrontation. This guy is trouble, just like Mia said. I should really listen to her more.

Carter doesn't look up from the note. "Hollis, Sunny. Sunny, Hollis." This tells neither of us anything, but the fact that she greets me with a warm smile and an extended hand indicates I may be in the clear and not accidentally playing the role of town harlot conspiring to steal boyfriends of beautiful maidens.

"I like your name," Hollis says as we shake. Carter is back to work.

"Yours too," I reply because it's not only the polite thing to do, but I truly do find it to be a nice name. Unusual. I wonder what the origins are. It's probably an English name referencing a holly bush.

Hollis turns her attention back to Carter. "Cash is looking for you. Something about a stout and not enough coffee flavor."

"I see the feud has passed," is all Carter says in return, looking to be in no hurry to address whatever issue Hollis communicated.

"I'm afraid your brother is officially stuck with me. And my dogs."

Carter's lips tick up at the corners, and I decide I like this woman. And now that I look at Carter more carefully, I believe the man trimmed his beard and brushed his hair —and he's wearing a form-fitting navy T-shirt I've never seen. Unfortunately, this makes him even more handsome.

"Well, Hollis, it's lovely to meet you. Do you happen to have any tips on getting this one to speak?"

She grins, her eyes alight with mirth. "I wish I could help you, but this Brooks brother is still a bit of an enigma. I could tell you what works on his brother, Cash, but I doubt it's legal to do that in public."

My traitorous cheeks light at her implication, and my eyes flash to Carter before I can force them to stay put. He's as cool as ever, twisting the wrench smoothly in one hand while he all but ignores us.

"Let me know if you figure something out," Hollis says over her shoulder as she heads back through the crowd.

I sigh. This is not going well at all. I suppose I have no choice but to force the matter.

I raise my voice so he can't ignore me. "Excuse me, Carter, but I think we need to renegotiate our agreement."

This grabs his attention, and he straightens to consider me. Whatever he sees results in a curt nod of his head and a gesture to follow him. It's April first, so I'm on high alert for pranks and tricks—being Duke's granddaughter and all—but Carter simply leads me to a set of glass doors that open to a patio and ushers me outside. He straddles the bench of a picnic table with a bright green umbrella and waits for me to sit on the other side. The table stands apart from the others lining the patio, all of which are filled with patrons enjoying the spring weather with their drinks.

"Sorry, I'm distracted." He shakes his head in a way that tells me he's no stranger to distraction and he's not pleased about it. This is no newsflash considering I've spent the last few months watching this man while he never once glanced my way or appeared to be aware of his surroundings at all.

"So, what is this mysterious case you're working on that requires a rendezvous with Knuckles and assistance from a bored senior citizen? Did someone poison your well? Are you in witness protection and a mob boss is after you? Or are *you* the criminal, and we're all going to jail for aiding and abetting?"

"Nothing quite so dramatic, I'm afraid." He glances back to the barroom, radiating discomfort. What could possibly be so hard to talk about? "The thing is, I'm not supposed to be a barman."

"Well, I'm not supposed to be a redhead, but we all have our crosses to bear." He's unamused, so I straighten my features. "Sorry. What are you supposed to be, then?"

"I'm supposed to be a congressman. Well, *eventually*, I was supposed to be one, but I got caught up in something that killed it."

I don't respond because the pain in his expression is glaring, and I suddenly don't feel like joking anymore. This guy needs help, and I'm going to do my best.

He goes on to explain that the congresswoman he worked with for the last decade unexpectedly flipped her position on some legislation that would clear the way for a harmful diet pill to be released to the public. Something about a study being buried that showed the supplement contains ingredients proven to cause kidney failure. I vaguely recall a fad diet pill from my teenage years that did the same thing and was pulled from the market, and Carter tells me it's the very same ingredient in new packaging.

He scrubs a hand through his hair, and I watch the sunlight bring out varying shades of rich chocolate and soil. "I've done a lot of research, and while supplement manufacturers are required to disclose ingredients before bringing a product to market, they don't always do it—especially if they know the ingredient would qualify as a drug instead of a supplement or if they have a team of expensive lawyers that can take the FDA on a wild goose chase. Dietary supplements fall under the 'food' part of the Food and Drug Administration and therefore have fewer regulations surrounding them. The further loosening of restrictions, along with a bunch of other changes, was the entire reason Congresswoman Hopkins opposed the legislation in the first place. It's not safe."

He goes on to tell me the manufacturer is controlled by donors with deep pockets who have the power to make or break careers. Carter's old boss is on a subcommittee influencing this legislation and was one of the only voices of caution—until one day when she suddenly reversed her position. It turns out another representative—a guy from Memphis—got to her, and he might even have his own money wrapped up in this manufacturer. Carter overheard the two of them talking about profits and about kidney failures being an "acceptable casualty." The profits would outweigh the cost of potential lawsuits.

What greedy cowards! Carter is much better off working at Blue Bigfoot where the atmosphere is less murdery.

At least now I understand the Memphis part and the role Knuckles can potentially play. When I ask Carter about Leonna Knotts and the address from the note, he explains she's the registration owner of the inspector's car—the one who tried shutting them down.

I inhale, my gut burning at not only the nerve of these pigs but at the thought of innocent people—already struggling with their bodies and health—being taken advantage of so cruelly, all in the name of the holy dollar.

"So, what happened when you told Hopkins you knew why she changed her mind?"

He squints at some invisible thing over my shoulder. "She tried blowing me off at first, but then I told her I'd been in her outer office while Cody was in there talking about it."

"I'll bet she didn't like that one bit."

"She didn't confirm or deny. Just said it was more complicated than it appeared. When I told her I couldn't keep my mouth shut about the conflict of interest or the buried study, she became agitated. She told me to take the night to think things over and understand what was at stake—meaning my future career in politics." He absently fingers the hem of his T-shirt while he relives the memory.

"I thought about going straight to one of the intelligence offices—I considered doing a lot of things that evening—but I was still in disbelief that this person whose integrity I'd admired for so long could fold so easily to a bribe. It made no sense." He shrugs and coughs out a mirthless laugh. "But I had no physical proof; only an overheard conversation, and not even a full one at that.

"I decided to sleep on it and thought maybe I could reason with her in the morning." He studies my face, his eyebrows squished together. I was right all along that this man is tortured. "Get her to change her mind, you know? I was hoping there would be a way to resolve things without either of us losing our jobs or going through the torment of being a whistleblower. It's all career suicide. But something had to be done."

"What happened when you went back in the morning?" I'm leaning forward now, my fingernails digging into my palms in anticipation,

His brows relax and I'm struck again by the beautiful hue of his eyes as I continue to watch him. "Nothing. I never got there." He shakes his head. "At two in the morning, a couple guys broke into my apartment, took my laptop and all the contents of my home office, stuck a gun in my face, and told me I had two hours to get the fuck out of town, keep my mouth shut, and never come back."

My jaw drops. "Holy buckets! This is like a James Bond movie."

His responding smile is rueful. "Only James Bond isn't sitting in a mountain town slinging beer instead of being the badass spy he was meant to be."

I can't blame him for being sore. I'd be livid.

"You said this was last year? What happened with the legislation? And what about the diet pill?" I don't think I've heard about anything called NutriSlender, not that I pay much attention.

"All still on track with no one the wiser, last time I checked."

I ball my hands into fists on the picnic table, not even caring when a loose splinter of wood pokes me. "And you're going to expose them all—bring them to justice and watch them rot in jail." I nod, liking the sound of that, despite my general inexperience with revenge fantasies. Who knew I was so dark?

"I hate to disappoint you, but I don't exactly want to get shot."

I ignore his comment because *yikes*! "We have to save all these poor unsuspecting people, right?" Obviously.

He's unmoved, his hands resting on his knees instead of in fists of rage like mine. I suppose he has had more time to process this than I have. "I'm honestly more focused on protecting my family at this point."

I gasp. "Did they threaten to shoot them too?" I haven't met any of his family, but I'm sure they're lovely people who don't deserve to be riddled with bullets in the name of fat loss.

He explains how the bad guys flexed their muscles to shut the brewery down when it looked like Carter was doing some investigating—which finally explains what he was doing at the library all this time.

I make another mental connection that has me nodding. "*Food* addiction! I did not see that one coming." I shake my head. "I assumed alcohol, what with the beer smell. And porn, but that's pretty common, I hear." He gives me a puzzled look I wave off. "So if you're not going to turn them in—which we'll talk about in a minute—what *are* we doing?"

He blinks at me, clearly still catching up while the sun dances over his skin. "Getting leverage—enough proof to make them nervous. I'll show them a copy and stash one in a safety deposit box with a key given to someone I trust and one of those handy 'In case of death, mail to the *New York Times*' fail-safes." He shrugs. "Obviously, I hope it doesn't come to that, but the whole plan is a work in progress."

I think about it and nod my approval. It works in the movies. "And how are you going to stop that diet pill from coming out?"

He exhales through his nose and gives his head another shake. "I'm not. If I go to the news or the feds, they'll come for me—and my family. It's too big to take on."

"But what about all the people, Carter?" I try and fail

to moderate my tone. "If you stay quiet, this poison will be unleashed on innocent people! And you know it's under-privileged women and minorities who will be targeted the most!"

His jaw tics and his eyes flash at me. "I'm aware, Sunny. But sometimes you just have to do the best you can. You can't save the world."

My heart sinks, and my mind immediately goes to Sebastian. He doesn't think that way at all. He lives every day on a mission to do exactly that—save the world. I inwardly sigh in anticipation of our upcoming evening of Netflixing and chilling. Then I feel guilty for thinking of myself when this massive danger is looming.

"I need to stay in my lane on this one or the people I love will get hurt." Carter doesn't wait for my reply, instead rising from his spot on the bench and striding back into the brewery.

I prop my chin on my hand and watch the customers laughing and chatting at the other tables while I frown at the thought of the long road ahead. Because I'm not giving up on Carter—and I'm certainly not giving up on the world. There's got to be a way to save both.

Sometimes being a librarian is *hard*.

CARTER

> RUTHANN:
>
> I need you to call me to arrange a meeting with Congresswoman Hopkins. It's urgent.

RUTHANN CAN FUCK RIGHT OFF, and so can Grace Hopkins. My mood is more sour than usual—which is saying a lot. Sunny's scolding tone and her naïve idealistic notions about saving the world are still shredding my brain like a cheese grater five hours later. These aren't some schoolyard bullies I'm dealing with; these people are powerful and very serious about maintaining that power. I was rude, as usual, shutting our conversation down and stomping out like a child who didn't get his way.

But I don't want to think about all the far-reaching implications of this mess anymore. I've wasted seven months of my life torturing myself over this shitstorm, and I just want to be free of it. If I can't have my old life back, I want to at least live my new one without having to look over my shoulder or slog through all the what-ifs every morning when I wake up.

I stab frustrated fingers through my hair and collapse onto the bed.

Sunny doesn't deserve my ire. In fact, I hope she's having a great time on her date with Sebastian right now. Hell, I hope he proposes marriage to her, and she tells me to go to hell.

But I know she won't. It was plain in her eyes and in the set of her stubborn mouth as she listened to my story. She's all in whether I want her to be or not. And now I have to make sure *she* doesn't get hurt either.

I must admit, though, it feels good to finally unload my burdens on someone, even if her pressuring me rankles a bit.

I thought she might throat-punch me last night when I kissed her in front of Sebastian. It honestly wasn't until my mouth was on Sunny's that I realized I hadn't so much as kissed a woman since D.C. The fact that I was so utterly oblivious to that tells me I've been even more of a walking zombie than I acknowledged.

And Sunny surprised the hell out of me. The half of me that wasn't on guard for that throat punch was expecting her to stand there frozen, but that girl got on board quick. Before I knew it, she was sliding her arms around my back and feeling me up. She had me hard in record time. If she hadn't pushed me back, I might have forgotten it was only a game and done some real investigating into what she's got hiding behind that doe-eyed exterior.

Yeah, I'd enjoy some more one-on-one time with a certain librarian, but that's not for me to explore. That's for Sebastian—or some other guy who's not an asshole like me.

Something furry brushes over my outstretched hand, and I look over to see Mango perched on my bed waiting for a scratch behind the ears. "You know you're not allowed on my bed, right?" I'm too tired to do anything but give him the scratch he demands, though. Once he's had his fill, he scampers off the bed and I remember why I pulled my phone out in the first place.

ME:

What's your ETA tomorrow?

The ellipses appear as Jeremy types his response.

JEREMY:

Early afternoon. Got a trailer all loaded with your shit and plan to leave early.

It's the first day of the April recess of Congress, which means staff is fleeing D.C. and heading for the representatives' district offices back home. Grace and company are Raleigh-bound, but they always take a few days off before reconvening at the district offices. Grace is probably on a ski vacation in Colorado or eating lobster on Martha's Vineyard with her ill-gained riches. Looks like Jeremy is spending his time off with me. Yet another person going out of their way to do me a favor. God, I'm a dick.

ME:

I really appreciate it. The bar is yours when you get here.

I'd be lying if I said I wasn't worried about hanging out with Jeremy again. It might send me into a downward spiral. I'm already anticipating the harsh sting of jealousy that he's still living the life I was meant for. But I've decided to look at it as a test of my character, and I'm curious about the outcome.

JEREMY:

Excellent. See you tomorrow, Brooks.

I wish I could talk to him about what happened; he's got to be dying to know—who wouldn't be? Your closest friend and colleague up and disappears overnight, leaving nothing but a key and a request to move their shit to storage?

But I've just added Sunny and Duke to my list of responsibilities, and I can't afford another addition. Besides, Jeremy can be a bit of a loose cannon, so his reaction to the news could range from cold-cocking Grace to busting through the walls of a federal building like the Kool-Aid man. Or, hell, maybe he'd say I should have sucked it up and kept my head down—that this shit happens all the time, and the only difference is that this time I found out about it.

Shit. Most people have one devil and one angel sitting on their shoulders; I've got an entire swarm of each buzzing in both ears.

A scratching sound catches my attention, and I pull myself up to sit. Mango is clawing at one of the loose floorboards in the corner. Dammit!

"Hey! Move it!" I hiss.

He flares his nostrils at me and stomps a few times before scuttling out the door. I feel a sudden kinship with Duke as paranoia spikes in the back of my mind, and I quickly rise to shut the door to the attic. Once it's locked, I move to the corner Mango just vacated.

I don't know why I didn't tell Duke—or Sunny, for that

matter—about the money. Or maybe I do, and I don't want to think about it.

I pull out my pocketknife and pry a board up by one edge to inspect the contents of my hiding place. Numerous stacks of cash, bound in bundles of five thousand and wrapped in plastic, line the inside of the shallow space. Eighty thousand fucking dollars.

Yeah, I know exactly why I didn't tell anyone about the money. Because who wants to admit to being an absolute hypocrite? One who demonizes others for taking bribes while holding onto their own stash of blood money all the while.

"HELP."

I spin around at the sound of a familiar voice and see Sunny standing in the doorway to the brewhouse. She's wearing overalls with a pink shirt underneath, and she wastes no time welcoming herself in and beginning a pacing pattern that takes her around the fermenters, past the boiling tanks, and right in between me and the table where I'm testing the stout. Cash was right. It needs more coffee flavor.

This is the fourth day in a row I've seen this woman, yet she never ceases to take me by surprise with her peculiarity. She's mumbling to herself this time, and I allow her to continue, not anxious to resume our conversation from yesterday.

It isn't until she's completed four full rounds of the brewhouse floor that she finally speaks at an audible pitch.

"The date was terrible. It was so… so… awkward." Her hands cover her face, but she keeps walking.

Relieved that we're broaching a new topic, I set the stout aside and give her my attention. Her news isn't all that surprising. From what I've witnessed thus far, putting those two in a room with romantic expectations playing the role of elephant would be akin to trapping a duck and a hamster in a box and expecting them to make a baby. Still, I hoped it might work anyway.

"It's day one. Baby steps, young Jedi."

She comes to a halt and eyes me, those gray irises flashing in a way I sort of enjoy. "I *so* didn't peg you as a *Star Wars* guy."

"Every guy is a *Star Wars* guy," I inform her.

She resumes her pacing.

I owe her, that's not in question. Duke already found the registration owner for the inspector's vehicle, and he's working on recruiting Knuckles. So with Sunny on board for the road trip, it's time for me to hold up my end of the bargain. Too bad Sebastian's not here right now because the beast in me wouldn't mind pulling Sunny in for another one of those searing kisses.

Her hair is down today, the waves brushing her shoulder blades, and she's free of makeup, as usual. With how easily she blushes and how naturally expressive her face is, it's not like she needs it. She's got that fresh-faced ingénue thing going on—with a side of quirkiness.

It's refreshing to see a woman who doesn't try too hard, but I do wonder what she'd look like if she tried at *all*. She'd likely blow me away. But that's irrelevant. And I've spent many an hour twiddling my thumbs on a woman's couch waiting on her to finish coiffing and primping, only to get the sense she was dressing to impress somebody who wasn't me.

"Come with me," I tell Sunny, shedding my apron and dropping it to the worktable. I lead her out to the hall and through the back door of the brewery, sliding my sunglasses in place as I walk. Along the way, we pass by the office where Cash is squinting at his laptop, but I don't stop. Stopping means possibly explaining, and I'm not ready for that.

"Is that your brother? Shouldn't you tell him you're leaving?"

"Yes. And no."

She glances over her shoulder, even though we're already out the door. "You guys look alike. It must be kind of fun working with your brother. I'm an only child." The oversharing begins, telling me she's letting herself get distracted from her Sebastian troubles. Good.

Miller emerges from the driver's seat of Cash's beat-up black sedan. I curse my luck, but my youngest brother only shoots me a two-fingered wave, along with a warning. "Mama's on the warpath. Don't say I didn't warn you."

Since that could mean anything, I don't bother replying as we pass one another and he disappears into the building.

"Exactly how many brothers do you have?" Sunny asks, shielding her eyes from the sun and glancing around as if an entire herd of Brooks kids might pop out from behind the bushes.

"Three. And a sister."

"Wow. That must have been a blast growing up."

"Yeah, I guess," I answer, directing her to the sidewalk leading up the street. She's not wrong, but it's always more complicated than outsiders know. It's the same with every family, I suppose. Miller and Lynn, the youngest, lost our dad when they were still kids. Hell, Denny was only 22, mostly a kid himself.

But Cash and I got to grow up to adulthood with our family intact. We both got time with our dad to learn shit —how to be a man, a father, a partner. I know I wish I'd paid more attention, and I'm guessing Cash feels the same. After he passed, Cash took on the father role for Lynn and Miller, which probably explains why those two brothers mix like a fork and a power outlet. For my part, I became even more driven to make a name for myself—for our family—and that's one piece of the Grace Hopkins fuck-off severance package I haven't yet allowed myself to unpack.

Sunny doesn't question me when I continue leading her down the sidewalk, past the rest of the warehouse shops and uphill to a grouping of small storefronts.

"I always wanted a big family, but I grew up with my grandparents, and my mom was an only child. My grandma said I used to prop my stuffed animals up on kitchen chairs and pretend they were my brothers and sisters. She passed away last year."

"I'm sorry." It's inadequate, but it's still true.

"Don't be. I got to have twenty-eight amazing years with her, and she was in pain at the end. She was ready. Even Duke knew that."

"I sometimes wonder which way is better—quick and painless or sick with time to say goodbye." I didn't mean to say that out loud, but it's not like I can take it back.

"I take it you've had some experience?" I realize she's walking double time to keep up with me, so I slow a bit.

"My dad went in for gallbladder surgery at fifty and never woke up."

"That's awful. I'm so sorry."

"Me too." I stop at the door of one of the storefronts and hold it open for Sunny.

She glances up at the sign for Pete's Café. "What are we doing?"

I prop my sunglasses on top of my head and motion for her to go in. "Taste testing."

CHAPTER
FIFTEEN

SORRY, BUT COFFEE DOES NOT CURE EVERYTHING

SUNNY

THE COFFEE SHOP is bright and airy and smells divine. I've never been to this place before, which is unsurprising since I live about thirty minutes away, but I always enjoy trying new places. I have no idea, however, how taste testing coffee is supposed to help me with my Sebastian dilemma.

I'd been so looking forward to last night—to finally being able to maybe enjoy some affection beyond the occasional hug or cheek kiss. Even an arm around the shoulder would have been a dream. But everything was off from the second Sebastian walked in the kitchen door last night.

Duke was sequestered in his room, the silent treatment working in my favor for once, and I'd prepared an array of snacks and treats, complete with a bee theme. I made vegan "honey" scones, and I even painted the popcorn bowl with black and yellow stripes and wore matching socks I unearthed from the bottom of my sock drawer.

Perhaps shaping the quinoa bars into a beehive was a little overboard, but I was excited.

The first sign that things were not going to plan was when Sebastian greeted me with only an awkward wave from his hip. No cheek kiss, no hug, no warm smile. But, hey, I was nervous too, so I pushed it aside. I handed him a glass of fresh-squeezed lemonade, assuring him that the lemons and sugar were organic and the water was filtered. But I should have known then that the evening was doomed when he didn't even ask me if the paper straws were recycled.

When I invited him to sit on the couch, he settled himself close to me, which was promising, but he was careful to maintain a very strict six-inch space between us that never narrowed. He did, however, enjoy the lemonade and popcorn. Although I got the impression he would have eaten cardboard if it gave him the opportunity to do something with his hands and meant he didn't have to speak to me.

At the hour mark, he paused the documentary and excused himself to the restroom—where he remained for the next twenty minutes.

Had I given him food poisoning? Was the quinoa rancid? Why wasn't he talking to me or commenting on the show like he usually did?

When he returned, we both pretended he hadn't just spent an inordinate amount of time in my bathroom, and I tried smoothing things over with chitchat.

I asked how the rally plans were going. I told him the story of the time I got stung by a bee in the middle of the forehead and thought I would grow a unicorn horn (the correlation between the two is a mystery, but I was seven at the time, so…)

I even asked him to tell me all about cow fart methane release, which I know from past experience he loves to talk about. But nothing! His answers were a few words at best, and he wasn't meeting my eye. When I asked if he wanted to finish the documentary, he begged off and excused himself, claiming he had an early morning. I didn't even get a chance to stand from the couch before he was out the door.

What happened to the warm, friendly vibe we've shared for the year since he moved in? I want it back. But I also want *him*. Is that so much to ask?

Carter nudges me, and I realize I've paused in the doorway to the coffee shop. He smells like pine needles and woodchips again, despite just having come from the brewing room inside Blue Bigfoot—which bore the same sweet, yeasty aroma he'd emanated the day I bashed my skull into his shoulder and designated myself his addiction counselor.

"I don't smell beer today," I inform him.

His brows draw together and he nudges me again with a hand to my back. "It's coffee." He omits the silent "you idiot" that his tone implies. I don't bother to explain.

"You're back. I'm flattered." The brown-haired guy behind the counter puts both hands over his heart and offers us a crooked smile. His name tag says Pete, so I can only assume he's the owner of Pete's Café.

Carter raises a hand in greeting, and we approach our cheerful host.

"Hey, man. How's it going?"

They exchange brief pleasantries, but Carter doesn't introduce me. This is a pattern today with the men we've encountered. I might feel slighted if I wasn't already familiar with Carter's generally laconic nature. In fact, I was almost shocked when he shared his father's death with me on our walk over. That strikes me as something I might have had to pry out of him with a set of emotional pliers.

"What can I get you?" Pete asks me first, exhibiting manners Carter could afford to take note of.

"Um…" I peruse the board above us and make my choice. "I'll have an iced dulce de leche latte with chocolate syrup and extra whipped cream. Oh, and sprinkles."

"Is there even coffee in that?" Carter eyes me from his elevated vantage point. Why is he so tall? And hot?

Pete and I both ignore him, Pete asking Carter for his order.

"How many kinds of black coffee do you have?"

Ah, I forgot about the taste testing that will somehow fix things with my maybe-future boyfriend.

The shop owner lists off several familiar varieties, and Carter asks for a tasting size of each one. If Pete thinks it's weird, he doesn't show it, instead telling us to have a seat and he'll bring our drinks out to us when they're ready. Carter insists on paying, which makes up for him not introducing me, I guess.

"How exactly is this supposed to help with my awful Sebastian date?" I ask once we're seated.

"Well, the two pounds of sugar and cream you ordered should set you up for a nice afternoon nap, for starters."

I glower at him, and he grins before continuing, "I'm looking for a specific coffee flavor for a beer recipe, and I thought we could kill two birds."

God, this would be so much easier if this guy had a phone.

He settles in and gives me his full attention, hitting me with that sienna and moss gaze. "Tell me what happened."

He's more relaxed today than he was during yesterday's visit, and I'm happy to see it. I know he's struggling, but we'll fix it. After we address my current Sebastian crisis, that is.

I relay the gory details of the date, pausing when Pete drops off our drinks, and ending with my forehead banging on the table in front of me. Carter slides his big hand between my head and the tabletop before I can do too much damage to either.

"Twenty minutes?"

"Yeah," I confirm with a sigh once I sit up again.

"Didn't you say he's vegan?" I nod again, still slumped in my chair, when Carter cocks his head to the side. "You didn't happen to put butter on that popcorn, did you?"

All the blood drains from my face as I bolt upright, my eyeballs threatening to jump from their sockets. *Shake in a shack! I did poison him! And he was trying to be polite the whole time!*

"There you go. Problem solved." Carter leans back in his chair and splays his hands like God showing off his handiwork over a beer at the end of day six.

"Problem solved? I forced the guy to break his long-standing commitment to sustainability and responsible stewardship of Mother Earth!" I lean forward to drown my sorrows in whipped cream and chocolate sauce. *Oh, wow. This is delicious. I'll have to remember this place.*

"Hey, nobody made him hog all the popcorn. My guess is he forgot how good butter tastes and turned into a bit of a glutton. That's on him."

I stare at Carter in incredulity, but he takes zero notice, instead holding a cup of hot coffee up to his nose and inhaling deeply. After he takes a sip and makes some weird motion with his lips, he returns his attention to me.

"The rest was probably nerves. For both of you."

I prop an elbow on the table and drop my chin into my hand. "Why do I feel like a kindergartner composing a 'check yes or no' note with my crayons?"

"Yeah, why is that?" Carter surprises me by entertaining the notion instead of teasing me. "Do you not date very often?"

"Try never."

He moves on to the next cup, considering me and the coffee in equal measure this time.

"I mean, I've dated. I just… haven't in a while." I feel the need to explain.

But there's no reason to share that I haven't had sex. It's not like I'm a freak of nature or anything; according to the internet, there are plenty of people my age who haven't had intercourse for one reason or another—and lots of people don't even define sex as intercourse. None of this means I want to remain intercourse-free for the rest of my life, though. I'm very much interested in some good old-fashioned penis and vagina action!

To Carter, I must be some strange extinct bird, complete with dusty tail feathers and legs that look like they were assembled backward. The way he kissed me the other night tells me this man is no stranger to a woman's body, something his rugged good looks could probably have told me on their own. And with a glimpse of this slightly more tailored version of him in the last day, I'm getting the idea that there's even more hotness hiding under all the hair and shaggy clothes.

"And we can assume the same about Mother Earth's number one steward?" Carter asks. Ah, the teasing is back.

"Well, he was sort of dating somebody last year, but it didn't last long. I think she moved or something." I only saw her in passing and was never introduced, but I think her name was Celery.

"Okay, well, if he doesn't make a move in the next couple days, I'll come over to your house again and we'll kick it up a notch."

My skin flames at his words because what he means is he'll come over and ravish me in front of Sebastian's window again! And kick it up a notch? Is he crazy? That's not what I want! I mean, it *is* what I want if it will light a fire under Sebastian's butt, but I want Sebastian to be the one making my toes curl. Not Carter. No. Even if he excels at it.

"In the meantime, I'll have some flowers delivered to the wrong door, and he'll have to bring them over to you."

Flowers? I want to laugh and cry at the same time. Of course, my first flower delivery from a guy will be part of a scheme and not in any way a romantic gesture. I should give up and get a dog. I lean in again and bite down hard on my straw, but Carter has moved on.

"This is the one," he declares, holding up the third cup of dark coffee.

Well, I'm glad one of us found the answer we were looking for. All I can do now is hope Sebastian comes around before Carter initiates "Make the Virgin's Head Explode v2.0." The only good the flowers will do then is provide a lovely decoration atop my casket.

OLD FRIENDS, NEW PROBLEMS

CARTER

"RICCI IN THE HOUSE!" a voice booms from the taproom, and I suddenly regret giving Blue Bigfoot's address to Jeremy. But I guess it's too late now.

It did occur to me that, simply by stopping to see me, Jeremy could be putting himself in danger, but they've got no reason to suspect him of anything other than what his texts stated—if they are hacking my phone at all, that is.

Wiping my hands with a rag, I get my ass down the hall and into the taproom where my old friend stands in the center, scanning the room from corner to corner, floor to ceiling. He's in a familiar uniform of blue button-down, black dress slacks and shoes, with dark aviators covering his eyes. His hair gel could withstand a North Carolina hurricane without breaking a sweat. A few patrons at nearby tables smile in amusement at Jeremy's boisterous entrance.

Jeremy Ricci is a guy who commands a room—sometimes through intelligence and verbal acrobatics, and other times through sheer volume. It's the latter today.

When he catches sight of me, he lifts the sunglasses, head cocking sharply and eyes narrowing for a second before he doubles over at the waist in laughter.

I roll my eyes and hurry forward to greet my friend. I guess it's a good thing I trimmed my beard yesterday and changed shirts.

"Help! The sasquatch got me!" he hollers as I grab his hand and pull him in for a guy hug and a back slap that hits a little harder than he's likely expecting.

"I see your sense of humor still sucks."

He pulls back and scans me, mouth set in a smirk. "You look like my grandpa Joe. Got any moonshine out back?"

I turn and head to the bar, throwing a friendly "Fuck off" over my shoulder. Oscar and Cash are tending bar while Kelsie and Jodi have the floor and Miller's on busing duty. Sunday afternoons are some of our busiest times, especially with the patio and the spring Asheville temps holding shy of the sweltering summer ones.

"Who do we have here?" Cash asks as he slides a *Squatch Blossom* across the bar to a patron.

"This must be Cash." Jeremy shoots me a grin. "You were right. He did get all the good looks in the family."

I lean into the bar from the patrons' side, starting to enjoy myself. "He looks like a big toe." I shouldn't have bothered worrying about Jeremy's visit affecting my mood. It's like hanging out with my brothers: all insults, bullshit, and beer.

"Then imagine what *you* look like, asshole," Cash volleys back to me, and he and Jeremy shake hands in solidarity.

I introduce them, and Cash pours us a couple beers. I

opt for a *Hop Squatch* while Jeremy tells Cash to surprise him. That's my brother's favorite kind of order.

"Man, I can't get over your new look. Hopkins would shit her pants if she saw you like this—and probably clutch onto her purse for dear life."

"It's just a beard. Get over it."

His responding eyebrow raise tells me I'm not fooling him. Sure, he's used to seeing me in tailored suits and expensive ties with my hair and face carefully groomed and polished. But it's only clothes and hair. I'm still the same person.

Sort of.

Jeremy begs Cash for some embarrassing stories about me, but a group of Asheville Arrows players walk in the front door, so Cash excuses himself. These guys have shown up a few times now, and while I don't know exact numbers, Cash says it's doing wonders for our bottom line. If we become a regular hangout, fans will routinely camp out and order drinks while they wait for a glimpse of their favorite players. And that spells good things for Blue Bigfoot.

The players grab a table in the corner by the Dutch shuffleboard table, and a few patrons wander over for selfies and autographs.

"What's going on there?" Jeremy gestures before taking a deep swallow of his *Legendary Larry*. All the beer names here are Bigfoot references, this one a salute to our mascot on the bar.

"Arrows players." Asheville recently got its own Major League team, and it's given a boost to the local economy, for sure. It hasn't, however, decreased the number of tourists clogging the downtown streets. But everything is a tradeoff.

"For real?" He glances over and gives me an impressed nod. "Damn, Brooks. You guys must be doing alright."

I can only shrug. The brewery was probably in a better position when I had a separate income to contribute—and we hadn't just dropped over twenty grand on useless inspection updates—but things have been picking up lately.

We shoot the shit for a while, and Jodi stops by to flirt with Jeremy, which he gobbles up with a spoon. Then he excuses himself to make a couple calls and hit the head.

I remember I still need to order flowers for Sunny, so I swipe Cash's phone from behind the bar and do some searching. No way I'm risking entering even Sebastian's address into my phone.

"Who are the flowers for?" Jeremy asks over my shoulder. Shit.

"Nobody." I drop the phone face-down on the bar top.

"You're such a shit liar."

I suppose he's not wrong. But I can sure manipulate the truth like a pro when I need to. This time, I don't need to.

"Sorry, I misspoke. What I meant to say was none of your fucking business, asshat."

"I see how it is." He sits on his barstool again. "So, is this why you haven't been back to the District? A woman?"

I change the subject. "How's the new ride?"

He lets it slide. For now. "Phenomenal. I might even let you drive it to your place to drop off your shit."

"Thanks again for that," I tell him, hoping he knows I'm being sincere. The idea of setting foot back in D.C. right now makes my blood start to boil all over again.

"I'll drive it!" Miller volunteers, appearing out of nowhere and dropping his bus tub on top of the bar.

"Get that shit off there," I growl at him. He knows better than that. I stand from my stool and round the bar to grab a clean rag and some spray before Cash notices and fires his ass. To Jeremy, I warn, "Don't let him touch your car. It's only been two weeks since he totaled mine."

"How many times do I have to tell you it wasn't my fault? There was something wrong with that piece of shit before I even started it!" He repeats the same bullshit he's been trying since the day he crashed it—probably looking out the window at some girl in a short skirt. I'll admit, seeing my kid brother all banged up in a hospital bed hit pretty hard, but he's had an excuse for everything since the day he was born. It gets a little old after a while.

But he gets easily distracted, as usual. "Did you see Cart's new ride yet?"

Before long, Miller pulls Jeremy out to the parking lot to show off the Olds. I finish wiping the bar before grabbing Cash's phone again to complete my flower order. Sebastian will *have* to make a move if he's forced to give Sunny flowers from another man. And if he's letting bro-code get in the way—even though we've only met once—I can fix that by staging a nice dramatic breakup with my partner in crime for his benefit. Once we're done with my project, that is.

"Not so fast!" This time it's Cash who interrupts me, snatching his phone out of my hand. "You think I was born yesterday? What did you do to it? Install a porn ringtone for whenever Hollis—" He cuts himself off when he sees the bouquet of pink and yellow flowers on the screen. I thought they suited Sunny with their cheerful colors. Even when she was lamenting over Sebastian at the coffee shop, she was still chatty and funny, that expressive face drawing my attention back every time it tried to wander.

An idiotic shit-eating grin washes over my brother's face. "Interesting."

But it turns out I won't need to find a hiding place for his dead body because he manages to straighten his features. "I'm a vault, you know that. But don't let any of these other morons see that or you'll never hear the end of it." He should know. Nobody cut him one inch of slack when he and Hollis began their weird-as-hell relationship.

Few things are funnier than watching a grown man pull a woman's pigtails while he thinks he's fooling anyone that he does not, in fact, want to fuck her brains out. So, watching that shit play out between Cash and our dog groomer neighbor, Hollis, kept everyone at Blue Bigfoot entertained for the last few months. They fought like WWE all-stars. But I swear my brother only picked fights with her so he had something to jerk off to at night.

"It's not what you think," I inform him. Hell, I'm not even lying.

"I don't think anything at all." He doesn't look up from the pint glass he's filling. This is why we're partners.

He lifts a chin at me and takes his beer plus two more from Oscar to deliver to the ball players. Unfortunately for me, Oscar's wearing the expression of a chihuahua who just heard the door of a delivery truck close and is preparing to alert the entire fucking neighborhood that we're under attack.

I stab an index finger his way. "Don't even think about it." Then I stalk to the parking lot to rescue my friend from my little brother before he lends him money. Or worse, his new car.

CARTER

"SO, THIS IS THE OLD HOMESTEAD," Jeremy comments as we pull into Mama's driveway a couple hours later. I'm driving the Mercedes, but only because Jeremy started working his way through our entire beer menu. He's determined to try them all before he leaves for Raleigh Tuesday morning.

The house has seen better days, but none of us can complain. It's a narrow clapboard structure standing two stories tall with a deep lot that backs up almost to the Blue Ridge Parkway. The place is up the mountain a ways, about a thousand feet above downtown, but only a twenty-minute drive east. Mama and Dad built it over thirty years ago, around the same time the neighbors to the left bought their lot, and our families have been thick as thieves since. Adrina Carmichael is about as headstrong as Mama, but her husband, Wes, balances things out by being a world-champion napper.

The properties are surrounded by forest with just

enough lawn space to throw a football around and have a backyard barbeque. Cash keeps the yard mowed—yet another of the hundred thankless tasks he takes on without anyone asking. There's no good reason I couldn't mow—or Miller, for that matter. I add it to my growing list of ways to get my head out of my ass as I precede Jeremy to the bright yellow front door.

It isn't until we cross the threshold that I remember Miller's warning from this morning about Mama being on a warpath.

"I told you to get off my property! You are trespassing, and I'm calling the cops if you don't turn around right this minute! How dare you walk into my—"

She appears around the corner, her expression shifting from fire-spitting to joyful in half a second flat. "Oh, Carter, it's you. I thought you were that damn developer thinking he can swindle me. The man doesn't have the sense to pound sand down a rathole if you ask me. Like I'd suddenly want to sell the house to him when I've made it clear for years we ain't never sellin'. Don't know what good our place would do him anyway with Adrina and Wes staying put on one side and Winston on the other. I think some people just enjoy stirring the pot, don't you?"

Jeremy doesn't even wait for her to shut up. He walks forward and folds Mama into a hug while all I can do is try not to lose my mind.

Mama hugs him right back. "I can't say I know who you are, but who am I to refuse a hug from a handsome young man?"

"Mama, this is my friend Jeremy from D.C."

"Well, isn't that nice of you to pay a visit. Come on in, Jeremy from D.C. I was always dying to meet Carter's friends and colleagues from his days as a hotshot, but he kept saying he was too busy."

"He wasn't lying," Jeremy supplies as we follow her to the kitchen. I drag two clothing bags from the trailer with me. "They work us like sled dogs. I barely escaped with my life to come down here."

"Jeremy brought my stuff from storage. He's heading to the district offices in Raleigh after this."

"I love Raleigh." Mama shoves aside a sketchpad and a pile of drawing pencils from the center of the kitchen table and grabs the bags from me before I can protest. "Tell me, do they still have that German bakery that makes those bee sting cakes?"

"I don't know. I've never been there, I don't think, but now I have something to look forward to." The guy is a shameless flirt, and Mama's no better, winking at him as she lays my bags over an empty chair and motions for us to sit.

"Oh, yes, you must try them and let me know what you think." A bowl of chips magically appears between us, and I tilt my head for a better look at the sketchbook. I immediately regret it when I recognize a crude rendering of a naked man.

"What do you think?" Of course, Mama catches me looking, so she reaches over for the sketchpad and holds it up proudly in front of her chest. "Lizzie is doing a unit on the human form at the senior center, and I thought I'd join in. Mitch makes an excellent model, don't you think?"

Mama works at the senior center when she's not hiking mountain trails, cooking, volunteering, riding her bike with Mango in the front basket, or reading kink with her book club. I'm guessing Lizzie teaches the art program— one of the many Mama oversees at the center. As for

Mitch, all I can say is he's a lucky guy if Mama's rendering is even marginally accurate.

Jeremy covers his grin with a mouthful of chips, leaving me to respond.

I choose to go with, "Inspiring."

"Oh, that reminds me, I told Regina you might be interested in moonlighting for her, and she gave me the number of one of her young men who can answer any questions you might have. Will something or other. Apparently, he's dating her niece. I have it in my purse. Hold on a second." She sets the pad back on the table and goes hunting for her purse.

"Moonlighting as what?" Jeremy asks over his mouthful of chips.

"Nothing," I answer in my most commanding voice, but he still hears Mama's response from the other room.

"An escort!"

"I'm moving in," Jeremy declares once he's finished choking on his chips.

Mama returns to the table and passes me a sticky note which I refuse. "Now, Jeremy, we're a little tight on space with all my boys, but I'm happy to make up Lynnie's room for you. Or you can take the attic and Carter can bunk in hers—or with Miller."

Not on my life or his.

"But I must warn you, the attic doesn't have a window unit, so it gets a little stuffy up there, as I'm sure Carter can tell you." Mama continues.

"Jeremy's staying at a hotel in town," I tell her.

Mama looks almost wounded at that, and my friend appears like he might rearrange all his plans for her benefit. But common sense finally returns to the kitchen. "I couldn't possibly impose. And hey, when Uncle Sam offers a stay at the Hilton, you take it, right?"

It does the trick. "Did you know they don't allow skunks at the Hilton—or at any hotels, for that matter?" Mama drops into the empty chair next to Jeremy and the two of them discuss pet accommodations while I head back outside to bring in another load from the trailer.

Looks like Jeremy fits right in around here on his first day. It makes me feel stupid for taking so long to come around myself.

Mama feeds us her famous butternut squash soup with a loaf of crusty bread, and we chat for a bit—or, I should say, Mama and Jeremy chat while I occasionally offer a few words before I'm cut off. I'm half thinking I'll be calling him Daddy by the time he takes off for the hotel.

Only then do I remember I never finished that flower order for Sunny. But there's no way I'm borrowing Mama's phone. She'd sniff it out in seconds, and then I'd have to come up with a story to keep her off my back about my "mystery woman."

Maybe I'll tell Sunny to invite Sebastian over tomorrow after work, and I can hand deliver some flowers while he's there instead. It'll have almost the same effect. Plus I'll get to be an eyewitness to her delighted smile and whatever goofy thing she'll undoubtedly say when she sees them.

I don't allow myself to think too hard about it and consider the matter settled. Besides, I've seen Sunny four days in a row now. What's the harm in five?

Sober again and full of soup and gossip, Jeremy takes off for his hotel. He leaves the trailer here, and I tell him I'll return it, seeing as he's done more than enough for me already. We make plans to hang out while I'm working in the brewhouse tomorrow, and he asks me if Jodi will be around. I give him the finger and tell him to get lost.

Since I plan on getting up early to work out in the morning, I hit the hay when Mama does. The house is dead quiet, which it won't be when Miller barrels in after driving the Olds home from work. Cash will probably stay at Hollis's place, and I don't blame him. It's hard to find privacy in this house sometimes.

The attic is warm tonight, and I hate to think how humid and sweltering it'll be come summertime. I suppose that'll give me the extra motivation I need to finally get my own place, although it won't be nearly as nice as my D.C. apartment. Cash and I are still at the point where we're putting almost every penny back into the business, so staying home has saved a lot of dough.

But I can't continue indefinitely as this pathetic, unkempt hermit who snaps and growls his way through the day just because things didn't work out the way I wanted them to. I need to man the fuck up.

I flip on the box fan and shed everything but my boxers before dropping into bed. I don't bother with the sheets. When I order myself to stop dwelling, the first thing that pops into my head is the image of Sunny in her overalls trying to scowl up at me from behind her dessert drink. I actually laugh out loud into the dark room. And her reaction when she realized she'd fed butter to a vegan? Priceless. Although she didn't find the whole thing as amusing as I did.

I've never been a subscriber to things like signs and fate, but my last thought before dropping off to sleep is that maybe there's a reason for Sunny Underwood's sudden appearance in my life.

"CARTER," she moans my name like a plea for something, and I know exactly what she needs.

I part her creamy thighs and she lifts her hips for me, placing her damp pussy at just the right angle to take me. Her fingernails claw so hard at the bare skin of my back that I'll have marks for days. Good. I want her mark on me. I don't finesse, lining my cock up to her wet entrance and plunging all the way into her in one hard stroke.

She gasps and squeezes around me, cradling all of me in her tight channel and locking her ankles behind my back. Fuck. I don't think anything has ever felt so good.

"Fuck me, Carter," she begs, and I draw my hips back until I'm almost fully withdrawn before plunging back in again. This time she cries out and scrapes her nails down either side of my spine, hitting every nerve ending along the way.

She's so tight and wet I repeat the same motions, reveling in the ecstasy of having her all around me. I push up to my knees so I can watch my cock pump in and out of her and enjoy the sight of her generous tits bouncing with every thrust. Her nipples are rose pink and tightened to sharp peaks at my attentions. I'll have to get them in my mouth soon.

But right now, nothing could stop me from fucking her hard and deep. Her cries get louder the harder I go, so I'm merciless, driving into her over and over. When she throws her head back and pinches her nipples with her fingers, I pick up speed. I can't decide if I want to come inside her or on her lush tits, but I'd better make my mind up soon.

She's panting now, her hips meeting every one of my thrusts, our bodies slapping together in a damp, sweaty slide as I fuck her over and over. Her pussy starts to spasm, and I bring my thumb to her clit to seal the deal. She shouts my name, and it sounds like she's claiming me, like I'm claiming her with every drive of my hips and spear of my cock inside her.

And then she comes completely undone, writhing under me and mewling as her pussy spasms wildly and sucks me into her and she climaxes hard. I want to wait until I've wrung every bit of pleasure out of her, but I don't know if I can.

I buck forward, my thumb still on that hot button of nerves, and I can feel it coming from the base of my spine. Fuck!

"Fuck!" I shout just as I'm about to come. My fist hits the bed and I spring upright, blinking into the dark, my breath coming in pants and my cock hard as a fucking stone inside my boxers.

But I'm alone. And Sunny was only a dream.

SUNNY

"I'M SORRY. You're right. It's not funny." Mia tries and fails to stifle her grin.

I just let her read Randy's notes about my *Dear Mona* letters, where he thanked me but suggested I shy away from using words like "prevaricator" and "protuberance" and go with the more common "liar" and "penis" in the future. He then emailed me seventeen new letters and said he'd prefer not to need a dictionary next time. I suppose I can see his point.

"So, how did the errand date with Sebastian go on Friday?" Mia asks.

I open my mouth to answer and realize how much has happened since I left work on Friday. And then I imagine the look on Mia's face if I tell her that not only did I run into the mystery library patron in a darkened park near my house, but I then escorted him back to my home and let him kiss me stupid! Oh, and while we're at it, how I made plans to go on an overnight road trip across state lines with the man before paying two visits in twenty-four hours to his job and sharing a very bizarre coffee date where I made private confessions about my love life and drank my weight in chocolate while he watched me have a nervous breakdown.

"Good," I answer. Cicero had an excellent point when he advised, "Brevity is a great charm of eloquence."

Mia gives me an expectant nod as she continues arranging books on the trolley for reshelving. She's wearing a silky emerald green top today, and it looks fantastic against her skin.

"Green is definitely your color."

She glances down at her top and smiles back at me. "Kwamie bought this for me. What can I say? The man has excellent taste."

"Of course he does; he picked you."

Her smile turns a little dreamy at the edges, and I can't help the little pang of jealousy that curls in my chest. Because Kwamie is head over heels for my friend, and I couldn't be happier for her that she has that. But I also want it for myself at the same time.

"Next week's schedule is posted." Meredith approaches the desk, and I quickly click my way to the employee page on my computer screen. Neither Carter nor Duke has figured out when this trip to Memphis is supposed to take place, and I'm worried I'll have to ask Meredith for time off at short notice.

I already lucked out by having a schedule that gives me weekends off, but in doing so, I'm essentially at Meredith's beck and call on weekdays and evenings.

I scan the schedule as Meredith engages Mia in a conversation about the community jobs program which hosts meetings every Monday. Mia's on duty for today's session.

I already told Carter I'm committed to the rally this coming Saturday, but I have Sunday off, and it looks like I'm working the late shift on Monday—which leaves a day and a half that could work out if Knuckles is game. I'm still unsure how Duke and Carter think Knuckles might procure some piece of proof of Clarence Cody's guilt or involvement, but I'm leaving that up to them.

I've got enough on my plate—I still haven't finished the goat pins, Duke somehow lost his cane last night, I need to figure out what to do about Duke if I'm traveling overnight, the new batch of *Dear Mona* letters are waiting, and the goat transfer is still in limbo. I talked to the farmer, and he said I can borrow a trailer, but I need to figure out if my hitch is the right size. And none of that takes into account all my usual daily duties.

"Sunny, did you make those scones? The ones in the break room?" Meredith asks, pulling me from my to-do list.

"I did." I figured the leftover scones were better left here than on my already generous hips. "They're vegan."

"Remind me to add the cookbook collaboration to your projects, would you?"

"Um, sure." It's always flattering when your talents are acknowledged and celebrated. But my head is so full of my current tasks, and the cookbook isn't even part of the library's official programs.

But I remind myself that helping people is a reward in itself, and I mentally add scheduling a cookbook meeting to my list.

I also ignore the meaningful look Mia sends my way as

Meredith traipses toward the break room to help herself to another of the souvenirs from my disastrous date night.

As I'm getting ready to leave for the day, Tanisha pops over to tell me there's a call for me on the main line. Taking personal calls on the library line is verboten, but what Meredith doesn't know and all that.

"This is Sunny. How can I help you?"

There's music and an indistinct clamoring of voices, making me think I picked up the wrong line, but just before I hang up, I hear a familiar voice.

"Sunny? Sorry. It's really loud in here." It's Carter.

"That's okay; I can hear you. I was about to blow this pop stand. What's up?"

"Hey, I was thinking I might stop by tonight if that's okay with you and Duke." Someone in the background starts singing out of tune and I press my ear harder to the receiver to hear Carter.

"Sure. I'm making dinner if you're hungry."

"Thanks, but that's okay. You should invite Sebastian though."

"Um, okay." It's not a terrible idea, if I can get over my embarrassment from the other night, that is. I already texted and apologized for poisoning him. He was very gracious about it but didn't suggest we schedule a redo of the date.

"Okay. See you all around eight?"

"Sure. See you then." I replace the receiver and hitch my bag up onto my shoulder. It's my favorite teal one with red pom-poms along the edges.

"Soooo," Mia coos. Darn it. I forgot she's right there. "The date must have been good if he's coming over for dinner."

"Um," is all I say. I don't want to lie to my friend, but I

also don't have the time to listen to another lecture about Carter eating my organs and wearing my corpse like a blanket.

A woman toting three kids and a stack of DVDs saves me, and I slip out while Mia helps check them out—promising to myself that I'll come clean to her tomorrow.

Since it's Monday and I always make Duke's favorite stir fry on Mondays, I pop into the supermarket on the way home to grab some tofu to make a vegan version. While I'm waiting in the checkout line, a coverline along the bottom of a tabloid catches my eye. "Miracle weight loss supplement on its way to your local health-food store. Melt the pounds away!" I snatch the magazine up without hesitating and add it to my small pile of groceries.

Before my car door even closes in the parking lot, I'm practically tearing the pages in search of the article. And there it is! My heart simultaneously sinks to the bottom of my gut and races like I've just swallowed a gallon of espresso.

NutriSlender.

No, no, no!

I break a dozen traffic laws racing home from the store, only to find Duke isn't there. A note on the kitchen counter tells me he's "patrolling the perimeter" which I take to mean he's gone for a walk. At least this means he found his cane.

With this new information adding urgency to our mission, I consider not inviting Sebastian to join us for dinner. But since I doubt Duke will discuss much with me anyway, there's no reason not to work on my Sebastian project until Carter arrives later tonight.

Once I assure Sebastian four times over that I've checked every ingredient and can promise him a 100%

vegan meal, he agrees to join us at seven. Then I start the rice cooker and open the new *Dear Mona* letters on my tablet.

The first is an easy one asking for advice about an interfering mother-in-law. I quickly jot down a reply in my notebook and move on to the next. Letter number two is not as simple. The author sent a two-page saga about her boyfriend's snoring and how it's destroying their relationship. Since the only person I've ever slept in the same bed with was my grandma—who slept so silently, I sometimes checked to make sure she was breathing—I'm at a complete loss on how to answer.

When the third letter presents a question about the rules surrounding the choking of one's partner during sex, I take a break to crochet some more goats in pajamas.

Duke returns in the middle of the Mona letters, informing me the neighborhood is drone-free tonight but that Ms. Dobson from a few doors down threatened his manhood. When he sees the package of tofu on the counter, he grumbles about me trying to turn him into a "granola bar" and goes to his room to listen to his podcast.

By the time the knock comes at the back door, I'm beyond ready for some company.

"Hey." Sebastian's smile is bright, and he leans in to kiss my cheek, sending my heart racing in a much more pleasant manner than the panic-inducing choking letter from earlier. Are we back to normal? I truly hope so.

"Hi," I greet him, closing the door after him. "There will be no animal protein or byproducts anywhere in this kitchen tonight, I promise." I extend my hands to display the countertop full of fresh vegetables. "But Duke might not be joining us."

"Do you want some help?" my future boyfriend asks,

and we proceed to chop and chat until the soy-marinated tofu is sizzling in the pan and the rice and veggies are done to perfection. Things are so easy tonight without the expectations of an official date over our heads. But I suppose this is exactly what really being with someone is meant to feel like. Comfortable and simple.

I call Duke in once the table is set for three, and he reluctantly leaves his crime solving to join us.

"Tastes like a salty sponge," is Duke's answer when Sebastian asks him how he likes the tofu. But he piles more on his plate anyway and grumbles a thanks my way for doing the cooking, so all I can do is smile. He's so full of it.

Sebastian starts telling us about the sharp decline of caddisflies in Europe that's threatening the future of the aquatic ecosystem, which has Duke staring at him like he's just grown a pinky toe in the middle of his forehead. Luckily, the doorbell rings, but I realize I forgot to tell Duke about Carter coming over.

I stand to go answer the door, and my pulse speeds up for some reason. I must really be out of shape. Duke insists on Sebastian joining me to answer it because Ms. Dobson will then have to go through both of us to get her hands on him.

But when I swing the door open, the sight that greets me isn't Carter at all. It's the most gargantuan bouquet of orange Asiatic lilies and coral roses I've ever seen in my life. My gasp is loud enough that it has Duke shouting from the kitchen, "Leave my granddaughter alone and take the granola bar instead, you witch!"

I'll be lucky if Sebastian doesn't move out before this week is over.

CARTER

WHEN I HEAR Duke's voice, I maneuver my head around the giant bouquet to see Sunny and Sebastian standing in the open doorway. My eyes go to Sunny first and, oh shit, is she crying? I knew this bouquet was overkill, but the flower shop was closing for the night and the lady gave me a great deal.

Hands clasped over her breasts and her lips frozen in a perfect O, her silver-eyed gaze flashes back and forth between me and the flowers. She's either a better actor than I ever imagined, or she's forgotten this is all part of the plan and thinks I've come to propose marriage. My ego ignores reason and hopes she's genuinely touched by my offering.

Sebastian, on the other hand, stands dispassionately blinking at the flowers, seemingly oblivious to my presence at all.

"Oh my god, Carter." Sunny rushes forward, enveloping both me and the bouquet in a fierce hug. Her soft body

pressed against mine takes my dirty mind straight back to my dream last night. I've never had a dream that hot in my life. After I woke up, I finished myself off to the residual images of a naked Sunny under me. I came so hard I lost my vision for a minute. But I'll be damned if I'm going to stand around with a raging hard-on in front of Sebastian and Duke, so I force my thoughts to duller things.

Luckily, Sunny's short stature protects the flowers from being crushed by her fierce hug. I can't say the same for my ribs. "They're so beautiful!" She takes the bouquet gingerly from my hands and cradles it to her chest, admiring the blooms like they're a newborn baby.

I've gifted my fair share of flowers over the years, but I can't say any recipient has ever been as enthusiastic or appreciative as Sunny. My chest puffs again before I remind myself this is all an act.

"Duke, look!" She retreats into the house, leaving Sebastian and me alone at the door.

"Sebastian." I nod.

He sighs, his straight nose wrinkling, and I wonder for a second if he's going to confide in me or get down to business about Sunny. But all he says is, "A local perennial plant would have been a more sensible gift. Do you know the carbon footprint of the cut-flower industry? It's catastrophic."

"Oh. Um. I guess I never thought about it." He's got me there. But I want to tell him that based on Sunny's reaction to the blooms, he'd be hard-pressed to find a bush that says romance in quite the same way. The thought that she'll never get another bouquet of flowers if she and Sebastian are together for the long haul strikes me as almost mean. The woman obviously needs flowers.

Duke stands from the table when we enter the kitchen, moving to position himself behind Sebastian so he can send me hand signals. Sunny skips around the kitchen humming what sounds like "Psycho Killer" by the Talking Heads as she gathers a large water pitcher and a pair of shears.

I excuse myself ostensibly to the restroom, and Duke follows me to the hall, leaving Sunny and Sebastian alone in the kitchen. Maybe she'll agree with him about the flowers, and they'll find their love connection over their shared disdain for florists.

Duke hobbles on his cane into the office and jots a note on a pad of paper before ripping it off and handing it to me. I notice he's wearing the same clothes as last time—a stained dark yellow cardigan over a white golf shirt and brown pants. I vow right now never to go back to wearing my same dirty clothes every day. I'm already paranoid and cranky; I can't afford to have one more thing in common with this guy.

I look down and read the note.

Knuckles is on it. Need to set up a meet-up next week.

P.S. Don't eat the tofu. It tastes nothing like chicken.

I nod because, honestly, what else can I do? But I get a familiar shot of adrenaline at the news about Knuckles.

Before I can hand the note back, Duke snatches it from my hand, crumples it up, and eats it. I stare, impressed at how fast he gets it down.

Maybe I should have let Jeremy come with me to Black Mountain instead of leaving him in the care of my brothers for my quick trip. He'd get a kick out of Duke, that's for sure. But there's no way I could bring him into this inner circle of insanity. It's not only nuts, it's not safe.

"Hey," Sunny says from the doorway. "I need to talk to

you after Sebastian leaves." She's wearing another of her T-shirts today, this one paired with a casual skirt and showcasing a horned llama with the words "llunicorn llover" under it. Before I can determine which one of us she's talking to, she's gone.

Duke and I return to the kitchen to find Sunny arranging her flowers in the pitcher and Sebastian watching in consternation. I almost feel sorry for the guy.

Duke studies his granddaughter before turning to me. "Last I checked, you don't buy flowers for someone you're not courting."

I shrug, my tone casual. "What can I say? I'm trying to win her over. Although I don't think people call it courting anymore."

I came prepared for some questions. Sunny, on the other hand, did not.

Her hands freeze on the flowers and her shoulders stiffen. "It's an odd concept when you think about it." Her gaze flips from me to Duke to Sebastian before starting over again. "Courtship, I mean."

I hope she'll leave it at that, but she releases a nervous laugh, which does not bode well. "You know it comes from the idea of showing the same degree of respect toward a woman that you'd display in court, which is strange when you think about it because usually a person in court is being accused of something and feels intimidated by the judge, so I don't know that I'd want a romantic interest being intimidated by me—or looking at me like a judge at all, for that matter. And I'm not sure anyone would feel *affection* for a judge, even if they ended up being on the winning side of a case. Gratitude, maybe, but you wouldn't want to go out to dinner and maybe kiss the judge goodnight, and you probably wouldn't think to bring them flowers, would you? Intimidation and gratitude don't sound all that romantic to me. So, yeah, an interesting word, courting."

A silence settles over the kitchen, and Sunny's eyes return to her flowers. I'm having trouble not smiling. I have to say this for Sunny, I'm never bored when she's around.

"I'm gonna head out," Sebastian says in a halting tone as he hooks a thumb toward the back door. "Thanks for the, uh, dinner, Sunny."

"Oh, of course." Sunny blinks at him, every one of her emotions written on her face.

"See you," I offer as the door closes behind him. Then to Sunny, I say, "I don't know about you, but the guy looked pretty *intimidated* to me—and *grateful* for the dinner too. Well done, Your Honor."

She bends at the waist, and her head makes a *thunk* as it hits the countertop. I guess she wasn't kidding when she told me she has a hard head.

"I don't know what the hell is going on here, but keep me out of it," Duke says, narrowing his eyes at both of us before dropping into a chair and tucking into what I can only assume is a tofu dinner.

"I THINK your plan is flawed, no offense," Sunny tells me on the front porch a few minutes later. She said Sebastian had suffered enough for one night, so we owed it to him to stay out of sight.

"In my defense, you could have gone with something like, 'I'm exploring my options, Grandpa,' instead of an etymology lesson that degraded into a personal reflection on romance in the judicial system."

"Whatever," is her bruising response. "Here." She shoves a tabloid magazine at me, and I take it from her.

"No more *Car and Driver*?" I glance down at it. "I'm not really into gossip."

"Look closer." She bites her lip, the little gap winking at me.

Any amusement I was enjoying dissolves when I scan the cover and spot the sub headline in the bottom. I quickly flip through the tabloid to find the article, and my heart sinks like an anchor when I see the word *Nutri-Slender*.

"Shit."

"My thoughts exactly."

I read the entire thing while Sunny continues chewing her lip and shifting from hip to hip. It doesn't give a release date, only mentioning an expected summer or fall timeline, so at least it's not available yet. It does name the manufacturer, though, a company called Starboard Nutrition and Wellness, something I'd already uncovered on my own before the warning texts began. But this brings new urgency to our plans—not that I think I can actually stop it from coming to market.

"We have to get moving on this," Sunny echoes my thoughts.

"Duke said Knuckles is already working on it, and we just need to arrange a time next week to meet. I can make anything work, so the schedule is up to you. The sooner, the better though, yeah?"

"How about Sunday? I have Sebastian's rally on Saturday, but I have all day Sunday plus Monday morning off."

"That works for me, but I don't see how we can be back

before Monday afternoon, even if our meeting is short." The drive to Memphis is probably eight hours.

Her lip looks like it might split any second, and without thinking, I reach forward and pull it from her teeth's grasp with my thumb. "Don't hurt yourself. We'll figure it out." My voice drops low, and I can't help but run my thumb over the red spot on her bottom lip.

Heat fills her cheeks as I caress her damp lip, and I can see her quick intake of breath and the darkening of her eyes. I'm about to lean in and taste her when she takes a step back, jarring me back to reality.

Fuck. I need to watch my step. I clear my throat and pretend I wasn't about to kiss her a second ago. "So, uh, I guess we'll have Duke communicate in whatever code he and Knuckles use, and we'll set up a time?"

She feigns a casualness that doesn't come off very convincingly, especially with the heat lingering in her cheeks. "I still don't understand why everybody can't just talk on the phone or through email like normal people."

I back up another step and bury my hands in my pockets to keep them from getting ideas. My attraction to this woman is almost as puzzling as it is compelling. She's absolutely not my type in any way apart from owning breasts and a round ass. Well, that and she's clearly intelligent. And she knows how to bite back when I tease her, even if her bite is more house cat than panther. But she's not a game player, and she's certainly no shark, nor does she appear to have any desire to impress anyone at all. She's an open book, and I usually prefer mine locked shut with a hidden key and an ostentatious bow tied around it.

Maybe it's this town, or maybe I'm really not the same person I used to be.

"Technology is too easy to tap into these days," I

explain. "In person is best. Besides, your grandpa said Knuckles would want to 'size me up' in person. Not sure what that will entail, but I'm inclined to do whatever he wants in return for his help." As long as the guy doesn't require a body cavity search to convince himself I'm no danger, I'm in.

"If I spent my life being as paranoid as the three of you, I'd go insane."

"It's not paranoia when you've been on the receiving end of their threats, Sunny."

"I guess." She sighs and crosses her arms over her chest. "All right. I'll ask my boss if I can take Monday off. She hates short notice, but I do have vacation days saved up."

"Great. Thanks again for your help."

"Sure." She's regained her composure. "Thanks for the flowers. They really are beautiful." Her smile returns, complete with her usual eye sparkle, and I take that as a sign that I didn't completely fuck things up.

"You're welcome. It's a small price to pay for you interrupting your life. I feel like I owe you more than flowers and the Sebastian thing. Is there anything else I can do to help?"

"You mean the Sebastian thing that had him running out of here like his hair was on fire?" She purses her lips. Yeah, she likes to bite back.

I can't hold back my laugh at that. "Trust me. He's plenty jealous."

"I don't want him feeling jealous—not if it's hurting his feelings."

"It's not. The guy has been oblivious for the last year. He can handle a little competition. By the time you tell him we broke up, he'll be ready to swoop in."

"If you say so. Although, I don't know how believable it will be that *I'd* dump *you*." She looks me over before pulling her lip in again. I resist the urge to stop her this time. She clearly has no clue the kind of effect she has on me. "If you're serious about offering help, I do have a couple things I could use a hand with."

"Lay it on me," I don't hesitate to respond. I can move her furniture or help her force-feed Duke whatever medication he's refusing. No problem.

"How do you feel about farm animals and dating advice?"

CHAPTER
TWENTY

GOOD FRIENDS AND BAD IDEAS

CARTER

APPARENTLY, I've volunteered myself to load goats onto a trailer on Saturday as well as something about an advice column Sunny is writing. Being a librarian isn't exactly what I envisioned.

The favor could be worse though; I wouldn't put it past her to involve herself in some strange matchmaking scheme involving sheep competing on a reality dating show. We've agreed to meet up tomorrow morning for coffee at Pete's again so we can dig deeper into it. Until then, I'm not thinking too hard about it.

I'm distracted enough as it is by Clarence Cody and Grace Hopkins's seeming impenetrability that I can't be bothered to worry about Sunny's side jobs. The tabloid she gave me is tucked into my rucksack for another perusal later tonight, and I've got that itchy feeling again.

On my way back from Black Mountain, I resolved to stop allowing myself to think about Sunny as anything but a friend anymore. It's better this way, for both of us. We're partners on this likely ill-fated mission, and that's it.

"This really is the life." Jeremy sighs and crosses his ankles over the corner of the table as he balances his chair on two legs. We're enjoying a beer at a corner table after closing time at Blue Bigfoot. I left Sunny and Duke a couple hours ago with the older man's promise to confirm things with Knuckles for this upcoming Sunday night or Monday.

If he can get access to Clarence Cody's office and staff, maybe he'll be able to uncover something for me to use. Some electronic correspondence, a financial statement, a staff member with a similar ethical conundrum to mine. It's probably a long shot, but it's all I've got. We can't afford another hit to Blue Bigfoot's bottom line.

Cash deserves to know what's going on—especially since I just gave him shit for keeping the inspection report to himself for so long. But I could have helped with *that* if I'd known. He can't do a thing about this, apart from adding it to his list of worries.

Maybe Jeremy can offer something helpful since I haven't risked keeping myself abreast of the goings-on in the District since the warnings picked up. If I didn't think it would endanger both of us, I might consider confiding the entire saga in him.

"So, how's Grace these days?" None of us would dare use her first name in her presence, but that doesn't prevent the familiarity when we're away from the office.

"You know her. Overworking everyone and always on a mission about something or other."

"Yeah." I choke out a humorless laugh and can't resist commenting, "Such is the life of the ethically untouchable."

Jeremy cocks his head and gives me a curious look. "I don't know if I'd say that, but yeah."

Miller sits himself down in one of the two empty chairs, and I notice he's drinking soda for once instead of beer. "What are we talkin' about tonight? Women? Booze? Gambling?" He's way too eager.

"Vasectomies," I answer without hesitation.

"I'm out." He's gone before Jeremy can even say goodbye.

My friend laughs and takes a pull on his beer. "All those times you talked about your family, I thought you were exaggerating, but you really weren't, were you?"

"Not even a little."

He grins over his beer and shakes his head. Jeremy never talks much about his past, but over time I've learned his childhood wasn't the best. The fact that he came from nothing makes him a good match for Grace Hopkins's staff, but he's always been impatient. It's the only thing that ever trips him up.

Cash ambles over, but when I gesture for him to take a seat, he declines. "Nah. I'm headed over to Hollis's place. Can you give Miller a ride home?"

"Sure. No problem."

"Hollis is the hot blonde I pointed out yesterday, right?" Jeremy asks me. "The one with the nice rack and the dogs?" I bite back a smile when Cash stiffens.

"Excuse me?" my brother asks, his tone tight as a suspension bridge cable.

"What?" On most days, I'd classify Jeremy as a sharp guy. Not so much today, though.

"Were you checking out my girl?"

Jeremy unwisely decides to continue poking the bear. "Kind of hard not to, man." Acting like the pig he is,

Jeremy brings both hands in front of his chest, mimicking squeezing his own set of invisible breasts.

Cash turns to me, a vein threatening to rupture in his forehead. "How much do you like this guy?"

"Not all that much." I take a sip of my *Cryptid Chaos*, a rich bitter double IPA.

Jeremy coughs in indignation, but I leave him swinging.

Cash opens his mouth to deliver what I'm sure will be a hilarious beatdown of our guest, but his phone rings from his pocket before he can begin. He holds Jeremy's eyes in a death stare as he answers the phone.

"Peach. Yeah. No. Yeah. Tell Betty I'm on my way." He hangs up without even blinking and addresses Jeremy. "Keep your eyes to yourself, asshole." Then he turns and stalks for the hall.

I'm grinning like a lunatic, especially when Jeremy watches him go, marveling as he asks, "Exactly how many women does he have waiting for him?" I don't tell him Peach is Cash's nickname for Hollis, and Betty is the name of one of her dogs.

We bullshit a little more until Jeremy finally asks the question I've been waiting on since he rolled into town yesterday. "Still not ready to share why you ghosted?"

I owe him something. "Let's just say I'm doing what's best for my family."

He watches me for a second before nodding. "I envy you, man. Being so tight and all, I mean."

"It comes with its drawbacks, believe me."

"I don't know. Your brothers are hilarious. And your mom is something else." He chuckles, and I can't help a small grin.

"You haven't even met Denny yet—or Lynnie." My

grin drops as something occurs to me, and I straighten in my chair. "And don't you ever get any ideas about her, you hear me?" I vow right now to do my best to ensure those two never meet. Lynn would likely flirt with him just to get a rise out of me, and Jeremy can not be trusted where women are concerned. That's been made clear several times over.

"And tarnish my reputation in the public eye? Not a chance. Isn't she still a teenager?"

"Damn right, she is." Although she's turning twenty in another month, not that I'm telling Jeremy that. I decide to switch subjects before I get all pissed off over nothing. "So, future Congressman Ricci, you still set on paying those dues and embracing the life?"

"You know it." He sends a pointed look at me. "I'm not about to throw away what I spent the last ten years building." I can't blame him for the jab. I owe him more of an explanation than the family bit.

I acknowledge his comment with, "It's complicated." Not that it's much better than my first excuse.

"I sure as shit hope so. I'd hate to see you making a move like that over something simple."

We both know I'm not being forthright, and part of me worries he could end up like me if he's not careful.

"Just... watch your back, okay, man?"

He purses his lips like he tasted something sour, but he maintains his relaxed posture, his ankles still crossed over the table corner. "That sounds awfully cryptic."

"Yeah, well." What can I say? He could have overheard that conversation as easily as I did. Wrong place, wrong time.

"Come on, man, what happened?"

I shake my head and sip my beer.

"I won't say a word, I promise. You know you can trust me."

He's right about that, at least. We've had each other's backs for several years. I can give him something more without risking his safety. "Okay. All I can say is Clarence Cody pulled Grace into some side hustle he's got going, and I… disagreed."

Jeremy's feet hit the floor as the two front chair legs make contact with the wood beneath us. "The FDA changes," is his immediate response.

I only nod, which has him dropping a fist to the table between us.

"I *knew* that shit was fishy! She fed me some bullshit about reconsidering the value of job creation outweighing potential risks of dangerous shit slipping through the cracks. Dammit, I knew it!"

"Slipping through the cracks? How about being shoved down the public's throats?" I say through clenched teeth.

"What do you mean?"

"Fuck. I really can't tell you more without putting you at risk." I've said too much as it is.

"I can take care of myself. You know that. Besides, it's not like Grace would try to off one of us over a piece of legislation or a few bucks in her pocket." When I don't reply, Jeremy's jaw drops. "No fucking way! Grace? Miss Let's-All-Consider-the-Ethics-Before-We-Decide?"

"I doubt anybody would go that far, but fuck with me and my family? Absolutely."

"What the hell happened?"

I lean into the table, glancing around the empty taproom. "They made it clear they have the power to shut down the business. And anything else they please."

"No shit?"

Fuck it. I tell him about the goons breaking into my apartment, the warning texts, and what I know about the inspector—including how close Cash came to not raising the money for the required renovations.

He asks a lot of questions, most of which I don't answer. I don't tell him about the money or any of my investigating, apart from saying I poked around a little and got my hand slapped. And I don't identify Starboard or NutriSlender or mention anything about Duke and Sunny's involvement, of course. I also leave out the part about the woman's name and address attached to the inspector's car that's sitting in my wallet. I still haven't figured out exactly what to do with it yet.

"I don't know what to say." Jeremy shakes his head when I'm finished.

"There's nothing *to* say." It's the truth.

"I understand now why you're steering clear. It's completely unfair, though."

"Yeah." He doesn't have to tell me about fairness. "I'm less than pleased, as you can imagine." My jaw tics.

"That sounds like maybe you're *not* so set on steering clear." He speculates.

I toss an arm out to the bar. "I can't see myself puttering around here like a sitting duck with Hopkins and Cody holding this over my head for the rest of my life, that's all."

"So what are you gonna do?" He asks this like a man looking for trouble to involve himself in. And I can't have that. One of us needs to reach the future we envisioned.

I relax back into my chair and force my jaw to release. "Nothing. Just wishing things weren't how they are. It is what it is, man. But like I said, watch your back."

He studies me while we both sip on our beers, and I'm thinking he'll press me, but he doesn't.

Instead, he says, "You know, you should come to Raleigh this weekend. Blow off some steam. We can pick up some girls, have a good time like the old days."

"I can't." I fail to inject any reluctance into my tone. I'm itching to get to Memphis.

"I knew it!" His amusement has returned, and it's the same old Jeremy looking back at me, shit-eating grin and all. "Some girl has you under her thumb." His voice echoes off the high ceiling.

"Not exactly."

"Oh please, this has beautiful babe written all over it."

"Yeah, well," is all I've got in return. Beautiful? Babe? Sunny's not a conventional beauty. Cute, absolutely, and she's got fire that lends her an understated sexiness. But she's missing that edge of ice and polish that qualifies a woman as beautiful to Jeremy—and usually me. I don't bother confirming or denying Jeremy's assumptions because he'd never understand what I'm doing running around with Sunny even if I could be straight up about everything.

"What have you got planned? A trip to Vegas? A weekend shacked up in that attic at your mom's?"

I laugh for real this time. "I'm helping her with an errand on Saturday, and then we're going away for a couple days." Herding goats and road tripping to visit a man named Knuckles. Very hot.

"Nice. Hotel sex is the best kind, as I'm sure you know."

I'm not letting my mind go down that road, especially after my unfortunate faux pas on Sunny's front porch. She's made it clear she's into Sebastian, and I promised her

I'd get him to open his damn eyes. The only thing she'd get from me would be a roll in the hay and a thanks for her help. I'm in no position to offer anyone anything, especially while I've got a bullseye on my back, and I'm still moping around bemoaning my station in life.

I check the time and confirm that it's late as hell. Jeremy has an early morning, and I've got to find Miller and get us both home. I know Jeremy is in agreement because he rises from his chair and carries his half-empty pint glass to the bar. I follow with mine.

"Well, it was great to see you." He holds out a hand for me to take and claps my shoulder with the other one. "I'm glad I made the trip."

"Don't be a stranger, okay?"

"I won't." He glances around the taproom. "You've got a good thing going here, Brooks. Don't fuck it up." He grins and dodges me like he's waiting for a punch. Then he turns to go. "Be sure to let me know next time you head up to D.C."

"I will. Have a good trip, man."

When the doors close behind him, I lock up and go in search of my brother, allowing myself to count my blessings for the record third time this week. Now, that's progress, if you ask me.

SUNNY

WHEN CARTER CATCHES ME STARING, I drop my eyes to the tabletop as fast as humanly possible. But it's not fast enough.

"It's just a chin."

I want to laugh hysterically at that. It is *so not* just a chin. The man has shaved his beard and exposed himself as none other than Superman. With dimples.

Superman's famous cleft chin is missing—which, strangely enough, is actually a fetal defect caused from the incomplete fusion of the jawbone—but he's got a square jaw that might have the power to make a woman ovulate all on its own. Add in the dimples when he smiles—which he's been doing way too much for my comfort—and I might pass out before we finish our coffees. All this time, I was hanging out with handsome but scruffy Clark Kent, and then off came the flannel and the beard and *wham!* Brutally hot superhero time!

The temperatures are hovering in the high seventies, so

he's wearing a clean T-shirt the color of rain-washed slate with a Blue Bigfoot Beer logo on it. Occupying center stage is a giant sasquatch holding a mug of beer. The shirt exposes the firm muscles of Carter's arms and stretches over his shoulders in a way I'm finding quite distracting. I don't have a habit of hanging out with conventionally hot dudes, and the familiarity and proximity we share is unsettling.

None of this does my already-fretting mind any good in the least.

It's the morning after the flowers and the vegan dinner, and I've been beating myself up since almost the moment Carter showed up on my front steps last night.

Not only did I let Sebastian walk out the door after my unfortunate case of verbal diarrhea, but I hugged Carter on the porch and mooned over his flowers as if he truly brought them as a romantic gesture. I'm supposed to be mooning over Sebastian and his shiny hair, lean physique, and moral character. Not Carter.

And then I almost swooned like a twelve-year-old with her first crush when he touched my lip with his thumb for half a second. It wasn't even meant to be intimate at all—he was only trying to keep me from bleeding out on my front porch. But, of course, my brain thought he was going to kiss me again and I went all Firestarter in the face. Ugh.

I should have stood tall and told him I'll no longer be requiring his help; it's honestly what I'd planned to do after Sebastian ran out. But what did I do instead? I roped him into *more* aspects of my life by recruiting him for goat trailer pickup on Saturday and *Dear Mona* letters today.

Why am I self-sabotaging like this? Imagining possibilities and making up fantasies is fun, sure, but I always keep one foot firmly in reality. I don't moon over men who look like superheroes and likely have the power to dissolve a woman's panties into dust in zero point two seconds—much less men who try recruiting me for espionage! I read about men like that, not swoon at their feet in real life. I may be an optimist, but I like to consider myself a realist to some degree.

I'm interested in normal, principled, mild-mannered men whose interests lie in watching documentaries and diligently working toward global sustainability and a greener planet. That's what makes me moon and swoon. Fawning over Carter and letting Sebastian walk out after we'd re-established our easy-going vibe last night was foolishness.

I need to finish this Knuckles business, bid Carter adieu, and tell Sebastian how I feel about him. No games, no espionage, no dimples.

"Seriously?"

I jump at Carter's question, afraid I've been speaking aloud, but his eyes are on my tablet where the *Dear Mona* letters are on display.

"Why would someone write this? And who's Mona?"

I was feeling so flustered by his dashing appearance when I walked in a few minutes ago, all I could do was thrust the tablet at him. That, and order myself another one of those chocolate masterpieces.

I scoot my chair in. "Our friend Randy's ex-wife. She used to write an advice column before they got divorced, and Randy was scrambling to replace her, so he gave it to Duke." I'm toying with my napkin to occupy my hands. Where is my drink?

Carter chokes on a laugh. "He's not the first person I'd go to for dating advice. And he said yes?"

"Kind of. He gave it to me instead, and now I need to

respond to all these letters." I pull the tablet from his hands and start scrolling aimlessly. "But half of them are impossible to even mentally process, much less reply to in any sort of helpful manner."

He nods and we both lean back as a barista sets our drinks on the table—chocolate and sugar overload for me, black coffee for Carter. No wonder he's so fit. The man lugs kegs around all day and the only thing I've seen him consume in the last week is black coffee and a handful of almonds.

I take my first sip and immediately feel better. Carter, on the other hand, cradles his coffee cup in both hands and watches me slurp.

"What?" He's making me self-conscious.

"Do you ever say no?"

I draw my chin back. "I happen to like sweets, and milk is good for you—it has protein and calcium, and everyone knows women need more calcium than men to prevent osteoporosis. And don't even get me started on all the studies about chocolate being good for women."

"I mean the advice column—and the goats—and this trip to Memphis, for that matter."

"You want me to say no? Okay. No. Bye." I shift in my chair like I'm getting up, even though we both know I'm not. I mean, my drink is in a real glass so it's not like I can walk out with it.

"No. Yes. Maybe." Carter runs a hand through his hair in clear frustration. "I don't know."

Before we can try exploring his crisis of conscience, he mentally brushes himself off and points to the tablet. "Okay. Let's knock this out."

"Are you sure?" I know my expression is the picture of hope, but I can't help it. I'm desperate here, and Mia is of no assistance whatsoever. When I asked her what choking could possibly have to do with sex, she asked me for Randy's number so they could have a talk.

"Yeah." He nods, completely oblivious to the customer who just walked into a trash can because she was too busy staring at his superhero jawline to watch where she was going. "Read me the first one. I'll answer, you type."

"Oh." I reach for my bag to dig out my notebook and pen. "I always prefer writing out a first draft by hand."

"Huh. Me too." His half smile causes one of the dimples to surface, and my womb constricts.

"I know," I say before I think better of it. But thankfully he doesn't appear to notice, which prevents me from needing to come up with an excuse for why I spent weeks watching him at the library.

I hurry to read the choking letter, impressed with myself for getting through it in one go.

Carter doesn't even hesitate, and my hand flies over the notepad, recording his answer.

Dear All Choked Up,

While experimentation in the bedroom is an excellent intimacy enhancer, activities that bring danger and possible death to your partner should be avoided. Have you tried handcuffs or ropes or nipple clamps? When administered properly, all of these can get the blood pumping in a way that won't risk permanent injury or death. If you or your partner are having trouble getting aroused through more conventional activities, there may be an underlying cause that you could explore with a therapist. Sex and experimentation are healthy and should be fun for both partners, but nothing spoils the mood like accidentally killing your partner and spending the rest of your life in jail.

I hurry to write down every word and then look up at Carter in amazement. "Wow. That's really good."

"Thanks. Just call me Mona." He blows on his coffee before taking a sip.

His confidence and obvious comfort talking about sex does the impossible by making me realize this is really no big deal. It's only words. I love words. And while I still don't understand what could make a near-death experience sexy in any way, I'm guessing now that I'm not the only one.

With a new sense of assurance, I scroll until I find a letter I haven't looked at yet. But as I'm about to start reading it to Carter, I stop.

"Go on," he urges.

My cursed cheeks fill with heat. There goes my newly acquired sense of cool. But I'm not frazzled because the letter is about sex—not really—it's because, well... I swallow and forge ahead.

> *Dear Mona,*
>
> *I'm not experienced in the bedroom, and the guy I just started dating has a definite advantage over me. He's pretty much sex personified. I want to please him, but I'm afraid my inexperience will make me a disappointment—or worse, a freak. I know I should just be honest, but what if it scares him away?*
>
> *Sincerely,*
> *Virgin Scary*

"Okay, that's easy." Carter shrugs, and I try to swallow, but there's a lump in my throat.

The writer's words sear through my retinas and travel down to my chest where they clog up my lungs. I can feel the person's fear like it's my own. Because it is.

Isn't this the very reason I find myself a twenty-nine-year-old virgin? For the last several years, I've psyched myself out any time I let myself think about getting involved with someone I'm attracted to. Heck, I've been crushing on probably the most approachable person in the universe for a year and have never even tried to hold his hand. This letter could have been written by me—except for the part about the writer actually having the balls to date someone.

Talk about self-sabotage. I tell myself I'm too busy or there aren't any men who interest me or none of the guys I like would be attracted to me. But when was the last time I actually tried? I'm officially my own worst enemy.

Carter is oblivious to my inner epiphany-slash-traumatization, so I have to scramble for my pen when he starts talking.

Dear Virgin Scary,

First, please don't call yourself that. A guy worth holding onto isn't one who'll care about your experience or inexperience. In fact, he'll probably be flattered you chose him to initiate you into the world of sex and intimacy—which is meant to be fun, not stressful. Just be straight with him and tell him you want to take things at your own pace. If he tries pushing you or suggesting there's something wrong with you in any way, tell him to get lost. You decide when and if you have sex, and the right guy will not only know it, he'll respect it.

My heart twists in my rib cage at his answer. The words are blurring on the page in front of me and I don't know why I'm crying. There's no way I can let Carter see how much this is affecting me. No way in hell. So I practically bury my nose into the page and continue scribbling.

"Does that work?" he asks.

"Um, yeah. Absolutely." I don't look up. I need to get rid of these stupid tears.

"Something wrong?"

"No." I blink until the page becomes clear again and answer him as honestly as I possibly can. "Everything's... perfect."

But it's not really. Because my self-sabotage has leveled up out of nowhere, leaving me to deal with the fact that I've developed one giant, ridiculous, disastrous crush on Carter Brooks.

CHAPTER
TWENTY-TWO
LIBRARIANS KICK ASS

SUNNY

WHEN I STROLL into work for my two p.m. to nine p.m. shift, I don't allow myself to procrastinate. I head directly into Meredith's office and tell her I'm taking next Monday off whether she likes it or not. And, by that, I mean I beg her to let me take it off and offer to babysit for her next time she and her wife have a date night. But, who cares, because she agrees, and I've secured two and a half days to wrap this Knuckles thing up—and maybe even take a little side-trip to Dollywood. Because, hello? Who doesn't love Dolly Parton?

The next item on my list is much scarier.

"Hey there. How's your day been so far?" I ask Mia as I lean into the customer side of the counter. I'm supposed to be tidying the children's section and preparing for Story Hour, but I need to come clean with Mia first. And ask her to look in on Duke while I'm gone.

"Oh, you know." She smiles up at me. "Tom tried serenading the patrons this morning with selected songs from

Phantom of the Opera, and a lady changed her baby's diaper on the counter—*right* about where you're standing. I guess you could say I'm living the dream."

I take an immediate step back. What is wrong with people? Tom, well, it's not his fault. He struggles with mental illness and happens to have perfect pitch. The woman on the other hand? Well, what do I know? Moms have it hard.

"Don't worry," Mia reassures me. "The area has been cleared by the hazmat team." She raises one hand. "Whoever said there's no 'I' in team never worked for the county."

I lean back in and prop my chin on my hand, going for casual. "So, I've been meaning to tell you something."

One hand goes to her chest and she gasps. "Oh my god, you're pregnant."

"What? No!" I hiss and glance around to make sure nobody heard her before I wrinkle my nose. "I'd have to have sex to be pregnant, Mia."

"But I thought things with Sebastian were coming along?"

"They were. They are." I shake my head and lose any semblance of casualness. When I realize I'm shifting from foot to foot, I force myself to freeze and cross my arms over my chest. "This isn't about that."

"Then what is it?" I've got her undivided attention now, which is unfortunate because it means her eyes are drilling into mine and daring me not to be straight with her.

"I, um, I'm going on a little road trip this weekend, and I wanted to ask if you'd check in on Duke."

"Oh." She sounds almost disappointed. "Yeah, of course. I forgot you had that rally thing."

I bite my lip, but the motion only reminds me of Carter's thumb pressing into my flesh, so I quickly release it. *Coke in a can! Focus!*

"Yeah. That's Saturday afternoon, but I'm actually going somewhere else too. I'll be gone Sunday till possibly my Tuesday shift."

Her eyebrows dance as she twirls her pen with her fingers. "You're going on a trip without Duke? Finally! I've been telling you to cut loose and stop fussing all over that man. Where are you and Sebastian going?"

"I'm, um, not going with Sebastian."

Her pen stills. "Then who are you going with?"

I chicken out, still standing there like a statue with my arms crossed. "Nobody."

"Okay, well, I'll be happy to check in on Duke as often as I can. You take your mental health holiday to whatever spa you've got planned. Hell, I might just invite myself along."

I can't handle it. She looks a little hurt I didn't invite her, and I can't have that—especially when I know the truth always comes out in the end.

I take a breath and lean in closer, uncrossing my arms and gripping the edge of the counter. "I'm going to Memphis with the artist to help him with a project I can't talk about, and don't bother asking me more because I really *really* can't share, but I promise you it's completely safe—well, probably safe—and I absolutely know what I'm doing and he's in no way a serial killer or even a one-off-manslaughter kind of guy. And Duke's already mad at me that he doesn't get to come along and go to Graceland, so you're not allowed to look at me like that because I can't have both of you mad at me at the same time."

Her eyes have gotten progressively wider throughout

my confession, and now she dips her chin to achieve the perfect angle at which to properly assess me and my mental state. Not that I can really blame her.

Her jaw is locked, but she pries it open enough to say, *"Excuse me?"* in a tone that makes me want to pee my pants more than a little.

But someone up above is looking out for me because two patrons approach the counter with the entire romance section balanced in their arms, and Mia is forced to paste on a smile and check them out.

I, on the other hand, retreat to the children's section and work on a strategy for avoiding my best friend for the next several days.

Did I already mention that being a librarian is hard?

Mia fails to pin me down in person before she leaves for the day, but by the time I clock out, my butt is practically numb from the constant stream of texts buzzing my way. I had to stop reading them after the one that threatened to come haunt *me* in the afterlife if I didn't give her Carter's name, number, address, fingerprints, and next of kin.

I'm just grateful he's stopped coming in to use the computers or my bestie might find herself jobless.

I call the goat farmer guy on Wednesday to firm up plans after arranging to borrow the appropriate size hitch ball from one of our neighbors. The farmer won't be there when I arrive, but he's leaving the trailer unlocked and says I won't be able to miss the goats. His only request is that I have them back before the next morning, which shouldn't be a problem. When I ask him if they have pajamas they'd like to wear, he mutters something unintelligible and hangs up.

Mia is off on Wednesday, but I finally call her back,

hoping she's had some time to calm down. She has not. I know this because I can hear Kwamie in the background begging me to stop whatever it is I'm doing that has his girlfriend yelling at him for having a Y chromosome.

I tell her not to worry and that we can talk about it at work on Thursday.

Mia has always been a warrior, and in the four years of our friendship, she's rescued me more than a few times—sometimes, admittedly, from myself. So I'm grateful to have someone who's looking out for me.

But if there's one thing I've learned about Carter so far, he's a protector as well. And he's not going to let anything happen to me. Now, to convince Mia of that.

When I catch her in the break room the next day, she pretends not to notice me—seemingly taking a page from Duke's book on silent treatments. But it doesn't last long after I bend down and squeeze her in one of my python hugs and tell her I love her.

I listen as she explains her worries and do my best to assuage them, sharing as much as I can without betraying Carter's trust. In the course of our conversation, she somehow comes to her own conclusion that our top-secret mission involves beer and possibly a secret recipe. I neither confirm nor deny, but I am impressed with her imagination on this one. When I finally tell her I'm more likely to be assaulted by women trampling over me to hit on Carter, she finally allows a grin to break through her stern expression.

"Would it help if I let you talk to Duke about him? If Duke, of all people, isn't worried about me going to Memphis with the guy, you shouldn't be either."

"Duke worries about you being abducted by aliens, not sexually assaulted by some library patron with a toe fetish." Well, now her imagination is getting away from her.

If Carter had a phone, I could call him, and he and Mia could hash things out right here and now, but the notion does give me another idea. I pull out my phone and bring up the website for Blue Bigfoot Beer, where I navigate to the "About Us" page.

There sits a large photo of Carter and Cash standing on either side of the carved wooden sign for the brewery. Cash is immediately recognizable in a flannel shirt, jeans, and a couple days' facial hair. Carter, on the other hand, wears pressed dress slacks and a blue button-down, his hair cropped short and neatly groomed with not a single lock out of place. I might not have recognized him if I hadn't been introduced to his Superman jawline the other day.

I clear my throat and read aloud from the page.

"Situated at the warehouse shops in the colorful River Arts District of Asheville, Blue Bigfoot Beer provides a wide selection of craft beers in a homey atmosphere carefully created by the duo of Cash and Carter Brooks. The brothers grew up in the foothills of the Blue Ridge Mountains and attribute their love of beer and brewing to their late father, who inspired much about the business. The family's love of all things Bigfoot is demonstrated by the eclectic assortment of sasquatch-themed décor as well as in the names of the beers, all tongue-in-cheek references to the creature who acts as a namesake to the brewery and taproom. Come on in, enjoy a beer, and tell them Bigfoot sent you."

I lift my eyes to Mia before turning the phone her way so she can see the picture. This time, I'm the one dipping my chin and wearing the expression it's impossible to defend against. "I need you to trust me, Mia."

Her head falls back, and she sighs. "I know I'm being

overprotective, but you're always so trusting and… and… *Sunny.*" She shifts forward again and extends her hands across the table. "And I *love* that about you. But I could never forgive myself if something happened to you."

"And I love that about you." I smile at my friend, tears pricking my eyes.

"God, we're pathetic," she says, wiping a tear from the corner of her eye while I do the same.

"I promise I'll bring you a souvenir. I'm already planning on an extra suitcase for all the Elvis stuff I know I'll get Duke."

"Fine." She raises her finger. "But if you see even a *shadow* of Mister Artsy-Bigfoot's penis—or a weapon of any kind—you call me, and I'll have the cops there in a millisecond."

"You have my word."

As the week has flown by, I've only caught glimpses of Sebastian as he and his co-organizer—a thin bespectacled woman named Michelle—worked tirelessly to prepare for the rally and get the word out. By the time Friday night rolls around, I'm kind of looking forward to both the rally and the road trip.

I caught myself looking for Carter at the library this week, but he never showed, although I'm certain he'll be at the farm in the morning to help me out with the trailer. I wonder if he'd be a texting kind of guy if he had a phone. I don't know why the thought occurs to me except that I maybe kind of miss him—even though I've sworn to rid myself of this silly crush.

Sebastian left earlier today for Raleigh so he could be on-site at the crack of dawn, so I'm driving the goats on my own in the morning. Mia and Kwamie are all set to come by once tomorrow and then at regular intervals while I'm in Memphis, and they've even promised to take Duke out to his favorite diner on Sunday. I'm so grateful things are working out that I don't even instruct Mia not to let him have too much salt.

As if I weren't already kicking enough ass, I turn in all my Mona letters to Randy with the confidence that he won't need a dictionary this time. I'm certain that all the recipients will find some form of comfort or wisdom in the advice Carter and I dispensed. Even the person asking if it was strange to have romantic feelings for a family heirloom that happens to be a taxidermied moose.

Duke has spent the last few days in a restless state, still upset at not being allowed to come along. I feel for him and am sure he'd be a much bigger help to Carter than I will, but his hip and his blood pressure won't allow it. Even the promise of Elvis paraphernalia and greasy diner food don't make a dent in his mood.

When my alarm goes off on Saturday morning, he's already left for another of his perimeter patrols, and I don't get to say goodbye before I load Delilah up and head out to pick up the goats. Carter is meeting me there to help me connect the trailer to my hitch and load up the goats, but he's staying in town to work while I head to Raleigh.

I know Mia is stopping by this afternoon and I'll be home again later tonight before leaving with Carter tomorrow, but I'm still tempted to ask Carter to stop by so Duke can feel more involved. It was his scheme to begin with, after all. Mind made up, I leave a note for Duke and grab my backpack, the goat pins, and my keys.

It's time to get my goat fix on! I hope one of them is named Billy or Ramsey—or better yet, Vincent van Goat. I can't wait!

CARTER

"I THINK THERE'S BEEN A MISTAKE," she says.

I look over at Sunny where she stands in front of the goat pen, hands on her hips and a concerned frown pointed my way. Her hair is in two braids today and her brow has more wrinkles than one of Hollis's Shar Pei clients.

"Pretty sure we're in the right place." I point to the big trailer propped on a cement block nearby with the words, "Goat Rental by the Week" printed on the side in block letters. That size trailer seems like overkill for three goats, but I don't know much about this venture. She only told me about the rally and her job to deliver some rental goats.

"Not the trailer. The goats." She directs her gaze toward the three mangy animals in the pen. I can't say they're remarkable in any way, and they sure do smell, but they look like goats to me.

"What about them?"

"Well, nothing, I guess. I just thought they'd be smaller —and cuter."

I hide my grin. "You're probably thinking of pygmy goats, but I don't think they'd be as useful in grazing, if that's the goal."

"I guess that makes sense. Oh well." She shrugs and addresses the goats, the largest of which stands perched on top of a plastic children's playhouse, horns protruding from the top of its head. "I'm sure you're perfectly nice." She glances around the gravel drive and weathered barn surrounded by tall grass before turning her gaze to me. "You got here before me. Was the farmer guy here? I forgot to ask for the goats' names."

"No." I look around as well. "Speaking of which, if that's the trailer you're hauling, where's the vehicle you'll be driving?"

"What do you mean? I brought Delilah."

"Who's Delilah?"

"My car." She says this like it should have been obvious.

I shake my head. "You can't haul a trailer that size with a MINI Cooper."

"Sure I can. I have a hitch. And before you ask, yes, I have the right size ball on it." She cocks a hip and crosses her arms over her breasts. Somebody is fired up this morning.

"It's not the hitch I'm worried about; it's the size of your engine—and the entire car, frankly." While that thing might have some zip, there's no way it can haul a trailer that big.

"Oh." Her mouth turns down. "I didn't know there were *rules*." She says it like she's offended.

I can't keep the grin to myself this time. "It's not personal, Sunshine; it's physics."

She frowns harder at my use of her full name. "I didn't say it was." Did she just stick her nose in the air?

I let her get away with it because she's fucking cute. My eyes sweep the trailer, then the goats, and finally Sunny before I make a decision. "Come on, I'm taking you and these goats to Raleigh."

"What? No!" Her arms drop to her sides and she's lost her sass. "You can't do that. You have to work."

"What good is being the boss if you can't take time off when you want?" I start for the Olds to check out my hitch.

She comes after me, her sneakers kicking up dust. "But you're already taking the next two days off. Don't they need you? I mean, you have to work sometime, don't you?"

"Are you calling me a slacker?" It's more fun teasing her than anything I can recall in recent memory. Probably because she gets so easily flustered.

"No, I'm just…" She inserts herself between me and my car, stopping us both with a hand to my chest. "Look, I'm sure Delilah is stronger than you think. Just help me hook the trailer up and load these guys, and it will all be okay."

My hands are on my hips now as I insist, "Sorry, I can't do that."

She faces off with me. "Sure you can. You're very physically fit." She gestures up and down my body, and I don't hate having her check me out. But she can't trick her way out of this one.

"That's not what I'm talking about, and you know it."

I can see the wheels continue to turn. She relaxes her

posture and toes the dirt. "The thing is, I was kind of thinking today might be the day Sebastian makes his move. You know, he's feeling a high from accomplishing his big plan, his blood starts pumping. *I* show up—with goats." She extends her hand to encompass the animals.

"As irresistible as a woman with a goat entourage sounds, you won't make it more than twenty miles before your car breaks down and you and the goats are stranded on I-40." This isn't happening, no matter how cute she is.

She looks at the goats and bites her lip again. I know I've got her when the smallest goat cocks its head at her and bleats.

Thirty minutes later, we're pulling out of the farm's gravel drive, three goats secured in the trailer and the Oldsmobile's radio tuned to a country station.

Sunny is frowning down at her shirt—this one clearly chosen especially for the occasion, with a goat wearing a pair of Nikes and a Chicago Bulls jersey, the letters GOAT emblazoned in an arch over the top. "I didn't expect him to spit on me." She swipes at the shirt with a tissue.

I laugh. "I think it was a female."

"I just got this shirt too. Did you know Pete's girlfriend owns the T-shirt shop next to his café? I stopped in there while you guys were gossiping." She balls up the tissue and tucks it into the makeshift trash bin behind the center console. "I almost got you one. It said, 'Sprinkles are for Winners.'"

"We weren't gossiping; we were catching up."

"How much can there be to catch up on? His shop is right down the street from you, and I've seen how much coffee you drink." She glances pointedly at my travel mug in the console.

"I don't get out much since I came back from D.C."

"Define much."

"Try never," I echo her statement from the other day when I asked her about dating. Based on her awkwardness with Sebastian, I'd already guessed as much, but I'm beginning to think there might be more to it.

"Why is that?" Sunny asks. "I'd be lying if I said I wasn't always a little curious."

I glance at her in question.

"At the library. You'd come in, frown at the computer for an hour, and then disappear without even looking at anyone, much less talking."

Shit. I really was a dick. "I guess the whole being run out of town thing threw me for a loop." Not to mention the weight of all that cash under my floorboards. I should have made a detour on my way out of D.C. that very night and dropped the duffel bag of cash on Grace's desk. I know it now and I knew it then. But I didn't do it. And I can make all the excuses I want, but there will never be a reason good enough.

Sunny lets me make light of it. "I suppose I can see that. I can't say I'd be eager to make new friends if I'd recently had a gun pointed in my face."

"It's not nearly as charming as it sounds." This time, I manage a grin.

"But you seem much more social since I've gotten to know you a little bit."

"I guess." I don't tell her that she's pretty much been the catalyst for any growth in that area. I went from hotshot up-and-comer to dour hermit in the flash of a gun to my face, and she's pulled me further out of myself in the last couple weeks than I've been able to accomplish in the last seven months. Who knows? Maybe she somehow has the power to get my whole life back if I hang around her long enough.

A thumping sound emanates from the trailer, loud enough to be heard through the windows of the Oldsmobile. Sunny spins in her seat, her braids snapping against the vinyl.

"What was that? Did we do something wrong loading them?"

"No. We followed the instructions to the letter." Each goat is secured in its own penned-in compartment. "They're probably just playing around."

"Or they're scared! What if one of them tripped and broke something? We should stop and check on them."

Since I doubt I can dissuade her, I promise to pull over at the next exit so we can look in on our charges. I consult the dashboard clock, noting that it's not even nine. The drive to Raleigh is only three and a half hours, so we can afford a stop or two and still stick to Sunny's timetable.

By the time I pull over at a truck stop, though, all is quiet. I yank the lever to open the trailer doors and gesture for Sunny to take a look for herself. All three goats are secure in their pens, the biggest one munching on some hay and the two smaller ones lying down looking chill.

"See. It's all good."

Sunny releases a relieved sigh and then excuses herself to use the restroom since we're already stopped. I pull my phone from my satchel in the back seat of the Olds and text Miller that I won't be in for a few days, so he'll need to catch a ride with Cash to work. I also ask him to tell Cash I'll be out today and I'll call him later.

There's a text from Mama telling me they're all gathering for a cookout with the Carmichaels tonight in honor of Adrina's family visiting from Greensboro. But Mama will use any excuse to throw a party, so I'm not too worried about missing this one. I might be expected to explain my absence, though, which will take some creativity.

The second Mama caught wind of Cash and Hollis hooking up, she was all over it, inserting herself right in the middle. If she gets the wrong idea about Sunny and me, I'll never hear the end of it.

A new text from the unknown number catches my eye as well, and I reluctantly open it.

UNKNOWN NUMBER:

Keep your nose clean to avoid visits.

Shit. Goddammit, I hate being right sometimes. I toss the device back in my bag and fasten the buckle as if the phone has the power to jump out on its own and smack me upside the head.

"I got you a drink," Sunny says as she approaches, extending a Styrofoam cup as big as my head, complete with giant plastic lid and straw.

I take it and crack the lid to inspect the contents, half expecting whipped cream and chocolate sprinkles. "Thanks. What is it?"

"Unsweetened tea." She makes a fake gagging motion with her free hand, then grins. "I took a wild guess."

"Thanks." I nod. "Better not let your boyfriend see these cups."

I regret my joke when her grin is replaced by an almost stricken look.

"I'm kidding," I hurry, squeezing her shoulder before I can remember I'm not supposed to touch her. "I'm sure we can find recycling somewhere for it." Which probably isn't true, but it fixes her frown and she's back to smiling, chatting, and sucking on whatever sugar-laden concoction resides in her cup when we get back on the road.

Her cheery mood chases away the rain cloud from my text, and it almost has me looking forward to our big trip tomorrow.

Almost.

TWENTY-FOUR

PROTESTS ARE A SCREAM

SUNNY

"GRAB GANDALF BEFORE HE RUNS AWAY," I grunt as I pry the latch open on the last goat pen.

"Which one is Gandalf?" Carter asks from behind me.

"The one with the beard, of course." The latch finally gives, and I lead Billie out of the trailer by her rope. I've decided that's her name because she's a little bit of a tomboy, what with the earlier spitting and all.

"Oh, of course. How stupid of me." Carter bends to grab both Gandalf and Ramsey's ropes, but both are happily sniffing the narrow strip of grass between the parking lot and the street. Finding parking for a massive Oldsmobile and attached trailer near the Capitol building was easier than I anticipated. Still, I was glad for Carter's company when he expertly parked in the only double spot available.

"You're not stupid," I tell him.

"I was being sar—never mind." He shakes his head.

I hand him the third rope and retrieve my paper sack of

goat pins and my yellow backpack before slinging the pack onto my shoulders.

The sight of Carter standing casually in sunglasses with that clean-shaven face and an assortment of goats in tow has me smiling. I'd take a picture if I thought he'd let me.

"So, where to?" he asks, glancing up and down the street.

"That way—to the Capitol building." I point down the street. "But first…" I pull a black and white goat with green pajamas from the sack and approach to pin it on his shirt.

"Wow. I'm honored," he says. "But hold on." He shifts the ropes from hand to hand as he removes his flannel, exposing that broad chest I'm still not used to. He's wearing the army green T-shirt again—the one that brings out the mossy hue in his eyes. "It's too hot for this thing." He tosses the flannel into the trailer and shuts it with one hand.

"Very hot," I agree absently, my eyes glued to his pectorals. What am I doing? I quickly pin the goat to his shirt, careful not to touch him any more than necessary. I can feel sweat beading above my upper lip, and I quickly add, "Looks like it's gonna be a scorcher, huh?" Good gravy. I sound like my grandma. I may as well ask him about his bowel movements next.

I grab another random goat and secure it to my own T-shirt before taking Billie's rope and leading our troop down the sidewalk.

I hear the rally before I see it, which I hope means Sebastian got the turnout he was looking for. And, sure enough, when we round the corner, there are a good hundred or so people milling around with cardboard signs, chanting "No way! Don't spray!" I grin when I see Sebastian standing on a wooden crate, leading them through a megaphone. Michelle stands on another crate next to him, her own megaphone at the ready.

"Come on!" I urge Carter and the goats as I pick up my pace. "Let's go."

My heart pumps fresh blood and adrenaline through my veins, and my lungs are filled with exhilaration. I'm so glad we came. I'm so glad my future boyfriend is such a fantastic person. I'm so glad he trusted me with the rally mascots. I'm so glad… for everything! Here we are doing something noble for our community, and my heart might burst with happiness.

As we reach the edge of the crowd, Sebastian spots us and I wave enthusiastically, shooting him my best smile. His returning smile is just as big, and it's like there's a cosmic connection between us as we gaze into one another's eyes from across the pavilion, over a hundred heads. Things are all turning out how they were meant to.

"They're here!" Sebastian shouts into the megaphone. "The goats are here!"

My smile falters the tiniest bit at that. He could have said, "Sunny *and* the goats," but whatever. He's happy to see me, I know it.

As if they're one person, the entire crowd swivels our way, a hundred pairs of eyes falling on me, the three goats, and my companion. I stumble back a step at the intensity of it all. These people are really excited about goats.

Then out of nowhere, a deafening screech thunders from right behind me—it almost sounds like someone stepped on a baby holding a megaphone of its own, I hate to say.

I turn to see Gandalf charge forward, screaming his

furry face off and whipping his head back and forth, horns waving threateningly. A woman at the edge of the crowd screams in panic, sending Gandalf charging her way and dragging Carter behind him.

I pivot to grab Ramsey's rope as it slips from Carter's grasp, but I'm jerked back when Billie suddenly turns rigid as an oak tree and tips over on her side like she's just faced off with a wily lumberjack and lost. Her body bounces as it hits the concrete, wobbling back and forth a few times like a coin before it stills.

I've killed her! I've killed Billie!

But there's no time to mourn her because Ramsey takes off into the crowd, parting it like Moses and the Red Sea while Carter regains control over a still-screaming Gandalf —who's now chosen a new target in a guy with a Hawaiian shirt and a sign saying, "Bring on the Goats." And while, technically, I suppose he was asking for it, I don't think he'll take it in good humor when he ends up impaled.

"Everybody, calm down!" Sebastian yells into the megaphone, his tone the furthest thing from calm. "Sunny! Can you get them under control?"

"Everybody stop screaming!" Michelle screams helpfully into her megaphone.

"I'm doing the best I can!" I yell in my least librarian-approved voice.

To my relief, Billie miraculously springs back to life and trots my way as if she hadn't just been lying lifeless on the ground. I don't question it; I take off in the direction Ramsey disappeared.

No offense to anyone at this rally, but you'd think that in a crowd full of do-gooders like these, maybe one or two could be of some help with the goat wrangling. But no. I finally spot Ramsey eating a bush in front of the Capitol building and drag Billie along with me to retrieve him.

Everyone is still shouting and looking around like they've been visited by a plague of locusts—wow, my Moses references are on point today—instead of a few harmless farm animals. Gandalf and his horns aside, I suppose.

I've lost sight of Carter and Gandalf, but just as I get ahold of Ramsey's rope, Sebastian comes jogging up to me, his fraught expression making my heart twist. But he's coming too fast for both Billie and Ramsey's comfort, and Ramsey lets out a scream that's somehow even shriller than Gandalf's, causing Sebastian to trip over his sustainably produced slides and Billie to collapse into another of what I now realize was only a faint.

I'm wheezing with exertion, deafened by Ramsey's screaming, and helpless to do much of anything useful at all. So I draw in a ragged breath and say the only helpful thing I can think of as Sebastian frowns up at me from the concrete.

"Goat pin?"

TWENTY-FIVE
DID I SAY I THRIVE ON CHAOS?

CARTER

IT'S UTTER MAYHEM, and my first thought is thank God Sunny drives a tiny fucking car, or she'd be here on her own trying to control these maniacs.

The goat she called Gandalf is stronger than he looks, with a set of horns I'm not anxious to be on the receiving end of. But once the crowd finally backs up and gives him some space, he stops screaming and calms down. When I look around for Sunny and the other two beasts, they're nowhere to be seen.

"Did you see where the girl with the goats went?" I ask a huddle of protesters gathered within earshot, but they only glance around blankly before retreating farther.

I drop my eyes to Gandalf. "Are you happy now?" He bleats at me and bends to inspect my shoelace. "That's not food!"

I find Sunny a few minutes later tending to a wound on Sebastian's knee while a pale woman with glasses gingerly holds the ropes of the other two goats as they fight over a paper sack. I hope it's not the one with Sunny's pins or we'll be making a pit stop at a veterinary hospital on the way home.

"Well, it's not a proper protest until someone gets hurt, right?" I ask as I approach. Nobody appears to be ready for levity. Sebastian rears back at the sight of Gandalf coming toward him at eye level, so I restrain the mangy troublemaker.

"Hey, Carter." Sebastian lifts a wary hand in greeting. "I didn't know you were coming."

I want to tell him it's a good thing I did and that it wasn't right of him to expect Sunny to deal with three unfamiliar animals and a giant trailer on her own. But I don't. The guy means well, I'm certain, and it's Sunny's business after all. Not mine. Maybe if I keep telling myself her life is none of my business, it'll erase this problematic temptation once and for all.

"It was a last-minute thing."

"Brooks?" A voice comes from behind me, and I turn to see Jeremy Ricci approaching. "What the hell, man?" He's taking in the scene and chuckling as he stands dressed in a navy suit with a bright blue tie and freshly shined shoes that could possibly blind a person at the right angle.

"Hey, Jeremy," is all I can really say because this situation is too ridiculous to bother explaining. And he probably wouldn't believe me anyway.

He steps closer, still chuckling, and wisely stops just out of Gandalf's reach. "I see you finally shaved, Grandpa Joe." His arms cross over his chest like he's settling in for a while. "I can't wait to hear this."

Damn. I guess I'll have to try explaining after all. "Jeremy, this is Sunny, Sebastian, and…?"

"Michelle," the woman provides.

"And Michelle. Everyone, this is Jeremy. We used to work together." I regret it as soon as the words are out.

"In Washington?" Sunny asks, her eyes flicking nervously back and forth between Jeremy and me. The woman has zero idea how to play it cool, and if I can read her mind, so can Jeremy.

"Yeah, *sweetheart*. Before I moved home." My tone is affectionate yet pointed as I silently beg her to act normal.

Sunny's gaze flashes to Sebastian before she stands and shifts closer to me, her smile wobbly. I snake an arm out and pull her into my side, speaking over her tiny gasp. "Sunny and I took a little detour to help out a friend before heading to the beach tomorrow," I lie to my friend.

"I love the beach," Sunny says in what I assume is her best imitation of a doting girlfriend. "Don't you?" She leans against me, and even though this is in no way the time or place, I can't help but enjoy the feel of her soft curves pressed up to my body.

"Uh, sure." Jeremy's tone is more than a little suspicious.

"It's crazy that we ran into you, isn't it?" Sunny shifts her gaze from Jeremy to look up at me, and I send her a surreptitious wink, hoping it will calm her nerves.

"Not really," I answer for Jeremy. "It's April recess, so all my old colleagues are at the district offices next door right now."

"I was literally a block from here when I saw that hideous hunk of junk from my office window," my old friend says. "I figured it had to be you—no way there's another one of those cars on the road. I was about to text you when I heard the screaming." He surveys the crowd and our little huddle of goats and people. "What was that all about?"

"The goats," Sunny answers. "They like screaming." She points to the smallest of the goats, the female. "Except Billie. She's a fainter, not a screamer."

"Aw, I seem to remember Carter being partial to the screamers." Jeremy's grin is sly, and I kind of want to knock it off his face. But he lets the joke go in the next second. "You should have told me you were coming, man. We can still make plans for the night though."

"We'd love to, but we have to take the goats home," Sunny explains with a nervous smile. "Then pack for the beach. And buy sunscreen. And a beach umbrella."

I cut her off before she can read out her entire fake shopping list. "Yeah. The goats were for the rally." I gesture to Michelle and Sebastian, who's holding a bloody tissue to his knee and watching Gandalf with a frown. "What exactly is this rally about again?"

"The Forest Service is poisoning us with its herbicide kudzu containment program. We're petitioning for goat grazing as a more sustainable alternative," Michelle provides before yelping in surprise when the female goat licks her hand. The goat promptly faints, a rigor-mortis-like rigidity consuming her body as she falls stiffly to the ground.

"Yup. That's it," I add as Jeremy stares wide-eyed at the dead-looking goat.

None of us move as we watch for a few seconds until the poor thing rights herself and goes back to sniffing Michelle's hand.

Jeremy's dumbfounded expression takes on a skeptical edge again, not that I can blame him. I need to sell this or he's going to know I wasn't being straight with him in Asheville—and he can't think I'm up to anything besides hanging out with my supposed girlfriend.

"I'm just here for Sunny," I explain, which has Jeremy's eyes sweeping up and down Sunny's curvy frame. She smiles at him, and while I find it adorable, it reeks of awkward. I give her an affectionate squeeze to balance things out, and she shoots me a more genuine smile.

The crowd has calmed and reorganized during our conversation with Jeremy, and Sebastian rises from his seat on the curb. "We're gonna get back to it." His gaze flips from goat to goat until he looks back at us. "Um, do you guys mind maybe…"

"Getting them the hell out of here?" I finish his question for him, and Sunny and I each take a rope when Michelle hands them over.

Relief is written all over his face, which I now realize is the only emotion—besides fear—that he's shown. I'm a little surprised there was no discernible dismay at my claiming of Sunny in front of him. I'm beginning to worry I might not be able to uphold my end of this bargain with her after all. What's wrong with this guy?

"Sorry, Sebastian," Sunny says from my side, and it sounds like she's apologizing for more than just the goat havoc—not that any of it is remotely her fault.

"Nothing to be sorry for," he says as he steps back toward the crowd. "Thanks for trying."

Sunny pulls from my side with a quick "Wait!" and goes after him and Michelle. "You forgot the pins!"

Jeremy's eyes drop to the tiny goat now drooping sadly from my T-shirt. "Nice pin."

I rankle for no reason, but it only lasts for the second it takes me to push it aside. "Sunny likes to crochet." I perch my hands on my hips and try getting a grip on the defensiveness that's trying to rear its head.

"Crochet?" His eyes go over my shoulder in the direction our group retreated. "Farm animals? Protests? What's going on with you, man? This isn't like you."

"What can I say? I'm not the same guy I was." The defensiveness muscles its way into my tone again.

"I'll say. The Carter I know would be chasing after some hot blonde at the Tune Inn right now, trying to figure out how much sleep he can afford to lose trying to get her to fuck him before he needed to be in the office in the morning."

Yeah, I probably did do that. I guess I was that guy. Huh.

When I don't respond, he shakes his head. "All right, if she—if *this*"—he throws his hands out to indicate the goats, the protest, Sunny, Sebastian, and probably the goat pins too—"makes you happy, who am I to tell you what to do?"

I nod because I realize I *am* happy. Well, kind of. I mean, I'm happy today. I'm happy hanging out with my new friend, that's all.

"We good?" he asks, and I don't hesitate to extend my free hand for a shake.

"Absolutely." Jeremy will always be my friend—we have too much history for anything to prevent it—but I think I'm getting closer to accepting that our lives have diverged into two different paths. And that might be okay.

When Jeremy comes in for the usual shake and back-pounding hug, though, Gandalf is most certainly not on board—which he's not shy about expressing as his screams echo over the Capitol building square.

SUNNY

BY THE TIME I pull in my driveway later that evening, I'm so exhausted I can hardly keep my eyes open. And the knowledge that I'll be getting right back in a car tomorrow for an eight-hour drive through Tennessee sounds like more than I can take. At least this time there should be less screaming—and fainting.

When we dropped off the goats and trailer at the farm, the owner was there to greet us. I thanked him for allowing us to borrow the goats but suggested that next time, maybe he could warn a girl about all the drama. He only laughed and said there was a good reason he never rents those three out. Carter didn't find it all that funny.

Carter and I parted ways, both of us clearly done in, but before we left, I remembered to ask the goats' real names. I was disappointed to hear that they only had numbers, not names. Poor Gandalf. Poor Ramsey. Poor Billie.

Duke is watching a spy movie when I walk in, and

when I ask if he's had dinner, he replies that real spies don't need dinner. Since that doesn't really answer my question, I make him a sandwich, which he accepts before yelling at the woman on the TV to stop being a cliché and to just leave the house already. He has a point. Especially when she gets caught by the bad guys only seconds after climbing the stairs to investigate—as we all knew she would.

I leave him to it and go run myself a bubble bath to wash the day away and soothe my aching muscles. Goat wrangling is quite a workout, it turns out.

When the tub is full, I sink into it and let the bubbles envelop me, sighing at both the warmth around me and the weightlessness of my body. The hot water instantly loosens any tension I was holding, and I allow my eyes to close as I settle in. Worries and regrets are strictly banned from this tub, and I will not tolerate them if they try ruining my bath.

As the jasmine scent of the bubble bath overtakes my senses, I allow my imagination to wander and my breathing to slow until I feel absolute serenity, somewhere between awake and asleep. It's heavenly here, and I don't give it a thought when my hands begin wandering across my body. My nipples are sensitive peaks protruding from the bubbles, and I skim my hands over them, enjoying the sensation so much that I trail a hand down my belly and between my legs, where I part my folds and find the sensitive nub hiding beneath.

My mind conjures Sebastian's serious expression and I go with it, stroking myself until a shiver runs up my spine.

"That's right," my dream Sebastian coaxes, but there's something off about his voice. It's too deep.

I'm feeling so relaxed, though, that I push the thought aside.

"Let me see you touch yourself," he whispers, and I swear I can feel his breath in my ear and smell his woodsy scent.

The sensation of his breath on my skin makes me squirm, and I circle my nub a little faster, caressing my breast with my other hand. I moan, and there's no telling if it's in my imagination or if my voice is filling the steamy bathroom.

"Come on, I know you can get there," my dream lover urges as his hand joins mine between my legs, a dark dusting of hair over his muscular forearm tickling my belly. Somewhere in the recesses of my mind, I try reconciling this dream version of Sebastian with the real one, but I get lost when the first faint spasm of my sex takes me by surprise.

"Come for me, Sunny." His voice is almost a command, gruff and rumbling, and my fingers move faster to obey as his hand works in tandem with mine.

The first wave of my climax overtakes me, and my back arches as I draw it out to find the next one. This one crashes over me like a massive tidal wave, sending my body undulating in the water as I cry out and ride it until I'm a deflated pool toy floating in the bubbles.

My breathing is ragged, my chest in a rapid rise and fall as the nerve endings in my sex and my breasts burn in the most delicious way.

And just before I blink my eyes open to come back to reality, I see him, eyes dark with desire and mouth set in an approving half smile as he gazes down at me.

But it's not Sebastian I see at all. It's Carter Brooks.

I gasp and thrash in the tub, my eyes popping open as

water splashes to the floor. He was supposed to be Sebastian, sensible and earnest crusader, not Carter, smirky superhero troublemaker! What have I done?

With no way to erase the spine-tingling memory of my Carter-induced orgasm, I do what any girl in my position would do. I dunk my entire head underwater and scream my lungs out.

"YOU HAVE A PHONE," I immediately accuse Carter when I open the front door the next day. I'm feeling a touch antagonistic after my unsettling experience in the tub last night, and I'm afraid I'm taking it out on him.

His brow knits. "Not *on* me."

"Wait, what?" I frown. "Your friend said yesterday that he was about to *text* you when he heard Gandalf screaming. You didn't appear to find that odd in the least. Which means *you* have a *phone*."

"I never said I didn't." He's completely unbothered, which I find annoying. Also annoying is the way the midday sun picks up the warmer brown highlights in his wavy, thick, fresh-potting-soil hair.

"Yes, you…" *Pink on a porcupine!* He's right. He said he didn't have a phone the day I helped him jumpstart his car, and I extrapolated that to mean he didn't have one at all. I realize I'm pouting. And whining. This won't do, so I try shaking myself out of it. "I made an assumption." There. That was very adult of me.

"When I want to maintain a low profile, I leave it at home. Which is what I did today and what you need to do right now." Carter gestures toward the inside of the house behind me, not even acknowledging my mature behavior.

I gape at him and bring both hands to the butt of my shorts to protect my phone from his greedy hands. He'll have to grope me pretty darn thoroughly to get this phone from me. "I can't leave my phone. I need to be able to reach Duke."

"I thought you said your friend was checking in on him."

I did tell him that yesterday on our drive back to town. The trip was a relatively quiet one, due partly to the fact that our day was a total bust but also because I fell asleep partway in. I can't help it; the rocking of the car and the hum of road noise puts me to sleep every time. It had only been my worry about the goats that had kept me awake on the morning ride to Raleigh.

And maybe Carter was a little on edge after the run-in with his old coworker. I played it pretty cool, but Carter seemed tense. When I asked him about Jeremy on the way back, he told me they're good friends, and he was being careful not to tip Jeremy off to anything that could get him in trouble—especially since Jeremy still works with the congresswoman and all. Carter stressed how important it was for his friend's career not to crash and burn like his own had, and I thought his concern was noble. I let him change the subject after that because I could see the frown lines digging themselves deeper into his face.

"She is," I tell him, hands still protecting my butt. "But that's not the same thing. What if he forgets to take his medicine?"

"Your friend can ask him." Oh, he has an answer for everything, doesn't he?

"He might lie. *I* can tell when he's lying, but Mia can't." Okay, perhaps I'm being a tad anal.

Impatience bites away at Carter's mellow mood, and

there are those frown lines again. "Sunny, I'm trying to protect you—and Duke. We need to work something out here."

I look up at the lines between his eyebrows and worry he's headed back to the gloomy beast he was before we officially met. It would be a shame if he covered that jawline and those dimples with an overgrown beard again. "Fine. Let me call Mia, and then I'll leave my phone. But if anything happens to Duke while I'm gone, I'm going to sick Mia on you. And you won't like that."

"I'm terrified." The mischief has returned with the slight uptick of his lips.

Ha! "You will be." He has no earthly idea.

"I need to be able to check in on things at least once or twice a day, though, regardless of how often Mia can stop in." I'd never forgive myself if Duke fell or something, and I wasn't able to take his call.

"Okay. We'll figure something out. I promise."

He appears sincere, so I nod and look over his shoulder for his giant chartreuse car. I'm disappointed to see a plain black sedan with a faded paint job and more than a couple dents instead.

"What is this?"

Carter turns to look at the driveway as well, but he doesn't say, "Hey! How'd that get there?" like I hoped. Instead, he explains, "Jeremy's comment had me thinking, my car is way too conspicuous to take on this trip. And since only half of me can fit in your ride, I borrowed Cash's."

"It has no side mirror," I state the obvious.

He shrugs one shoulder. "I'll check my blind spot."

I know Delilah is small, but she's mighty. "Are you sure this thing can make the entire trip?"

"We'll see, I guess."

"You're not exactly inspiring a whole lot of confidence, just so you know."

He grins at me, and there go the dimples. Paired with the sculptor's cheekbones, they have a direct telepathic connection to my thighs because my muscles actually quake. Oh, this is so not good.

"Uh, let's get going." The sooner I can sit the better this will go, I can only assume.

I turn to find my grandfather for a goodbye hug and give Mia one last call to somehow explain why I won't have my phone, but Duke is already in the doorway.

"Have fun at the *beach*!" he shouts, over-enunciating each word and using a volume that ensures every last neighbor knows our destination. "Don't forget to bring me that *thing* I wanted."

Carter bends his head so his breath brushes my ear. He smells like coffee and fresh pine chips. "Am I supposed to know what that's code for?"

"He means Elvis stuff." I cup a hand over my mouth so Duke doesn't scold us for being careless.

Carter only nods. "Ah, of course."

Duke steps out onto the porch and gets right up in Carter's business, whispering, "You know it's all a cover-up. He's alive and well and living on Mars." He then slips Carter a note and steps back again, returning to his previous volume. "Watch out for *sharks*!" He shoots both of us a weighty look, and I can see the restraint it's taking for Carter not to roll his eyes.

So, maybe neither of us Underwoods are destined for subterfuge and espionage. But, honestly, I'm okay with that.

I go in for a hug, causing Duke to grunt when I take it a

bit too far. But this is the first time since Grandma died that we've been apart. And even if Carter and I get there and wrap everything up tonight—which I doubt—we'll still have the eight-hour drive back home. Maybe this was all a huge mistake.

"You're acting like a barnacle, Sunshine," Duke scolds in my ear, but his tone holds more affection than annoyance. He's such a marshmallow, even if he has that prickly cactus coating.

My eyes well with tears, and this time, Duke coughs when I squeeze him.

"Please don't kill him, Sunny," Carter pleads from behind me.

"Listen to the boy," Duke agrees, and I surreptitiously swipe at my tears before releasing him and stepping back.

When I look up at Carter again, I can tell by the return of his frown lines that I didn't do a very thorough job of it.

"I'll go call Mia." I slip down the hall in search of privacy.

When I return a few minutes later—thankfully having caught Mia's voice mail instead of the real thing—Carter has Duke's phone in his hand and passes it back to my grandfather. The fact that Duke let someone besides me touch his phone is shocking, but they must have been comparing notes on how to safeguard devices from UPS. Or aliens. Or, worse yet, Ms. Dobson.

I don't stop to hug Duke again, instead offering a weak parting smile as I pass by on my way out the door. Carter follows behind me and then opens the passenger door for me. It makes a popping sound followed by a drawn-out squeak as he pulls it fully open. I throw my stuffed backpack in the back seat and stow my other bag at my feet as I get in and buckle up. Well, at least the seat belt works, so there's that.

Carter climbs in the driver's seat and turns to me, offering a reassuring smile I appreciate. When he adds a wink, I start feeling a little drunk. "You ready?"

As ready as I'll ever be, I suppose.

CHAPTER
TWENTY-SEVEN

JUST SIT THERE AND LOOK PRETTY

CARTER

THE NOTE DUKE passed me on their porch holds an address, time, and date. It also says, "Memorize and burn/eat." Since I'm not eating a Post-it note or starting a fire in Cash's car, I tuck it in my pocket for the time being. The scribbled date is tomorrow, and the time is noon, so we now have our official meet-up with Knuckles on the books.

We'll get to Memphis tonight, grab a cheap motel that takes cash, and meet with Knuckles tomorrow. If all went according to plan, Duke's friend was able to do a little investigating around the federal building housing Clarence Cody's district offices in Memphis.

Since activity surrounding the office would naturally pick up with Cody in residence over the April recess—instead of in D.C.—the assumption was that they'd require some added security. That's the opening we've been counting on. If Knuckles was able to snag that assignment, it would be his ticket in, providing not only access, but protection from any suspicion. It remains to be seen if it worked out the way we wanted since Knuckles is even more tight lipped than Duke is. I guess we'll see tomorrow at noon.

Sunny sings along to some Maren Morris and Eric Church, having a good old time making my ears bleed. The car is filled with the subdued, sweet, vanilla scent I've come to associate with her, and despite her awful singing voice, I am somewhat entertained by her seated dance moves that have her loose fiery hair swinging all over the front seat.

When she's exhausted herself, she quizzes me on my favorite music artists. I blow her mind when I reveal my parents named all of us Brooks kids after country music legends. Starting with the famous Carter family and me, they next chose Johnny Cash, John Denver, Roger Miller, and finally Loretta Lynn. That's how we ended up with Carter, Cash, Denny, Miller, and Lynn.

"My name's origin story isn't nearly as interesting," she shares, watching the tall evergreens on either side of the highway fly by. "When the nurse told my mom they needed a name for the birth certificate, she was looking out the window at the sunny day and wishing she were outside. Grandma said she was always a bit wild—letting the wind take her where it chose."

"Does that mean you moved around a lot?"

"No. Actually, I've lived in that same house in Black Mountain my entire life. My mom wasn't wired for raising kids—in fact, she didn't even know she was pregnant with me until she was six months along."

"I'm sorry." I'm not sure what to say. I knew she didn't have much family, but growing up without a mother couldn't have been easy, especially for someone as sweet and full of life as Sunny.

"Don't be. Duke and Grandma were great parents to me. I'm lucky. I could easily have ended up in the foster system."

"I live with my mama too, you know."

She turns her smile my way. "Aren't we a couple of moochers? And here everyone thought Gen Zers would start outnumbering us millennials taking permanent residence in our parents' basements. Way to represent!" She raises a fist.

"I'm getting an apartment soon. I swear."

She wrinkles her nose, showing off her freckles. "I'll bet your mom likes you being home."

"Probably. But I don't know how much longer I can let her feed me and do my laundry. I'm guessing in your case, you're the one doing all the heavy lifting."

"I don't mind."

I've seen the way she dotes on Duke. "I know you don't."

An Old Dominion song comes on, and she cranks the radio up and starts singing again at the top of her lungs. Then she pulls some yarn and a crocheting tool out of her bag and starts making what she tells me will be a gnome named after me. I'm not sure how I feel about that.

We stop for gas before passing through Nashville. Cash's car gets much better mileage than the Olds, and Miller jumped at the chance to cruise around town in that monstrosity when I traded keys with Cash this morning. But there's a reason I handed the keys directly to Cash and not him.

Sunny is asleep by the time we get back on the interstate. I'd be lying if I said I wasn't jealous—not that having her drive would make any difference. I can't remember the last time I fell asleep when I wasn't completely alone behind a closed door. Hell, I've been sleeping like absolute shit since the day I returned from D.C. And while it does give a guy time for a quiet workout in the twilight hours, I'd trade it in a second for a full night's sleep and a rested feeling when I wake up in the morning.

But I won't begrudge her this nap, especially since I'm the one dragging her along on this wild goose chase for my own insurance. And her napping does offer something I enjoyed very little of on yesterday's voyage: silence.

By all rights, this woman's voice should sound like a dude with a five-pack-a-day habit with how much she exercises that thing. In the course of our seven hours in the car yesterday, I learned all about her best friend, Mia, and a guy named Kwamie who is "the Percy to her Mary Shelley." When I asked about the Frankenstein element, Sunny only laughed, but it had an evil edge to it, I swear.

She also shared her famous cornbread pudding recipe, a story about her childhood pet fish whose ashes now reside in a jar on her bookshelf, confessed to having crocheted over two hundred tiny gnomes—and toadstools, of course—and told me everything I never wanted to know about honeybees. When she nodded off for ninety minutes of the drive home, I didn't protest.

It's not that I don't appreciate the company—or her general cheerfulness. I've already acknowledged the positive influence she's had on my grumpy ass. But when you've been alone and in your head for as long as I have, it can take some getting used to.

She reminds me of Mama in a lot of ways—in terms of her disposition and outlook—but I feel a certain protectiveness over Sunny that Mama would laugh off if

I aimed it at her. Mama is unafraid, bold, a little nuts, and doesn't give a single shit what people think about her.

Sunny, on the other hand? While I don't think she gives much thought to how other people see her, I get the sense that it's because she assumes nobody notices her. If she were like me and was *trying* to fly under the radar, that would be one thing, but she's smiling at everyone and doing favors for people left and right—she's in everyone's direct line of sight. But she projects a certain acceptance of being invisible. And that ain't right.

Sunny mumbles something from the passenger seat, and I glance her way. "What's that?"

"Your toast is ready," she says a little more clearly this time.

It takes another couple of glances to realize she's talking in her sleep, her sweatshirt bunched up between her shoulder and ear, and the upper strap of the seat belt falling over her nose and forehead. She can't be more than five foot one at most, although she does her best to fudge it a little with her platform sneakers.

"Thanks. I'll eat mine later." I heard somewhere that you're not supposed to wake a sleep talker or a sleep-walker; instead, you play along and steer them back to sleep. So I figure she can make me toast if she wants.

"But it's breakfast in bed. Must eat now." She's sounding a little salty now.

I grin when I see her lips firm under the seat belt. Even in her sleep, she's arguing with me.

"Okay, okay. Hand it over."

She doesn't move, of course, or hand me anything at all. "I put butter on it even though you don't eat fat."

"I eat fat," I rebut like I'm having a real conversation

with her. She's never seen me eat Mama's chicken and waffles.

"No. You've got pectorals and glutes and... abdominals."

I chuckle to myself because this is turning into true confessions. It seems innocent little Sunny *has* been checking me out.

"Well, technically, everybody has them."

This makes her frown. "Stop talking."

I laugh out loud this time. "You're the one who started it. I was only being polite."

"Just sit there and look pretty."

This time I laugh so hard I accidentally jerk the steering wheel and have to right us before I drive into the median. Sunny startles upright. "What happened?! Is it Duke?!"

I don't bother answering specifically because a simple glance around will put her at ease. "Just driving," I reassure her, biting back my smile.

She squints first at me and then the road before straightening the seat belt so it rests across her chest and shoulder again.

"Speaking of Duke, I called someone to see to him tomorrow," I tell her.

Sunny blinks at me, a blank expression plastered on her face as she continues returning to full consciousness. "What does that mean? I already asked Mia to add another couple stops in if she can."

"Yeah, but you said she's working all day tomorrow, so this will give Duke a little more company."

"Um, perhaps you got the wrong impression of my grandfather."

"I don't think so." I watch the road ahead, the highway

stretching out before us, green hills rolling in the distance and nothing but farmland on either side. "Just trust me."

"Unless it's Elvis himself—or maybe JFK Jr.—he won't let them in."

"Oh, I think he'll let this one in."

"Who is it? Jesus?"

"Not quite. It's my mama."

I don't need to look over again to know that she's getting worked up. "Your mother? What happened to not involving more people or using phones?"

"I used Duke's phone. And if you saw my mama's text communications, you'd understand. My text about checking in on my date's grandfather while we grab a couple nights away is the least incriminating thing anybody caring to look would find." It's true too.

When I saw how worried Sunny was about Duke, I figured letting Mama loose to nose around in my love life was a small price to pay for Sunny's peace of mind. I'll figure out later how to tell Mama that Sunny and I didn't work out.

"That's both frightening and fascinating."

"Don't I know it."

"Let's set aside for a second that she'll never get in the front door. Why would she agree to this?"

"Mama's more of an act-first, ask-questions-later kind of person." It's no mystery where Miller got that particular trait. "And she loves helping people." Just like Sunny.

"So you... what? Texted her some strange man's address and said, 'Come hang out with this dude while I whisk his granddaughter away to the beach'?"

"Pretty much. Although I did say please."

"Well, Carter, your mom sounds great, but I hope she

doesn't get her feelings easily hurt." Sunny slaps her bare knees in exasperation.

"Nope."

The fight leaves her, and she sighs in resignation. "Remind me to apologize to her if I ever meet her."

"No need. It'll work out. You'll see."

Sunny's gaze swings my way, and when I glance over, her eyes are sparkling. "Look at you manifesting."

"Excuse me? What is it I'm doing?"

"Manifesting. You know, thinking positively and visualizing a desired outcome—willing it to be."

"No. That's not what I'm doing." That's a bunch of made-up bullshit people use to make themselves feel good.

"Yes, you are," she insists.

"No, I'm—never mind. I just thought I'd let you know I arranged something to make you feel better."

"And the considerate gestures? What is happening with you?" She's enjoying herself now.

I scowl at her. "It's not unheard of. I did drive to Raleigh and back yesterday to help you traumatize some unsuspecting environmental enthusiasts—and some goats."

"True. I guess it's becoming a pattern."

"Maybe." My agreement is reluctant for reasons I don't understand.

"So, where are we?" Sunny asks, looking out the window as if the vast farmland could disclose our precise location. "It's weird not having GPS to consult."

"We're somewhere between Nashville and Jackson, which should put us into Memphis in around two ho—"

I'm cut off by a loud thump and the violent shake of the steering wheel. Sunny yelps and I let off the gas, white-knuckling the wheel until we roll to a stop on the shoulder.

It's Sunny's turn to manifest. "I'm sure there's a spare tire in the trunk. Duke taught me how to change it."

If only that new-age shit actually worked.

TWENTY-EIGHT

I'LL TELL YOU WHAT DOLLY WOULDN'T DO

CARTER

"LOOK ON THE BRIGHT SIDE. At least you know what to get Cash for his birthday."

Oh, I've got some ideas. We're trudging down the shoulder of I-40, Sunny having refused to stay behind with the car in case I needed help. With what, I have no clue. With only a paper map to guide us, I used my best guess as to our exact location, estimating an exit three or four miles further up the highway. Sunny is kind enough not to remind me that if we had a phone, we could call for a tow or a ride right now.

When she tried flagging a car down, the driver nearly ran her over, so I'm keeping us to the far edge of the berm where she won't get flattened by a distracted driver.

"It would be a nice gift. Tires aren't cheap, you know."

Of this, I'm aware. I was determined to only spend cash on our trip, but with this added expense, I may have no choice but to use a credit card—which defeats the entire purpose of going digital-free.

At the last minute this morning, I dug all the cash out of the attic and stuffed it in the duffel bag in the trunk. I'm not sure why, apart from some vague notion that I might somehow run into Clarence Cody in Memphis and it would feel great to throw it in his face. But I know it'll just stay where it is until we get back and I return it to its hiding place.

"So, how far out of the way is Pigeon Forge?" Sunny asks, red sunglasses perched on her nose as we head toward the sagging sun. Her hair is wild and tangled, but it's still damn pretty.

"At this rate? About five days on foot. Why?"

"It's probably a moot point, but I thought if we had time on the way back, we could stop and see Dollywood. I've never been."

"No." My tone is harsher than I intended.

"Fine. Like I said, it was only an idea."

"Sorry." I'm hoping she'll leave it alone. She doesn't, of course.

"Do you hate Dolly Parton or something? Because I'll have you know she's a wonderful humanitarian and philanthropist as well as a talented singer and actor."

"I'm aware." One of Mama's favorite mantras is WWDD—What Would Dolly Do?

"I would hate to have to leave you stranded on the side of the road for disrespecting her," Sunny threatens.

"Luckily, that won't be an issue." My boots crunch some stray gravel as I pick up my pace.

The early evening sun is relentless. Of course, the warmest day so far this year is the one day I find myself walking on the hot asphalt shoulder of an interstate. I don't mean to be short with Sunny; it's just that this trip isn't starting off on the best foot, and unless she can manifest us a tire store, I'm worried it will only be downhill from here.

"So, why the negative attitude toward Dollywood?"

I open my mouth to say something I know I'll immediately regret, but before any words sneak out, I glance over at my companion. She's stranded on the same hot asphalt I am, walking to an exit ramp that could be a half mile from here or hundred for all she knows. And she's got the same positive attitude and patient demeanor she always leads with. She's only here in the first place because she's doing me a favor, so why am I determined to be an asshole to her?

"You banned for life or something?" She squints up at me as she speed-walks to keep up with me, our height difference requiring her to take two steps for every one of mine.

I make a point to slow my pace as I exhale and summon a fraction of the patience she deserves. Then I give her my most serious look. "As a matter of fact, I am. My entire family is."

Sunny stops in her tracks and cackles like a hyena, her red hair flying all around and her smile brighter than the sun bearing down on the blacktop. "I was joking!"

"Well, I can tell you the good people working security at Dollywood back in 2005 were not." Ain't that the truth.

She reclaims her spot beside me, and we soldier on. "Oh, this I've got to hear."

So I start the story like I start pretty much all my stories that end badly. "It was all Miller's fault…"

Two hours later, even Sunny has stopped talking. The sun disappeared beneath the horizon a half hour ago, and the only sounds filling the night air are the buzzing of insects and the occasional passing motorist—well, that and the intermittent rumbling of Sunny's stomach.

One guy did pull over to ask if we needed a ride, but he was giving off some serious tweaker vibes, so I declined before Sunny could climb in. She argued that he probably just had an anxiety disorder and could use some company. I told her his pupils and erratic movements told a different story, making me glad I hadn't left her alone with the car. She'd likely give Freddie Krueger the benefit of the doubt.

"Soooo hungry," she groans from beside me.

I throw her a grin, doing my best not to let my growing anxiety show. Not bringing a phone was utter recklessness —I could easily have bought a burner. Or I should have let Sunny bring her phone. What had I been thinking, putting her at risk like this?

I'd been trying to do the exact opposite by not exposing her to any prying eyes that might be tracing me, but now she's stranded in the dark in the middle of nowhere Tennessee with no oasis in sight and an empty stomach that, from the sounds of it, might be devouring her entire body from the inside out as we speak.

The least I can do now is try buoying her spirits. In true Sunny fashion, however, she beats me to it.

"What's the best meal you've ever had?"

I try for her sake, but I come up with nothing. "Guys are pretty easy. Usually our next meal is our favorite."

"Oh, come on."

When I still come up empty, she speaks up. "I'll go first then. Best meal I ever had was a full Easter Sunday spread at a hotel in Charlotte. I've never seen so much food in my life—carving stations, scalloped potatoes, every kind of salad you can think of, crepes, sausage, you name it." I think she might be drooling on her T-shirt. "To this day, I have no idea why we went there or how we could afford it. But I'll never forget it."

"Do you need a napkin?"

She scoffs but does wipe her mouth with the back of her hand, which makes me laugh.

"Okay. Now that I think about it," I say, "one of the best meals I've had was on Easter too."

"Oh, yeah? A giant ham? Deviled eggs? Oh, man, I'd kill for a deviled egg right now."

"Rabbit," I answer.

Her smile drops and she stumbles a little, her eyes hitting the asphalt. I worry for a second that she twisted an ankle or something.

"What's wrong?"

When she brings her eyes back up, she's wearing the exact same expression she had when Billie the fainting goat spit on her yesterday. "You had rabbit?"

Oh, please. She's not even a vegetarian. "Yeah. It's delicious. Especially that day—there was this wine and garlic sauce and all the fixings. Haven't you ever had it?"

"Um, no. At least I don't think so."

Growing up without a lot of money means eating whatever meat is cheap and whatever your mom puts on the table. I'm certain she grew up the same way. "It's really not unusual. People eat all sorts of game—elk, rabbit, alligator, you name it. Award-winning restaurants serve rabbit."

My argument has the opposite effect I intended, with Sunny's lips now firmed into a thin line. "I'm aware, *Carter*. But most of them don't serve the Easter Bunny on a plate on his one big day of the year!" She stalks ahead of me, and I realize this is the first time I've seen her truly mad.

It's also the first time I've seen her ass in shorts. I must admit, it's a good view.

I give her a couple minutes to mourn, repressing the urge to reason with her that a rabbit has about as much to do with Jesus rising from the dead as a pig or a cow would. I pick up the pace and rejoin her as we round a curve in the highway and finally—*finally*—see the exit ramp and a tall, battered sign bearing the words TRUCK STOP.

"Oh, thank God. I'm starving!" Sunny starts jogging, meaning that I can walk at my normal pace again as the worry drains from my chest. We're both hungry, thirsty, and covered in dust and dirt from our longer-than-expected hike, but that doesn't matter anymore.

"I'm going to order two supersized value meals. No, three!" Sunny throws her head back and her arms out. "Mommy's coming!"

I ignore her delirium, choosing instead to scan what I can see of the truck stop so far. It's not a chain, that's for sure, but it looks to have gas pumps, a small store or restaurant, and an attached roadside motel that gives off some genuine *Psycho* vibes.

"I'm thinking it will be more of a breakfast-all-day diner instead."

"Even better. Bacon! I could eat an entire pig right now."

"But certainly not a rabbit," I can't resist saying. When she ignores my comment, I add, "Let's hope they have tires in addition to bacon, yeah?"

"Oh, right. Of course. Sorry. I get a one-track mind when I'm hungry."

"You should see Cash when he's hungry—or hangry, as my sister puts it. He'll bite your arm off if you put it between him and a plate of food. And I'm only being partly facetious."

We both pick up speed, anxious to reach our destination, but the closer we get, the faster my hopes fall. The interior lights at the diner and the gas station are dimmed, and only the parking lot lights flicker in the dark sky.

"Shit."

"Oh no!" Sunny comes to the same conclusion I just did. "But wait—the motel!"

There is indeed a lit vacancy sign outside what must be the lobby or office. We take a shortcut down the long grassy embankment and jog the rest of the way to the door. I release a giant sigh when I pull on the handle and it easily gives way.

SUNNY

"HELLO?" I ring the bell for the third time as Carter stands like a Greek god statue at my side, his darting eyes the only evidence that he might not be made of stone. I turn to him as I hit the bell again. "Relax. They're not going to hurt you."

"And how exactly do you know that?" he asks through clenched teeth.

"They're just birds. The worst they might do is poop on you—and that's actually considered a sign of good luck so, hey, win-win."

A chubby brown bird flickers its wings from its perch on a Ficus tree in the corner, and I swear Carter whimpers. My hero. I've chosen to forgive him for the whole Easter Bunny thing, but mostly because I'm too hungry to hold a grudge right now. He could, however, be doing a better job of earning my mercy.

"I'm so sorry!" comes a voice from somewhere behind the small counter. "You caught me in the loo." A woman

I'd estimate somewhere between one hundred and three hundred years old emerges from around the corner with a head of tight white curls and a floral silk caftan. Fur slippers cover her feet, complete with fabulous pink pom-poms. I know immediately that I like her very much.

"That's okay." I smile at my new friend. And because Carter is clearly frozen in fear over a few harmless birds, I take on the duty of project leader. "Hi there. We got a flat tire down the highway a bit. We were hoping we might be able to get some help—a spare or a ride maybe? We'll pay, of course."

"Oh dear." She frowns and brings a hand to her chest. "I'm afraid the service station is closed until morning. Folks around here don't like to work Sundays, you know, it being the Lord's Day."

"Oh." I nod in understanding. "Okay, well, we left our phones at home. Do you have one we could use to call a cab or an Uber or something?"

"Where to? You're already at a motel, honey."

"And it's lovely. The birds are a nice touch. But we were hoping to get to Memphis tonight."

"You won't be getting to Memphis tonight—even if you did find a service station that was open—or a taxi to take you there. The highway's closed. Didn't you hear?"

"What?"

"It's all over the TV. A tractor-trailer full of chickens jack-knifed and caught fire. Feathers and flame-broiled chicken all over both sides of the interstate. On the bright side, at least nobody will go hungry."

"Oh no." I chew on my lip. Thank goodness our rendezvous with Knuckles isn't until tomorrow.

"Well, they're already dead. It would be a shame to

waste them." My god—she probably has rabbit for Easter dinner too.

I'm unsure how to respond to that. Or any of it, really. I look to Carter for help, and I notice one of the birds—a finch, if I'm not mistaken—has landed on his head and made itself at home. I press my lips together to keep from laughing. I would kill for my phone right now.

"Carter?" I manage to speak without losing it. "What do you want to do?" I have no clue what his master plan entails apart from meeting up with Knuckles, but I have to imagine this puts another kink in it. And if we miss the meeting, we have no way to get in touch with the guy. Heck, I still have no secret-agent-approved way to contact Duke yet.

"*Get. It. Off,*" Carter hisses, and I'm impressed at how still he manages to remain. He could work as one of those living statues in Vegas or New York City. All we need is a bucket of silver paint.

"Is the bird bothering your husband?" the woman asks in a tone one might use on a four-year-old.

"He's, um, allergic." He owes me for shielding him from humiliation like this.

As soon as the woman whistles, the finch flits from Carter's thick hair to her shoulder before flying to the Ficus to join the brown one.

"Aww. He's so cute." I look around and count the birds, finding two in the corner I missed before, making it a dozen. Is that an actual nest? "Don't they try and get out when you open the door?"

"Of course."

When I cock my head in question, she laughs. "Oh, they're not *my* birds. They're wild. I leave the door open most of the time, and they keep showing up."

Now I'm certain the whimpering sound is coming from Carter.

I give the bird lady my best smile. "Can you give us a minute?" I ask as I jerk Carter out the door behind me. Sure enough, the brown bird flies right over our heads and takes off into the night sky.

"What the fuck was that? It's like the Amazon in there!"

"And people say women are melodramatic." I roll my eyes at him.

"I'm sorry, but do you know how many diseases and parasites birds carry? They're essentially flying rats."

"Well, our hostess in there has been sharing an office with them for a good hundred years or so without being poisoned, so I think you'll be okay, big guy." I pat his shoulder and he actually shudders.

"We've got a more serious problem than birds, as I'm sure you heard."

He releases a breath and shakes out his thick hair, running a hand through it, presumably to check for stray birds or maybe eggs—which, honestly, I'd kill to eat right about now. "Yeah, I got that."

"So, what should we do?"

Carter glances around, and I follow his gaze, taking in the dimly lit service station and the large empty parking lot. The headlights of one lone car illuminate a patch of interstate before disappearing a second later. It's so quiet, all I can hear is crickets and katydids chirping.

"I guess we're stopping for the night." He jabs a finger at me, and I instinctively raise my palms. "But if there are birds in the rooms too, we're walking the rest of the way to Memphis."

"Aye, aye, captain."

"HERE YOU GO." The woman—whose name is Rhonda, we learn—unlocks the door to room nine and swings it open.

"Oh, Rhonda, I forgot to ask, is there a way to get any food around here by chance? Maybe a pizza delivery?" Carter offers one of his dazzling dimpled smiles, having regained his composure now that we've created some distance between him and the flying rats.

"Oh, I'm afraid not, dear. Sunday, you know. But there's a vending machine on the far side of the service station."

At this point, I'll take anything. "Okay, thanks."

Still playing the role of bird-slayer, I reach in and flip on the light. A single queen-sized bed rests against the wall, with a nightstand and armchair occupying the remaining space in the small room.

I turn back to our hostess. "Um, do you have any rooms with two beds?" I glance up at Carter before adding, "Or maybe we'll just take two rooms." How expensive could it be, really? We both stocked up on cash before leaving home.

He nods in agreement, but when our eyes go to Rhonda, she's wearing a frown. "Now, whatever it is you're fighting about, never go to bed angry."

"We're not—" Carter and I begin simultaneously, me finishing the sentence with the word "together" and Carter with "fighting."

"Oh, come now." She's not dissuaded. "I can spot a lovers' quarrel when I see one." She turns to me. "What did he do? Refuse to stop for directions? Leave your suitcase on the bed at home?" It's Carter's turn next. "Or did she distract you while you were driving, and you hit a pothole and popped a tire? Whatever it is, it's only a bump in the road, no pun intended." She laughs and tries ushering us into the room as if her ninety-pound frame on fur slippers could stand a chance against Carter—or me, for that matter. I outweigh her by a good fifty pounds.

"I don't think you understand, Rhonda. Carter and I are just—"

"Having a rough patch," she cuts me off. "Believe me, I know. But the best way to the other side is going straight through it, not around it. You'll thank me in the morning, I promise."

With that, she hands me the key and takes off for the lobby with more speed than I'd ever have guessed possible.

"This is ridiculous." I hold the key like Carter would hold a bird—with an overly dramatic sense of horror. What if I fart in my sleep?

"Don't worry," Carter says. "Let's get some food to prevent you morphing into whatever creature you become if you're not fed before midnight. Then I'll go talk to Rhonda and get us another room."

"What are you going to do, sweet-talk her?" I cross my arms and eye him.

"If that's what it takes."

I'm not usually one to go bear-poking, but hunger does things to a girl. "Oh, yeah? Maybe flirt a little? Or go all alpha and get her to roll over?"

"Anything is possible." He shrugs those broad shoulders. His T-shirt today is navy blue with a white beer logo.

"I see. Okay."

His eyes narrow. "I'm not planning on *seducing* her. Why do you look so… scandalized?"

I point to my own face. "Oh, that's not what this expression is."

"Then what is it?"

"I'm just thinking about the look on your face when you remember that office is full of blood-sucking rats with wings."

His shoulders drop. "Fuck."

"Yeah, I thought so."

CARTER

SHE'S ENJOYING THIS.

Good-natured, agreeable Sunny has checked out of this motel and been replaced by a version with enough sass and salt to make a serious dent in my manhood. I'm a pig, clearly, but this woman has more sides to her than a Ginny Brooks rabbit dinner.

Sunny would have no way of knowing I enjoy a challenge in a woman, and I enjoy confidence. Her throwing these little digs and flashing her gap at me with that smart-ass tone is an absolute turn-on.

But letting my mind even begin to wander in that direction is unwise. We're on a mission. I don't know how many times I'll have to tell myself Sunny is into Sebastian —and not me—for it to sink in. And I have no business looking at her as anything but a partner in this venture.

I didn't dare disobey when she sent me on a vending machine run while she went to straighten things out with Rhonda, the avian marriage counselor. I managed to gather a feast of granola bars, Funyuns, PowerAde, water, and some fruit snacks called YumZees. I assume it's a delicacy of the finest kind.

Since I'm clearly at Sunny's mercy tonight, I don't even think about starting without her, however much the water is calling my name. Luckily, the wait isn't long.

Sunny pushes the door open and stands at the threshold like a miniature Valkyrie fresh from battle. "You want the good news or the bad news first?" She obviously hasn't noticed the pile of snacks on the nightstand yet or I assume she'd be sharing any and all news around a mouthful of deep-fried onion.

I prop my hands on my hips and face her. "Bad news." I mean, as long as the bad news isn't that we're on bird-sitting duty, I can take it.

"We're stuck with the one room." She glances pointedly to the bed I haven't yet touched in case we were switching rooms. "And the one bed."

Hmm. Worse things have happened. A lot worse. I stop myself before I get any ideas.

"And the good news?"

"Rhonda has decided to allow us to conduct tonight's Bible reading in the privacy of our own room instead of with her—and the birds."

I force myself not to wince at the mental image of that. "That's awfully gracious of her."

"I thought so."

Sunny exhales, her shoulders drooping, and I can read the exhaustion on her face.

"I think I've got something that might cheer you up." I gesture to the nightstand. The second her eyes find the vending machine haul, the familiar sparkle is back.

"Oh my god, I love you!"

It's unclear if she's talking to me or the food, but I think I have my answer when she tears open a granola bar wrapper with her teeth and shoves the entire bar in her mouth. "Nth ush na mus snin im ema namud."

I reach for a water bottle and twist it open. "Sorry?"

She raises her finger while she chews and swallows. "This is the best thing I've ever tasted!" She goes for a Powerade next. "You're my hero."

This time, I know she's talking to me, and I can't help the little burst of pleasure in my chest. "Well, it's my fault we're here in the first place."

She scrunches her nose. "What? No, it's not." Her eyes skip around the room and she shrugs as she takes a long drink of blue liquid. "Stuff happens. It could be a whole lot worse."

She's right. I could be here alone with my grumpy asshole self instead of having her here to save me from my drowning in my own pessimism.

She sets down the bottle and goes for some of the fruit snacks, moaning and dropping her head back as she chews. The woman has zero idea where that takes a man's mind, and I finally sit on the bed, if only to hide my body's reaction to her antics.

Wrapping up her food orgasm, she asks, "So, what's the sleeping arrangement?" I must look confused because she continues, "There's no way either of us is sleeping on this floor, so how do we share this bed without... you know?"

I bring my hand up to stroke my missing beard. "It *is* possible for a man to lie in a bed with a woman without his dick magically finding its way out of his pants."

She blushes. "Duh. I just mean... you know."

No, I really don't. Is she afraid to sleep next to me? "Your virtue is safe. I'll sleep on top of the covers—and I'll somehow manage to keep my clothes from shedding themselves."

Her gaze rakes down my body like I just invited her to evaluate said clothes, and my dick likes it way too much. This woman might kill me before I even get a chance to contemplate sleep. Sunny is such a contradiction. She's the most curious person I've ever met, her mouth is a loud-speaker for every one of her thoughts, yet she blushes at even the mention of anything remotely sexual or intimate.

"My virtue? Ha!" She says it like a challenge, and my mind goes on a journey of its own making.

"How do I know *my* virtue is safe?" I tease, knowing better but saying it anyway.

Her laugh is nervous, and she busies her hands, tearing the snack wrapper to shreds. "Right. I'd guess you were born luring women into your lair."

I lean back on the bed a bit, my weight on my hands now. "That's not a very nice thing to say about a baby."

"Pardon me, then. I guess you sprang to life in full man form, schmoozing your way around like a true politician."

This time, I fail to play along. She wasn't trying to wound me, but she hit a sore spot nonetheless. "You know, not all politicians are shady."

I'm not naïve enough to think all people in public office are selfless idealists who got into politics to make a differ-ence. But I've also never been a true cynic who views the entire political theater as a cesspool of power-hungry char-latans clutching knives behind their backs. Most politi-cians I've met linger somewhere in that gray area in between. Me included, as it turns out.

"I know." Her tone is all sincerity. "I'm sorry. I was just joking around."

"It's okay. I can't blame you, especially given the circumstances surrounding our trip." I did give her the impression that my colleagues may all be a bunch of conniving assholes.

"Way to spoil the mood, Underwood," she mumbles.

I much prefer her throwing me sass, so I get over myself and wade back into dangerous territory. "And what mood was that?"

The blush returns. "I don't know." She's rattled again, but she's already shredded the snack wrapper, so she starts playing with the ends of her hair instead.

Leave it alone, Brooks. Go take a shower and go to sleep. "If I didn't know better, I'd say you're flirting with me, Miss Underwood."

Her responding laugh is strangled. "Yeah, right. I don't even know how to flirt."

Like hell she doesn't. She might not know that's what she's doing, but she's got all kinds of natural talent.

And I have no idea what possesses me—maybe it's her comment on politicians that got me riled up, or the frustration of the evening, or her vanilla scent filling the car all day, or even the damn birds—but the words are out before I can stop them. "Then why am I so fucking turned on right now?"

Two bright pink spots light up her cheeks and her mouth drops open, giving me way too many ideas. Fuck, what am I doing? I can't sleep with this woman. But it's not like she and Sebastian are dating right now, right? And I know she's attracted to me from her inability to hide anything. She may not view me as a love interest, but that doesn't mean she doesn't want me.

"Turned on, like how?" She steps closer, pulling that

bottom lip between her teeth. Fuck. Her guilelessness is pure kryptonite.

I don't mince words. I want to see her cheeks redden and her pulse catch fire. "I'm hard as a rock just lookin' at you." My voice comes out in a scratchy rasp and my dick strains for freedom from these clothes.

She tries hiding her little gasp at my words, but her eyes drop right to my crotch, and I adjust myself like the animal I am before sitting fully upright again.

I seriously contemplate that I'm dreaming this entire thing when she inches even closer and blinks those wide eyes at me. Her pupils are already dilated. "Can I...?"

She can fill that blank in with anything she wants, and I'll say hell yes.

When she steps between my splayed knees and extends a hesitant hand toward me, I take it in my own and bring it down to my pants, cupping my hand over hers as she settles it over my rock-hard cock under the zipper.

"Wow. You weren't kidding."

I want to growl and laugh and yank her on top of me all at the same time. She's set something loose in me that's been pent up and festering, and I don't want to bottle it back up, no matter how fiercely logic is telling me to.

From my seated position, with her standing between my thighs, she's taller than me for once. I reach my free hand up to cup her cheek and she dips her head until our lips meet. She immediately presses down on my dick, making me grunt into her mouth and shift my hand so my fingers slide through her hair to the back of her head. My other hand releases hers and moves to her hip, gripping the soft curve beneath her shorts. We're both covered in dust and dried sweat from our hike, but her lips are sugar-sweet from the snacks and her body is all warmth and invitation.

My hand slips to grip her behind her neck and draw her in closer as I slant my head for a better angle. I swipe the tip of my tongue along her bottom lip, catching more of the sweet, and her mouth opens to invite me in. I should have guessed her natural curiosity extended to the more intimate side of things, but the way she starts stroking my cock through my pants is an unexpected surprise. My hips shift up to meet her hand.

I slide my tongue along hers and she matches me taste for taste, melding our mouths together as she releases a little moan. Between the moan and her hand, this has a chance of being over before it starts, so I pull her closer until she has to remove her hand from my cock. Without any urging from me, she climbs onto the bed, her knees cradling my hips and her round ass settling on my lap.

Fuuuuck.

She grinds down on me, our mouths never parting, and it's my new mission in life to make this woman come while I watch. Somewhere in the back of my head, I know I don't have a condom, so I can't fuck her like I want to. But I sure can have a whole hell of a lot of fun doing all kinds of other things with her.

She lets out a little mewling sound as she dry humps me and fists my T-shirt with both hands at my back. I release her lips to trail my tongue down her throat, then back up to taste the spot just beneath her ear. Her taste is salty and sweet, like the rest of her. She tilts her head back, squirming and thrashing like I'm licking her clit instead of her neck, but she manages to keep her rhythm. At this rate, my dick might get zipper burn, but I don't give a fuck right now. I can feel the warmth of her pussy through the fabric of our clothes, and the saltiness of her skin brings a kind of thirst that water can't fix.

"Carter," she pants my name as she moves over me. I urge her on with both hands moving to her hips as she rides me, head thrown back and tits right in my face. Fuck, yes. I grasp her hips harder and bring my mouth to her throat again.

I need to get my mouth on her breasts, so I move to pull her T-shirt up, but before I can, she cries out, her voice cracking as she starts thrashing again, her body almost vibrating as she climaxes on top of me.

"That's it," I coax her. "Fuck, you're hot." I pump my hips up to meet her as she rides out her orgasm, gradually slowing her movements until she comes to rest. Her head drops down, her forehead landing on my shoulder, hot quick breaths bleeding through the fabric and heating my skin underneath.

I'm wearing an idiotic grin as I stroke her back and ass with my hands and her breathing evens out. But just as I open my mouth to tell her how fucking sexy it was seeing her ride me, she stiffens in my arms.

Well shit.

THIRTY-ONE
WHO NEEDS ENEMIES WHEN YOU CAN BE YOUR OWN?

SUNNY

CORN ON A FREAKING COB! What did I just do?!

I'll tell you what I just did: I rode Carter Brooks like my own personal hobby horse and had an orgasm on his lap like he's nothing but a giant dildo!

Why am I so impulsive? I swear, the man told me I turned him on and the next thing I do is reach out and yank on his penis? Who does that?

This is so profoundly embarrassing. And now I'm sitting here, still on his lap, my vagina fluttering like a butterfly's wings after that orgasm. Can he feel that? Please tell me he can't feel that.

It's not like I can stay here with my head buried in his shirt for the rest of my life, now can I? I need to find a way to gracefully extract myself not only from my position but from this entire situation. *Bird in a bobsled!*

I lift my head, spine straight as a yardstick as I awkwardly climb off his lap and stand, careful not to add insult to injury by kneeing him in the groin. "Um, I'm so sorry, Carter." There. I'm still an adult. Even if I can't bring myself to look at him.

"What for? That was hot as hell." I can see him run a hand through his hair and adjust himself in my peripheral vision.

"I just… basically used you to… get off." I stab my fingers into my own hair, feeling the dust from the interstate coating the strands. I can't even contemplate what a trainwreck I must look like right now.

"Sunny." I capitulate to his demanding tone and meet his eyes before I can stop myself. When I do, he finishes with, "You getting yourself off on me is something I'd gladly welcome any damn time of day or night. Guys really aren't that complicated."

I bite my lip and examine him for signs of dishonesty, but I can't find any.

His eyes are on my mouth as he shakes his head with a half grin. "She says she doesn't know how to flirt."

"I…" I start but have no idea what to say. Maybe I *am* sexy, and I just didn't know it. I must admit the thought has me feeling sort of… powerful. The only way I can think to end my sentence now is, "Thanks."

Carter's back hits the bed, and he busts out laughing. And since I'm now kind of feeling myself, I join in too. "Well, this day certainly didn't turn out how we expected, did it?"

"Not exactly," Carter responds, still chuckling as he turns his head to look at me. The man should always smile; it does amazing things for his already devastatingly handsome face. If I'm a hot mess, he must be into hot messes because there's nothing but contentment and pleasure in his expression. Who knew?

"And now we have a good story to tell."

His eyes widen, and I hurry to clarify.

"The night we got stranded in a creepy bird-infested motel and had to survive on Funyuns and YumZees?"

He grins, my partner in crime once more. But I never have learned how to spot a good time to stop talking.

"One to tell the grandkids," I add. Because it would have been way too easy to shut my mouth and enjoy the moment.

Carter's grin fades, and I can read his mind like one of my favorite books, only this is a horror story, not a Jane Eyre novel. *Pork in a pie!* Now he thinks I'm some clingy lunatic who's going to start stalking him for orgasms.

I throw my hands out, desperate to explain. "Not *our* grandkids. *The* grandkids. You know, me to mine and you to yours. Two separate sets. Of grandkids, I mean." I gesture. "Unless you don't plan on having kids because, hey, you do you." I can hear my tone approaching manic, but there's nothing I can do to stop it. "And, really, given my track record, my eggs are likely to shrivel up and die before I even get laid!"

The words echo off the motel room walls like we're smack dab in the middle of the Grand Canyon. My face turns cold, I imagine because every drop of blood has drained from it.

"Shit! Forget I said that!" My frantic gaze pinballs around the room, looking for anything to focus on except for Carter. When I spot my bottle of blue Powerade on the nightstand, I snatch it up like a lifeline and bring it to my lips. I chug the entire contents, not stopping even once for a breath.

Gasping for air, I lift the empty bottle between us and declare, "I'll go find the recycling!" before sprinting out the door of room nine, leaving Carter on the bed to contemplate exactly how he ended up on this doomed voyage with the likes of me.

The door shuts behind me with a *bang*, and I don't stop. To think, not thirty minutes ago, I was feeling all cocky, teasing Carter about the birds, kicking ass and taking names. Now, I'll have to beg Rhonda to let me sleep with her and her feral friends for the night. Because it goes without saying that I'm never talking to Carter again for the rest of my life.

Nice knowing you, dude, but I won't be able to take the pity I'll see any time our eyes meet now. Or, worse yet, his patronizing tone as he pretends things are business as usual. I had him looking at me all sexy and flirty and then I had to go and drop the virgin bomb like that.

I haven't even confided in my best friend—who would be required by the official BFF contract to be supportive and tell me there's nothing wrong with me. To lie, basically.

I turn at the end of the brick motel building and head for the empty service station, trying to shake myself out of it and get my head on straight. There's absolutely nothing wrong with me. My research said so. It's just been a matter of the wrong guy at the wrong time—on repeat—that's all. I'm perfectly normal. And the last thing I need is anyone's pity. Oh, the horror.

Most people don't live in the same headspace I do. I know that, and I'm fine with it. I've never felt the need to be the center of attention or force myself to fit in. I don't mind being different, not that I've ever made it a goal to strive for. I like who I am. I shouldn't have to apologize for what I wear, what hobbies I enjoy, whom I choose to spend my time with, and certainly not for my sex life, or lack thereof.

So, why *haven't* I confided in Mia, then? And why do I care what Carter thinks? We made out, and I had an orgasm. So what?

I always tell myself I've kept it private because not having done "the deed" is the least interesting thing about me. Or it's nobody's business but mine. Or it's some stupid arbitrary physical act that's been assigned way too much importance by people who have no right to dictate such things. All of which is one hundred percent true.

But so is the fact that I *want* to feel intimate with someone in a way I've never had the chance to. Not simply the pleasure of an orgasm—I can give that to myself just fine. But knowing that I choose to be vulnerable with someone and they appreciate that and make themselves vulnerable to me. That we put a special trust in one another. I want that.

And I've been a coward in not putting myself out there to find it. Every year that goes by, I add another ten-pound weight that makes it harder. I've allowed it to become a stigma, even as I've rebelled against the notion. I've never been a quitter—or a coward—but I've let this turn me into both.

Not that I haven't contemplated getting drunk and grabbing some stranger to get it over with. I know sex can just be sex, and you can do it with anyone—quite literally. I could go to a bar right now—if I weren't in the middle of nowhere on a Sunday night—and have sex with a random guy if I chose to. But everything that makes me *me* won't let me enjoy a stranger putting his hands on me—in me. Much less his penis. Not a chance.

So here I am, twenty-nine and never been laid, lying to myself that my lackluster pursuit of Sebastian is me giving it my best shot. And now I've not only gotten more intimate with Carter Brooks, aka Superman, than almost anyone before, but I've inadvertently confided in him—the one person in my life who's already proved himself to be leagues outside my sphere—socially, physically, professionally, everything. The guy is even a foot taller than me, as if that's fair.

This confession can't be undone. All the lecturing myself won't change it. Rationally, I know there's nothing to be embarrassed about, but emotionally? Forget it. I may have a sturdy countenance, but even I won't be able to withstand the humiliation waiting for me in that motel room. If Rhonda and the birds won't have me, I'll break into the service station and sleep under the slushie machine.

I'm sure I've mentioned it before, but being a librarian is really, *really* hard.

I CHOOSE NOT to bother Rhonda again. Not so much out of respect for the hour as my already knowing she'll only usher me back to my fake husband's side. So I pace, hum some girl-power anthems, and read all the warning labels on the gas pumps—even the tiny print. I also add the word "evaporative" to my list of fun words to say.

By the time forty-five minutes have passed, I've recovered my sanity to a point where I've pushed the embarrassment down and replaced it with defiance. I've also decided to redefine sex as having an orgasm, which means I've been having sex on the regular since I was twenty. So there!

What am I doing out here? And why in the world did I leave Carter with all the snacks? I make my way back to room nine and pause in front of the door to shore up my courage—and any extra defiance I can muster—then push it open.

Carter has not only left the door unlocked for me but has turned out all the lights and is lying on top of the duvet, scooched all the way to the far side of the bed. His eyes are closed, and he's perfectly still.

I know what he's doing, and I should have expected it. He's trying to make this as painless for me as possible.

There's nothing left to do but wash all the road dust off under the shower, rinse my mouth out, and climb under the covers on the other side of the bed—all of which I accomplish in near silence.

He's pretending to be asleep, and I let him.

The bed is lumpy, but I nestle into my pillow as I do some controlled breathing to unwind and clear my mind for sleep. After a few minutes, I flip to my back and focus on relaxing each part of my body, starting with my toes and ending with my forehead. When that doesn't work, I roll to my side and count backward from one hundred. Then I move on to counting sheep. Then goats. I consider suffocating myself with the pillow to finally get some rest, but before I can, Carter's voice comes from beside me.

"I took money."

Since this statement makes zero sense, I assume I heard wrong. "What?"

"The guys with the gun. They gave me a bag full of money."

I don't respond because I don't know what to say. Here I was expecting my sex life to be on his mind, and he's been thinking about dirty money this whole time.

"I haven't told anyone. You're the only one who knows."

My breath whooshes from my lungs. *This guy.* While I don't understand his reasons or the scope of this money deal, I understand that he's kept it private for a reason, and it's not something he wanted to talk about. But he told me anyway because *I* told *him* my most private secret—even if I didn't intend to.

"What did you do with it?" I ask.

"Nothing. It doesn't belong to me."

I remain silent because he's right. It's blood money. I blink into the darkness and wait for him to say more.

"At first I told myself getting out of town alive was the most important thing. I threw the bag in the trunk of my car. When I got to Asheville and felt the finality of it all, I told myself I deserved the cash for being forced to give up my life."

Temptation is a tricky beast.

"And now?"

"Now I want to throw it in Cody's and Hopkins's faces."

My lips quirk. "I vote for that one."

"I knew you would." I can hear a little bit of a grin in his voice as well.

I roll to my back again, eyes to the darkened ceiling. "Or you could go to the feds or something, couldn't you?"

"Not if I want to stick to my plan."

Right, that plan for leverage to protect his business and family—not the hundreds of thousands of strangers who'll be ingesting poison in a few months. He thinks it's a choice between the two; he's being practical.

But practicality is the enemy of imagination. Maybe I have something to teach Carter after all. But not tonight.

"Thank you for telling me," I say into the still air. "I'll keep it to myself, I promise."

"I know." I can hear his movement, and I know he's looking at me when he says, "Me too."

I allow myself a tiny smile before I roll to my side and finally nod off to sleep. In my dreams, Carter kisses me while a yellow-toothed gnome hands Sebastian a suitcase full of money, telling him he can have it if he allows the kudzu to take over the forests. But Sebastian rebuffs him, telling the gnome his integrity is not for sale. I watch him go and continue kissing Carter.

CARTER

MY FIRST INDICATION that I'm not in the attic at home is the mattress spring digging into my back. The second is the warm hand on my junk that doesn't belong to me. I may have just awoken this second, but my dick has beaten me to it by several minutes, at least.

When I blink my eyes open, sunlight filters through the closed curtains of the motel room, allowing enough illumination for me to make out the body of my bedmate—the very same one whose hand has wandered during the night. Sunny's hair is splayed over my shoulder, and she's using my chest as a pillow.

My dick jumps because that's what dicks do when they're being felt up. It clearly remembers last night as well as I do. But instead of causing Sunny to withdraw her hand, the movement only appears to encourage her. She burrows her face into my chest and throws a bare leg over my thigh. In other words, she's trying to kill me.

I'd love nothing more than to roll her onto her back

and explore all the skin and curves I didn't get to last night, but after her confession and that panicked exit, I can't touch her until we talk. And I doubt she'll be happy if she wakes up like this.

I try carefully sliding to the side so I can stand, but as soon as I start moving, she grabs onto me like a spider monkey and pulls me closer, using my dick as leverage. I bite down on my cheek to keep from howling.

"No," she says, her tone scolding.

Here we go again.

This time, I gently pry her hand from my junk, one finger at a time until I'm gripping her hand just above it. So, of course, that's the moment she awakens.

I witness as each synapse fires and she comes fully awake to find me holding her hand over my obviously aroused dick. Thank God I'm still dressed at least.

"What are you doing?" She jerks her hand out of my grip.

"Nothing, I swear."

She lifts her head from my chest and retreats until she's back on her side of the bed. "It didn't look like nothing."

This is ridiculous. I was trying to be sensitive to her emotions, but she can't honestly think… I throw my hands up in exasperation. "Look, I just woke up, and you were holding my junk and using me as a pillow. That's all I know."

She eyes me skeptically. "What happened to the covers?"

We both inspect the bedding and while my side of the bed is as tucked and neat as it was when I first lay on it last night, hers is a mess of twisted sheets and blankets, both pillows buried somewhere within.

"I have no idea."

She glances around for a few more seconds and then untangles herself. "Oh. I guess I must have moved around a little in my sleep."

"A little?"

Unfortunately, I still have the issue of the tent in my pants, and now that Sunny is fully awake, she is not shy about looking, which does nothing to help the problem.

"Did I...?" She trails off, pointing at it now. Jesus.

"While it does usually make its presence known first thing in the morning, it's never this... cheerful."

She tries and fails to hide her self-satisfied grin. "Sorry about that."

"No need to apologize. I think I'll survive." My tone is as dry as my mouth is.

She stretches, and the motion pulls her T-shirt tight across her breasts, highlighting the fact that she's braless. My dick jumps again, and I figure this is as good a time as any to talk about last night. But not with a hard-on, so I avert my gaze, glancing at the clock on the nightstand that reads 8:29.

"Shit!" I fly to my feet, not understanding how I possibly slept this late. I haven't slept past seven in probably a decade.

And that's when it hits me that I didn't wake up even once last night. Which means I somehow got about nine hours of uninterrupted sleep. That's unheard of.

But there's no time to marvel because we need to haul ass if we're going to make it to Memphis in time for our meet-up with Knuckles. And we still have to figure out the tire situation.

Sensing my urgency, Sunny glances at the clock before jumping out of bed on the other side. Her shorts have ridden up, exposing more of her thighs than yesterday, and my hands itch to slide right between them. When she bends over to pick up her shoes, my cock threatens to take matters into his own hands.

Snap out of it, Brooks!

We each take a quick turn in the bathroom and then stumble out the door and to the office to find Rhonda—and hopefully a phone.

I only spot two birds before Rhonda comes to greet us. "Well, look at you two this morning. Pink cheeks and all." We do not have time for this.

"What can I say? You were absolutely right." I yank Sunny into my side and place a loud kiss on top of her head. She nearly stumbles. "The wife and I are good as new. Now, about that phone…"

Thirty minutes later, we're pulling back onto the interstate, one brand new tire in place and enough time to comfortably make our noon meet-up. It turns out Rhonda wasn't so bad after all—despite the whole bird thing. She'd taken the liberty of telling the service station manager about our situation first thing this morning, and he was all ready to drive us back to the car and fix us up with a tire. Maybe I've seen one too many Alfred Hitchcock movies.

Unfortunately, I spent almost all my cash on the motel and the tire, leaving maybe enough to afford the gas for the return trip, but certainly not another night in a motel. If we can't wrap this up today, we're sleeping in the car tonight. Because I'm not touching the cash from the duffel bag.

Miraculously, Sunny remains awake for the entire two-hour drive and treats me to some more car karaoke and the origin story of her love of gnomes—something about her grandmother and a giant gnome that looked just like Duke.

We don't talk about last night—the making out or either of our confessions. But I'm relieved that there's no real awkwardness; I'd hate for her to regret last night or feel self-conscious about the whole thing. It feels like we've come to a silent agreement to leave all of that behind the door of room nine for now. But it can't stay there forever.

Instead, I tell her a couple stories about my dad and his love of Bigfoot, and she decides she might open a yoga studio just so she can call it Gnome-aste. However, she confesses that she doesn't, in fact, know much about yoga at all. Which we both decide could present some issues.

At a quarter to twelve, we pull into a parking spot outside The King's Diner off Austin Peay Highway in Memphis. The address matches the one from Duke's note, but since Sunny doesn't have the best recollection of what Knuckles looks like—apart from being "kind of big maybe"—we're relying on him to identify us.

I hold the diner's glass door open for Sunny, and we walk into an Elvis carnival with a side of French fries. Anything not covered in chrome is plastered with Elvis's face at various stages of his career. At the end of the breakfast counter stands a gleaming floor-to-ceiling statue of The King striking a pose in his infamous white jumpsuit, flashing lights studding the suit like diamond glitter.

"Wow," Sunny says, echoing my exact thoughts.

"And here Cash and I thought we'd nailed the whole homage-to-a-theme thing." We might need to up our game beyond the Sasquatch décor and the Bigfoot-themed beer names.

An older waitress with a frilly white apron tells us to

take a seat at the breakfast counter, so we grab two empty stools and wait.

I order coffee, and Sunny asks for hot chocolate, but we're just buying time. At exactly noon, the waitress—whose name tag identifies her as Mabel—slides our check across the counter and winks at me. Her dyed blond hair is piled in an updo on top of her head, and she's so tan, her skin resembles my leather rucksack.

Sunny sips her hot chocolate while I look down at the check. Instead of a summary of our order, it says, "Excuse yourselves to the restroom one at a time. Go through the door at the end of the hall and wait."

I pass the check to Sunny so she can read it. Then I stand from my stool and proceed to the restrooms on the other side of the diner, leaving her at the counter. This can't possibly all be necessary, but it looks like we have to do it Knuckles's way or no way at all.

When the door at the end of the hall closes after me, I'm in another pitch-black hallway. Two minutes later, Sunny is at my side.

"This is just like in the movies," she whispers. "We're definitely getting murdered." Why does she sound excited about that?

Part of me wants to reassure her she's safe because everyone knows the virgin is the only one to survive in a horror movie, but of course, I don't. Instead, I go with, "Where's your optimism now?"

"This way," a deep voice commands from somewhere to our right, and Sunny pulls her spider monkey moves again by digging her nails into my arm and holding on for dear life.

I hear the flip of a light switch, and illuminated in a doorway is a giant man with a barrel chest, full sleeve tattoos on both arms, a frown signaling some deep-seated dissatisfaction with the world, and a wicked scar down one side of his face.

Well, lucky for Sunny, I'm not a virgin—which means I'd better start saying my goodbyes.

HAGRID'S BROTHER IS A TOTAL BADASS

SUNNY

"IS THAT LITTLE SUNNY?" Hagrid's twin brother rumbles as he looks me over, his mouth spreading into a grin that shows off two rows of straight white teeth with a single gold one on the upper left.

"Present." I raise my hand before Knuckles lumbers forward and swallows me in a bear hug. "Hi, Knuckles." The guy actually may have giant blood in him, he's so huge. I feel positively dainty right now. My only memories of him are vague at best, but I know my grandma always liked him.

"Look at you!" He pulls back, repositioning me in front of him like I'm nothing but a ragdoll. "You've got your grandma's smile. Beautiful!"

I can't help but smile wider. That's the best compliment I've ever received. I can feel Carter's eyes on me, so I introduce him. "This is my friend, Carter. The one Duke told you about."

Knuckles's smile drops as his eyes move to my

associate. He scans him carefully from head to toe, and then the two men engage in a staring contest for some reason. Neither flinches nor blinks until Knuckles finally nods his head. "I know who you are."

I have no doubt he and Duke both vetted Carter in their own ways since he came onto the scene, and I'm relieved he's been deemed "safe" or whatever. But perhaps I spoke too soon.

"So, Carter Leland Brooks, what are your intentions with Miss Sunshine, and why should she and Duke want to help you out?" Leland?

Carter looks to me and then back at our burly friend. "I honestly can't think of one reason Sunny would want to help me apart from it being her nature to want to right wrongs. As for Duke, you likely know better than I would." He's got a point. And I'm relieved he didn't disclose anything about Sebastian or Knuckles might feel the need to go vet him too.

Knuckles watches Carter, eyes narrowed, as if he's a human lie detector. "And?"

"My intentions are to repay Sunny in any way I can and to keep her out of harm's way." He shoots me a reassuring nod. I'd probably be shaking if I were in his shoes right now, but he's cool as an emperor penguin.

"You gonna nail Cody?" Knuckles asks in a ragged tone, this time laced with a new intensity. Uh oh.

When Carter opens his mouth to answer, I panic and cut him off. "Absolutely." I can't let us come this far only to have Carter fess up that he's only after leverage, not justice.

Luckily, it takes Knuckles a fraction of the time to assess my honesty than it did Carter's. I don't want to lie to Duke's oldest friend, so I silently reinforce my vow to devise a plan that will help everyone.

Satisfied with our answers, Knuckles steps aside and motions for us to come into the room. It's an office with a similar setup to our one at home with a few folding chairs, a desk, and enough cords and electronics to make a hacker chartreuse with envy.

"How is Duke these days?" Knuckles asks. "I was real sorry I couldn't come to Helen's funeral. I was in the middle of an op."

I nod in acknowledgment, not daring to contemplate what an "op" might entail. "He's alright. Had his hip replaced earlier this year, so he's not quite in fighting form yet, but he's working on it."

"Aren't we all." Motioning for us to have a seat, Knuckles rounds the desk to sit on the other side, the overhead light reflecting off his shaved head. Then he opens a drawer, extracts a file folder and a flash drive, and sets them on the desk in front of him.

Elbows propped on the desktop, meaty tattooed forearms on display, he leans in and starts talking. "Here's the 4-1-1. That Cody asshole has his hands in more pots than you clocked. This diet pill business is the least of it. Took me a day to swap security details with the guard outside his personal office and another couple to get the lay of the land."

He lifts two of his giant sausage fingers. "Two things I learned straight off the bat. One, Cody likes pie, and two, there's more paper shredding going on in that office than there should be."

"Oh my." I straighten in my chair.

"Lucky for you, my Mabel makes the best pie in Memphis. Also lucky for you, I happen to know that an industrial cross-shredder gets jammed up nice and good when you drop a quarter into it."

My lips spread into a grin as I reconsider my dismissal of some of Duke's stories over the years.

"Cody's got this kid Nielson who does everything but wipe his ass for him. The guy never sleeps and has a coffee habit worse than mine. No question, he knows everything his boss is mixed up in. Ten times a day I see the kid walk in and out of Cody's office, file folders in hand on the way in but not on the way out. Once before lunch, then again at the end of the workday, Nielson spends ten minutes at the shredder inside Cody's office. I made my move on day four—Friday.

"I do my regular morning sweep of the offices, only I make sure to do a close pass of the shredder so I can drop the quarter in. The day moves like clockwork. Nielson goes in to see Cody with another stack of folders an hour before lunch. I slip a few drops of extra-strength laxative into his coffee. He comes back out ten minutes later, downs his coffee, and I wait. Twenty minutes go by, and the kid runs past me toward the hall looking like he's trying to hold an egg between his knees.

"Another fifteen minutes, and Cody buzzes Nielson's desk phone. I give it a minute till he buzzes again, then knock on the congressman's door. I tell him Nielson ran to the john with a face greener than Shrek's ass. Ask if I can do anything to help. He declines, and I leave the door cracked.

"Without Nielson there, he takes a stack of papers to the shredder. Only the thing makes an awful racket when he tries feeding it. I knock again and enter without his express permission seeing as I heard a concerning noise, and it's my job to protect him. He drops the papers face-down on his desk and tells me the problem. I tell him I'm a handy sort of guy and it's likely a paper clip or staple, and I got him covered. And, by the way, I saw homemade blueberry pie in the office kitchen, and he may want to grab a slice before it's all gone.

"Seeing as Nielson is out of commission and can't fetch it for him, Cody weighs his options and decides on pie. He scrams, leaving his laptop open and the stack of papers on his desk. I take the liberty of copying his downloads folder onto a thumb drive, sifting through the papers, and taking a few snapshots. Then I fish the quarter out and go back to standing guard. Easy as the wife's pie."

All I can do is stare, and it seems Carter is equally impressed because he hasn't taken his eyes off Knuckles's face.

Duke's friend slides the file folder across the desk. "Printed copies here." He hands the flash drive over next. "Digital here. I hope you nail his ass."

Carter opens the folder and starts scanning the photographs, increasingly creative expletives pouring from his lips with each new one.

"We really owe you for this," Carter says, stopping to meet Knuckles's eyes again.

"You don't owe me nothin'. Like I told Duke, I've had it in for Cody since he was doing his lawyer thing back in the early 2000s. That ambulance chaser put my favorite tattoo artist out of business." He lifts his left arm and points to his bicep, where a merman winks at us. "This was supposed to be a chick, not a dude. Took me forever to find someone half as decent as Morty."

"Oops," is all I've got.

He stands and shrugs a white button-down over his T-shirt. "I'm on my lunch break, but I gotta get back to

Cody's office to ride this gig out and avoid suspicion. You let Duke know if you need anything else since I'll be there for another week."

Carter and I stand. "We will."

Carter extends a hand. "Thank you so much. I really appreciate everything you've done."

The two of them shake hands, and I don't miss the tensing of Carter's jaw as Knuckles squeezes his hand like a vise. "Get yourselves a slice of pie on your way out. Nobody makes it better than Mabel, I can promise you."

"We will," I tell him as he finishes buttoning his shirt, dons a dark jacket, and rounds the desk again. This time, his hug has me gasping for breath.

"You take care, kid. And say hi to Duke for me."

Knuckles disappears out the exterior door at the other end of the hallway, and I look to Carter, my eyes equally as wide as his, I'm certain.

"Whoa."

Carter answers with a wink. "Another one for the grandkids."

CARTER

"I CAN'T DECIDE between the snow globe or the TCB license plate." Sunny holds both items up for my inspection, one containing a snowy scene of Elvis surrounded by a blue landscape and the other bearing the acronym of his favorite catchphrase, "Taking Care of Business."

If I thought anything I said would help us get out of the Graceland gift shop any faster, I'd randomly pick one for her, but this isn't my first day hanging out with a female.

She already bought some Elvis playing cards and a "He Lives" scarf with an image of Elvis on Mars from Mabel at the diner, but she insisted we come to the official gift shop at Graceland as well.

I'll go anywhere she tells me now, though, since Knuckles handed over the goods at the diner. I'll read everything more thoroughly later, but from what I saw at The King's Diner, I've got evidence of insider trading, among other things. Even if I don't have enough to nail him on the NutriSlender deal, I've definitely got enough to buy my family and me some peace at least.

Now I need to get Sunny home safe and sound before I work out my next move. And there's still the Sebastian part to finish. I'm torn down the middle about that one, but since the choice isn't mine to make, I'll do my best to get it done like I promised.

"I'll just buy both," Sunny decides, taking her spoils to the line at the register. We stopped at an ATM on our way out of Asheville so she wouldn't have to use plastic, but the way she's spending, she can't have much left. And since I'm low as well, we'd better split before we go broke.

"Aren't you getting anything?" she asks.

"No. Elvis isn't really my thing."

"But it's nice to bring people souvenirs. I got cards and a bookmark for Mia, and a bunch of stuff for Duke."

"My family thinks I'm at the beach with my new girl-friend. Believe me, they're not expecting presents." I'm under no illusion Mama kept her mouth shut—or Oscar for that matter.

"Speaking of which, you promised we'd find a way to contact Duke today. We should have asked Knuckles when we had the chance." She bites that lip again.

"That's why I picked up a burner phone when we stopped for gas this morning."

She shoves her Elvis stuff at me, and I have no choice but to take it. "Can I have it?"

I dig the phone out of my pocket with my free hand while she pulls some folded bills from her bag, and we trade. "Here. Pay for this stuff and then meet me outside." Bossy, that one.

When I bring her bag of souvenirs outside ten minutes later, she's smiling into the phone. The sun on her hair makes it look like the auburn waves are alive with flames. We really do need to have that talk at some point.

"Yes. I did, and you're going to love it. Uh-huh. I won't. Duke, we're driving back this afternoon. Yeah, hang on a second." She extends the phone to me. "Your mom wants to talk to you."

I exchange the bag for the phone and bring it to my ear while I watch Sunny wander over to inspect a flowerbed. She changed into a loose turquoise top and jeans at the gas station earlier, and I kind of miss the shorts. "Mama?"

"Hi, darlin'. I just wanted to hear your voice and tell you everything is fine here. Marvin and I are getting on famously. I'm learning all about unsolved crimes in North Carolina—I never imagined there were so many. And we're doing target practice in the backyard later this afternoon too."

I won't be telling Sunny about that one. "That's great. Thanks again for going over there." I can only assume by "Marvin" she means Duke.

"I had nothing else planned for my day off besides walking Mango and doing some grocery shopping—but I can do that tomorrow."

"A friend is coming over to check on Duke later, like I said, so you don't have to stay the evening."

"We'll see. We're having fun. Will I be seeing you—and maybe your young lady—when you get back?"

Sunny is taking a picture for a couple by the flowers and laughing at something one of them said. She and Mama would get on like a house on fire—all the more reason not to raise Mama's hopes. "Um. I'll have to see. We're getting back really late tonight," I hedge.

She lets me off the hook. "Okay. I'll leave it alone, baby. Just a second." I hear her move the phone and then Duke's voice in the background before she comes back on. "Marvin wants to know where Sunshine hid his whiskey." She drops her voice to a whisper. "I'll tell him she's in the bathroom and can't talk now."

"Okay, thanks. Talk to you soon."

"Love you."

"You too." I hang up and slide the phone back in my pocket before walking over to join Sunny. "Marvin?" I ask.

Her eyes go wide. "How did you know that? Nobody —and I mean nobody—calls him that."

"Well, apparently my mother does."

"That's bananas," she marvels. "You know, he told me she brought him soup and marched right into the house when he answered the door." That sounds about right. "And then she fixed the pipe under the kitchen sink, made sandwiches, and beat him at Gin Rummy. If she can get him to take his pills and stop drinking, I'm asking her to move in."

"I guess that manifesting shit really does work after all," I tease, and she beams up at me.

Ten minutes later, we're in the car heading back to the interstate when something occurs to me. "You said you like bringing people souvenirs?" She nods, so I continue, "Why didn't you get Sebastian anything?" It's the first time his name has come up since last night's encounter, but it's pointless to ignore his role in all of this. He's who Sunny is going to be with; I'm only an extracurricular activity along the way. "And now that I'm thinking about it, why didn't you ask Sebastian to check in on Duke instead of Mia? He's right next door." That would have made more sense.

"Duke… isn't the biggest fan of Sebastian."

"I get the picture he's not a big fan of most people," I tell her. "So, he likes Mia?"

"Not necessarily, but it makes no difference to her if he likes her or not. She's doing it for me, not him."

"And the souvenirs?" Why am I pressing the issue?

She shrugs beside me. "I guess I didn't really think about it."

I don't know if that's supposed to carry some unspoken meaning or not, but I force myself to leave it alone. Only trouble lives down that road.

"Sebastian… he's different. Kind of like me, I guess," Sunny says, pulling her crochet stuff out of her bag again. "He dances to the beat of his own drummer, and I don't want to change who he is. I'd rather make allowances to let him be himself without that pressure."

I get what she's saying—when it comes to friendship maybe. But a partner? "Does he make allowances for you?"

"Of course. I mean, he must, right?" She looks to me as if I have the answer. I want to tell her she's coddling him and that shit will get old fast. She's so willing to take care of everything and everyone, she won't ask for anything in return.

I don't answer her direct question, instead asking another of my own. "So, you feel like wanting him to step outside his comfort zone is too much to ask?" I'd absolutely hate it if a woman I was dating didn't challenge me.

"What's so wrong with that?" She waves her hook thing in the air.

"Nothing, I guess, but if you're always doing things his way, when do you get a turn?" Her entire relationship with the guy thus far has been one-sided as far as I can tell, and here she is setting herself up for a future of the same damn thing. I'm starting to get angry on her behalf.

"This is ridiculous." She shakes her head and starts unwinding her yarn. She's likely to give my namesake gnome a giant wart on his nose after this conversation. "We're not even dating yet. He's just… awkward about some things, and I don't want to put him in a situation where he feels out of sorts or intimidated or like he's being tested."

"So you want to coddle him." There. I said it.

"I didn't say that." Her yarn unwinding turns to yarn jerking as she scowls down at her project.

I've already pissed her off; I may as well go all in. "What makes you want to be with him? I mean, besides his moral character." Because, Lord knows, nobody can fault that.

I have her full attention now. "Isn't that enough?"

Is she serious? No, it's not enough! He should make her laugh, make her curious, make her excited, make her believe she can do anything or be anything or conquer anything. He should care for her and help her and want all the best things in the world for her. And he should put her first. That's what she deserves. Plus all the flowers she wants.

But since telling her that wouldn't do any of us any good, instead I say, "Yeah." But I can't help adding, "If it's enough for you."

SUNNY

WHAT HAS GOTTEN INTO HIM? He's been ornery since we got back in the car. If I didn't know better, I'd say he's acting jealous of Sebastian. Which is ridiculous.

Carter may be attracted to me, which is flattering, no doubt. But that's all it is. Attraction. It's biology and pheromones, not romance. And I want romance. I want a guy to be so gone over me he gets tongue-tied with a stomach full of butterflies. No, Carter might make out with me, but he doesn't want to *be* with me. Which is fine by me. I don't want to be with him either.

He's really not my type. Despite the taciturn troubled loner I first met, Carter claims that's not the real him at all. He misses the person he was in D.C., and I'm guessing he'd do anything to get him back. I saw his friend Jeremy at the rally. Flashy, smooth, a little conceited, maybe even superior. It was like a window into Carter's past—the one he identifies with the most. And that kind of guy is pretty much the opposite of what I find attractive.

And then he had the nerve to suggest good morals aren't enough to make someone datable. Ha! If I thought it was worth arguing, I could have told him I like Sebastian's calm demeanor and how cerebral he is. There's something to be said for predictability. And I like Sebastian's hair too. And his eyes. Sure, his hair isn't as thick and wavy as Carter's and his eyes aren't as beautiful as Carter's sienna and moss swirls. But I still like them just fine, thank you very much.

And, speaking of morals, Carter's ethics could use a little work if he's not worried about all these people he could potentially save. I mean, that's not very attractive in my book—despite his arguably valid point that he's decided to focus on his family first. I mean, Sebastian would never in a million years lose sight of the need to care for all Earth's creatures equally. But, then again, I suppose he doesn't have much family to speak of. Hmm.

I try envisioning what I would do if a train were barreling down on Duke, a stranger, and a box of kittens. Before I can think better of it, I open my mouth. "Carter, what would you do if a train were coming, and you see Cash, a stranger, and a box of tiny kittens tied to the railroad tracks?"

"Is there a sinister madman twirling the ends of his mustache anywhere nearby?" It seems someone's mood has improved.

"Just answer the question."

He shrugs as he holds the steering wheel with both hands. "I'm not a monster. I'd untie them all."

"Of course," I agree. "But what if you didn't have that kind of time?"

"Then I'd save Cash. No question."

It's what I knew he'd say, so asking was pointless. Really, would I have liked a different answer any better?

We sit in silence for another few minutes, me crocheting the ears for Carter the Grumpy Gnome and Carter staring ahead at the road. I find myself a little irked that he doesn't seem the least bit curious about what I'd do in that same impossible train situation.

"Aren't you going to ask what I'd do?"

His response is immediate. "I already know what you'd do. You'd untie Duke, then you'd keep at it until the train hit you, the stranger, and the kittens."

I gasp. "No, I wouldn't!"

He swings his gaze my way, giving me a look that says I'm a liar.

"Okay, fine. I'd consider it."

He grins and turns his eyes back to the road.

When I try to think about what Sebastian would do, I'm at a loss for the answer.

THIRTY-SIX
FRENCH FRIES AND TATER TOTS

SUNNY

I'M FEELING a hundred times better after we stop for food, and I can admit to myself that some of my earlier irritation may have stemmed from low blood sugar, not so much my companion. The fact that I finally witness Carter eating French fries doesn't hurt either.

When he nixes my idea of a detour to check out an antique shop called Dead People's Things, we spend the next hour with me reading the folder's contents out loud while Carter listens, alternately slapping the steering wheel and cackling menacingly in a way that has me somewhat concerned Mia might have had a point.

There's enough information to prove Clarence Cody participated in some insider trading, netting himself some nice investment earnings with a public company called Victrolo Sciences. There's also some reference to the manufacturer of NutriSlender, called Starboard Nutrition and Wellness, but no financial statement or record of any personal investment that could prove a conflict of interest with his job as a congressman. But the fact that he's exchanging correspondence with executives at a company poised to benefit from his legislative vote can't look good. We haven't gone through any of the electronic files yet, and who knows what could be hiding in those? We'll have to wait until we get to Duke's computer for that.

After storytime, I offer to drive, but Carter insists on staying behind the wheel. I'm unsure if it's chivalry motivating him or some mistaken notion that I suffer from a case of narcolepsy that might result in our fiery death, but I'm okay with the decision. I'm a little afraid Cash's car might fall apart if I hit the brakes too hard.

We fall into a comfortable silence, and I mull over all that's happened in the last couple weeks. I can't comprehend what it's been like for Carter to have lived with the weight of his situation for seven entire months. He doesn't deserve the bum deal he's gotten, and I wish more than anything for him that he could have his old life back if it is indeed the one that fits him the best. A life in politics holds no interest for me, but as I've observed before, we belong to two very different spheres.

And everyone deserves to live their dreams, whatever they are—within limits, of course. If you tell me your dream is to ride bareback on a wild gorilla at the Super Bowl halftime show, I might suggest you take a moment to reevaluate your life goals.

I watch Carter for a few minutes, but he's too lost in his own thoughts to notice. The man is so ridiculously masculine. I shiver at the memory of last night and the feel of him under me, the caress of his fingertips, the guttural sounds of his pleasure. My womb flexes inside me. He'll probably forget about it by next week, but the memory is mine to keep. I almost wish I didn't find his company so enjoyable. It would be a lot easier if I had reason to find all memory of him distasteful when this is over.

He's absently stroking his chin with one hand, probably still getting used to not having the beard—either that or he's sharpening the edge of that jaw so he can use it as a weapon.

"What made you want a career in politics in the first place?" I ask, breaking the silence.

He blinks and glances over at me. I wonder what he was thinking about. Part of me wishes he was thinking about me, but the other part knows that's both foolish and dangerous. Carter Brooks and his dimples could break my heart into a million pieces if I let my imagination convince me of a connection that's not really there.

He drops his hand from his chin and puts it back on the steering wheel. "I don't think there was a single moment of epiphany or anything like that, if that's what you're asking."

I shake my head and wait for him to say more.

"I guess I've always enjoyed being a leader. First born into a family of five kids didn't hurt." He shrugs. "I spent my childhood in student government—all the way through college, actually. I liked being at the table when decisions were made or changes enacted. I also liked feeling important; I can't lie." He smiles at the road in front of us. "I remember when I was president of the student body in high school, I was determined to leave a legacy—something tangible that I could point to and say, 'I did that.'" He stabs his finger in the air. "Maybe something students coming after me would be in awe of or aspire to top when it was their turn. We tried everything from getting the school's name changed to instituting a scholarship fund to changing the school mascot."

He coughs out a laugh and grins over at me, those dimples popping like a one-two punch to my already warm chest. "You know what we finally ended up with?"

I can't help but smile in anticipation. "What?" His answer could be tarantulas for all I know.

"Tater tots every day of the week in the cafeteria instead of just on Fridays."

I snort and cover my mouth. "The Carter Brooks Memorial Tater Tot."

"I wish." His eyes go back to the road. "I learned that enacting change takes time and tenacity. That you need to take small steps before you can take big ones. But even the small ones make a difference. The year after I graduated, I was still getting emails from students thanking me for the tater tots."

"Being a huge fan myself, I should hope so."

He checks his blind spot and changes lanes. "I like a challenge; I like working toward a goal; and I'm not afraid of hard work. Imagining what I could do on a larger playground had me hooked. I was never under the illusion that I would change the world, but I could change things for the better for *some* people at least."

The warmth has spread from my chest to my whole body. His story helps me understand a little more about his leverage plan. "Well, it's a lot more than most people would do. You'd have my vote, Captain Tater Tot."

"Well, thank you kindly, Ms. Underwood." He dips his chin and winks at me. My heart squeezes because it didn't escape my attention that his frown lines failed to make a comeback when he was talking about the future that's now lost to him.

"How about you?" he asks. "Why a librarian?"

"Nothing quite so profound as yours, I'm afraid. I just

love to read. I love stories and using my imagination, and I love that books make the entire world accessible to everyone, no matter where you come from. The library is an equalizer."

"Sounds pretty profound to me." He reaches over and squeezes my hand but releases it right away as if maybe he didn't mean to be so familiar. He doesn't need to tell me last night was a one-time thing. I already know we're not meant to be anything more than two people doing one another favors.

I'll say one thing for the man, though: he knows how to say all the right things at the right time. Was he born that way, like I accused him of last night? I envy how easily it comes for him. Honestly, I should hand over the entire *Dear Mona* column to him. He'd be able to complete a month's worth of letters on a single coffee break.

And maybe it's the knowledge that I probably won't see him again after this week—or the relatable image of a teenage Carter who worked his tail off only to end up with potatoes—that makes me brave enough to make myself vulnerable again.

"Carter?"

"Yeah."

"You know what you said in that *Dear Mona* letter?"

He smirks. "About death not being sexy? Or you mean the one where the guy called out his mom's name during sex?" I'd almost forgotten about that one. The poor girlfriend.

"No, the other one. From the inexperienced girl."

"Yeah." I can tell from his change of tone that he's guessed the direction I'm headed.

I swallow and watch the fields fly by. "Did you mean it?"

"Which part?"

"All of it, I guess." I don't want to rehash the whole thing because, logically, I already know what he said is true. But logic and emotions are two different things.

"Absolutely, why?" He's looking at me now, but I'm still choosing to focus on the farms and trees around us.

"Because I'm terrified of finally dating Sebastian and having to tell him." There. I said it.

He's silent for a few seconds. "Are you afraid it will change the way he sees you?"

I can only shrug because I honestly have no clue how Sebastian sees me as it is. "I don't know. Maybe."

"You're worried it will intimidate him." It's not a question. Carter knows.

I finally look his way, but his eyes are back on the road. "It's a lot of pressure to put on a guy."

Carter's jaw tics at that, and I can tell he's holding back.

"What?"

"Nothing." It's a curt response.

"So your jaw just cracks for no reason now?"

He bites out his reply. "Yes."

"Liar." I don't know why, but I feel a need to explain myself and what it is I'm looking for. I don't need the moon and stars and a bed of roses like he might be assuming. "I'm not 'saving myself,' you know. It's just never happened. I don't even care if I'm in love with the guy; I just want to feel safe. Familiar. Comfortable."

"And nobody has ever given you that?" His tone is almost strangled now, his jaw shifting like he's grinding his teeth to dust. Perhaps this was a bad idea.

"Please don't read anything into that. People have always been well-intentioned. But I guess not."

He's silent, so I assume he has nothing else to say, but a minute later, he does respond, this time with a loosened jaw and a sincere tone. "Well, maybe Sebastian can give you that."

I sigh and sink back into my seat as my eyelids droop shut. "Maybe."

CHAPTER
THIRTY-SEVEN
WHAT WOULD DOLLY DO?

CARTER

I WAS *this close* to saying exactly what I was thinking. That if Sebastian has inspired such a small degree of confidence by this point, it should be a no-brainer to cut him loose and start searching elsewhere.

And if I thought it would do anything but make her mad, I would have. But everything I know about Sunny says that if I tell her something can't work, she'll try twice as hard to prove to me it can.

She doesn't want to put the "pressure" of her inexperience on the guy? If I didn't want to punch something so badly, I'd laugh my fucking ass off. This woman is determined to put the whole world on her shoulders and remain cheerfully upbeat while she stumbles around under its weight.

When was the last time she put herself first?

Hell, I've practically made a full-time job out of putting myself first since I left D.C., and that shit has got to end. Things need to change right the hell now.

And the perfect place to start just happens to be only a quick detour away.

"SUNNY."

Her head is lolled to the side, the seat belt over her chin this time and the gnome doll's head resting on a pile of yarn in her lap. I'm relieved to see she hasn't added the wart I deserve.

"Sunny." I try again. This time, her long eyelashes flutter. She opens her eyelids all the way, and when she sees me, her mouth stretches into a warm contented smile that hits me directly in the solar plexus.

"Hello there, handsome," she murmurs, making me grin back at her. Whatever had me thinking this woman wasn't beautiful was so far off base I can't comprehend my own idiocy. She blinks a few more times and starts to straighten. "Did I sleep the whole way?"

I lean in and unbuckle her seat belt. "Come on." Taking a step back, I hold out my hand, and when she takes it, I pull her from the car.

"Where are we?" She squints at the bright sunlight as she glances around the huge parking lot full of cars, but I pull her by the hand in the direction of the ticket booth. "Oh my god!" She's clearly spied the Dollywood sign. "I thought you were banned after your brother peed on the performers!"

"I'm guessing it's a little hard to enforce." I drag her along until she falls in step with me, her hand still in mine.

"You're being sweet to me," she teases with another flash of that smile.

"Well, I figured I owed you for being an asshole earlier." I owe her a hell of a lot more than an amusement park visit.

She shakes her head and squeezes my hand. "No, you weren't. Annoying, maybe, but an asshole? No." She lets me off the hook.

"They close in an hour, so we don't have much time."

"But we spent all our cash at the last gas station."

I shake my head as we round the last row of vehicles. "We're so close to home now, I'm not worried about using a credit card. It'll just look like I took my girlfriend to her favorite celebrity's playground." I ignore the satisfied hum in my chest at the notion.

"You *are* being sweet. Don't try arguing."

I let go of her hand when we reach the sidewalk, having no good excuse to keep holding it. When we get to the ticket counter, Sunny balks at how much it'll cost for us to go in for less than an hour. She even yanks the credit card from my hand when I try passing it over to the clerk, so we finally compromise by going to the gift shop—which Sunny claims is often the best part anyway.

I spend my time watching her as she shops, declining when she tries buying me a hideous pink camo hat that says, "Good Golly, Miss Dolly." I claim it clashes with my shirt, but I really mean it clashes with good taste in general.

It doesn't escape my attention that she still fails to buy Sebastian a souvenir, despite me bringing it up earlier. She does, however, buy a magnet for Mia that says, "Jolene, you can have him!"

The sun has just set when we get back to the car. The entire population of Pigeon Forge appears to be exiting the parking lot at the same time, so we sit idling while we wait for our turn.

"Thanks for stopping," Sunny says, throwing me a smile I could read a hell of a lot into if I let myself.

"Maybe we'll actually go in next time," I reply, and deep inside, I know I want there to be a next time of a lot of things with Sunny Underwood. Too bad that manifesting shit doesn't work in the real world.

She doesn't comment on my mention of a future where we still know each other. "I think I'll call Duke again," she says instead.

I pull out the burner and hand it over as I inch the car forward. The A/C is having trouble keeping up with the heavy heat outside.

"Your ears must have been burning," Sunny says into the phone, followed shortly by, "Hello to you too. You doing okay? Did Mia come by tonight yet?"

She immediately extends the phone my way with a frown. "Duke wants to talk to you."

I wonder if Knuckles contacted him with more news. "Duke," I say into the phone.

"Your mother got a call an hour ago. Somebody broke into her house."

"What?!"

"She took off right away to go check things out," he tells me in his usual raspy tone.

She probably called my phone, but I don't have it on me to answer. Dammit!

"Shit! Was anybody hurt?"

Sunny's wringing her hands next to me, asking what's going on, but I wave her off.

"Not that I know of. Whoever called her said the place was torn up and the cops were on their way."

I need to get home. "What else did she say?"

"Just that I wasn't supposed to tell you about it, but

that's a bunch of bullshit." She *what*? Why wouldn't she want me to know?

Sunny rolls her window down and sticks her head out, looking for a way out of this ant march of a car line.

"We're still another two and a half hours away," I tell Duke. "But thank you for telling me." I hang up the phone and stare at the back windshield of the car in front of us, reality settling in like a piano on my chest. My mother didn't want to burden me with the news that her house was burglarized and trashed! How have I let myself become a man so pathetic that his own mother can't count on him for support during an emergency? Fuck!

"What happened?!" Sunny practically screeches from my side, and I realize she's been waiting for an explanation.

The car rolls another few feet forward as I grind out, "Somebody broke into my mama's house."

Sunny gasps and grabs my shoulder. "Oh my god. Was anyone hurt?"

"Thankfully, no. But the place was torn up and the cops came to investigate."

"Did they steal anything?"

"I don't know yet—not that there's a whole lot to steal." Ain't that the truth. Why would somebody break into our house when there are million-dollar houses a few miles up the mountain?

"Still. It's scary." Sunny's worrying her lip now.

"Duke said Mama got a call about an hour ago from someone and headed home to check things out and talk to the cops. That's all he knows. Except that she told him not to tell me." I smack the steering wheel hard enough to bruise something. Shit! I'll bet my phone is blowing up with messages from my brothers—or maybe not. Maybe they're treating me with the same kid gloves.

I dial Cash's number and wait while it rings. It's the only one besides Mama's I know by heart. But he doesn't answer, probably because he doesn't recognize the number.

"We shouldn't have stopped," Sunny says, "Without Graceland and Dollywood, we'd be home by now."

My anxious scanning of the vehicles before us stops, and I close the phone and turn to her. "How could we have possibly known? The important thing is we're heading back now." She doesn't need to worry herself about any of this. The cars in front of us start moving a little faster. "Finally!" I maneuver the sedan to an open lane and buzz by some slower vehicles.

"Why wouldn't she want you to know?"

I can feel my jaw tense again. At this rate, I'll give myself lockjaw. "Because I'm an asshole." I speak nothing but the truth.

"Shut up. No, you're not. Maybe she wanted you to enjoy your trip without worrying about it until you got home." Sunny would extend grace to the devil himself.

"I don't think so." I swallow and tell her how it is. "I'm a fucking hypocrite. I give you shit for coddling Sebastian when I've spent the last seven months letting—no, practically *demanding*—my family coddle my ass. They've all been walking around on eggshells while I've been feeling sorry for myself and not sharing a damn thing with any one of them."

"You're being too hard on yourself," Sunny pleads. "What you went through was a huge deal. It would take anybody time to recover."

I cough out a wry laugh. "Now you're the one being

sweet—not that it's a surprise. But Mama didn't tell me because she's trying to protect me. *I* should be the one protecting *her*."

Sunny throws her hands out. "Isn't that exactly what you're doing?" Her voice has risen and I have no clue what she's talking about. When she sees my questioning look, she continues, "With your plan? You're doing all of this to protect your family from any more surprises from these horrible people. To shield them. None of this was your fault—you have to remember that, Carter. You were in the wrong place at the wrong time, and you stood up for what you believe in. Any mother would be proud of that."

I fall silent because nothing I say will stop this saint of a woman from fighting for my soul.

"We just need to get home," I finally say as we turn onto a main road and race back to the interstate.

CARTER

"CARTER!" My little sister bursts out the front door of the house and rushes to me, long hair swinging in a ponytail. I wrap her in a hug and hold on a little too long.

"Were you here?"

"No," she answers into my shoulder. "Miller called, and I drove down from school. Mama's pissed he told me, but I don't care."

I release her and step back. She looks more grown every time I see her, but she's wearing the same expression now that she had when she fell off her bike at six years old. "And everyone's okay, yeah?"

She nods. "The place is a mess, but we're all okay. Mango's missing though." She frowns up at me.

"That little mongrel is always missing. He'll turn up," I reassure her. And I hope it's the truth. That skunk loves exploring more than anything, but he always comes back eventually. Still, I imagine breaking into someone's house and being confronted by a skunk might cause a criminal to… never mind. "Where's Mama?" I ask.

"She's in the den." Lynn nods toward the house.

I turn to see Sunny approaching from the car. "Sunny, this is my baby sister, Lynn. Lynn, can you—" I don't finish my sentence before she moves toward Sunny.

"Absolutely. Go see Mama."

I give both of them a stiff smile and jog for the front door. "Mama?!"

"Carter?" Her voice comes from beyond the kitchen where the den is, but I have to pick my way through broken dishes, picture frames knocked to the floor, over-turned chairs and more to reach her. When I finally do, she wraps me in her arms. "Everybody is fine, don't you worry. I'm sure it was a shock coming home to all this."

I don't tell her I got the tip-off from Duke, instead just hugging her back and thanking God she's okay.

When she pulls back, I can see both the strain around her eyes and how hard she's trying to make light of the situation—probably for my sake. "It's only things. Things can be replaced."

"Mama." It's not only things. It's a violation. It's scary as hell. What if she'd been home?

She shakes her head and pats my chest.

"What did the police say?"

"Not much. They took a report and told us to make a list of anything missing. And to contact our insurance company, of course. They did go over to see the Carmichaels and Winston, but nobody saw anything. There was a bent screen at Adrina's, though, and the front door lock at Winston's was tampered with. I guess our house was the easiest to break into." She shrugs and goes for a smile that doesn't quite work.

"And Winston didn't see anything?" That guy never leaves his house. In fact, we hardly see him except for when he does his morning stretches on his back deck in his underwear. The woods go right up to his house in the back, and it's as if he thinks they shield him from view—either that, or he likes messing with us.

"No. He said he was napping. And Adrina and Wes aren't even home. Luca came up earlier to have a look around. He's the one who found the bent screen."

My eyes scan the den. The coffee table is overturned, the rug is flipped over, and Mama's books are strewn across the floor along with the couch cushions. Thankfully Larry the Bigfoot carving is at the brewery—it's the one thing of real value our family owns. An old sculptor friend of our dad's gave it to him before his work started gaining value. Mama said Larry belonged at Blue Bigfoot and brought him there on our opening day. He enjoys a spot right by the register, and patrons have started rubbing his head for good luck.

I pull Mama into my arms again, and she hugs me back just as hard. When she tries reassuring me again, I cut her off. "Mama, I'm so sorry I've been absent, oblivious, you name it." She tries pulling back, undoubtedly to argue, but I don't let her. "That's done. I'm here and I'm not leaving you hanging ever again." She doesn't try arguing this time, so I know she heard me and got my meaning.

"Cart."

I turn to see my brother Denny and his girlfriend, Rosie, coming down the stairs. "Hey, guys. Anything missing up there?"

"Not that I can tell," Denny replies, coming forward to pull Mama into his side. She smiles up at him, showing off her brave face.

"Is that your friend outside with Lynn?" Rosie asks. "I saw somebody out the window."

"That's Sunny." It's my entire explanation.

"She's here?" Mama's face lights. Good grief. She grabs Rosie's hand and the two of them take on the obstacle course to the front door.

Denny throws his palms up. "I'm leaving it alone." His sandy hair is a mess and he looks like he just rolled out of bed.

"Damn right, you are." I frown at him. "Were you around when the police were here?"

"Yeah, but it doesn't sound like they can do a whole lot. They dusted for prints at the entry point, but with as many people as we've got going in and out of this place?" He shrugs.

"Yeah." While he and Rosie have an apartment closer to town, they're still over here a lot—especially since Rosie is Adrina and Wes's daughter and grew up right next door. Between Mama, Cash, Miller, Denny, Rosie, Adrina, Wes, Luca, me, and any of Mama's friends who drop by, this house is lousy with fingerprints. Besides which, I'd imagine the intruder wore gloves if they were any good at their job.

"Are Cash and Miller here?" I ask.

"Cash was here earlier for a bit, but he went back to Blue Bigfoot, and he made Miller stay there. You should go up and see if any of your shit is missing." Denny throws a chin to the stairs.

"I'll do that." I clap a hand on his shoulder and head up, taking the stairs two at a time.

The attic is an even worse mess than downstairs. My mattress is shredded, the sheets piled up on one end, and my makeshift nightstand is on its side, the contents all over the wood floor. I see my phone among the items nearby. All the shit from my storage unit has been largely left alone, but the old dresser along the wall has been hacked to pieces and all the family's storage boxes have been ripped open and dumped out. What the hell is the point of all this? Vandalizing someone's entire house for the fun of it? It's not like we're the kind of people hiding precious jewels in a wall safe behind a fancy painting.

I freeze before swinging my eyes to the far corner of the room. I can see from here that one of the loose boards is out of place. When I hurry over to inspect, it's been pulled up and out of the way.

Is that what the intruder was looking for? The money? As far as I know, the only people with any knowledge of that money's existence include me, Sunny, and those bastards who love to mess with me.

Fuck!

Do they know about Memphis? About Knuckles? About Sunny and Duke?

Shit!

I snatch my phone from the floor and turn it on. I scroll past the texts from my family, and there it is.

UNKNOWN NUMBER:

It seems you need a reminder.

I race down the stairs to see Denny still in the den where I left him, so I walk right up into his space and hold him by the shoulder. "Lock up and take Mama and the girls to your apartment and stay there," I tell him, just above a whisper but with as much intensity as I can inject. How did my life end up like this? "I'll explain later, but just do it."

He pulls back, giving me a baffled look. "What's

going on?"

I squeeze his shoulder harder. "Just do it. Please, Denny."

"Okay."

As soon as I see his nod, I take off for the front door, vaulting over all the debris along the way.

"Sunny!"

She turns from where she, Lynn, Rosie, and Mama are gathered in a circle. They're all chatting and smiling, but every last smile drops when they see the look on my face.

"What is it?"

"Is it Mango?" Mama clutches her chest.

"No, it's not anything to do with Mango. I really need to get Sunny home, that's all." I grab her hand and pull her with me toward Cash's beater, and she doesn't protest.

"Maybe he's anxious to get her alone," I hear Rosie suggest.

"They just spent the night shacked up at the beach," Mama argues.

"Bye! It was lovely to meet you all!" Sunny yells out the window as I shove the car into drive and spit gravel, taking off back down the mountain.

"What's going on? Doesn't your mom need you?" Sunny fights with her seat belt and finally gets it latched.

I hold up a finger and then unlock my phone. I hit Cash's contact.

"Cart, man, I've been callin' you."

"Sorry. I didn't have my phone. I was just at home though."

"So you know?" he asks. I can hear the bustle of customers and music in the background.

"Yeah, man. Was anything of yours missing?" I ask as I round another curve, going faster than I should.

"Not that I could tell, but I didn't go through everything." Shit.

I try to temper my voice. At this point, I have to assume they're monitoring everything of mine. "I've got an errand or two to run, but you and Miller stick around at Blue Bigfoot, okay? I'll be there in about an hour to talk shop."

"Carter, you're making me nervous," Sunny whispers from beside me, and I cover the mouthpiece. I hate the fear I hear in her voice, but I can't have anyone else hearing it.

"Where else would we be?" Cash chuckles before we hang up.

Now I can talk to Sunny. When I turn, her face is ashen, so I reach my hand out and take hers. "It's okay. But I need you to call Duke on the burner and then Mia. I'm exercising an abundance of caution here, so don't be scared, but you need to stay with Mia tonight."

"What? Why?"

I give her hand another squeeze before I explain. "I got another text message. This was no random break-in." She gasps, but I continue, "Nothing was stolen, but whoever broke in was looking for something. The place where I hid the cash from those goons was searched."

"Did they take it?"

"No, but only because I had it in the trunk this whole time."

Sunny smiles, despite the circumstances. "You *were* going to throw it in Cody's face."

I can only shrug. "If we assume they were looking for the money, they weren't happy when they didn't find it because the house was completely trashed—my room in particular. They were definitely sending a message."

"Oh my god! Do you think they know about Memphis?

About Knuckles?"

I knew she'd get there like I did. "They know some-thing, but I don't know how much. I'd rather be safe than sorry. We'll go to your place, have Duke contact Knuckles to warn him, and then you and Duke will go to Mia's."

"What are *you* going to do?" She's gripping her seat belt with both hands as I make another turn down the mountain.

"Don't worry about that. Just get yourself to Mia's."

"I can come with you." She straightens in her seat.

"No, you can't, Sunny." There is no way on God's green earth I'm pulling her in any further than I already have. I never should have involved her in my dirty past in the first place.

"Why not? I came this far with you. You might need help."

It takes work to keep my tone calm. "What would help me is you staying safe and sound at Mia's."

"But—"

"But nothing. You're not coming with me." So much for calm. "This is *my* shit to take care of, and I don't need you sticking your nose in where it doesn't belong. Just… mind your own business for once in your life!"

Fuck. My mouth moved faster than my brain on that one, and I know the damage is done.

Sunny sinks down in her seat and doesn't say another word. When we reach the point where I'd turn right to downtown Asheville or left to Black Mountain, I pull over to the side of the road and open my door. Then I take my phone and hide it behind a rock where it's out of sight.

We finish the trip to Black Mountain in silence.

When we pull into Sunny's driveway, we both open our doors, but she stops me.

"No. Don't come in." She gathers her yarn, her backpack, her purse, and her various gift bags. "I can take care of it. I know what to do."

"Sunny," I protest. "Let me at least come in and talk to Duke."

"No!" Her voice is sterner than I've ever heard it. "I said I'll take care of it, and I will. I'm a perfectly capable person, and Duke and Knuckles are *my* business."

"I know you are. Sunny, I—"

She cuts me off with a slam of the car door, and I stay where I am as I watch her unlock her front door and disappear inside.

It's better this way. Hanging out with me has only brought her trouble thus far, and who knows what's on the horizon. She needs to go back to being a librarian and a caretaker.

She doesn't need my help to win Sebastian over. She's not inept in any way, despite her claims. In fact, she's probably the sexiest, most amazing woman I've ever met. She deserves everything she wants, and that's always been Sebastian.

I'd only bring her trouble, heartache, and probably danger. It's not even worth thinking about.

All I can hope for now is that they reach Knuckles, and that Cash's car hasn't somehow been tracked. Based on Knuckles's sheer size and experience, I doubt he needs any protection, but a heads-up never hurts. As for Duke and Sunny, I think they're in the clear unless someone saw her in Memphis.

I wait down the street for the next twenty minutes until I see the MINI Cooper pull out of the drive and head east. When there's no sign of anyone pulling out to follow them, I turn back for Asheville.

SUNNY

"SPILL."

I glance up from my spot on the couch to see Mia standing on the other side of the coffee table, her hands propped on the hips of her satin pajamas and her braids gathered up in a scarf. The tight line of her lips tells me she has not come to play games.

In no hurry to rehash the evening's events—as much as she deserves the truth—I start simple. "His mother has a pet skunk."

"Do I look like someone you want to toy with right now?" she asks.

"Um, no." I pull a throw pillow onto my lap and hug it to my chest. Mia takes mercy on me and drops onto the other end of the couch with a sigh.

"Just start at the beginning and tell me what's going on. You're scaring me, Sunny."

Rat in a roost! I don't want my best friend scared. After all, I am the one who showed up at her front door saying it wasn't safe for us to stay at my house. Duke is already asleep in Mia's guest room, the excitement from our grand escape having exhausted him. I haven't seen him so animated since before Grandma died. Half of me thinks he'd welcome bad dudes chasing us across town.

"I don't actually think I'm in any danger, Mia, but Carter insisted I be careful. He said he was exercising an abundance of caution, and I didn't want to mess around with Duke's safety just in case."

"God forbid you worry about your own." Mia rolls her eyes. "Sunny, I swear, you're the most giving person I know, but you have *got* to start looking out for yourself."

"I am," I protest. "I'm here, aren't I? I was very careful on the entire trip too—I looked both ways before crossing every street." She's unamused. "And I'm looking out for myself by not being stupid and catching feelings for some hot guy who looks like Superman. All I seem to be doing these days is looking out for myself."

She throws her hand up between us. "Hold up. Are we talking about the same Sebastian here? Awkward guy with a tiny man bun and thighs skinnier than my biceps?"

I cock my head. "*Sebastian* doesn't look like Superman."

"That's what I just said. Wait. Who are we talking about?"

"I'm talking about not letting myself fall for Carter even though it would be *so* easy to do. The man is ridiculously sexy—and sly too."

"Carter, as in your 'platonic acquaintance' who needed your help pilfering a secret beer recipe from the competition?" She cocks her head too and momentarily drops her scolding tone. "Hmm. I guess he kind of does look like Clark Kent in that picture you showed me. I'm more into

Black Panther, if you know what I mean." One corner of her mouth lifts in a naughty smirk.

"Believe me, he has the entire superhero thing down pat. The chest on that man—and don't even get me started on his jawline or his dimples."

The smirk stays put. "But you're not interested in him."

Oops. "No."

"Uh-huh. Okay." She leans back into the cushions and shakes her head.

"I'm not! I may think he's handsome, but he's not my type at all. Sebastian is my type."

"Seb—" She cuts herself off. "Stop trying to sidetrack me and get back to the part where you tell me what the hell is going on!"

"Fine. Whatever." Feeling no particular loyalty to Carter after he acted like such a jerk in the car, I spill the entire thing to Mia—except for the money. And the part where I rode Carter like a rodeo pony.

To Mia's credit, she only interrupts three times to scold me and once to do the sign of the cross. She also accepts her souvenir gifts with a very heartfelt thank-you. By the time I'm done talking, she's slumped down on the couch with her own throw pillow, looking almost as tired as I feel.

"So, do you think this break-in at his mom's house really is connected, or is he going down a Duke-style paranoia spiral?" she asks, playing with the fringe on her pillow.

"I have absolutely no idea."

She doesn't know that whoever broke in found his hiding place for the money. But the more I think about it, the more preposterous it seems that people dealing in millions of dollars would go to all that trouble to reclaim eighty thousand dollars. I'd expect them to do something much more drastic if they knew what we've been up to. But maybe the break-in was meant to be another warning and there's more on the horizon like Carter appears to think.

"I'm worried he's going to do something rash and get himself in even more trouble," I confess to my friend.

"Sunny, not every battle is yours to fight. I say you steer clear and count your blessings that things didn't go south while you were running around playing spy with the guy."

"That's exactly what Carter would tell me to do." It's pretty much what he *did* tell me, only not in so many words. The words he used stung like nettles. But despite what I've told myself all night, I know they came from the same place of concern as Mia's gentler ones.

"Then I take back what I said about him being a moron." Mia sends me a tired smile.

"Nobody should have to go it alone, Mia. You wouldn't let me face something this big and scary by myself."

"Next time someone points a gun in your face, you watch how fast I run in the other direction." She yawns.

"Liar."

"Yeah, well. I'm your best friend. This guy is just... some stranger from the library."

Only he's not. He's my friend. Even when he tries pushing me away.

If Carter won't let me fight *with* him, I can still fight *for* him.

"Mia, what do you know about the dark web?"

CHAPTER
FORTY

IT'S A BROTHER THING

CARTER

"NOW CAN I GO HOME?" Miller asks Cash the moment he sees me walk through the back door of Blue Bigfoot. The place is closed, but Cash still stands behind the bar.

When he turns to me, I toss him his keys. He catches them easily and sets them on the bar. "Miller's worried the intruder stole his weed." He smirks into his pint glass, this one full of water instead of beer.

"It ain't the cheap shit. That's gonna set me back if they cleaned me out," Miller complains, brushing his hair out of his eyes.

"I think your weed is safe," I tell him, dropping my rucksack and duffel bag on the floor and settling myself on a stool across from Cash.

"While I appreciate the positivity, I'd like to check for myself, if you don't mind." He goes for the keys, but Cash swipes them out from under our little brother before he can grab hold.

"I wasn't trying to make you feel better. I have an actual reason I think your stash is safe." I've got both my brothers' attention now. "Lemme use your phone." I hold my hand out and Miller drops his phone in my hand without question for once.

I hit Denny's contact, and he picks up on the first ring. "Yo."

"It's Carter. Call Luca to stay with Mama, Lynnie, and Rosie and then get your ass down to Blue Bigfoot." Luca is Denny's best friend, Rosie's big brother, and Adrina and Wes's oldest. He's also a damn good artist and a decent human being. He designs all our beer labels in exchange for free beer, and sometimes I'm unsure who makes out better in that deal.

"All I'm saying is this had better be worth all the cloak-and-dagger shit."

I hang up without replying.

"What the hell is going on, Cart? I know you've been holding out on us, so don't try talking in circles to get your way out of coming clean." Cash's eyes drill into mine from across the bar.

Miller looks back and forth between Cash and me. "What did I miss?"

"Where were you the last two days? And don't tell me you were at the beach with some girl because we both know that's not true."

"Wait." Miller hops onto the barstool next to mine. "You weren't going to pound town in Carolina Beach? Dude, how long has it been? Do you even remember what to do with it?"

We both ignore Miller, and I answer Cash. "You're right. And I'll tell you everything as soon as Denny gets here."

"Let me guess, you're running for local office," Miller says, clicking his tongue piercing against his teeth. "You're officially announcing your candidacy for Sanitation Director of Asheville."

"Will you please shut up?" Cash glares at Miller.

"Fuck off. You guys never take me seriously."

"Maybe if we thought you had a serious bone in your body, we'd be more likely to," Cash retorts.

Miller chokes out a laugh. "Says the guy who asked the fucking health inspector if he likes boning sheep or horses better. You almost got your own bar shut down!"

"I already apologized for that," Cash snaps back. Shit, I guess there's one more thing I'll have to add to my list of confessions.

"When did you two get so old—and oblivious?" Miller scoffs. "I could tell you shit that would shrivel your balls."

"Oh yeah? Like what?" Cash challenges. I should stop this, but at least they're not staring at me anymore. As soon as Denny gets here, I'll get down to business.

"Like I know who messed with Carter's car the day I crashed into that fence." Miller's smug expression is way too much. Cash and I look at one another and it's impossible not to laugh, even in my current mental state.

"Oh yeah?" Cash asks over his laughter. "Who was it? Your drug dealer? You owe him some money, little brother? Or let me guess, was it Agent Smith? Are you about to reveal that we're actually living in the Matrix?"

"Fuck you. Never mind. I'm not telling you shit."

"That's what I thought."

While it never gets old giving Miller shit, I'm the one who should be in the hot seat tonight, so I finally intervene. "Okay, enough!" They both turn their glares to me.

"Let's just wait for Denny and then we'll get this over with."

"Why wait?" Cash asks, clearly still riled up from tangling with our baby brother. "I, for one, think I'm owed an explanation. I believe it was only two weeks ago that we promised we wouldn't keep secrets from each other anymore."

"And I told you my shit was different," I reply, my usual defensiveness trying to rear its head.

"Ha! Your shit don't ever stink, does it, Mr. Congressman? How you think you're better than all the rest of us, I have no clue, but you've always looked down your nose from your lofty pedestal. The rest of us are just simple folk to you, working our jobs while you were the big man with a fancy 'career' instead. Face it, you can't come to terms with living like the rest of us now that the whole politician thing didn't work out. You've been moping around feeling sorry for yourself while the rest of us have been working our asses off!"

"Yeah!" Miller chimes in, putting a hand up in front of Cash. Cash high-fives him without taking his eyes from me.

Well, it seems I'm in the hot seat after all. May as well embrace it. "You're one hundred percent right about everything."

When I don't say anything else, the wind in Cash's sails dies a quick death. He drops an elbow to the bar, propping his chin on his hand. "Well, that was unexpected."

Blessedly, I hear the back door close, and we all swing our gazes to Denny as he saunters into the taproom. He comes to a stop when he realizes we're all staring. "What?"

I shake my head. "Nothing. Come on over. We need to have a talk."

And then I do what I never could have imagined doing just two weeks ago. I confide all my secrets in my brothers, including every detail of the last twenty-four hours. Well, almost every detail. The sounds Sunny makes when she comes are still only my business.

Miraculously, they let me talk without interrupting even once. When I'm finished, I retrieve my bags from the floor and lay the folder and thumb drive on the bar before dumping the eighty thousand out of the duffel and onto the bar top.

"Holy shit!" Miller reaches for a stack of cash, and I grab his wrist in a vise grip.

"You really want your fingerprints on that, little brother?"

"Oh, right." He pulls his hand back with a sheepish tone.

"Um, Cart, uh." Cash stumbles over his words, and when I look up at him, he radiates guilt. "You may want to count that money again."

"I told you I didn't spend a dime. It's eighty thousand."

"*You* may not have spent any, but I'm pretty sure *I* did."

Before I can jump to conclusions and lose my mind, he tells me how he and Mama found Mango with a bundle of cash and thought it was one of our dad's secret stashes he liked to leave around the house. The man inherited a distrust of banks from his own father, and it always drove me batshit when he'd forget where he hid money that we couldn't afford to lose.

In this case, Mama told Cash that Dad had been saving

for a newer truck when he died, and since she never found his stash, she assumed Mango had finally uncovered it five years later. Cash used it to get Larry out of hock a couple weeks ago. He'd been so desperate to save the brewery that he'd leveraged our family's one true heirloom instead of asking for help. We're way more alike than I think either of us would ever admit out loud.

"I'll get the cash to replace it tomorrow," Cash says.

"Fuck it," I tell him. "They're the ones who cost us money over this whole bogus inspection. They owe us."

"Yeah," Miller agrees, reaching for the bundles of cash again. This time Denny puts him in a half-nelson hold from behind.

"Money aside, what's our next move?" Denny asks, still holding a struggling Miller with what appears to be very little effort. His use of "our" instead of "your" doesn't escape my attention. "Go to the feds?"

"I think a newspaper would be faster. The sooner it's in the public eye, the harder it is to sweep under the rug."

They all look to me.

"If y'all keep a vigilant eye out here, I think it's finally time for me to pay Grace Hopkins a visit. That's where this clusterfuck started. Maybe I can end it there too." I'd prefer having a way to inspect the digital files before confronting anyone, but there's no safe way to look at them without Duke's secure setup. And, hell, it's possible not even his security has worked.

"And who's watching after your girl and her grandpa?" Cash asks. I don't bother to correct him about Sunny not being mine. Because she's still mine to protect.

"They're staying at the friend's house tonight, but knowing Sunny, she won't let this get in the way of going back to business as usual come morning."

Denny releases Miller, and my brothers all exchange looks.

"The senior center has security, so I can take Mama and Rosie to get the grandpa in the morning, and they can hunker down at the center tomorrow," Denny suggests.

"I can take the library. Probably wouldn't kill me to read a book." Miller shrugs.

I nod, and Cash offers, "I can stay here and keep an eye out. Maybe recruit Lynnie to take a shift on the floor so she doesn't go rogue and try tailing you to your thing with Hopkins. I don't want Hollis out of my sight while this shit is going down either."

"Sounds like a plan."

I then tell them my Hollywood-inspired idea about stashing a copy in a safe deposit box, and all three of them are on board. We make copies of the file folder contents on our office printer, and Cash takes one set as well as the thumb drive, planning an early morning trip to the bank while I stash my folder and the stacks of money in the duffel for my trip in the morning.

I just hope to hell I don't run into Jeremy on my way to Grace.

Adrenaline pumping, we part ways with bro hugs all around. I'm crashing in the brewhouse, Cash is headed to Hollis's, Denny takes off for his apartment, and Miller promises to skip the weed search at home in favor of crashing at a friend's for the night.

With any luck, this will all be over tomorrow, and my family can finally be free of my fucked-up past. I'm long overdue for a new chapter.

SUNNY

"IF YOU WON'T LISTEN to me, will you at least listen to Carter?" I plead with my mulish grandfather.

He's insisting he needs to go home today to do some more research and check for any response from Knuckles, but I'm torn. As much as I'm concerned for Knuckles's safety, the guy looks much better equipped to take care of himself than any of the rest of us.

"Go ahead and ask Brooks! He'll be on my side," Duke argues.

Mia watches us bicker from her kitchen island, where she stands calmly sipping her coffee. "As much as I'm enjoying this heartwarming family breakfast, we need to be at work in a couple hours, so can you two come to a decision soon?"

I scowl at my friend. "You're supposed to be on my side." So much for the BFF code.

"I'm on the side that gets us all where we need to be today safely. How about all three of us head to your place

—Duke can do what he needs to do first, then we all go to work together?"

I consider that before glancing Duke's way. He's frowning at Mia, but I don't sense any outright hostility, which tells me he might accept the compromise. "Fine. Let's do that."

"Fine," Duke agrees, hobbling toward the hall. "I'll get my things."

Forty minutes later, our caravan pulls onto my street, but when I see a strange car parked in our driveway, I pull over a few houses down and motion Mia to do the same. Before I can huddle with Mia on what to do, however, I recognize Carter's mom, Ginny, stepping out of the driver's side. She's followed by Rosie—the neighbor I met yesterday—and a tall young man who I'm guessing must be either Denny or Miller. I signal Mia with a thumbs-up and proceed to our house where I park on the curb.

"Hello, Sunny!" Ginny greets as I open the car door. She heads straight for Delilah's passenger side and opens Duke's door. "Good morning, Marvin." She smiles at him, and I'm dumbstruck when he responds with a calm, "Hi, Ginny," instead of asking who the hell she thinks Marvin is. This woman is clearly a miracle worker.

Mia joins us, and we all congregate in the driveway for introductions. The tall guy with dark blonde hair and a contagious smile turns out to be Denny.

I finally get the opening to ask the question I've been holding onto since the moment I spotted their car in my drive. "Um, what are you all doing here?" I ask in my friendliest and most welcoming tone since I don't want to be rude.

Rosie and Ginny immediately turn twin scowls at Denny. "Yes, *Denver*, what *are* we doing here?" Rosie pins him with a searing tone before turning back to me and smiling brightly. "Not that we aren't thrilled to see you all."

Denny throws his hands up. "I'm just doing what I'm told." His eyes swing to me. "Carter told me to find Duke here or at your library and bring him to work with Mama."

As soon as he says it, I realize that's actually a brilliant idea. Ginny works at a senior center and it's clear she has a better handle on my grandfather than anyone else on this earth.

"And we'd love to have you, Marvin." Ginny links her arm with Duke's. "We're doing an art series that you might enjoy." Duke frowns at her, but she ignores it. "However, *someone* won't tell us why we're all being escorted around town."

"It ain't mine to tell!" Denny defends himself again. Well, this is just plain ridiculous.

"Why do *you* get to know and *I* don't?" Rosie asks, hands on her hips.

"I don't make the rules. Come on, let's get going." He tries guiding her to the car, but she shakes off his hand.

"I need to get to my office." Duke steps toward the house, cane in one hand, Ginny attached to his other side.

"But we've got to go," Denny protests, still trying to lead Rosie.

"I'm not going anywhere else until someone tells me what's going on!" Rosie insists, retreating behind me where Denny can't reach her.

"All I'm trying to do is keep everyone safe!" Denny's hands are in the air again.

Ginny starts arguing with Duke while Denny and Rosie keep at it, and Mia sidles up to my other side. "If I'd known how normal these people are, I never would have given you a hard time about road tripping with one of them."

I narrow my eyes at her, but before I can respond, a new voice joins the fray.

"What is going on here? I can hear all the shouting from next door."

I turn to see Sebastian standing at the edge of the driveway, his feet bare and hair loose. With his wrinkled clothes and messy hair, he looks like we just woke him up.

"Hey, Sebastian," Mia greets him, and he turns to her with a blank look. She leans into me to say, "I think I'll wait in my car." I don't blame her one bit.

"Sorry, Sebastian," I say as I approach him. His arrival has prompted Rosie and Denny to tone their argument down, and Ginny has halted Duke on the front porch.

"Who are all these people?" He looks decidedly uncomfortable, and something about his demeanor hits me as irksome—as if he disapproves.

"These are my new friends," I tell him before raising my voice and turning to my guests. "Ginny, Rosie, Denny, this is Sebastian. Sebastian, meet Denny, Rosie, and Ginny." I swing an arm out to indicate Mia, who's already reached her car. "And Mia, you've already met." She lifts a hand but doesn't turn around.

"I have?" he asks, still appearing overwhelmed at the gathering.

"Yes, you—" I begin but cut myself off. This is not the time. "We were all about to head inside. I'm sorry we disturbed you."

When Denny tries protesting, I cock my head and assume my absolute best don't-mess-with-me stare. It appears to work because everyone files through the front door behind Duke, leaving Sebastian and me in the driveway alone.

"So, uh, how did the rest of the rally go?" I ask.

His expression brightens. "It was great, actually. We got over five hundred more signatures on the petition, and we handed out a thousand flyers. I think we might be getting closer to some sort of resolution."

"That's great!" I am genuinely happy for him. He works exceptionally hard, and he never gives up on what he believes in.

And neither do I, it turns out.

"I'm really happy for you, Sebastian," I tell him. "But I've got to go."

"Oh, okay."

I shoot him a wave and a smile as I turn toward the door.

"I'll call you later!" he yells as the door closes behind me.

Duke is already in the office and the Brooks crew makes themselves comfortable in the kitchen. I pull out a jug of iced tea and set a pot of coffee brewing before I excuse myself to the office as well.

"What did Knuckles say?" I ask Duke.

"Nothing suspicious or unusual going on. It's business as usual."

"I guess that's good, right?" I'm honestly not sure.

But Duke nods, so I leave him to it and get back to our guests. Denny is missing, and when I ask where he went, Ginny and Rosie both roll their eyes and say he went outside to make a private phone call.

Since it's clear what's going on here, I join in on the eye roll. Then I bring this crew out of the fifteen hundreds and spill most of what I know to the two women—keeping anything personal about Carter and me private, as well as the bit about the money since I'm not one to break my promises. I also skip the part about the goons breaking in and pointing a gun at Carter's face since I don't want Ginny passing out on my kitchen floor.

Denny's not wrong that the story wasn't his to tell, but I figure I've played a big enough role that it's half mine to do with as I please. I know Carter was only trying to protect his loved ones, but the man obviously has more things to learn about women than I imagined.

I only feel a little guilty when they both start in on Denny upon his return from my yard.

Two hours later, all my guests—plus Duke—are at the senior center, and I'm at computer station eight at the library with Miller Brooks at my side and Mia at the circulation desk keeping one eye out for Meredith.

"Are we ready?" I ask Miller.

"Let's do it," he says, sending me a grin so naughty I just know he kept Ginny on her toes when he was younger. The guy is adorable with messy dark-blond hair and brown eyes framed with ridiculously long lashes. His build is leaner than his brothers', and it's clear from his torn jeans and the various piercings on his face and ears that his taste runs edgier. But he's got the same Brooks handsomeness they all do in their own way.

He also, as it turns out, knows a bit more about the dark side of the internet than I'm guessing his mother or brothers would like.

Of course, Carter sent him to the library to keep an eye on me, giving me yet another sign that the man will never escape his protective nature, no matter how hard he tries convincing himself he's nothing but trouble to his loved ones.

When Miller saw me frowning at the computer and messing with my flash drive, he came to investigate. Since he already knows all of Carter's business, I told him what I was trying to do, and he was immediately on board.

I warned him Carter might be mad, but that only had him more excited to join me.

It was remarkably easy once I found what I was looking for. Who knew finding a mobile number with only a last name to go on would be so simple?

We decide a text message is the best way to go, so I log into the online tool Miller showed me that allows us to send one safely through the dark web.

I enter the number and begin.

ME:

Is this Patrick Nielson who works for Congressman Clarence Cody?

(555) 732-1197:

Who is this?

ME:

Consider me a friend. Is this Patrick Nielson?

(555) 732-1197:

What do you want?

Excellent.

ME:

Cody is going down. If you go to the authorities first, you can keep yourself from going down with him.

(555) 732-1197:

I don't know what you're talking about.

He's playing the good soldier. For now. But Cody is going down sooner or later, of that I'm certain, and this guy has an opportunity here. Miller and I grin at each other before I continue.

ME:

Don't play games, Patrick. Save yourself.

(555) 732-1197:

I'm blocking your number.

"Go ahead and try, asshole," Miller gloats from beside me.

ME:

Go ahead.

The dark web is kind of fun with all the tools you can find. Like this one that lets me send block-resistant texts with no chance of being identified.

ME:

I'm still here. And I know all about Victrolo Sciences. Did Cody share any of his take with you?

I'm killing it with all the badass lingo.

I'm not about to mention NutriSlender and invite suspicion on Carter, so I take my pick from Cody's widespread corruption hobby without endangering Carter. The files Knuckles handed over had the most info about the insider trading with Victrolo, so I decided that one was best. But Patrick is still scared, so I need to light a fire under him.

ME:

How's your stomach?

(555) 732-1197:

What are you talking about?

ME:

On Friday you came down with that stomach bug right before lunch. You spent an awfully long time in the bathroom. Just wanted to see if you're feeling better.

(555) 732-1197:

How do you know that?

Miller cackles and Mia sends us a glare from circulation.

ME:

I told you. I know a lot of things. Just like you do.

(555) 732-1197:

What do you want from me? I'm just an assistant.

ME:

That's why I'm giving you the heads-up. Save yourself, Patrick.

(555) 732-1197:

Why would you want to help me?

ME:

Somebody's got to look out for the little guy, right?

I keep typing.

ME:

> Do it today. I can't promise the shit won't hit the fan by morning. I won't be able to help you then.

He doesn't respond, not that I expected him to. If I were in his shoes, I wouldn't want an electronic record of me agreeing to turn my boss in to the feds either. But I'm fairly certain he'll do it now that he knows Cody's secrets are out.

I exit the site and get my butt out of the dark web entirely before returning the desktop to the welcome screen.

"Well, I imagine that should do it." I can't help my grin. "And can I say I'm proud of us for not lying even once?"

"Carter is gonna shit his pants when he finds out," Miller says with that same naughty grin.

I sigh and look Miller in the eye. "Clarence Cody deserves to go down, and I can't in good conscience let that assbadger get away with one more thing. Carter's got nothing to do with it." So much for not lying.

Miller nods and wiggles his lip ring. "Assbadger. Nice. I like it."

"Me too." I grin back at him.

Miller turns his chair around and straddles it this time as he faces me. "You know, Carter's not the only one attracting intruders and bad dudes. Somebody's after me too," he tells me in a conspiratorial tone.

I blink at him. "Are you messing with me?" After all, I've been warned about Miller and his antics.

"No, I swear. I'm actually being followed." Why does he look pleased about this?

"By whom? You need to tell Carter! It's probably the guys from D.C., Miller!"

He shakes his head. "No, it ain't them. I know who it is."

"Who? What do they want?"

He winks at me. "I've got it covered."

I lean back in my chair and eye him. Now I'm pretty sure he's messing with me, so I don't press him on it anymore. I just poke his knee and say, "If *I* were being followed, I'd go to the cops."

But he only sends me an eyebrow wiggle that has me feeling sorry for Ginny all over again.

I stand to rejoin Mia at the circulation desk where I was supposed to be this whole time. "You don't have to stay here, you know," I tell Miller. "Nobody is coming to the public library to kidnap me, I promise."

He shrugs from his spot on the chair. "Better safe than sorry. Besides, Carter would have my head if I didn't keep his girl safe."

I shake my head and blink at him. "I'm not his girl." Carter already came clean to his brothers, so there's no reason to continue this charade.

Miller stands and pushes his chair in. "You'd better tell *him* that." He winks at me again and wanders over to the fiction section before I can even think of how to respond to that.

FORTY-TWO

SO LONG, SUCKER

CARTER

"RUTHANNE." I nod at Grace Hopkins's assistant as I approach her desk outside the congresswoman's office.

There was a time when I would have chatted amiably with the woman before even asking her to let Grace know I was there. But those days are long gone.

Nonetheless, she gives me a half grin as she picks up her desk phone. "It's about time you showed up, Slick." She hits a button and speaks into the receiver. "Carter Brooks to see you, ma'am."

My appearance here isn't a surprise. The security guard had to buzz up before I was allowed in, and my cell phone has been resting in the breast pocket of my suit coat the entire drive to Raleigh. If these assholes have indeed been tracking me, I wanted them to know I was coming this time. I'm all done hiding.

I spent the drive to Grace Hopkins's district offices alternately rehearsing what I wanted to say, watching for suspicious vehicles that might be trailing me, and replaying the entire past few weeks in my mind. But there's been a new calmness inside me since I unburdened myself last night and my brothers rallied around me.

Whatever happens now, there are enough copies of evidence and fail-safes in place that I'm confident I can do what it takes to protect my own. I'm through acting the put-upon victim.

"Go on in," RuthAnne says.

I approach the double doors to Grace's office, take a deep breath, and walk in. She sits behind the wide wooden desk, wearing her favorite "casual day" ensemble of white blouse and red cropped jacket paired with what I'm certain are her navy pinstriped pants and heels. Her hair is expertly styled in a short brown bob, and her makeup looks like it was applied by a professional just this morning. When she stands, I see my prediction about the pants is spot on. I know this woman. Or, at least, I thought I did.

"Carter. I'm so glad you finally decided to come." Her tone is a mix of relief and hesitation.

"Well, I have something I need to discuss." I come forward, stopping several feet in front of the desk. I'm wearing my best power suit, and my hair—while still longer than she's seen—is combed into a neat sweep to match my clean-shaven face. I'm the very picture of a D.C. staffer on his way up. Only that's not where I'm headed.

"As do I," she responds, gesturing for me to take a seat on the sofa along the wall. I sit in a chair opposite her desk instead and set my briefcase on the floor next to it.

She doesn't argue, rounding the large desk and turning the chair beside mine until it faces me before seating herself. "As I'm sure you know, I've been trying to reach you."

"I'm aware." I don't waste time with pleasantries,

instead extracting a manila folder from my briefcase. I extend the folder to the congresswoman, but instead of looking inside or even eyeing me with curiosity, she immediately sets it on the edge of her desk, never taking her eyes from me.

"I owe you more of an apology than I can ever possibly convey."

I open my mouth to begin my prepared speech when her words register. My momentary confusion gives her the opening to continue speaking.

"You were never anything but loyal to me, and I threw it in your face to save myself and this sinking ship." She coughs out a mirthless laugh before continuing. "I almost came to Asheville to track you down, but I was worried I'd only bring more trouble to your door. I figured asking you here at least gave you the option of refusing."

"Excuse me?" I finally ask, unbuttoning my suit jacket and shifting in my chair. This is not going even remotely as I imagined. In fact, I'm more confused than ever. I expected her to lead with defensiveness or threats.

She shakes her head. "I behaved appallingly. And I was a coward." She straightens her posture again and gathers herself before looking me straight in the eye. "I should have stood up for what was right instead of protecting myself—and my family."

"I—" I stutter. "I'm afraid I don't understand."

"I know." She nods. "You see, about a year ago, I found out Antoni had an affair." Her tight-lipped smile holds zero amusement. I always got the sense that Antoni didn't enjoy having a wife more powerful than him, so this isn't a huge surprise. "A very colorful one, as it turns out. I won't bore you with the details, but the parties involved contacted me and threatened to go to the tabloids with all the gory details if I didn't pay them off."

Good old-fashioned blackmail. You can't beat it. I decide to let her continue. There's plenty of time for my news.

"The amount was much more than I could possibly gather on short notice—or probably at all. So when Clarence approached me, ostensibly to give me a friendly warning that he'd seen Antoni at a hotel with someone who wasn't me, I unwisely shared my troubles. He, being the thoughtful man he is, offered to lend me the money and said that I could pay him back over time." Her sarcasm is impossible to miss.

She sighs and shakes her head, sending me a look that says she knows exactly how unwise a move that was. "I jumped at it without thinking at all. It was utter foolishness. But I was blinded by the mental image of the pity, the scorn, the humiliation I'd face if that story came out. And our poor children." She frowns before huffing out another humorless laugh. "I'm sure you can guess the rest."

"Cody came collecting for something other than money." It actually makes perfect sense. Her moral code didn't crumble overnight; it corroded over time like seawater slowly working at a steel bridge.

She only nods. "And you overheard enough to put yourself in a precarious spot." She leans forward in her chair and rests her hands on her knees. "When you told me you were going to turn us in, I panicked. I can't begin to tell you how much I regret it, but I thought I could reason with Cody and tell him we all needed to back down or it was going to come out. When he asked me who knew, I didn't tell him, but he guessed. He knew how close you and I were."

A part of me feels for her, but the bigger part doesn't give a shit about her anymore. "And this confession is supposed to make things all better somehow?"

She shakes her head and begins speaking again, but I cut her off.

"Have you come clean to the feds? To your colleagues? Have you stood up to Cody?"

"I—" She falters before closing her mouth and shaking her head no. I used to idolize this woman; I wanted to be her. Now all I want is to be better than her.

I force my jaw to unclench enough to speak. Each word comes out like a slash of a whip. "They broke into my apartment. They held a gun to my face."

She gasps, but I only continue, even though her reaction reveals that it was all Cody all along.

"They told me to get the fuck out of town and never come back. Then they followed me home. They tracked me. They tried running my brewery out of business." I spew the words through gritted teeth now. "They broke into my *mother's* house and trashed it. And I'm now starting to wonder if they may have messed with my car to try sending another message. My brother was in that car, Grace!" I'm standing now and shouting while she sits there dumbstruck, hand to her chest and lips quivering.

"I had no idea! Y-you have to believe me, Carter. I figured they threatened you and that's why you left and didn't turn us in. But I didn't know. I swear!"

"You cost me my entire career!"

Rapid knocking sounds at the door.

"It's fine, RuthAnne!" Grace yells, trying to pull herself together.

The knocking stops.

"I know, Carter, and I'm so so sorry. But I can fix it. I know I can."

All I can do is shake my head. She has to know that sorry is only a word; it does nothing at all. I take the folder from the desk and hand it to her again. "I imagine you will be."

She opens the folder and starts flipping through the pages.

"My next stop is Cody's office, but I figured you'd enjoy a preview. This is how it's going to go. I don't give a shit how he does it, but Cody is going to stop that diet pill from hitting the market. It's poison, and all of us know it. *If* he does that, then the information in this folder—plus more I've collected and am happy to share with him—will stay between us. If he *doesn't*, you can all say goodbye to your careers and hello to a nice cozy jail cell. And the same goes if I see *any* sign of someone keeping tabs or if *one* hair on *one* head of anyone I've ever met is touched. You got me?"

Her nod is more of a jerk while she stares up at me with unblinking eyes. I bend to get in her face before continuing, "You let Cody know I'm coming. But tell him not to get any bright ideas about sending his goons to intercept me. He'd better hope I don't get in a car accident on my way, because if I get so much as a broken pinky toe, I've left instructions for every last word of incriminating information to go straight to both the feds and the *New York Times*." I stab the folder in her hands with my finger. "This isn't the only copy, and this isn't my first day playing this game."

I straighten and pick up my briefcase. Then I hold it over her desk before turning it upside down. The plastic-wrapped bundles of cash cascade onto her desk in a pile.

"And you can tell Clarence fucking Cody that I can't be bought."

I fasten the buckle on my case and turn for the door, ready to get the hell out of here and never come back.

Grace stands to intercept me. "Carter, I'm sorry." She drops a manicured hand to my arm. "And I'm more relieved than you can know that this drug won't make it to market with all you've done. Please, stay. We can fix this and get your career back on track! I promise. You were born for this. We both know it." Her voice is pleading, and at our close proximity, I can make out tiny clumps of her makeup caught in the wrinkles around her eyes.

"The only thing I was born for was making my own damn decisions." I shake her hand off and head for the door. But just before I open it to leave, I turn one more time. "I'm reminded of something my dad used to say, and I think he'd agree with me when I tell you to shove your sorry *and* that career in your bunghole and cork it."

I'm out the door and back in my car less than a minute later, my expensive tie and pressed suit coat crumpled in the back seat of the Olds and the radio cranked up as I hightail it out of town.

One down, and only one more to go.

SUNNY

"UH, SUNNY?"

I glance up from my position on the floor where I'm reshelving picture books by the beanbag chairs in the children's section. Sebastian stands there, hands shoved in the pockets of his cotton pants and a hesitant smile pointed my way.

"Hey, Sebastian." I scramble to my feet with a responding smile. This is the first time he's ever come to visit me at the library. "What are you doing here?"

"I don't know." He shrugs and glances around. "I mean, you talk about the library a lot, so I figured I may as well come and check it out."

"Who's this?" Miller appears at my side out of nowhere, arms crossed over his chest and a frown that's way too similar to his brother's in place. He and Sebastian are around the same height, but there's no question who would win in a fight. Not that there will be one—now, or ever.

"It's fine, Miller. This is Sebastian. Sebastian, this is Miller." I don't offer more details.

My neighbor lifts his hand in a halfhearted wave. "Hey there."

"What's he doing here?" Miller asks me, ignoring Sebastian's greeting.

I shove him away with both hands. "If you'd leave us alone, I can find out." He does walk away then, but he does it backward, eyes trained on Sebastian the entire time. I can't stop my eyes from rolling.

"Sorry about that," I say, still not explaining.

"So, um." Sebastian's hand goes to the back of his neck and his eyes drop to his feet. Oh, I recognize this look. It's the sheepish guilt schtick—the very one Carter has down to a T. Sebastian is about to ask me to haul more goats. Or maybe kidnap some methane-farting cows this time. Or drive him to pick up Michelle for a march on the Governor's mansion to demand equal rights for groundhogs.

But I stop myself right there. Sebastian isn't responsible for my crabbiness any more than Miller is. And I actually enjoy lending a helping hand when I can—especially for a good cause. I shove my negativity to the side and send him my best smile. "Whatever it is, I'm up for it."

His eyes snap up to mine and his brows spike. "Really?" His smile is the same warm one I've adored since the first time he sent it my way over an overflowing recycle bin.

"Absolutely." I nod.

"Well," he begins, the hand back on his neck, but eyes and smile on me now. "I've been thinking, and I know you're kind of seeing Carter, but if you guys aren't exclusive or anything, I thought I could take you out to dinner. At a restaurant. Like a real date."

My smile falters the tiniest bit, and I have no idea why. This is exactly what I've wanted for the last year. And Carter was right. Sebastian would never have made his move if he hadn't been kicked in the pants by a little dose of competition. Everything is working out exactly as it's supposed to. The bad guys are going down, Carter's family will be safe, and I'll be with Sebastian. It's perfect. Absolutely perfect.

I shore up all my generous reserves of positivity and beam at my soon-to-be boyfriend. "I'd love to."

"WE HAVE A PROBLEM." Miller all but crashes into the circulation desk as he catches my attention. He's holding his phone out to me and worrying his lip ring.

I take the phone and bring it to my ear. "Hello?"

"Oh, Sunny, it's Ginny. Carter's mom."

My lips twitch. "I know who you are, Ginny. What's up?"

Mia pretends not to be listening from the chair next to mine, but she's a terrible faker.

"Honey, I am so *so* sorry, but I seem to have misplaced your grandfather."

"What?!" My volume is way too loud for a library, but I can't help it. "What do you mean?"

From the corner of my eye, I see Meredith poke her head out of her office, but I don't give two hoots if I get fired. Duke is missing!

"Well, he said he left something in the car, and I was busy helping Lizzie with the class, and Mitch was already naked, so I told Marvin where the keys were and to find Denny to go with him, but when I went looking ten minutes later, Denny said he hadn't seen him. And when we checked the parking lot, my car was gone!"

That sneaky old grouch is up to his old tricks! And this time he stole someone's car!

"Ginny, I am so sorry. I can't believe he stole your car!" Actually, I can, but I'm not telling her that. "Do you have any idea where he went? Did he say anything earlier that might give us an idea?"

"Well, now that you mention it, he did say something about wanting to help Carter with the investigation—no, *inspection*. That's the word he used. I figured he meant whatever you said he's been helping with on his computer. Does that help? Maybe he went home?"

"The health inspection!" Oh, Duke, what are you doing? Trying to kill me, that's what. And I already decided I'm not dying before I get good and laid. "Thanks, Ginny. I'll call you back in a bit. And sorry again about your car."

"No worries, darlin'. I'll wait for your call."

I hang up and dial Duke's number, but it goes straight to voice mail. I immediately click on Miller's contacts next, scrolling to Carter's name and hitting the call button. "Does Carter have his phone?"

"I think so," Miller says.

The line starts ringing, and I see Meredith hurrying my way. Shit! I don't have time for this right now, so I start backing up, as if she can't simply detour around the counter. Just as she turns to come around, though, Mia intercepts her. "Meredith, we need to talk. Now." My best friend takes our boss by the arm and ushers her back to her office while Meredith points at me over her shoulder and whisper-hisses at Mia.

I officially owe Mia my firstborn. Which I may eventually have if I can locate Duke before my head explodes.

Carter picks up on the fourth ring. "Yeah?" Thank God.

"Carter! It's Sunny. Duke has gone missing. Your mom said something about not being able to ditch a naked guy to take Duke to the car, so he stole her keys and took off in her car, and he was talking about an inspection, and I know—I just *know*—he got it in his head to go after that inspector or that Knotts woman you two tracked down. He's pulled this kind of thing before, which I'm sure is no surprise, only I have no idea where he's going since I don't have a photographic memory, so now I'm calling you because you're the only one who knows where he's headed and thank God for once you finally have your phone on you!"

I gasp for breath, ignoring Miller's unhelpful snickering from the other side of the counter. We've attracted the attention of some patrons, so I offer them an awkward smile and cup my hand over the phone this time. But Carter speaks before I can say anything else.

"Sunny, I'm pulling over now and changing direction. I'm outside Morganton so I might not beat him there, but I'm on my way."

"Wait! Come get me first."

"Sunshine, that will only give him more time. You know it's true." His voice evens and his tone drops low. "I swear to you I will go get him and bring him back to you, do you hear me?"

Tears are clogging my throat too much for my words to come out.

"Sunny?"

"Yeah," I finally croak.

"Don't you worry. I'll have him back giving you a hard time about his liquor before you know it."

I choke on a laugh. "Okay." I'm not sure which one of us needs it more—if I need to say it or Carter needs to hear it—but I exhale and say, "I believe in you, Carter."

He hangs up and I drop the phone to my hip before bursting out into tears in the middle of circulation.

I know you're sick of hearing it, but being a librarian is a hell of a lot harder than it looks.

CARTER

I'D LAUGH if Sunny weren't so distraught. Duke could drive the Dalai Lama insane. I just hope the guy can drive with that hip, because coming back to Asheville without him is not an option.

I break about eight dozen traffic laws on my way to D.C., and I nearly go out of my skull when a fender bender blocks traffic for over thirty minutes outside Greensboro. Duke will beat me there for sure now, as I assume he took the fastest route from Asheville via I-81.

I should be concerned that Sunny spilled her guts out over my phone line, but I already showed my hand to Grace and provided my warning. I have to trust now that they'll all take me seriously. There's no telling what I'd be capable of if someone so much as looked wrong at Sunny.

Miller's number pops up on my phone again, and I almost don't answer. I'm not sure I can stand hearing the pain in Sunny's voice again without being there to pull her into my arms and reassure her. But when I hit the accept button, it's Miller instead.

"We checked the house just in case, but the old guy isn't there. I know you're driving, but I thought you'd appreciate a heads-up."

"Yeah, thanks."

"That wasn't the heads-up I was talking about. Some dude was here movin' in on your lady earlier today."

"Sunny does, on occasion, talk to men. They're called patrons." I don't know why I don't just tell him she's not mine and she never will be.

"Nah, this was somebody she knows. Sebastian something or other."

"Oh."

"That's it? I heard the dude ask her out, man! You gonna put up with that shit?"

"Miller, I've got to concentrate on the road. I'll talk to you later." I hang up before he can say anything else.

So, Sebastian finally manned up and asked her out. Good. It's what she wanted, and she deserves whatever she wants.

She's way too good for me anyway.

Without her, I doubt I would have chanced demanding Cody take on the NutriSlender thing. And there's a good chance it could still come back to bite me in the ass if he can't make Starboard kill it on his own. I'll have no choice but to follow through and go public with the evidence from Knuckles, and that means putting trust in a system I don't have a whole lot of confidence in these days. I could end up in a worse spot than I am now.

But it was the right thing to do. And Sunny knew that all along.

With hours of open road ahead of me, I've got

nothing but time to conjure up one regret after another. But I've already wasted enough time on regrets these past months. Shit happens to everyone, no matter if you're a member of Congress or a bartender from the Blue Ridge Mountains, and life goes on—if you let it, that is.

I've still got something to offer, and I'm far luckier than most people. It's time I count my blessings instead of bemoaning the ones unavailable to me right now. Working my ass off toward a goal is what I do best. It's what I've always done best. And it's time I set a new goal for myself—whether that's carving out a new career or becoming the best brewmaster this side of the Mississippi. I owe it to myself—and the people who care about me—to set my sights anew.

There is one regret I will allow myself, though, and that's not being upfront with Sunny and telling her everything on my mind when I had the chance. But if I really want to put her first like she deserves, I won't interfere with the life she wants. And putting that woman first is something I won't ever regret.

"I TOLD you I'm not stealing anything!" Duke's familiar voice overshadows the chatter from the police officer's belt radio.

"This is all a misunderstanding, like I said," I reassure the officer standing between me and the front door of the townhouse in Brookland off Route 1 in D.C. I have yet to lay eyes on Duke, but from what the officer has told me, he showed up to the door an hour ago and scared the housekeeper who then called the cops—after hog-tying him when he let himself in, that is. Thank God the owners are out of town.

The cop looks unconvinced.

"He didn't mean to trespass. He had the address wrong and got confused," I lie. "He's just stubborn, not dangerous. Have you seen him?" I straighten my tie and summon my most confidence-inspiring tone.

There's more chatter from the radio, and I can tell the officer is becoming distracted.

"Did I mention Mr. Underwood is a veteran?"

The guy frowns at me, unclipping his radio and raising it to his mouth. "1A-41. Copy that. We're wrapping up." He lowers the radio, speaking to me this time, "Escort him off the premises. I'd better not see him again."

"You have my word. Thank you." I nod at the officer and slide past him to get to Duke, who's still grumbling from a room just inside the townhouse.

"Brooks!" His eyes light when he sees me. Another officer is talking to the housekeeper while Duke rubs his wrist from his spot on a plush sofa. "I've been manhandled!"

I'm not lingering any longer than we need to. The last thing I want is for these officers to realize Duke drove himself here and arrest him for driving without a license. "Not another word," I mutter as I help Duke up. I hope to hell he didn't tell the housekeeper his name. "Where's your cane?"

He frowns over at the housekeeper. "Ask her. She was about to beat me with it."

She turns to scowl at Duke. "No, I wasn't, old man, and you know it!" She points to a bookshelf beside a writing desk. "It's right there."

Duke shakes me off and scowls back at her before

hobbling over to get his cane. I take the opportunity to glance around the room, and sure enough, there's a family photo on the wall of our friendly inspector flanked by a thin middle-aged woman and two teenagers—complete with the Eiffel Tower as a backdrop.

But the inspector is the last thing on my mind. All I care about right now is getting Duke out of here and back to Asheville as soon as humanly possible. I usher him out the door and down a few yards where we can talk in private.

I reach my hand out, palm up. "Keys."

He mutters under his breath but does reach into his pocket for the keys and drop them into my hand.

"Where's the car?"

He points farther down the street, so we walk in that direction. "You stole my mother's car? Really?" I'll have to figure out a way to get the Olds back to Asheville. Or, hell, I might just go to my insurance agent's office and tell them to go fetch the hideous beast themselves.

Heading for the car, I pull out my phone and text Miller that Duke is fine and we're on our way back.

It isn't until we're both buckled into Mama's Toyota and I've pulled onto the street that he speaks. "They left me no choice. Nobody listens to an old man."

"Duke, do you know how worried Sunny is?"

"She worries for no reason."

"She worries because she loves you, and you're the only family she has left," I tell him, trying not to yell. "You need to call her."

He continues to scowl but does as I say. I can hear Sunny's voice on the other end, but I can't make out any of her words, which is probably for the best. Duke spends the majority of the short call listening, and when he tries to argue, it's clear she cuts him off. I'm encouraged, however, when his last words before hanging up are, "You too, Sunshine."

We drive in silence, each of us in our own thoughts for the time it takes me to calm down enough that I won't shout at him. I'm sure Sunny has enough scolding stored up for the both of us and more. When I do speak again, it's information I'm looking for.

"What was the point of coming all this way when we already have what we need from Knuckles?"

He turns to me. "You don't have what you need to nail *this* guy. And you said he basically stole from you with the whole inspection hoax."

I shake my head. "That's the least of my worries. I'm focused on the bigger fish pulling his strings."

He reaches under his cardigan—the same dark yellow one as always—and pulls something out. "Well, here's your puppet anyway." He hands me an old Polaroid picture in a frame. Since I'm driving, it takes a few glances to recognize a younger version of the balding inspector wearing a graduation cap and gown. Standing with an arm slung over the graduate's shoulder is a younger version of none other than Clarence Cody. Cody is beaming in the photo as he looks at the young inspector with what is, without a doubt, fatherly pride.

"No way." The guy is Cody's son? I wonder how much time you get in jail for impersonating a government officer. I mean, I knew Cody could easily pull strings to fake just about anything, but sending your own kid in as an accomplice?

"The car is the wife's. Leonna Knotts. Some women these days don't take their husbands' last names," Duke informs me, ever so helpfully.

The close family connection might up the stakes if Cody finds out we went to his son's house, but maybe it's a good thing. It shows him we're not bluffing, and he'd better fall in line quick. I'm guessing he's already heard from Grace and isn't having the best day as it is.

I turn left at a T in the road and head for the interstate. "If you already figured it out, why did you have to steal a car and come all the way up here?" The man sometimes appears to live on his own planet.

"Physical proof, Brooks." He snatches the photo from my hand. "There's something to be said for doing things the old-fashioned way. And besides, you and Sunny and that damn doctor spoiled my chance for the Memphis gig."

"Sunny was looking out for you. And, I promise, there wasn't really all that much to it. We talked to Knuckles for twenty minutes and then stopped at the Graceland gift shop. Didn't she give you your souvenirs?"

"I don't want souvenirs!" he shouts loud enough to make me flinch in surprise. Silence falls over the car. He doesn't say anything else for a few moments, and I give him the time. This is a new kind of anger I haven't seen. It's not an act or an exaggeration for Sunny's benefit. He's truly upset.

When he does speak again, he's regained some control over his temper. "I don't want souvenirs or a trip to the diner to placate me. I'm not a child. I'm a grown man who needs more than a radio show and the same four walls day in and day out." He shakes his head and looks out the passenger window, shielding his expression from me. "Did it ever occur to any of you that maybe I wanted to see my old buddy after all this time?" His eyes drop to his lap, roaming the length of his legs in the familiar brown pants.

"My body may be giving out, but the rest of me isn't ready to give up—not even close."

When I'm certain he's done talking, I ask, "Have you told Sunny any of this?"

He only shakes his head.

"Duke, I promise you she'll want to know. She loves you and wants you to be happy. She'd do anything for you." And anyone else, for that matter.

"She's the one who deserves to be happy. My Helen raised a good one, she did." There's a trace of a smile now.

"The best one," I agree. And it's true.

Sunny is a remarkable human being and a beautiful woman. She may wear glasses a little too rose-colored for me sometimes, but when I get a glimpse of the world through her eyes, I can see all the brightest and most beautiful spots. The woman never complains or assumes the worst in people, and even when she's talking about something as painful as being abandoned by her parents, she refuses to focus on anything but the blessing of her grandparents in her life. When she detects a problem, she never even considers it can't be solved, volunteering herself to be the first one to try.

And she believes in people. She thinks Sebastian really can change the world. She thinks good people will always prevail in the end. And she sees good in *me*—the part of me that has nothing to do with being in the spotlight or holding a position of power or influence. She believes in Carter the brewer, the brother, the son, the friend, and even the spy. I can't imagine any gift better than having her in my corner.

"You know," Duke begins, grinning now for real, his bushy eyebrows dancing. "I don't really believe in all that bullshit I go on about. Don't get me wrong—the government is definitely spying on us—but I like picking fights with the neighbors about drones and floating some colorful conspiracy theories for Sunny to laugh at. It always tickled Helen, so I ham it up a bit for fun."

I knew it.

"So you don't really think Elvis lives on Mars."

"Oh, that one's God's honest truth. The King is up there, mark my words."

I can't tell if he's pulling my leg or being sincere, but either way, it's nice to see him back to himself.

I adjust my grip on the steering wheel and merge into the traffic speeding down the highway. "How about we get you home so you can tell your granddaughter how you cracked the case of the fake inspector and his crooked congressman dad?"

Duke raises his hand and points to the road ahead. "Onward, my boy!"

SUNNY

"THEY'RE HERE!" I shout, flying past Sebastian at my kitchen counter and almost tripping over the rug on my way to the front door. I yank the door open to see Ginny's car come to a stop in the driveway, headlights illuminating the house.

I leap down the steps and sprint for the passenger side, tears clouding my vision and a huge smile plastered across my face. "Duke! Thank God."

He grumbles as I dive at him and squish him in my arms, the seat belt tangling both of us up into a heap.

"I'm sorry I worried you, Sunshine. But I'm fine."

I pull back and stare at him with wide eyes, part of me thinking there must be something wrong if he's apologizing right off the bat like this. "I don't care as long as I have you home safe. Are you okay?" I go back in for another hug, but this time I undo his seat belt first.

"Let a man use the facilities before you squeeze him like that!" He extracts himself from my hug and I pull him to standing before escorting him into the house. Carter stays by the car, watching from a distance.

"I'll be right back!" I tell him. I owe him such a massive thanks, and I have no idea how I'll ever repay him. Although maybe getting the heck out of his life for good will be the best payment of all.

I finished out my shift at the library yesterday, fretting and pacing through most of it. Meredith miraculously left me alone, something I have Mia to thank for, and my bestie doted on me the entire time, telling me stories to distract me and sending all the patrons my way so I'd have something to do with my brain and hands.

Miller stuck around until I left, and when he tried following me home, I told him to go back to Blue Bigfoot. When he refused, I asked him if he really wanted me on the radar of whoever is following him. It was a long shot, and the fact that it worked tells me he may not have been lying to me earlier.

Sebastian stopped over later in the evening, and when I told him about Duke, he offered to stay with me while I waited. We watched two documentaries, ate cold pizza, and he finally fell asleep on the couch at midnight. I stayed up crocheting, reading a romance novel, and biting my nails to the quick.

Now it's five in the morning, and I'm buzzing on caffeine and happiness that my grandpa is back home safe and sound.

Sebastian yawns over his coffee while Duke hurries to the bathroom, and I excuse myself outside to talk to Carter. When I approach—this time more calmly—I can see the dark circles under his eyes, even in the dim light reflected off the house.

I don't even stop; I walk right into him and hug him

tight around the waist. This is probably the last time I'll see him or touch him, so I memorize the sensation to keep with me when he's gone. His warm firmness, his strong hands on my back, his woodsy scent.

"I can't ever thank you enough." I squeeze him harder.

"I was happy to do it. I'm the one who brought all this trouble to your door in the first place. I should be apologizing to you."

I only shake my head and inhale once more before letting go and stepping back. "Tell your mom I'm sorry about the car. I'll reimburse you for the gas and anything else, obviously."

"Absolutely not." His tone is final, and I don't argue.

"I'm sure you're exhausted and want to get home and crash," I tell him. "The last time I stayed up all night, I was making a paper mâché eggplant piñata for Mia's cousin's daughter's birthday party, only to find out when I showed up that she'd asked for an elephant, not an eggplant. The cousin wasn't amused. Mia, on the other hand?" I shrug, knowing I'm just dragging this goodbye out.

Carter smiles at my story, even though he's probably only being polite. "You gonna be okay by yourself? Need me to send my mama over to play drill sergeant?"

I smile back. "Nah, we'll be okay. Sebastian's here anyway." There's no reason for him to put himself out for me any more than he already has.

"Oh. Okay. I guess I'll, uh, see you, then." He nods, opening the door to the car again.

I want to ask him about the evidence and what he's doing next. I want to tell him about Patrick Nielson and share a conspiratorial laugh as we rub our hands together in tandem like evil mastermind partners. But I don't.

Instead, I raise a hand in farewell. "Okay, see you."

He pauses halfway to the seat. "By the way, when you talk to Duke, make him tell you why he took off like that. Don't let him bluster his way out of it, either. We had a talk on the way home, and I think it would be good for him to open up."

"Okay, I will." Duke has never been much of a sharer, but I think this stunt warrants a nice long talk. "Oh, and there might be someone following Miller around, in case he doesn't tell you." Carter's eyes widen, so I explain, "Or he could have been messing with me. I'll let you figure it out."

He nods and lowers himself into the car. I assume we're done here, and I don't want to watch him drive away like the heroine in one of my books, so I turn for the door.

"Sunny?"

When I turn around, he's standing again behind the car door, one of his handsome half smiles—complete with a single dimple—aimed my way. "You deserve everything you ever want, and I hope you get it all."

I have no idea what to say in response, so I stand there dumbly as he sits down, closes the door, and pulls out of my driveway. Then I watch him drive out of my life exactly the way I said I wouldn't.

Sebastian has his nose buried in his phone when I come back inside, so I go down the hall to check in on Duke. He's fallen asleep on the toilet, so I wake him up and make sure he stays conscious for the walk to his bed. Our talk will have to wait.

I'm thinking of napping myself since I'm not on at the library until this afternoon, but I can't exactly leave Sebastian standing in my kitchen alone—especially when he was kind enough to keep me company all night.

"Breakfast?" I ask.

He glances up from his phone. "Oh, uh, sure."

I open the refrigerator and frown at the contents. What do vegans eat for breakfast anyway? "I have toast and jam. Does that work?

"Sure." He shrugs. "Can you believe how the West tries dodging responsibility for all the climate change issues suffered by developing nations? It's abominable. It's *our* fault."

"It is terrible. I agree." I grab a jar of raspberry jam and close the refrigerator door before hunting down the bread. "I have some news of my own, in fact." I've decided to tell him a little bit about the corruption since it's going to come out anyway. "I'm helping to expose a corrupt politician from Tennessee who's engaging in insider trading, among other things." I open the bread bag and pull out four slices as I wiggle my eyebrows at Sebastian. He's not the only one cleaning up trash these days.

He looks up at me. "Oh, can you check to make sure there's no dairy in that bread?"

My proud grin teeters, and I almost repeat my news since he was obviously distracted the first time. But instead, I turn the bread bag over and read the ingredients to myself before responding, "Nope. No dairy."

"Okay, great." His eyes are back on his phone screen.

I stand holding the bread bag and watch him for a good minute before dropping the bag to the counter and cocking a hip. "Sebastian?"

He glances up, eyebrows raised. "Yeah?"

"What would you do if a train were coming, and you see me, a stranger, and a nest of baby birds tied to the railroad tracks?" I decide to change the scenario to include baby birds instead of kittens since Sebastian is allergic to cats and I wouldn't want that to influence his answer.

He nods, clearly paying attention this time. "Train travel is one of the more sustainable modes of transportation, you know."

"Yes, I know." I wave a dismissive hand and shift to the other hip. "But answer the question. And, before you ask, you don't have time to rescue more than one."

He looks up at the ceiling as he considers his answer for way too long, if you ask me. When his eyes finally drop back to mine, he asks, "Are the birds an endangered species?"

Jam in a jar! What am I doing here? And what was I thinking letting Carter drive away without telling him how I feel?

CARTER

THE STOUT STILL HAS ISSUES. I know it, Cash knows it, Oscar knows it, and he hasn't even tasted it. He just hangs around Cash too much.

The base malt is fine, but maybe I need to use chocolate malt with my caramel and Munich malt.

"I thought you were supposed to be asleep for your trip to Memphis in the morning," a voice comes from the brewhouse doorway. I look up to see Hollis adjusting her glasses and watching me.

Does everyone on God's green earth know my business now?

"Sorry, *mom*, but I wasn't feeling much like sleeping, so I stopped into work." I drop my pen onto my notebook. "I figured Cash might appreciate it if I showed up to do my part once in a while." I muster up a half smile so she doesn't take my crankiness personally.

Lord knows there's a surplus of people on security detail at Mama's house, so they don't need me there. Rosie called her cousins Ponch and Ari, and they both showed up with Ari's husband, Jax, and some girl named Andie in tow, as well as two dogs and more than a couple of baseball bats. Nobody's getting near the Brooks family for the next few days, at least.

And Sunny doesn't know it, but Miller and Luca are trading shifts in Black Mountain until I get back from Cody's. When I asked Miller about being followed, he blew me off, so I tipped Luca off and he's keeping an eye out.

There's been no more word from the unknown number since the night of the break-in, and I'm not sure how to interpret that yet. I hope to hell it means they've given up and Cody is playing ball. I guess I'll find out tomorrow.

Lynn is back at school in Boone, and everybody else is pitching in on cleanup at the house between work and other responsibilities. Rosie even found Mango in one of the kitchen cabinets, feasting from a bag of sunflower seeds. One thing's for sure, there's no shortage of people willing to lend a hand and come to our rescue, and for once, I'm taking the time to truly appreciate how lucky I am.

Hollis shrugs and leans into the doorjamb, her blond ponytail falling behind her. "Maybe, but I doubt he cares all that much as long as he knows you *want* to be here."

I abandon my recipe and turn my stool to her. "Of course I want to be here. I wouldn't have sunk my life savings in the place if I didn't believe in it."

She crosses her arms like she's preparing for one of her fights with my brother. "You know exactly what I mean."

I'll leave the fighting to Cash. All I want is to fix this stout recipe and get my ass to Memphis tomorrow to wrap shit up. Hell, I should just buy an RV with how much time I'm spending on the road. Who needs an apartment?

But she is right. I do know exactly what she's talking about; she didn't need to make the special trip from next door. Cash and I will be okay, but I'm glad he got shit off his chest the other night. I needed to hear it as much as he needed to say it.

And I can give Hollis something, especially knowing she'll report it right back to my brother. "I hear you. And I'm done looking behind me. You can tell Cash that I'm officially a full-time brewmaster and business partner from here on out."

But Hollis isn't done. "He just wants you to be his brother and be happy. That's it. You think you can manage that?"

When I look up at her this time, I hope she can read my sincerity. "That's the plan."

"Good. Then my job is done." Her smile is the kind that tells me my brother is in for a challenge. And I couldn't be happier about that.

She shoots me a little wave and disappears, so I get back to jotting in my notebook. Maybe it's the timing, and I should try adding the coffee after the yeast is finished working. I make a note and see from the corner of my eye that Hollis has returned to impart more wisdom.

Except the voice doesn't match my neighbor's. "You're not going to believe it!"

I turn to see Duke shuffling through the brewhouse door, cane in hand, ugly sweater right where it belongs. So much for the Luca and Miller surveillance team. "What are you doing here? Does Sunny know where you are?"

He waves a hand. "Yeah, yeah. She's out there talking to somebody or other." The jolt to my pulse at the knowledge that Sunny is so near shouldn't be a surprise. But Duke won't be ignored. "Knuckles contacted me. You won't believe it."

"What?" I pull another stool over and Duke settles himself before placing his cane on the worktable.

"When he got to Cody's offices this morning, things were in an uproar." Wow, this is a lot faster than I anticipated. "Turns out when Cody's assistant left work last night, he took half the office with him. Cody's laptop, file folders, you name it. Gone! Knuckles said Cody was fit to be tied, screaming at everyone and ranting all over the place."

"Wait. Did he say the assistant's name? Was it Nielson?"

"Yeah—that was it. Nielson. Knuckles was having a hard time keeping a straight face. Said everyone was sequestered for interviews, but he sailed through his and was dismissed."

I shouldn't be all that surprised that I wasn't the only one with a crisis of conscience, I suppose. I wonder how long Nielson was playing both sides.

One thing's certain now, though. Cody is going down —and maybe Grace too—and they don't even have me to blame for it. Ha! I guess things do work out better than you plan sometimes.

"We did it!" Duke declares with a crooked grin and a raised fist. "Case closed!"

I don't know that I'd go that far, but I, for one, am more than ready to put this all behind me. I extend my hand. "Couldn't have done it without you, Duke." That's for sure. "Thank you."

We shake hands and he slides off his stool again. "How about a free beer for my troubles?"

That has me chuckling, and I figure something light couldn't hurt. "Right this way." I gesture for him to precede me to the taproom, and when we turn the corner, Sunny is standing in the hall smiling at Duke as he all but prances toward her—well, as much as he can with a bum hip and a cane.

She's changed from her earlier outfit of pajama pants and T-shirt and is now wearing another pair of those shorts with a white sleeveless top that has little penguins printed on it. Of course it does.

"Duke wanted to tell you the news himself." She turns her smile to me, and I feel it like a hit in the chest. "I hope it's okay that we stopped by unannounced."

I shake my head. "Absolutely. Anytime. I mean it." She can move in if she wants, although I suppose Sebastian would have something to say about that.

"Brooks is buying me a beer," Duke announces, bypassing his granddaughter and heading for the bar.

Sunny rolls her eyes, and I don't take my gaze off her when I shout to Oscar, "Give the man whatever he wants, Oscar!"

She steps closer and laughs when Duke lets out a *whoop!* I stay where I am because I probably can't be trusted.

"Nielson, huh? I gotta say I did not see that one coming."

She shrugs, eyes sparkling now. "Well, he may have had a little encouragement."

My eyes widen. No way. She didn't? Did she?

"By the way," she continues, hands in the pockets of her shorts now. "Miller is a terrible spy. It took less than thirty seconds to figure out he was following me and another two to ditch him at a red light."

I drop my head back and groan at the ceiling.

Sunny laughs again, the sound like bells chiming. "But he's pretty handy with a computer, I have to say."

When I bring my head back down, I ask, "Do I want to know?" but she shakes her head. Good grief.

Her expression evens out. Even in the hallway lights I can see the freckles scattered across her nose and cheeks, and my thumbs itch to brush over them. "He said you went to see Congresswoman Hopkins. I'm sure that was hard."

"It actually felt great." I shove my hands into my own pockets so I don't give in to temptation or tuck the stray strands of red hair behind her ear for her. "You would have especially liked the part where I shoved the money in her face."

Her hands come out of her pockets and she does a little clap as she hops my way. "Seriously?! That's amazing. What did she do? Pass out?"

"Not quite, but I definitely made my point. I was heading back to Cody tomorrow, but I guess Nielson—and maybe you and my brother?—saved me a trip." I grin this time.

She only shrugs, but the mischief in her eyes tells me I'm at least partly right. This woman never ceases to amaze me.

And I know I should leave it here just like I know I'll regret asking, but I need to get back to reality. "Where's Sebastian?"

She purses her lips like she's thinking hard about it, and she's so close now that I can smell her vanilla lotion. "Um, I believe he's either weeding at the community garden or saving baby birds from an oncoming train. I'm really not sure."

"I guess I never did follow through on the dramatic breakup scene," I remind her. "But, uh, Miller told me it looked like things worked out regardless."

More lip pursing makes it impossible to keep my eyes off her mouth. "Your brother likes to jump to conclusions. I actually decided I didn't like the idea of dating a guy who was already in love with another woman." My confusion must be written on my face because she goes on to explain, "Mother Earth is a hell of a woman to compete with, so I told Sebastian to go follow his heart. Honestly, he seemed relieved." Her nose wrinkles and it takes work not to smile.

"I'm sorry." My emotions refuse to come to order in my head. I'm sorry she was hurt, but just knowing she isn't with him means there could possibly be a window if I ever clean my act up enough to deserve a shot.

She inhales and shrugs. "I'm not. It feels good to know myself and know what I want."

"Then I'm glad. I already told you that you deserve whatever you want in life, and I meant it."

"Really?" She looks up at me and meets my eye like she's genuinely seeking my assurances.

"Of course. You're the best person I know, Sunny Underwood, and don't you forget it."

One corner of her mouth lifts and I can just spy that little gap between her teeth. "You're not so bad yourself, Carter Brooks." She continues, "I've actually learned a few of your tricks."

"Oh yeah? Like what?" It feels incredible to be across from her teasing her again. "Flirting with bird ladies?"

She props her hands on her hips. "Like asking for what I want instead of apologizing for wanting it."

"Impressive." I nod. "Do I assume this means you've also learned how to say no?"

She puts a finger to the middle of her chin like it will help her think. "Well, that depends on the question, of course. If it's Meredith asking if I want to work a double shift, that's a hard no. If it's you asking if I want to go out on a date, then it's a definite yes."

In the seconds it takes for her words to register, she continues, "You're what I want. And it's okay if you don't feel the same, I promise. But I needed to tell you."

"I—" I start, but she puts both hands up and interrupts me before I can get more than the one syllable out.

"And no matter what you say, I won't be sorry I told you. Personally, I think we make a great team, and we already know we travel well together. I even finished your gnome last night while I was waiting for you and Duke, and I think I managed to capture a good balance between grumpy Carter and flirty Carter, although it was impossible to get those dimples just right. But what I really mean to say is I think you're the bee's knees, Carter Brooks, and I think we'd be great together."

Since she's already said more than enough for the both of us, I only grin at her and close the space between us. When she sees me coming, her smile is the most beautiful one yet. I almost hate to cover it, but nothing can stop me when I finally drop my lips to hers.

EPILOGUE

SUNNY

"WHAT'S THAT LOOK FOR?"

"We're not doing this," he says. "I already told you."

"Yes, we are."

"No, we're not."

"Carter, I have waited almost thirty years for this, and I'm not waiting another minute! Take me now, you beast!"

The man has already strung me along for weeks now—although, I suppose giving me countless orgasms doesn't technically count as stringing me along—but tonight is the night or I might lose my ever-loving mind. He has taken me to the brink on more than one occasion before backing down at the last minute and using his tongue and clever fingers to distract me until I forget my own name—in addition to the fact that his very nice penis has yet to be officially introduced to my very desperate vagina.

"Do I need to call your mama?" I threaten from my seated position on the edge of the bed.

This has him flashing a terrified expression down at me —and probably doing nothing for his state of arousal. But I'm reaching the end of my rope here.

"Because you know she'd be on my side." We've spent a lot of time with the Brooks family these past weeks, and I've learned that Ginny Brooks loves speaking her mind. She also loves her kids—fiercely so. And that makes me happy for everyone.

We all worked to get their house back in order, and now it's all about family barbeques, bickering siblings, nights hanging out at Blue Bigfoot, and watching Carter embrace his role as brewmaster and true family man. Even Mia has been won over, although she thinks he should grow the beard back.

Duke has become a regular at the senior center, where he's struck up a new friendship with another older veteran named Fuzzy. I'm pretty sure they both have a crush on Ginny, but hanging out there gives him something to do besides listening to his podcast and missing my grandma. We had a long talk a few days after his grand theft auto stunt, and I realized I needed to loosen my death grip on him a bit so he could enjoy life a little more. I know he won't be around forever, but now, instead of smothering him, I'm focusing on enjoying our time together. And he gets a kick out of his guy time with Carter too.

Ginny has been a wonder. Not only has she taken over the *Dear Mona* column—which she's sharing with a friend named Regina—she told Duke he's banned from the center on days he doesn't do his physical therapy exercises and take his medications. As a result, his health has shown some steady improvement in just a few weeks. He might even be ready soon for one of Ginny's Bigfoot hikes—

although a beginner one—where she takes a group to hunt for signs of her family's favorite cryptid in the forest.

I told Carter I was nominating her for sainthood when she convinced Duke that vintage personal care products are not a thing and it was finally time to throw out his bottle of TUMS from 1982. If she can get him to stop hiding booze, I'll give God a call myself. I've already crocheted a sasquatch and a little Mango skunk for her as a partial thank you, but she only hugged me and said she was the one who owed me for bringing Carter back home to her. I don't think I had all that much to do with it, but it's always nice to get hugs from kind people.

The biggest wonder by far, however, has been Carter.

He told me what he did in Grace's office, insisting on NutriSlender being pulled, and I think I bruised his ribs hugging him, I was so proud. Of course, I shared all about my foray into the dark web, and we've enjoyed watching interviews with Patrick Nielson where he plays the part of honorable whistleblower who sacrificed his career to do the right thing. He may be full of it, but we'll gladly hand over the credit if it means keeping our privacy.

Especially since the information he shared with the feds ensured Congressman Clarence Cody's immediate fall from grace. Cody took off the same day Knuckles contacted Duke, clearly seeing the writing on the wall. He escaped overseas before he could be arrested, so he's currently camped out in Iceland fighting extradition.

Since Grace's situation was blackmail and she never voted on the legislation, she escaped any charges but resigned from all her subcommittees. She's still in Congress but not enjoying the same lofty status any longer. Carter told me she filed for divorce from her cheater husband. When her assistant called Carter on her behalf to ask where to donate the dirty money, my cheeks hurt from smiling so hard when he told her to give it to Sebastian's kudzu goat initiative.

Ginny chose to go the insurance route instead of dragging things out trying to link the break-in back to Cody. And, even though Duke protested, Carter and Cash let the inspection hoax go for now. Once Cody is back in the States, they may pursue it, but for now, everyone is happiest to put it all behind them and get back to normal. Even the unknown texter has fallen silent, the nasty jerk.

NutriSlender is dead, of course, and good riddance. The board of directors at Starboard started from scratch with all new executives to avoid tangling with the FDA. I'm sure it's only a matter of time before the next scandal, but it will hopefully steer clear of Asheville next time around.

Carter hasn't heard from his friend Jeremy, despite calling and texting. He's worried how Grace's demotion will affect his friend and guesses that Jeremy might be sore he wasn't brought into the inner circle on our little mission. I told him to give his friend space—just like he was given when was thrown a curveball, and he hopes that's all it will take.

Carter frowns at me from his elevated position. He stands shirtless by the nightstand in the bedroom of his new apartment in West Asheville, and I'm enjoying how the light from the window plays over the muscles of his arms. He has an extremely sexy smattering of dark hair over his arms and chest that makes me go a little weak in the knees when I let myself stare too long. He is all man, and he's also all mine, as it turns out.

Except for this one little issue that needs to be

addressed. Carter is of the opinion that I'm not ready for intercourse; however, he's mistaken. But I think I know what's going on here, and I'm ready to take the reins.

"You're afraid of hurting me." I set my chin so he knows I mean business.

"No, I'm not."

"Liar." I shift to my knees so I'm taller and place my hands on his bare chest. He's firm and warm, and that spot under this jaw that I love to nibble on is *right* there so—*no! I must remain focused.* "I'm not made of glass, Carter." I slide my hands up to his shoulders. "And what happened to a woman deciding when she's ready?"

He frowns at me but doesn't say anything because he knows I'm right. When he tries staring me down with his mossy sienna swirls, I lean in and brush my lips against his. But I pull back before I get carried away.

"I choose this." I point to the bed beneath me. "And I choose you." My finger pokes him in the chest. When he still looks like he's on the fence, I decide to employ some of my newfound flirting skills by dropping back down to my butt and letting my hand wander up my thigh and under my shirt.

When my fingers skim my nipple under my T-shirt, I sigh and say, "Unless you don't find me attractive," before sinking down onto the bed and arching my back.

He lands on top of me in .02 seconds, grazing my chin with his lips and laying enough of his weight on top of me that I can feel his arousal while still being able to breathe. "You play dirty."

I beam at him as a little shiver runs over me. "I know. Isn't it great?" I'm very much enjoying my sexual confidence.

"It's not any of that," he says against my neck. "I know

you're ready and I know I won't actually hurt you." He drops a kiss into the hollow of my throat. "Sometimes I just can't help thinking you could do a hell of a lot better than me."

I pull my head back and shove him up a little so he has to give me his eyes. When his hair falls into his face, I brush it aside. Is Carter Brooks, smooth operator and undercover superhero feeling insecure? This will never do.

"You are my favorite person—aside from possibly Malala Yousafzai, but I don't want to date her. I love you. You stand up for what you believe in, you take care of your own, you admit your mistakes, and you believe in the goodness of people." I poke him. "And don't try to lie and say you don't. You can't hide from me, Carter Brooks."

"You love me?" His brows draw tight, and I don't think he's ever been more handsome than right now with the light filtering in through the window and his focus centered entirely on me. Me! I'm the luckiest woman in the world.

"Of course. And you're not hard on the eyes, either." I run a finger along that ridiculous jawline.

He rolls to his back and drops an arm over his eyes with a giant exhale. "Thank fuck." Then he jumps back on top of me again and hits me with a huge grin, both dimples framing that sexy mouth. "You have completely stripped me of any game I ever had. I've been stumbling around like an awkward disaster because I am so fucking in love with you, and I've been determined not to rush you into anything you weren't ready for."

"Seriously?" My eyes pop.

"One hundred percent." Those dimples might be the death of me.

"I have not once seen you awkward—except with the birds. You are always the picture of cool and collected otherwise." He's clearly exaggerating.

He leans in for a quick kiss before pulling back too soon. "Then you must be blind. My entire family has been having a field day making fun of me."

"How did I miss this?" I think I might have enjoyed witnessing that. I love how his family interacts, and I love that I get to be a part of it too now.

"No idea. Didn't you see the look on my brothers' faces when I announced the name of the new IPA?"

I think back to last week at the release of a new beer. "I guess I thought it was a little weird that it's the only beer name without a Bigfoot reference."

He groans, and it makes me smile at him. "I've been getting nonstop shit for naming it after you instead."

"Me? You didn't tell me that." I can't believe he did that. Or maybe I can. I *knew* he was sweet!

"Why else would I name a beer Eternal Hoptimist?"

"You're a fan of puns?"

He glares at me, but it's all for show.

"Hm, I guess I'm sorry I didn't tell you sooner then." I shrug and start feeling him up.

"You knew before today?"

"Of course. I've known since you told me about the tater tots and took me to Dollywood."

His back hits the bed again, but this time he pulls me on top of him. My T-shirt rides up and the hair on his chest tickles me in a delicious way. My nerve endings love this man almost as much as I do.

"I guess this means I'd better give the lady what she wants." His lips lift in a dirty grin.

"Yes, please." I give him my most exasperated look but

quickly drop it when he comes in for a kiss and flips us so I'm on my back.

My hands wind around his shoulders as his tongue brushes mine in a sensual slide. The time for talking is over as he kisses me stupid like he always does. His hands roam down to my thighs as he presses his erection against me through his jeans and my underwear. I ditched my skirt and bra earlier, and it's time to get rid of the rest of our clothes. But I can tell Carter is setting his own pace, so I let him.

Nevertheless, I bend my knees and cradle him between my thighs as I explore the muscles and warm skin of his back and he works me up into a frenzy with his kiss. The man has talented lips which he eventually drops to trail down my throat as I tilt my head back and squeeze him between my thighs. He groans against my neck, sending another shiver over my skin.

"Vanilla," he murmurs, and I smile. I know from experience that he's a fan of my body lotion.

"Pants," I reply, gliding my hands down his back and reaching for his pants. Of course, my arms are too short, so I give up and allow him to nuzzle me through my T-shirt as he drags his chin down to find what's hiding beneath.

When he exposes my naked breasts, he pulls back to enjoy the view for a second. "Fuck."

"Yes, please," I ask, and he dips his head to pull a nipple into his mouth. The combination of suction and bite mixed with his hands' caress over my skin has my back arching off the bed and my eyes rolling back in my head. He could probably make me come from sucking my nipples alone. My sex thrums and my clit throbs with his ministrations, and I start clawing at his shoulders.

He releases my nipple with a pop. "I love how aggressive you get when you're turned on." It's not the first time he's told me this, nor is it something I consciously do, but I really can't help myself with this man.

His hips come forward, pressing his hardness against me in an unconscious move, and I groan with want. I need him inside me. I'm done waiting. I'm done talking. I'm done fooling around. Let's do this thing.

"Carter, I need you." I don't care if I'm begging at this point. "I want you inside me."

I'm not sure I've ever seen his jaw this hard, though I know it's only from trying to restrain himself. But I don't want his restraint. I want all of him. Hot, hard, thick, deep. I want it all.

"Anything for you, Sunshine."

I would smile at his sweet words, but I'm way too turned on right now, so I pull him toward me instead. Carter has other plans, however. He easily resists my puny muscles and sinks down to his knees at the bedside before yanking me to the edge so my butt hangs off the bed, my shirt gathered above my bare breasts.

My underwear disappears in the next second, and Carter's tongue plays my clitoris like he's a concert violinist and my little nub is a freaking Stradivarius. Pleasure rockets through my womb and I buck into him. He moans against my wet folds and slides a finger inside me. My open palm hits the bed and I buck again. This time, Carter palms my butt and squeezes hard as he adds another finger inside me with his other hand. My back arches and I start to pant.

The way his tongue toys with my clit and his fingers delve in and out has me coming out of my skin. I moan his name, which only has him lapping at my wetness and groaning in pleasure. He twists his fingers inside me and hits a spot that I realize has to be the famous G, and I'm a sweaty mess, thrashing under him and fluttering around his tongue and fingers.

He comes up for a breath, and I hear him encourage me. "That's right. I want you to come on my tongue." The words alone have me beginning to spasm, and he dives back in to taste me some more.

I climax around his fingers and tongue, writhing and moaning as each wave crashes over me. Carter is relentless with his movements, never letting up or giving me a break until my muscles exhaust themselves and I deflate on the bed in pure satiation.

But if I think he's up to his old tricks, I'm pleasantly surprised when instead of gently kissing my belly or stroking my thighs, he unbuckles his belt in a flash and shucks his jeans and boxers, standing before me buck naked with an impressive erection bobbing between us. Finally!

I forget my tiredness and reach out between my splayed thighs for him. I want to taste him like I've done a couple times now, but I'm afraid if I don't pounce on him now, he might change his mind again.

"You're grinning like the cat that caught the canary," he says, and when I look up, I see he's grinning right back at me.

"You'd like that, wouldn't you?" I tease him. "One less flying rat on the earth."

He chuckles, but it's not his normal relaxed one. I guess it's hard to stay loose when you've got a raging hard-on. So I reach for him again, ready to get the rest of this show on the road.

"Condom," he reminds me, pulling away.

Man, it's a good thing someone is paying attention here. Oops.

He opens the nightstand and removes a condom. See, he knew we were going to do this all along, the big faker. When I try helping, he brushes my hand aside and turns so I get a prime view of his sexy butt.

"If I let you put it on, we'll never make it," he says as he turns back, condom in place.

He lets me pull him on top of me then and kisses me so sweetly I almost want to cry. I can taste a bit of myself on his lips, and it makes the entire experience even more intimate and special.

"I love you, Sunny," he tells me, and darn it, I *am* tearing up now.

I never thought I needed sex to be about love, but I'm finding that I wouldn't want it any other way now.

"I love you too." He brings a thumb up to catch a little escape-artist tear, and I kiss him hard, hoping he feels every bit of my adoration and emotion.

He reaches down to adjust himself at my entrance and presses a first inch into me as he keeps my eyes. "You tell me if you change your mind, yeah? No matter when."

I shake my head. "I won't. Please, Carter."

He pulls back before pushing forward again ever so slowly. He stretches me in an entirely new way as he inches forward. It burns but I'm desperate for more of it, so I lift my hips, forcing more of him inside me. He groans and closes his eyes for a moment before opening again and holding my gaze.

"I want all of you. Now." My voice is almost a command, and I'm a little surprised at my own brazenness, but it obviously turns Carter on. His pupils dilate even more, and he pulls back before thrusting inside me, harder this time.

I groan at the sensation—the burn is like an addiction. My nerve endings clamor for more. Carter recognizes my sounds as those of pleasure because he withdraws again and thrusts forward, plunging even deeper into me this time.

I cry out and grasp him, lifting my hips in encouragement. "More."

"You're so fucking tight," Carter says, still watching me as he thrusts again, his teeth setting as he tries to maintain his control.

My legs circle him as I move with him, bringing him into me with each curl of his hips. I'm completely full, yet I want more, and I can feel my inner muscles clench around him.

"Sunny," Carter groans, his head tilting back now as he powers forward and sets a new rhythm.

It's beautiful and breathtaking, this connection between us. I never imagined experiencing so many feelings, emotions, and sensations at the same time. It's an absolute revelation. And I can't get enough.

He continues his thrusts as I meet him move for move. Sweat drips down his temple and I feel the dampness of my own skin as we slide against one another. I'm so wet for him, I can hear the sounds melding with the slapping of our bodies as we connect over and over. It's almost animalistic, but mostly it's just plain hot.

"Carter." My voice comes out as a whimper as I start losing control. It only makes him move faster and harder, his breath more of a growl now.

Instead of its usual gradual approach, my orgasm hits

me all at once like a giant tsunami. It rockets up and down my spine, taking over every muscle south of my eyebrows. I constrict and buck and curl, my body completely out of my own control as I spasm wildly around Carter. My fingers claw and my teeth clench, my tongue releases words I don't recognize, and my toe joints crack they curl so hard. Every hair on my body stands on end as Carter pumps into me a few final times and finds his own release.

He shouts and bucks against me, and I revel in the idea that I did this to him. I made him lose control just like he made me. We're both sweating and panting as he finally collapses onto one elbow so he doesn't suffocate me. I lock my ankles at the small of his back and kiss him, smiling against his lips.

When I pull back, I know my eyes are shining. "This is my new favorite thing. Prepare yourself because we'll be doing a *lot* of this."

He grins at me and drops his forehead to my shoulder. "I'm happy you approve," he pants.

"We've got tons of time to make up for, so I hope you're hydrated, Brooks," I tease. Before I can expound on the glories of sex, his phone rings from the nightstand.

"Ignore it," he says, and I'm happy to if it means I get to keep holding him.

When mine rings next, though, I frown. Carter lifts his head and looks at me with sex-drunk eyes. "Ignore it," he mutters. And, really, who am I to argue?

The phones go silent, but Carter interrupts our snugglefest anyway, saying he needs to deal with the condom. I reluctantly allow it. But before he leaves me entirely, he drops the softest of kisses on my lips and says the absolute sweetest thing yet to me.

"Thank you."

The earnestness in his eyes is achingly strong, and I'm certain I've got stars in my eyes and little birds with bunting and flowers flying around above me when Carter walks his sexy butt to the bathroom.

But dang it if his phone doesn't start ringing again.

"I'm not answering," he yells from the bathroom.

I sit up, some of my underused muscles protesting, and peek at his phone. "It's your mother."

"Then I'm definitely not answering it. Stay where you are, and don't you dare put any clothes back on!"

I grin to myself, thinking about how lucky I am. How lucky *we* are. As unlikely a pairing as we might be, we still managed to look past expectations and assumptions to see that we were meant for each other all along. And I won't ever take that for granted.

Both phones start ringing at the same time now. Carter comes back in only his boxers, and I hand him his phone while I pick up mine. His says "Mama" while mine says "Lynn Brooks." She and I exchanged numbers a couple weeks back because she wants me to teach her how to crochet her school's mascot—well, that, and she said her brother sometimes ignores her calls. That's no surprise to me.

"Hello?" Carter and I say at the same time.

"Is Cart with you?" Lynn asks, panic in her voice.

My eyes flash to Carter to see him bring his hand up to cover his eyes as he listens to his mom and asks, "Are you serious?"

"Yeah, he's right next to me," I tell Lynn.

Carter's jaw does that clicking thing, telling me I won't like Lynn's next words if they match whatever her mama just told Carter. Unfortunately for everyone, it turns out I'm right.

"Miller's in jail."

And here I thought being a librarian was rough.

NEXT UP IS Miller's story. I know you're dying to know how he ended up in jail! Find out in *Deja Brew All Over Again* (*Love on Tap*, Book 3 - Coming Winter 2023)

CATCH CASH and Hollis's story in *Ale's Fair in Love and War* (*Love on Tap*, Book 1 - FREE with Kindle Unlimited)

Want some side character tea? Check out the *Asheville Collection* (Standalone Stories from the *Love on Tap* World)

Have you read **Denny and Rosie**'s story? Get a **FREE** copy of *Full-On Clinger* at **sylviestewartauthor.com**

EXCITING UPDATES, **freebies, new releases, swag, and more when you sign up for Sylvie's newsletter: http://bit.ly/sylvie-nl**

WE HOPE you enjoyed *Smooth Hoperator*. The best way to support an indie author is to leave a review and tell your friends! Thanks so much!

. . .

IF YOU'RE **interested in signed paperbacks or merch (stickers, pins, bookmarks, pens, bags…) hop over to my website: sylviestewartauthor.com**

WANT TO HANG OUT? Join my Facebook Group, Sylvie's Spot for the Sexy, Sassy, and Smartassy!

EXCERPT FROM ALE'S FAIR IN LOVE AND WAR

LOVE ON TAP, BOOK 1

**Hollis Hayes is the worst neighbor in the entire history of neighbors.
She's also the hottest.
F.M.L.**

I don't have time to fight with the dog groomer next door. There's a brewery to run, siblings to rein in, and a mom to look after. So if Hollis thinks I'll roll over and let her drive me out of business, she's not nearly as smart as she thinks she is.

Sure, I enjoy the little pranks we play on each other, and I don't hate watching her prance around in those tight leggings. But she's gone too far this time, even if she pretends to know nothing about it.

I'll do whatever it takes to save my business from going under, and if that means playing dirty with the girl I love to hate, game on.

CHAPTER ONE
VIRGIN SAYS WHAT?

CASH

"Blue Bigfoot Beer," I bark into the phone, tucking the receiver between my shoulder and ear. The customer across from me holds out his hand as I count his change from the drawer.

A breathy voice on the other end of the line has my hand freezing in midair.

"Is this Cash?" she purrs.

Hmm. Seems like my day might be about to turn around.

I drop the change into the customer's palm and toss him a chin lift.

"That's me. What can I do for you?" I have a few ideas if the voice matches the body.

She lets out a little giggle that has my dick twitching in my jeans. "I'm calling about your virginity."

My hearing must be going because it sounded like she just said I'm a virgin.

Turning away from the prying eyes of my brother a few feet down the bar, I take the receiver in hand and press it firmly to my ear this time. "Sorry, come again?"

"Your virginity," she repeats, her voice still filled with sex but carrying a tinge of amusement now. "I'm interested in relieving you of it."

I squint at my reflection in the mirror of the back bar, wondering if I always look this tired and trying to figure out which of my three brothers is fucking with me. I settle on Denver because that asshole has been way too jolly since he talked his girlfriend into moving in with him.

"Very funny, Rosie. Tell Denny I'm gonna kick his ass next time I see him." The phone drops back in its cradle with a heavy *clang*. I don't have time for jokes today. There's a brewery to run, a taproom to serve, a newbie to train, and a pale ale release tomorrow that I haven't promoted nearly enough.

I glance down the bar just in time to see Miller, my youngest brother, slosh water all over the floor mats as he drops a bus tub in the sink. The towel I throw hits him square in the face. "You *trying* to create a hazard, or does it just come naturally?"

He sends a glare over his shoulder, a new eyebrow piercing glinting at me as I brush past him to serve another customer. It's a regular named Smitty, so there's no need to ask for his order. I press a pint glass onto the glass rinser, then pull back the tap on *Squatch This*, a golden wheat with a crisp finish. It's one of our most popular beers.

The phone rings again, and I'm somewhat encouraged to see Miller answer it without any prompting while I get a card to start Smitty's tab.

"It's for you." My little brother thrusts the phone in my direction.

I gesture for him to make the rounds of the taproom as I grab the receiver. If I've got to work with him, I'm at least gonna train him right. Family can be a real pain in the ass sometimes.

"This is Cash."

"Oh, uh, hey." The masculine voice on the other end stumbles. I'd half expected it to be Denny cackling at his own stupid joke, but this voice doesn't belong to anyone I know. I wait another second for him to speak, but time is money.

"Who is this?" I demand, knowing I'm taking my busy day out on a stranger and hearing my mama's voice in my head urging me to be patient. It's never been my strong suit.

"Tom."

I rack my brain looking for any trace of a Tom but can't recall a soul apart from the guy who runs the smoke shop a couple spaces down. This is not that Tom, and I know this because that Tom is always high as an eagle's nuts and only refers to me as "Cool Money."

"Do I know you?" I glance out into the taproom to see Miller parked on his ass at a four-top of attractive brunettes. That little…

"Uh, no," Tom mutters.

Jesus, get to the point. "What can I do for you, Tom?" I repeat, impatience bleeding through.

"I was, uh, hoping *I* could do something for *you*."

For the love of Larry.

My eyelids drop closed as I brace a hip against the back bar. "Oh yeah? What exactly can you do for me, *Tom*?"

"Pop your cherry?"

When the receiver hits the phone's base this time, the clattering echoes through the entire taproom.

Someone is definitely fucking with me.

And I'm pretty sure I know who.

Recognizing the look on my face and the mood it signifies, Miller hauls ass back behind the bar, hiking his jeans up his hips as he goes. My little brother's contempt for belts is one of life's greater mysteries.

I take my agitation out on Larry, the Bigfoot statue that stands beside my register and watches over the patrons, scrubbing at some beer residue on its base with my towel. The ring of the phone has my molars gnashing, and I leave the receiver right where it is.

"Aren't you gonna get that?" Miller asks.

"Don't touch it!" I throw the towel onto my shoulder and stalk down the hall to the office.

If she wants to start something, I'll only bite back harder. My eyes narrow to slits as I attempt to bore a hole through the wall separating my brewery from the neighboring pet groomer.

Happy Tails Salon. The name is just as sickly sweet as her fake-ass smiles and fluttering eyelashes behind those misleadingly innocent glasses.

Miller's disembodied voice breaks through the speaker of the desk phone. "It's Mama, jackass. Line two."

Well, shit.

"Hey, Mama." I do my best to brush off my irritation. She doesn't need to know about any of my frustrations.

"Hello, darlin'. How are you?" Her concerned tone has me instantly wary. My eyes dart around the office, but I haven't one damn clue what I'm expecting to find.

"I'm great. How are you? Did you find Mango?" Mango is the love of her life, and everyone knows it.

She clucks her tongue. "You know, he showed up in the kitchen a few minutes after you left. I don't know what he got himself into, but he's here now, safe and sound. *Aren't you, my little sweetheart*?" she coos at the mongrel, and I realize I'm just being paranoid.

"That's good to hear." I glance at my watch. "Hey, aren't you late for work?" It's already halfway through the afternoon and I haven't gotten shit done.

"I'm leaving in a few. We're doing pizza and movie night," she replies. She works at the senior center coordinating activities and generally causing trouble. "I just wanted to call about your problem."

My butt drops into the desk chair, and I smile into the phone. "I wouldn't say he's *my* problem. I like to think of Miller as *all of our* problem."

"Oh hush, you. I'm not talkin' about your brother—although I am so glad you took my suggestion and hired him."

Took her suggestion? More like folded to her edict. Hiring Miller was not my idea at all, but the asshat crashed his bike and got fired from yet another job, so my hands were tied. Blue Bigfoot Beer is a family venture in many ways, but my oldest brother, Carter, and I are the only ones left holding the bag at the end of the day.

"Yeah, well." There wasn't much more to say than that. Mama always did teach us if you don't have something nice to say, don't say anything at all. "So, what problem are you talking about?"

"Your virginity, darlin'."

Fuck. My. Life.

Twenty minutes later, I'm staring at a Craigslist ad on my laptop that has both my name and Blue Bigfoot's phone number on it.

"Looking for someone gentle to break my guymen. I just haven't met the right person, and it's become a burden. Please be kind because I'm hideously ugly."

"Dude, there are easier ways."

Miller's voice sends me jumping. The bastard is leaning over my shoulder reading the screen and breathing his nicotine dragon breath in my face. I give him a good shove.

"Fuck off. I didn't post this," I grunt. "And who's manning the bar?"

Hitching his jeans up again, he snickers, enjoying this way more than I'd like. "Relax. Oscar's got it covered."

I only glare in response. There's no way I'm telling him that Mama just offered the services of her buddy Regina to help me out with my so-called problem. The same Regina who runs an escort service catering to Asheville's elite and hard-up.

Of which I'm neither, thank you very much.

"Any idea who did it?" Miller flicks his tongue ring against his teeth, sending my already raw nerve endings buzzing.

There's only one person on this earth who can get this far under my skin and make me take my eye off the ball like this.

I grit my teeth around my growl of an answer. *"Hollis."*

Find out what happens next in ***Ale's Fair in Love and War***
(FREE with Kindle Unlimited)

EXCERPT FROM THE NERD NEXT DOOR

CAROLINA KISSES, BOOK 1

New town, new job, new neighbor... new crush.

I've got a serious problem and it goes by the name of Ted Jones. Even his name is nerdy! Combine that with his glasses, lean runner's frame, crazy smarts, and superhero addiction and he's got my lady engine revving hard.

What can I say? I've got a thing for hot nerds.

But our shy glances and awkward exchanges in the elevator aren't going to cut it. This nerd is mine; he just doesn't know it yet.

Grab your copy now and start the sexy, laugh-out-loud Carolina Kisses Series today!

CHAPTER ONE
HALEY

… Pulling up to our building in a dark blue late-model Mazda is the object of my… fascination? Obsession? Slightly stalkerish tendencies? The car settles in a spot by the curb, the driver's side door opening shortly after. And out steps Ted Jones.

My Ted Jones.

Well, he would be if I had my way about it.

Tilting my head to the side, I admire him for a moment or two while Tank sniffs a dandelion. Now, here's a man who knows how to rock an elbow patch. *Oooh, yeah.* I don't know what it is about Ted Jones' particular brand of nerdiness, but it is friggin' hot. I've done a little, let's call it… investigating and discovered he teaches in the liberal arts school at NCUW, so I know he's whip smart. He also wears the sexiest black-framed glasses over brilliant blue eyes, has little to no affection for his razor, and exercises a habit of smoothing his hair down to fight a stubborn cowlick. It never obeys, much to my delight, making him sport a constant just-rolled-out-of-bed look.

In contrast to that, he is always dressed neatly, often in a traditional tweed jacket with elbow patches which he pairs with jeans that do amazing things for his ass. Something about that combination of tweed, leather, and denim sets off an odd Pavlovian response in my uterus. I can't explain it. To top that all off, he's a runner, and I've seen the muscles of his thighs and calves bunching as he powers through his evening runs, leaving him coated in sweat and me with plenty to think about when my head hits the pillow.

It's safe to say I'm gone over Ted Jones.

The only problem is we've never actually had a single conversation.

To be fair, we *have* spoken to one another—on several occasions, in fact. But you couldn't exactly call these interactions conversations. As I recall, my first word to him was, "Hi." To which I got zero reply.

It was the afternoon I moved into my apartment, the unseasonably cool temperatures making my fingers ache from cold. I'd just returned a borrowed cart to maintenance and was trying to remember which walkway would take me to my building when I got my first glimpse of my future boyfriend (positive thinking is always recommended). Although, to be honest, it was the teenage girl speaking to him who first caught my attention and caused me to do a double take.

The two stood on the sidewalk while the brisk early-spring temperatures caused us all to tighten our coats around us. When I first saw the girl, I could have sworn a bag of cotton candy rested on her head—the classic dual pack with sugary clouds of half pink and half blue. But, no, it was just her hair, so my attention quickly shifted to take in the man beside her.

He wore a dark wool coat, and I could see the puffs of his breath on the air as he laughed at something the girl showed him. It was a magazine of some sort, called *The Weatherman*, although I'd never heard of it. Both the girl and man were seemingly enthralled, and neither one noticed me as my insides turned to mush. His laughter skipped toward me on the breeze and made my stomach flip—and this was before I'd ever even seen him in his tweed, denim, and leather trifecta of hotness.

The two spoke animatedly, the girl gesturing with wide sweeps of her arms as her cotton-candy hair swished around her ears. He flipped some pages until he found what he was looking for and they both buried their noses —and every other sense, it seemed—into the magazine. I felt oddly left out, even though I'd never laid eyes on either of these people before in my life. After a few moments, I stole one last look and retreated down the cement walkway to what I was almost certain was my building.

So it was no surprise that I all but gasped when I found myself on the elevator of my apartment building not two hours later with the very same man—sans teenage girl this time. I mean, what were the chances of him living in the same building as me in such a huge complex? It was clearly a sign, as was the uptick in my heart rate as I got my first close-up view of him. I drew in a breath and uttered my very first word.

"Hi." Yes, I am available to teach flirting lessons should anyone need my brilliant advice.

He didn't even glance my way. Here I was in an enclosed space with this delicious guy who immediately pushed all my buttons—making *me* want to push the emergency button on the elevator and make out with him in a really dirty way—and he wouldn't even acknowledge me.

I've never been great with guys, but I do okay. Certainly well enough to spark up a casual conversation in an elevator. When he left me hanging, I felt a sharp pang that this guy who was friendly to *Weatherman* girls and was my type in every way was actually kind of a rude jerk. That was, until I noticed he was wearing a pair of those wireless earbuds. This discovery brought some relief, but I still stood awkwardly until we reached the third floor where I got off.

Refusing to concede defeat, I waited until the elevator was about to close behind me and turned to give him my best smile and a friendly wave. Unfortunately, I missed the small fact that he had stepped out after me. Which meant when I whipped myself around, my forehead made audible contact with his very defined cheekbone, causing us both to stagger back.

"I'm so sorry!" I put one hand to my head and one out toward him, as if my hand held a magical power that dulled the pain from blunt-force trauma.

He held his cheek and blinked a few times, his jaw working as if to test the level of injury. Then he pulled out an earbud and shook his head, his gaze dropping to the floor.

His voice was a deep, quiet rumble when he spoke. "No problem."

Then he snatched a set of keys from his pocket like he thought I might attack again and made quick work of the lock to apartment 3-C. The apartment right next to my 3-B. Ack!

"Happens all the time," he mumbled before disappearing behind his door. I continued to stand in the hallway, unsure of what had just happened and wondering if I should run to the store for some frozen peas or something. But I got the distinct feeling that would just make things more awkward.

Little did I know, awkward would be our go-to vibe for all subsequent encounters.

Like the time my grocery bag split, sending a bottle of wine, a huge roll of chocolate-chip cookie dough, and a box of panty liners tumbling out at his feet. Instead of just picking them up like a normal person, I, for some unknown reason, felt compelled to share that I was

PMSing. I believe my exact words were, "Gotta love that time of the month."

You know, because those are the exact words that will make your crush confess his undying love for you. *Oh, Haley, there's nothing I find sexier than the mental image of you stuffing your panties with cotton personal products before binge drinking and shoving raw cookie dough in your face. Come to daddy!*

Yeah. That's pretty much how things have gone since.

But not today! Today, I'm going to have a real live conversation with Ted Jones if it kills me—which is a distinct possibility at this point.

I straighten my back and then glance down at my clothes. The old t-shirt and capri leggings can't be helped. I take a quick sniff in the general direction of my armpits and resolve to just keep my arms glued to my sides during the course of our scintillating discussion. Hell, he's a runner. Maybe he's into girls who work up a sweat.

I stride forward, pulling Tank along as I watch Ted stop at the communal mailboxes on a grassy patch of lawn. He stands with his back to me, his legs shoulder width apart and covered in the familiar denim.

I can do this. I'll be confident and charming and not even a little bit weird—I'm sure of it. That is, until I actually reach the mailboxes and catch Ted's scent. Lordy, he smells like pencil shavings and leather. I want to bite my fist and then lick his neck. Instead, I pretend to search for my mailbox key which I know to be sitting in a dish on my entry table at this very moment.

Ted doesn't turn his head or acknowledge me in any way, instead closing his mailbox and removing his key before sifting through the stack of white envelopes and coupon fliers.

It's now or never. I take a deep breath and turn to him, one hand on my hip and the other gripping the leash as Tank circles our feet. "Beautiful evening, huh?"

Dammit! *The weather? Seriously?* I'm a walking cliché, but it's too late, so I widen my smile. Ted turns to me and, upon taking in my overly enthusiastic smile, takes a step back.

Right into the pile of shit my dog just dropped behind him.

Find out what happens next in **The Nerd Next Door**
Also available in audiobook

EXCERPT FROM PLAYING BY HEART

FROM THE ASHEVILLE COLLECTION

Music lover Kat has spent a lifetime hiding in the shadows. When her hot guitar-playing crush needs a songstress to save his show, can he convince her to give life under the spotlight a try?

KAT:

The cat's whiskers twitch as her watchful gaze turns menacing.

That's my cue to back away—an instinct honed from an entire life's history of unfortunate feline encounters.

I don't care if her name *is* Duchess von Snuggle Pants. Names lie all the time, my own being a prime example.

I hum a few bars of "White Christmas," hoping it will get her to trust me. It doesn't. Duchess VSP makes a run for it, clearly forgetting she's tied to the giant aluminum basin by a leash. She boomerangs, smacking her already-smushed face on the metal and treating me to a terrorized *hiss* and a whiff of the awful stench that earned her a trip to my wash tub.

"Oh, Duchess, why won't you let me love you?"

"I'm going to pretend I didn't hear that," a familiar voice cuts through the din of the crowded park.

I don't dare look up from my charge, lest she take advantage of the diversion and extract a kidney with a sharply chiseled claw. "I just realized you have the perfect name, Jade."

My bestie snorts. "What a news flash. Have you drowned any animals yet this morning?"

I choose to ignore her question. "Isn't she beautiful?" I sigh, gazing at the cat's generous silver coat and grumpy face as she glowers at me from the bottom of the tub. "Even if she does hate me."

"Of course she hates you; you're giving her a bath. What moron asked you to bathe a cat?"

I reflexively glance up for a split second—long enough to take in Jade's raised eyebrow and downturned lips. It's her go-to expression.

I slide to the other end of the basin and flip the sprayer on, careful to keep the nozzle pointed down. Duchess tries to strangle herself again. "She's a Persian, and her owner says long-haired cats love baths. He saw we were doing this charity pet wash, and he'd much rather give his money to us than their regular groomer." My gaze flips up again to find Jade's expression has now shifted to one I'm painfully familiar with. I go still.

Dammit.

The sprayer drops with a tinny thud, spewing an arc of warm water over both me and Duchess before Jade jams the spigot off. I throw the cat an apologetic smile, to which she narrows her eyes and hisses again as she continues to plot my death.

Instead of verbalizing what I know Jade is thinking— that *I* am, in fact, the one-and-only moron in this situation

—she sidles up beside me and rests a hip against my basin.

My nose wrinkles. "No wonder all the other volunteers disappeared when Duchess and her owner signed in." My dad used to say I'd buy a magic drop of water if I were drowning in the ocean.

Jade's elbow bumps my shoulder, bringing into full relief our vast height difference. "Well, maybe the view will cheer you up." Duchess VSP sniffs Jade's hand and proceeds to mash her face into her palm with a contented *purr*. Seriously?

"I've been to this park a couple hundred times. I doubt it." My gaze follows the movement of her fingers as they absently stroke the silky fur. Duchess moans as if climaxing in a kitty orgasm. This is ridiculous.

"I'm not talking about the park." Jade's elbow jabs me harder this time.

I swivel, thinking maybe Jade has somehow conjured up the very person I've been hoping to spot all morning. But all I see is the same throng of people swarming the park in holiday garb, leading all manner of pets to the washing stations manned by red-shirted volunteers like me.

When the director of the event asked for volunteers, the idea sounded like a blast: raise money for women's heart disease by hosting a pet wash and pageant during Christmas in July. What's more fun than a park full of soggy dogs prancing down a makeshift runway trimmed with holiday decorations? Somehow, I forgot to factor in the universal human compulsion to show off *all* of one's pets at every given opportunity, no matter the species.

So far today, I've shampooed two dogs, a pig, a ferret, and a chicken. Yes, a chicken. The ferret was the smelliest,

Brewster the chicken was surprisingly agreeable, and Jon Hamm the pig was over it before it began. But none of them hated me quite like Duchess von Snuggle Pants.

"Since when have you been a pet person?" I ask. "I thought you only showed up to bug Pete." Jade's boyfriend owns a coffee shop—cleverly called Pete's—and is one of the sponsors of the Have a Heart Pet Wash and Pageant.

Clearly frustrated at my lack of comprehension, Jade abandons the cat's adoration and physically directs my gaze to a huddle of shirtless men gathered under one of the shade trees dotting Pack Square Park.

"Oh. Them." I shrug, batting her hands away. They smell from petting Duchess.

"That right there is a harem of hot peacocks looking to get laid. They're probably a bunch of idiots, but, hey, who says they need to talk?"

"Gross." I scrape a swath of wet hair from my cheek. Big showy guys don't interest me. The thought has my eyes scanning the crowd for the hundredth time since I got here. *Where is he?*

"You were just saying the other day that it's time to put yourself out there."

"No. That was you. You said, and I quote, 'If you don't get nailed soon, I'm sacrificing Pete to the cause.'" I swing back to face my friend again. All this talk of guys is getting my nerves worked up. Maybe it's better if he doesn't show —not that I was really going to speak to him anyway.

But Jade's not paying attention. Instead, she's got her palm to her nose, her lips twisted in revulsion.

"What is that smell?" She glares at Duchess.

I bite my lip to suppress a grin. "He said she rolled in something. Likely something dead."

"I'm out." Jade turns on a heel and stalks away, her hand extended as far out as possible without dislocating something.

I drop my eyes back to poor Duchess and use my most soothing tone. "I'm sorry, sweetheart, but I might have to kick your dad in the dick."

"I-I can come back," a new voice stutters behind me, just as something cold and wet presses into my arm. I glance down to see a black nose and a pair of enormous chocolate eyes gazing up at me.

My stomach drops to my knees when I realize I know this dog's cute face. Almost as well as I know the one belonging to its owner—the very same guy who just caught me threatening a stranger's manhood with my knock-off Birkenstocks.

Suffice it to say, this is so not how I envisioned finally meeting my crush face to face.

Find out what happens next in *Playing by Heart* from the **Asheville Collection** (Standalone Stories from the *Love on Tap* World)

ALSO BY SYLVIE STEWART

Ale's Fair in Love and War (*Love on Tap*, Book 1 - *Free with Kindle Unlimited*)

Deja Brew All Over Again (*Love on Tap*, Book 3 - *Coming Winter 2023*)

Asheville Collection (Standalone Stories from the *Love on Tap* World)

* * *

Poppy & the Beast (*Free with Kindle Unlimited*)

* * *

Between a Rock and a Royal, Kings of Carolina, #1 (*Free with Kindle Unlimited*)

Blue Bloods and Backroads, Kings of Carolina, #2 (*Free with Kindle Unlimited*)

Stealing Kisses With a King, Kings of Carolina, #3 (*Free with Kindle Unlimited*)

Kings of Carolina Box Set

* * *

The Fix (Carolina Connections, Book 1)

The Spark (Carolina Connections, Book 2)

The Lucky One (Carolina Connections, Book 3)

The Game (Carolina Connections, Book 4)

The Way You Are (Carolina Connections, Book 5)

The Runaround (Carolina Connections, Book 6)

Carolina Connections Box Set 1

Carolina Connections Box Set 2

* * *

The Nerd Next Door (Carolina Kisses, Book 1)

New Jerk in Town (Carolina Kisses, Book 2)

The Last Good Liar (Carolina Kisses, Book 3)

* * *

Full-On Clinger (FREE for a limited time)

Then Again

Happy New You

About That

Nuts About You

Booby Trapped

ACKNOWLEDGMENTS

Thanks to all my readers for welcoming the Brooks family so enthusiastically! I hope you love Sunny and Carter as much as I do. Big hearts are always the best.

Big thanks to Ellie at My Brother's Editor and to Regina for her sharp eye. I also owe the entire rom-com author community a huge thanks for all the support.

And, of course, I couldn't do anything without Sparky, Crash, and Jabberjaw. You guys are everything and I love you to bits!

ABOUT THE AUTHOR

USA Today bestselling author Sylvie Stewart loves dad jokes, hot HEAs, country music, and baby skunks—preferably all at the same time. Most of her steamy contemporary romances and romantic comedies take place in North Carolina, a.k.a. the best state ever, and she's a sucker for hugs from her kids and a good laugh with her hot-nerd hubby. She also cusses like a sailor and can't bring herself to feel bad about it. If you love smart Southern gals, hot blue-collar guys, and snort-laughing with characters who feel like your best friends, Sylvie's your gal.

facebook.com/SylvieStewartAuthor

twitter.com/sylvie_stewart_

instagram.com/sylvie.stewart.romance

bookbub.com/authors/sylvie-stewart

tiktok.com/@authorsylviestewart

pinterest.com/sylviestewartauthor